tiny titans

GROWING UP TINY!

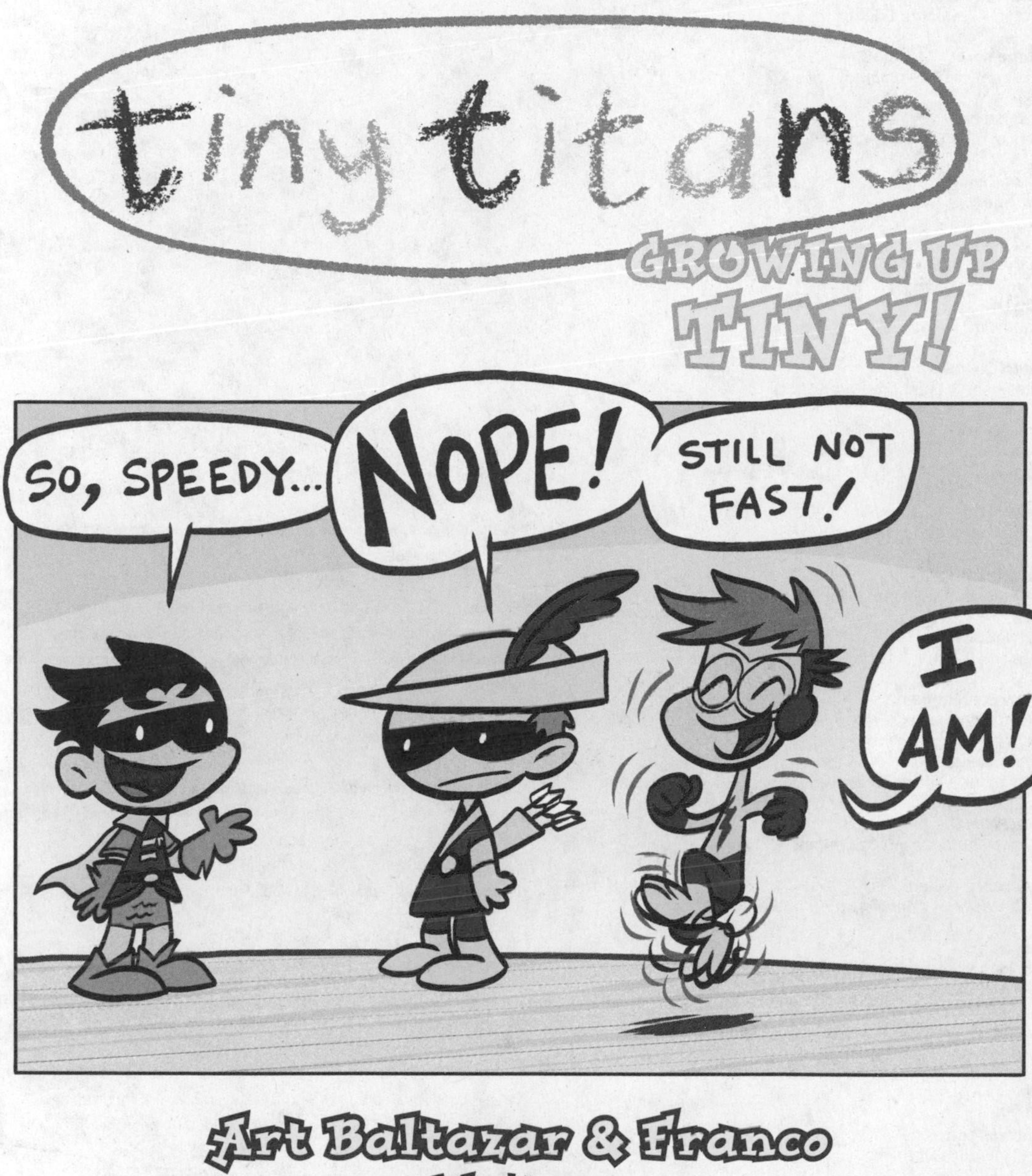
SO, SPEEDY...
NOPE!
STILL NOT FAST!
I AM!

Art Baltazar & Franco
Writers

Art Baltazar
Artist & Letterer

Franco
Artist — Flashback Scenes

TINY TITANS: GROWING UP TINY!

Published by DC Comics. Cover and compilation Copyright © 2012 DC Comics.
All Rights Reserved.

Originally published in single magazine form in TINY TITANS 34-44
Copyright © 2011 DC Comics. All Rights Reserved. All characters, their
distinctive likenesses and related elements featured in this publication are
trademarks of DC Comics. The stories, characters and incidents featured
in this publication are entirely fictional. DC Comics does not read or accept
unsolicited ideas, stories or artwork.

DC Comics, 2900 W. Alameda Avenue, Burbank, CA 91505
Printed by Transcontinental Interglobe, Beauceville, QC, Canada. 1/6/17.
Fourth Printing. ISBN: 978-1-4012-3525-3

Library of Congress Cataloging-in-Publication Data

Baltazar, Art.
  Tiny titans : growing up tiny! / Art Baltazar and Franco.
    p. cm.
  "Originally published in single magazine form in TINY TITANS
34-44"—T.p. verso.
  Summary: "These all ages tales from the DC Universe, beautifully
written and illustrated by Art Baltazar and Franco, will entertain new
readers and seasoned fans of comics"—Provided by publisher.
  ISBN 978-1-4012-3525-3 (pbk.)
  1. Graphic novels. [1. Graphic novels. 2. Superheroes—Fiction.] I.
Aureliani, Franco, ill. II. Title.
  PZ7.7.B334Tiv 2012
  741.5'973—dc23
                                              2012002201

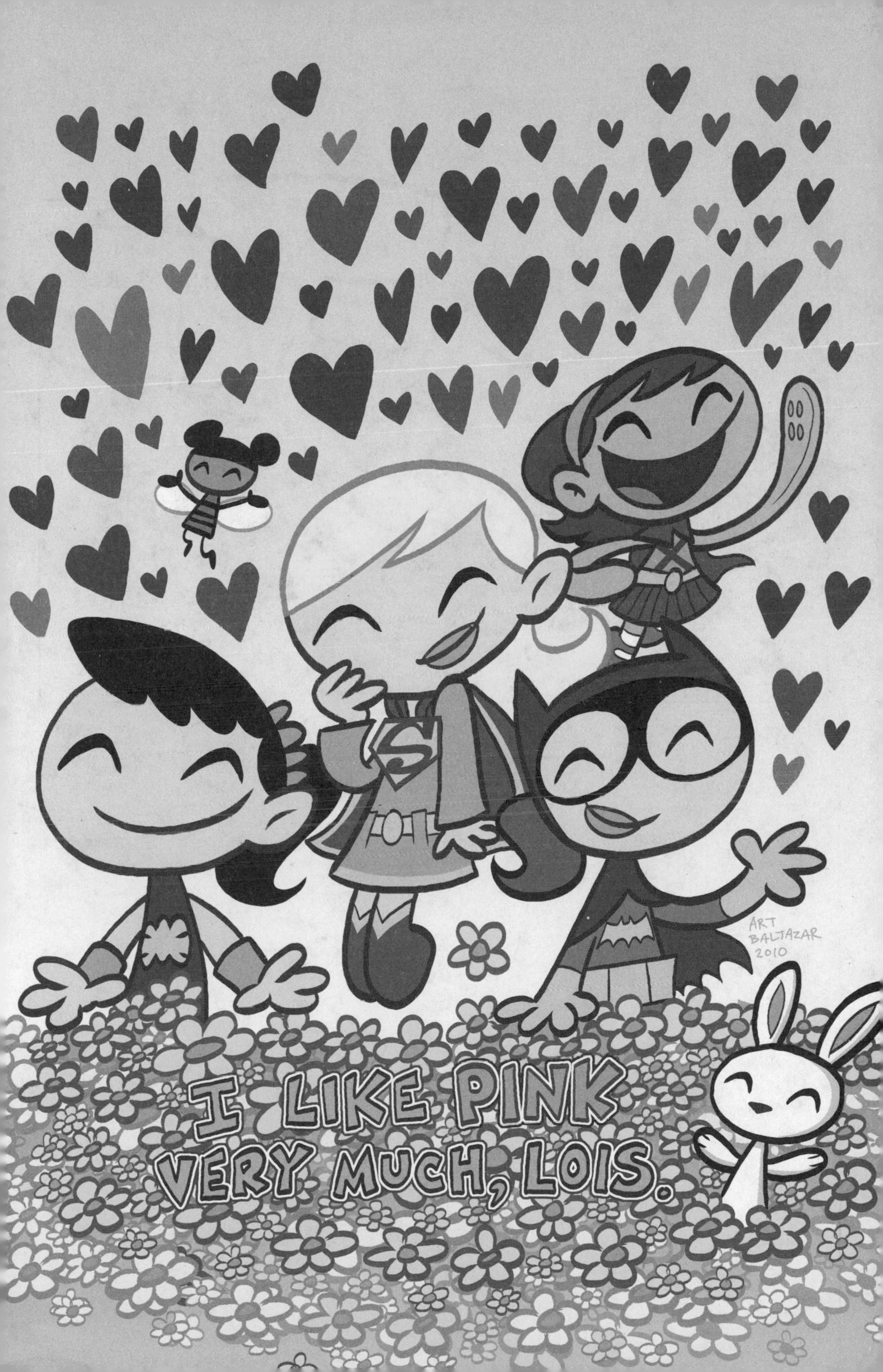
ART BALTAZAR 2010
I LIKE PINK VERY MUCH, LOIS.

tiny titans

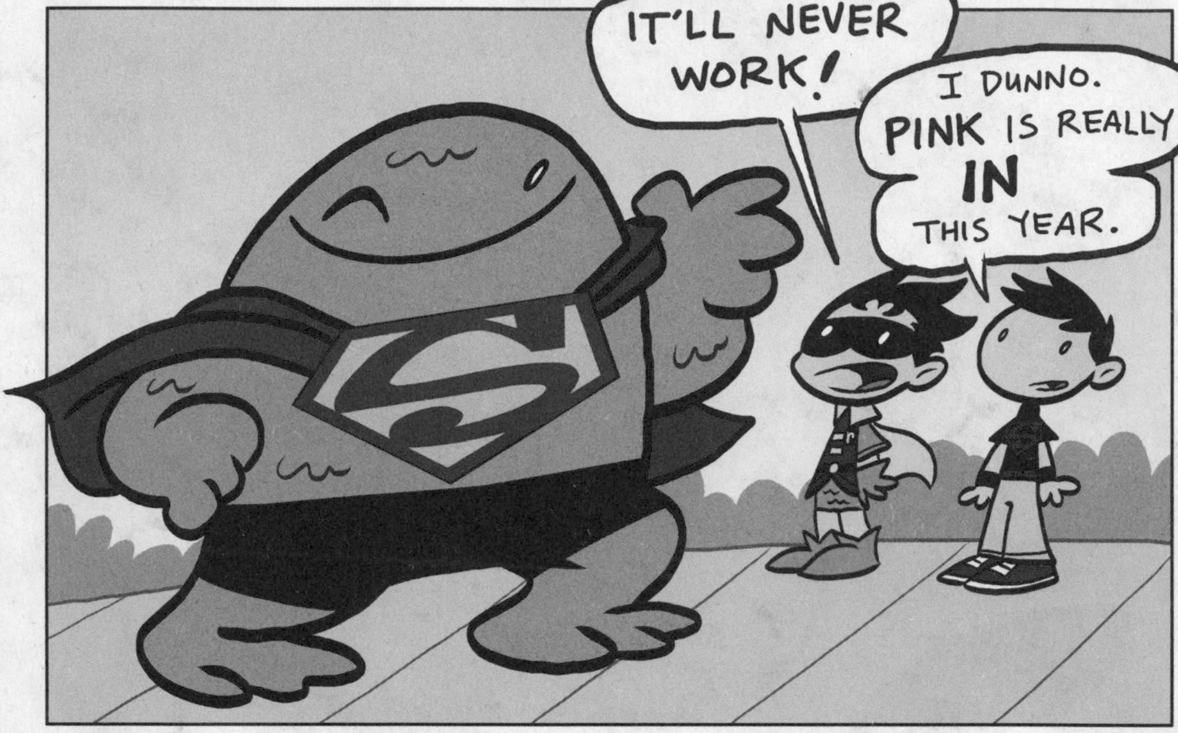
IT'LL NEVER WORK!
I DUNNO. PINK IS REALLY IN THIS YEAR.

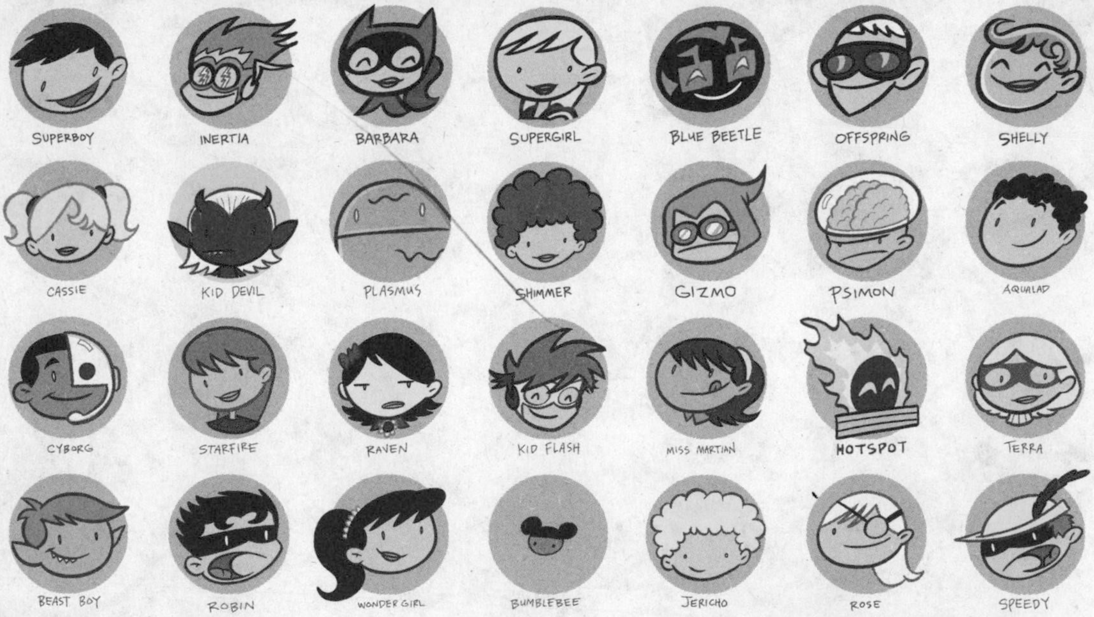
SUPERBOY
INERTIA
BARBARA
SUPERGIRL
BLUE BEETLE
OFFSPRING
SHELLY
CASSIE
KID DEVIL
PLASMUS
SHIMMER
GIZMO
PSIMON
AQUALAD
CYBORG
STARFIRE
RAVEN
KID FLASH
MISS MARTIAN
HOTSPOT
TERRA
BEAST BOY
ROBIN
WONDER GIRL
BUMBLEBEE
JERICHO
ROSE
SPEEDY

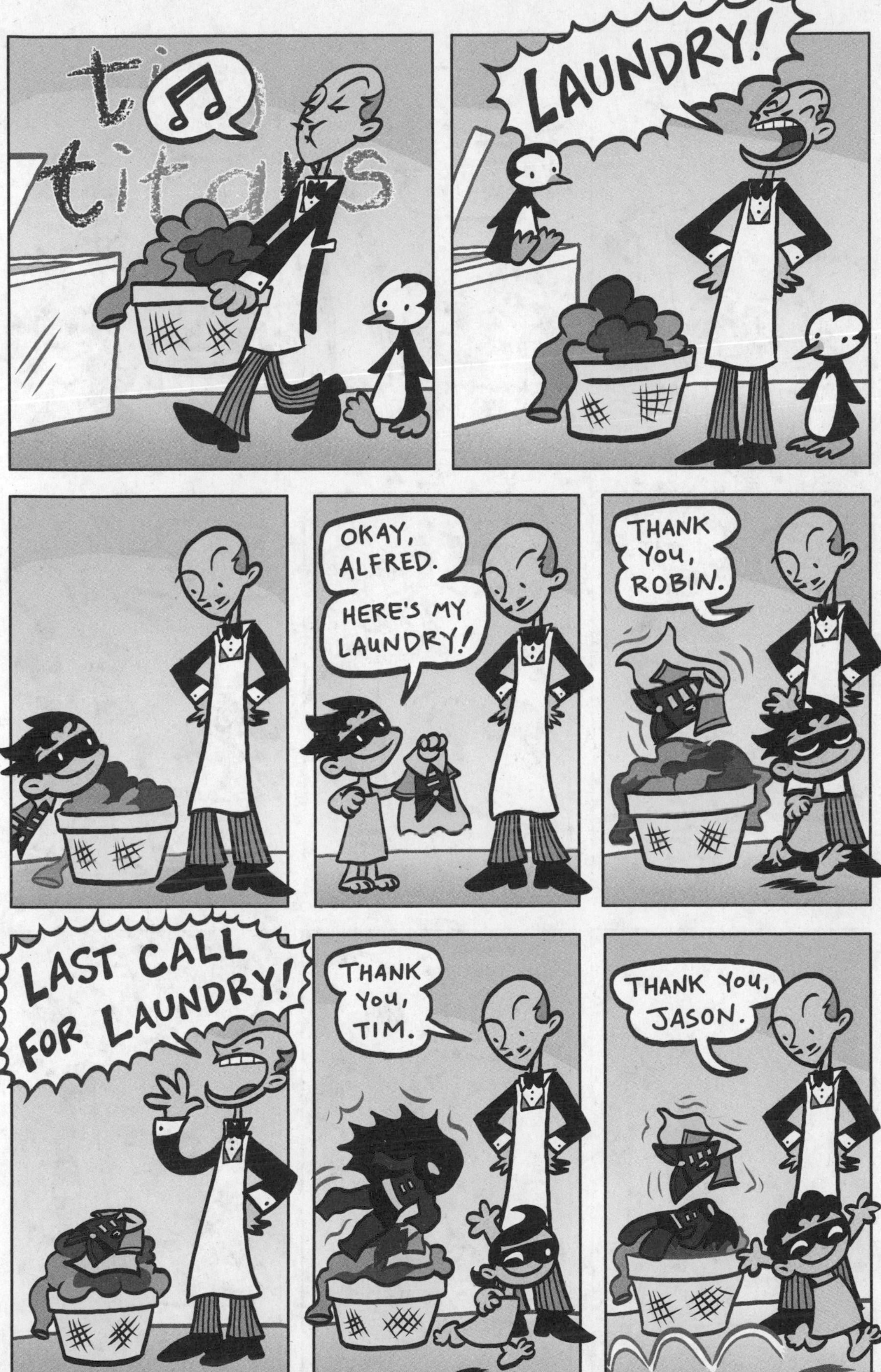
LAUNDRY!
OKAY, ALFRED.
HERE'S MY LAUNDRY!
THANK YOU, ROBIN.
LAST CALL FOR LAUNDRY!
THANK YOU, TIM.
THANK YOU, JASON.

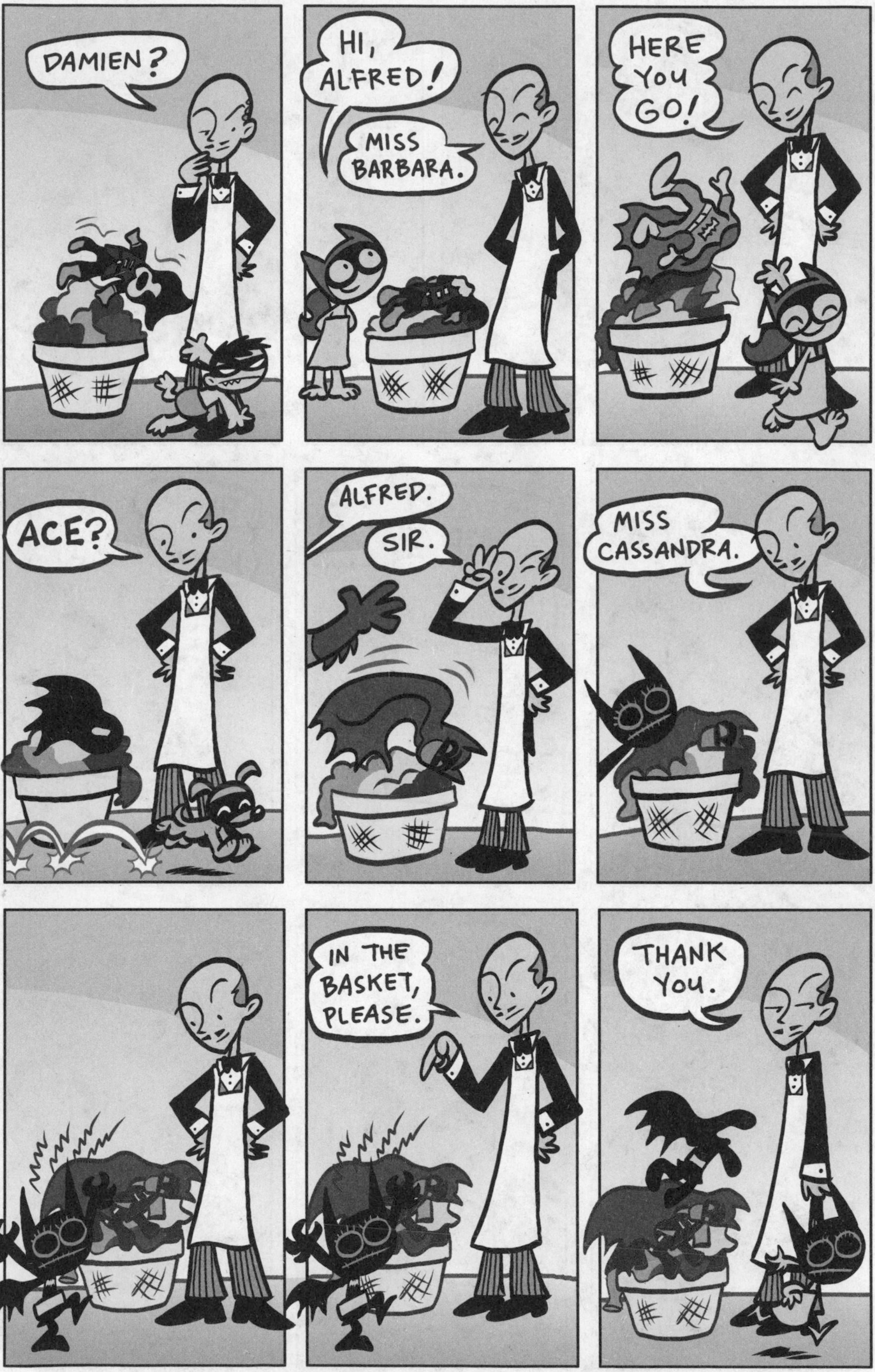
DAMIEN?
HI, ALFRED!
MISS BARBARA.
HERE YOU GO!
ACE?
ALFRED.
SIR.
MISS CASSANDRA.
IN THE BASKET, PLEASE.
THANK YOU.

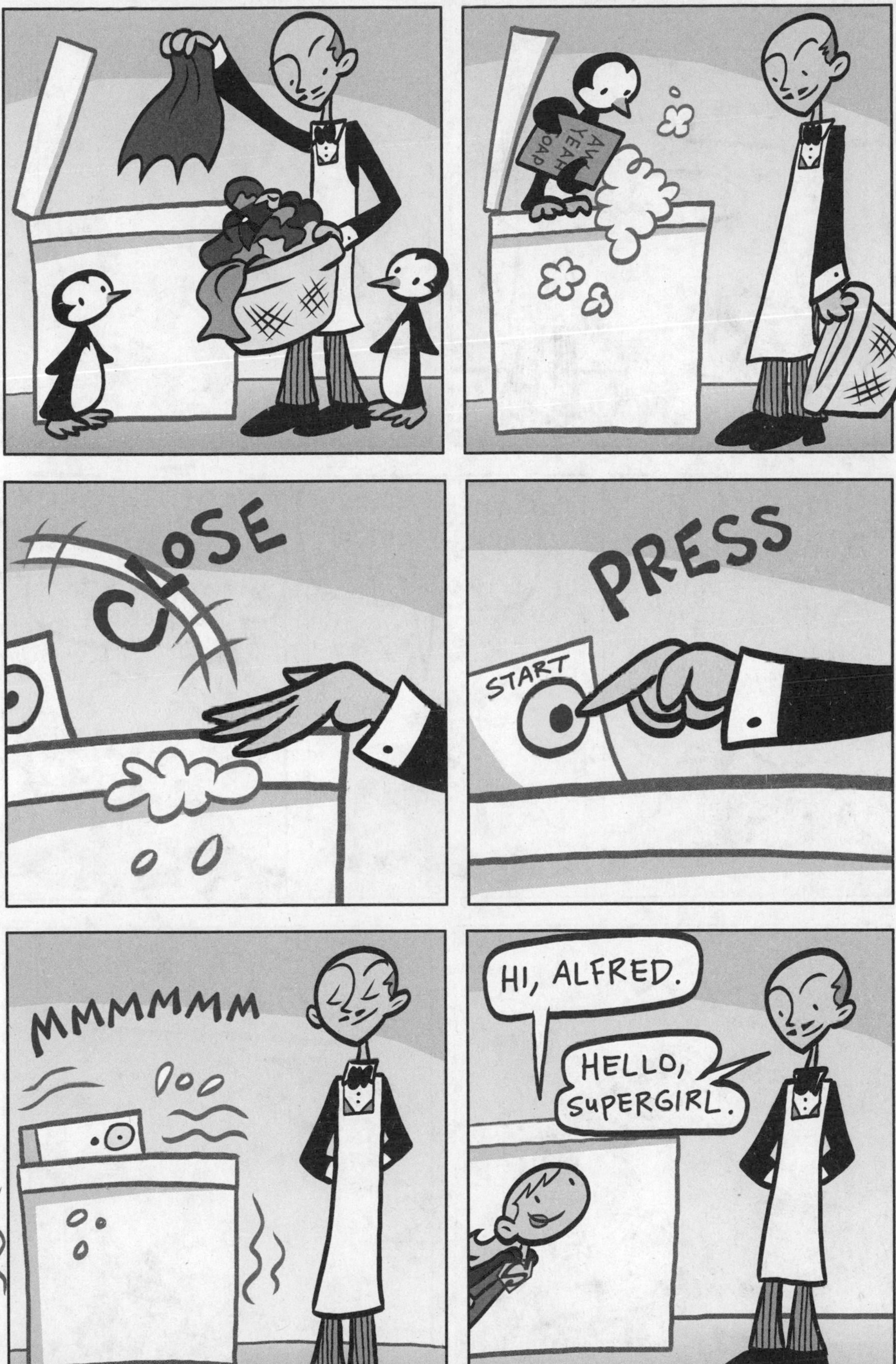
AW
YEAH
OAP
CLOSE
PRESS
START
MMMMMM
HI, ALFRED.
HELLO, SUPERGIRL.

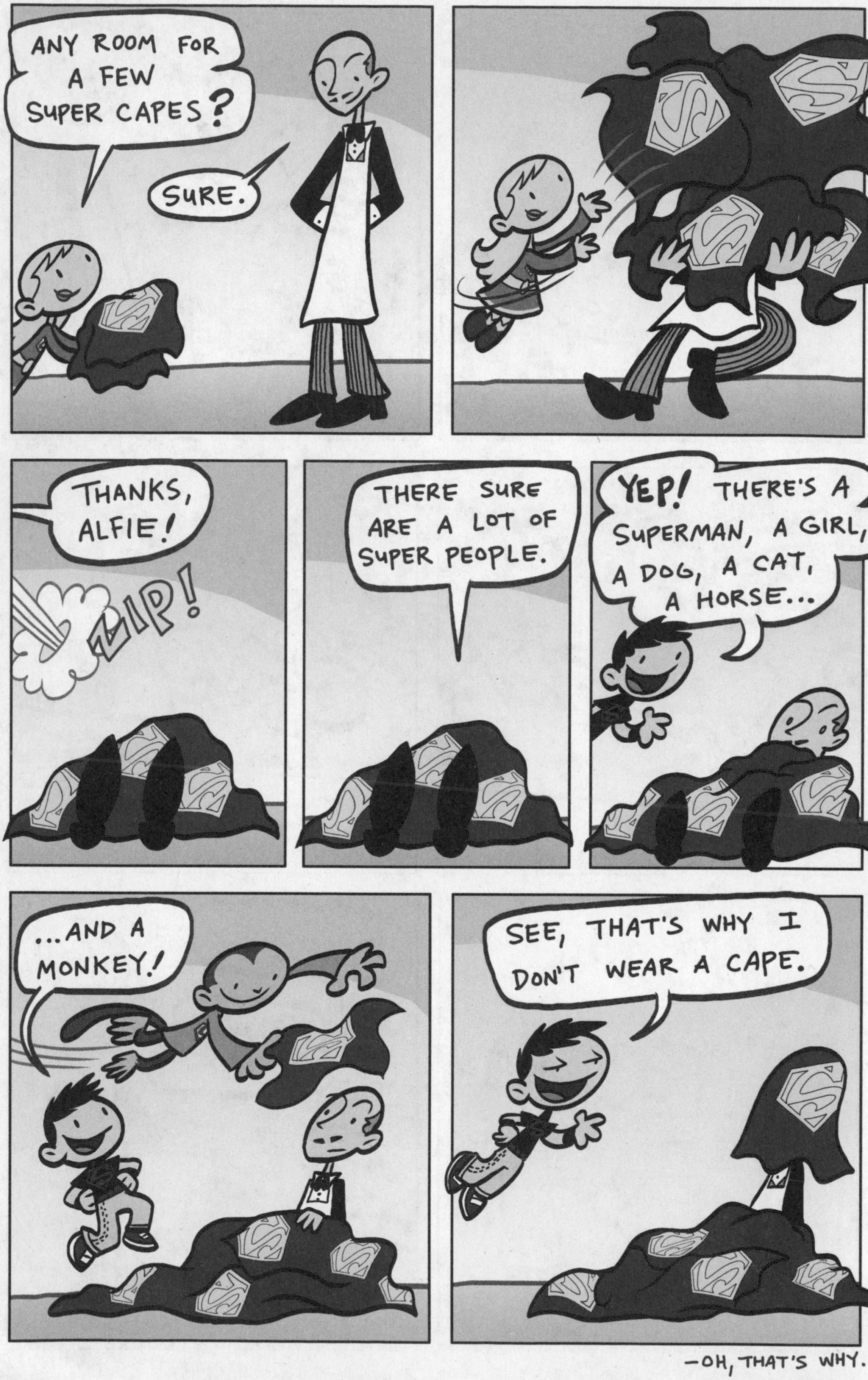
ANY ROOM FOR A FEW SUPER CAPES?
SURE.
THANKS, ALFIE!
ZIP!
THERE SURE ARE A LOT OF SUPER PEOPLE.
YEP! THERE'S A SUPERMAN, A GIRL, A DOG, A CAT, A HORSE...
...AND A MONKEY!
SEE, THAT'S WHY I DON'T WEAR A CAPE.

—OH, THAT'S WHY.

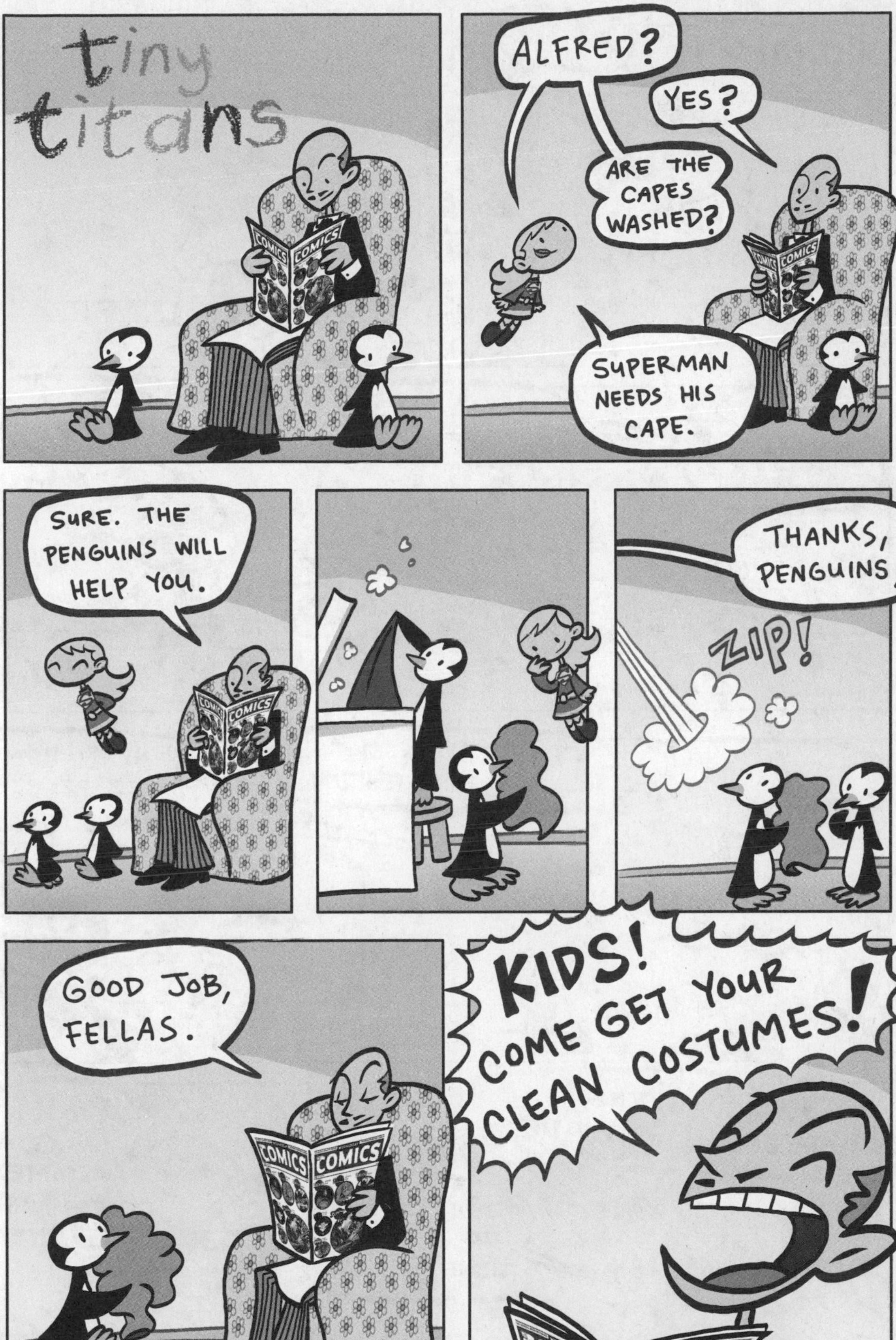
tiny titans
ALFRED?
YES?
ARE THE CAPES WASHED?
SUPERMAN NEEDS HIS CAPE.
SURE. THE PENGUINS WILL HELP YOU.
THANKS, PENGUINS!
ZIP!
GOOD JOB, FELLAS.
KIDS! COME GET YOUR CLEAN COSTUMES!

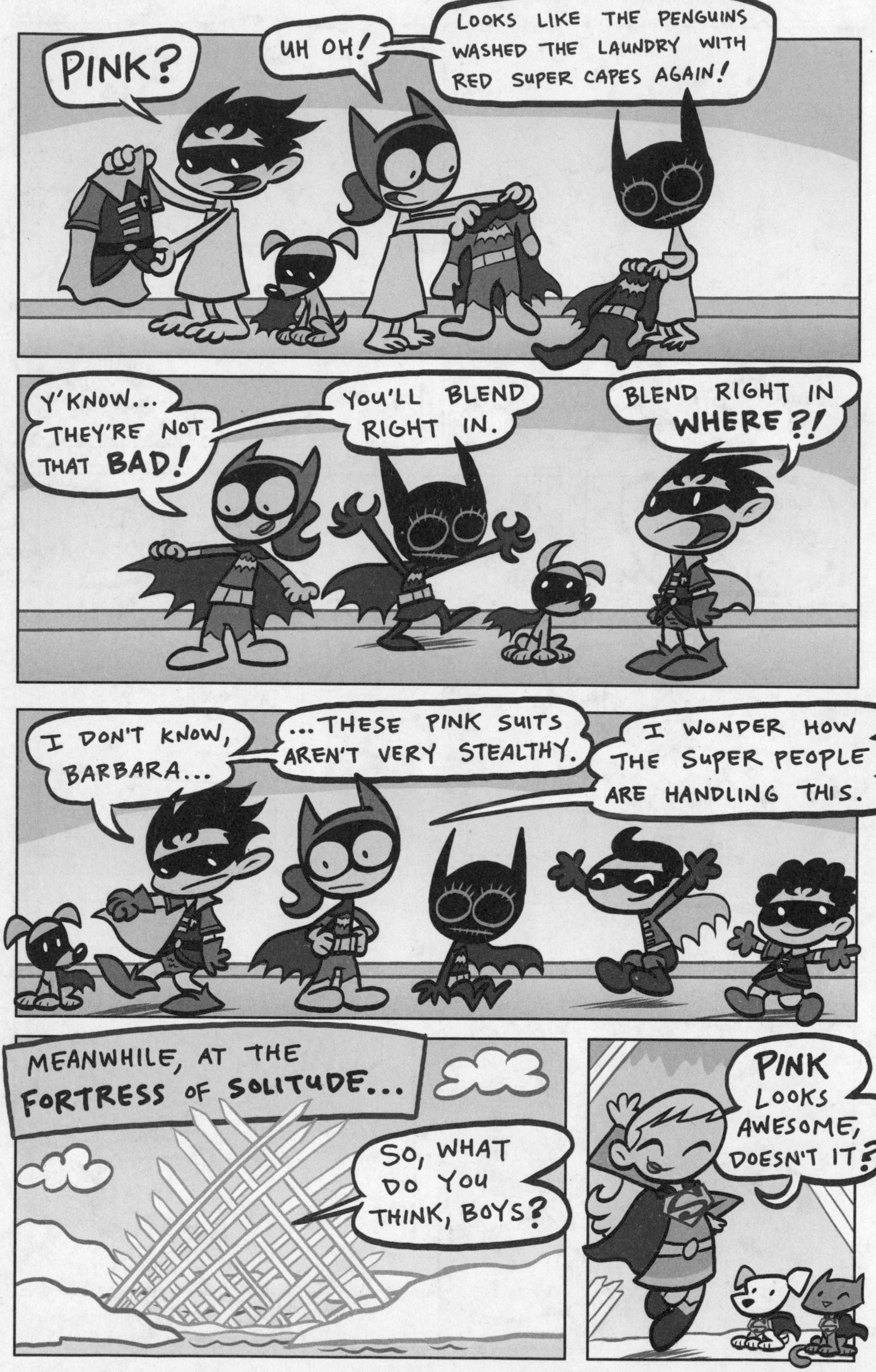
PINK?
UH OH!
LOOKS LIKE THE PENGUINS WASHED THE LAUNDRY WITH RED SUPER CAPES AGAIN!
Y'KNOW... THEY'RE NOT THAT BAD!
YOU'LL BLEND RIGHT IN.
BLEND RIGHT IN WHERE?!
I DON'T KNOW, BARBARA...
...THESE PINK SUITS AREN'T VERY STEALTHY.
I WONDER HOW THE SUPER PEOPLE ARE HANDLING THIS.
MEANWHILE, AT THE FORTRESS OF SOLITUDE...
SO, WHAT DO YOU THINK, BOYS?
PINK LOOKS AWESOME, DOESN'T IT?

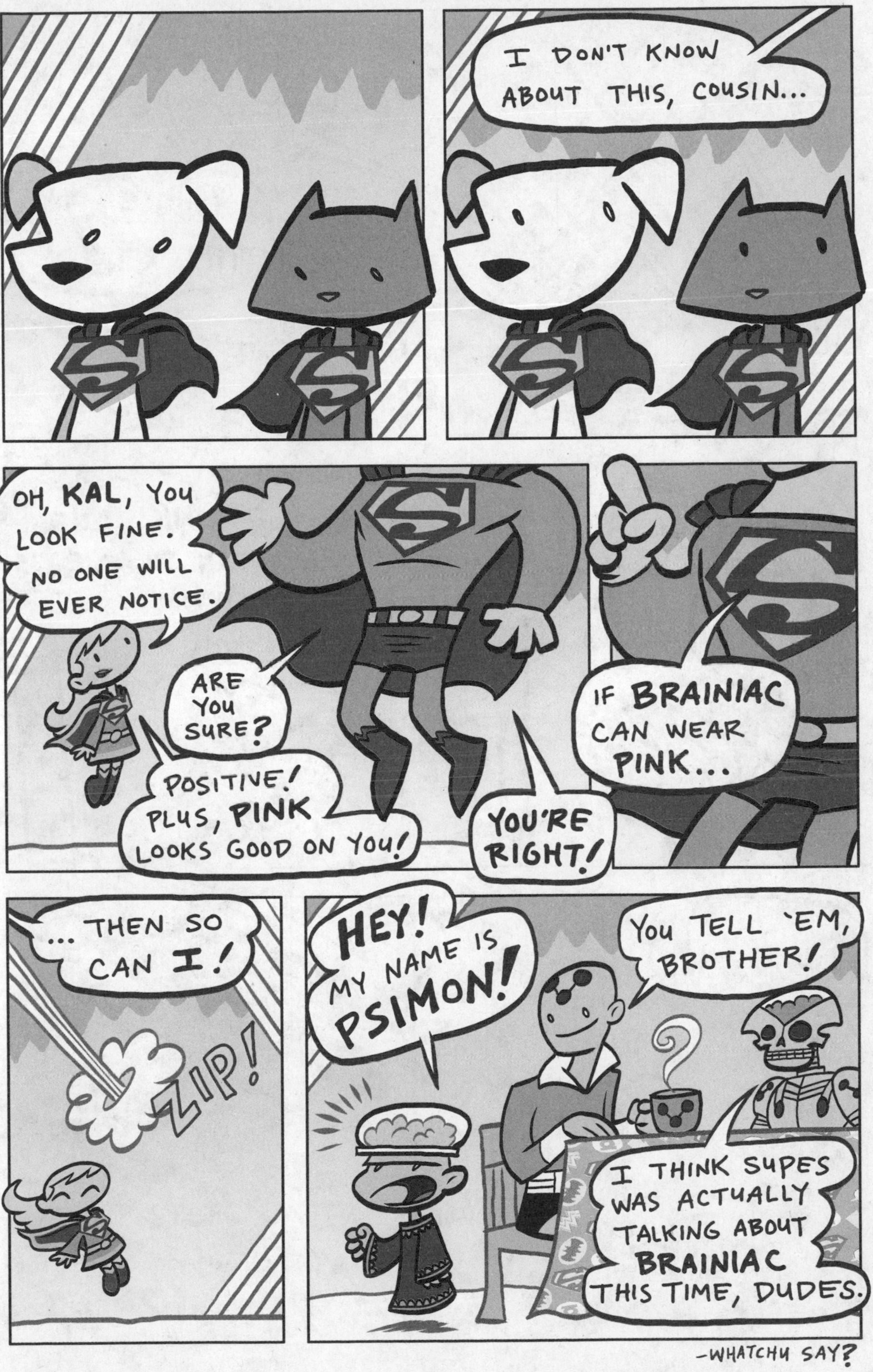

I DON'T KNOW ABOUT THIS, COUSIN...
OH, KAL, YOU LOOK FINE. NO ONE WILL EVER NOTICE.
ARE YOU SURE?
POSITIVE! PLUS, PINK LOOKS GOOD ON YOU!
YOU'RE RIGHT!
IF BRAINIAC CAN WEAR PINK...
... THEN SO CAN I!
ZIP!
HEY! MY NAME IS PSIMON!
YOU TELL 'EM, BROTHER!
I THINK SUPES WAS ACTUALLY TALKING ABOUT BRAINIAC THIS TIME, DUDES.
-WHATCHU SAY?

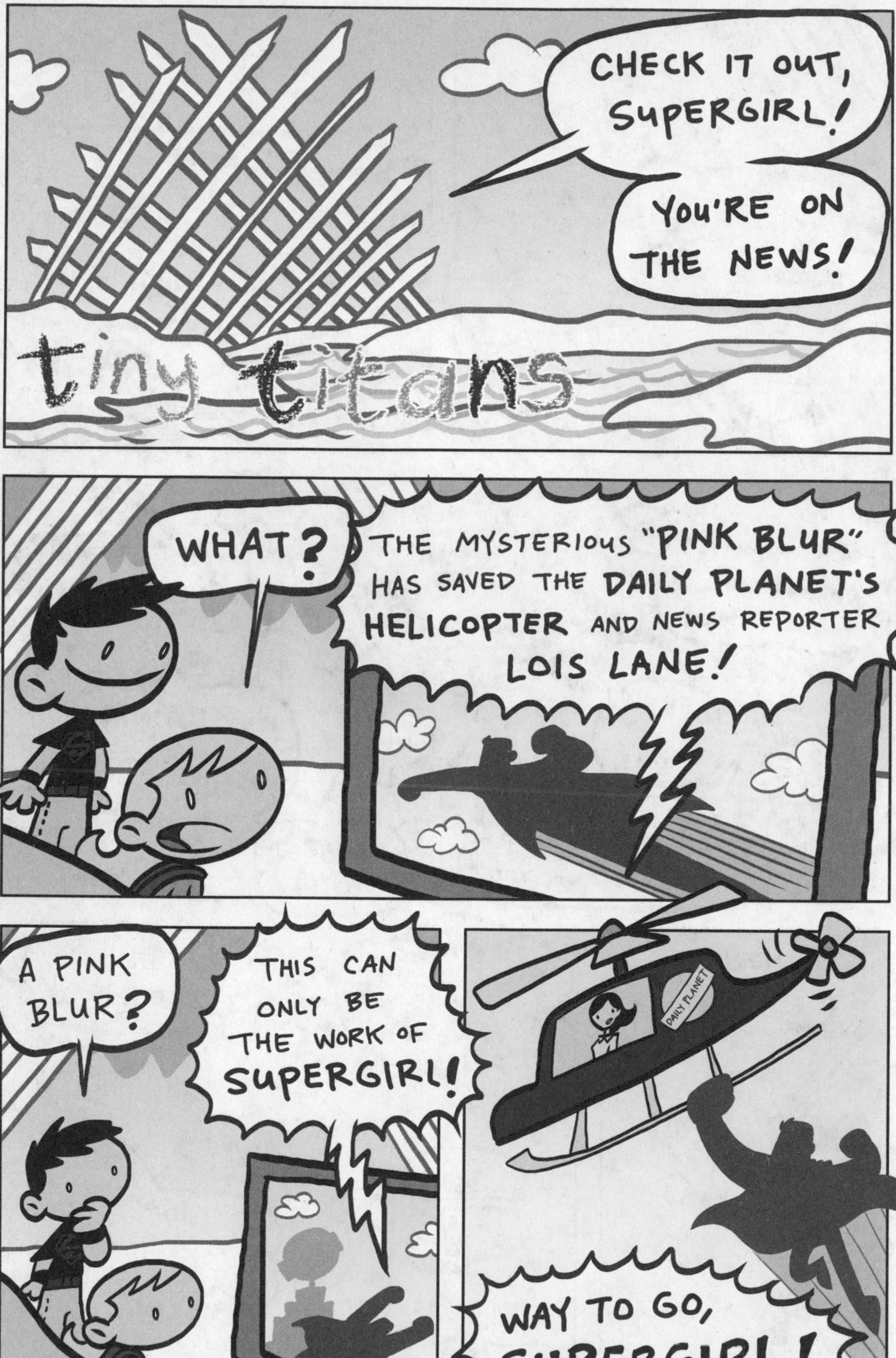
tiny titans
CHECK IT OUT, SUPERGIRL!
YOU'RE ON THE NEWS!
WHAT?
THE MYSTERIOUS "PINK BLUR" HAS SAVED THE DAILY PLANET'S HELICOPTER AND NEWS REPORTER LOIS LANE!
A PINK BLUR?
THIS CAN ONLY BE THE WORK OF SUPERGIRL!
DAILY PLANET
WAY TO GO, SUPERGIRL!

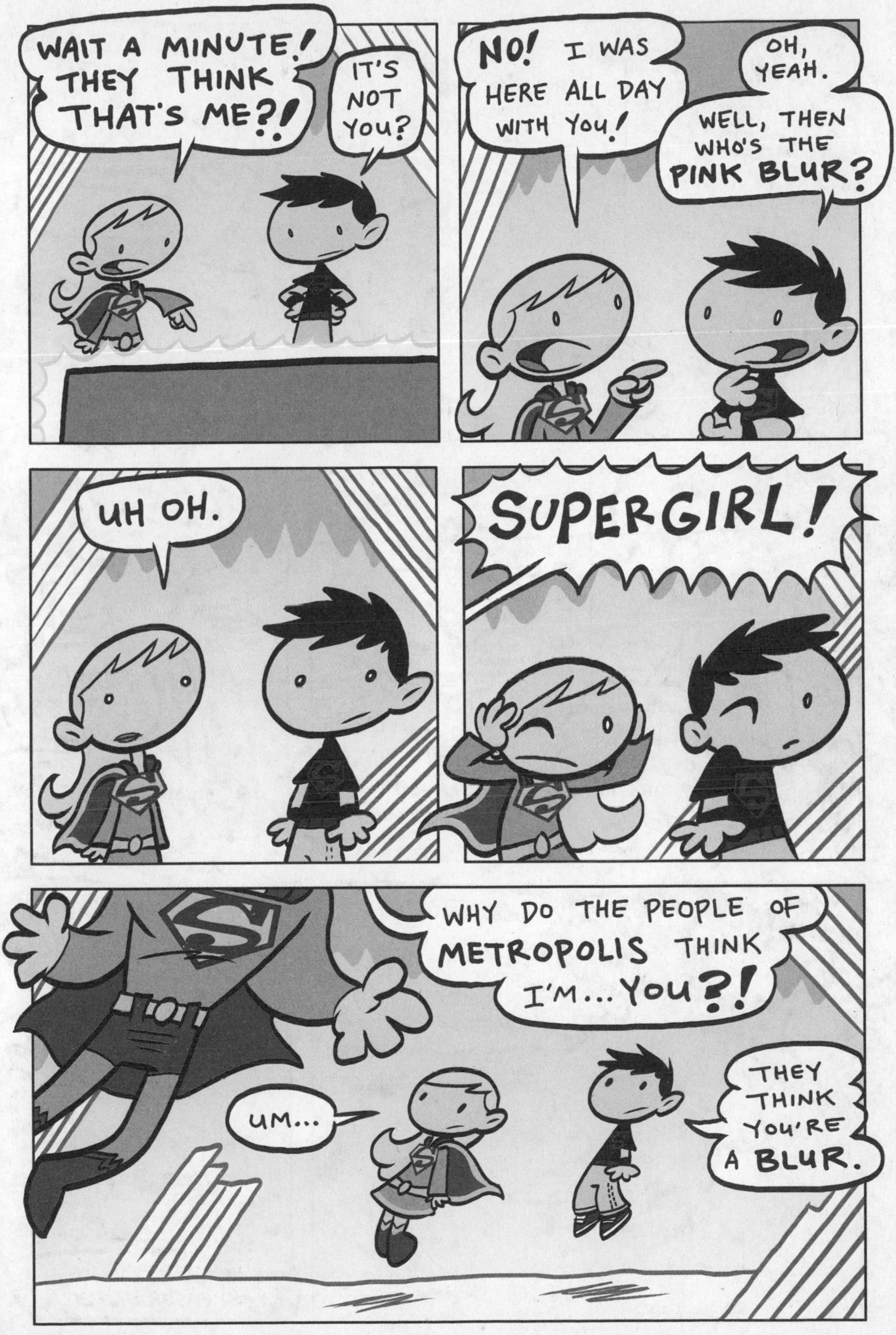
WAIT A MINUTE! THEY THINK THAT'S ME?!
IT'S NOT YOU?
NO! I WAS HERE ALL DAY WITH YOU!
OH, YEAH.
WELL, THEN WHO'S THE PINK BLUR?
UH OH.
SUPERGIRL!
WHY DO THE PEOPLE OF METROPOLIS THINK I'M... YOU?!
UM...
THEY THINK YOU'RE A BLUR.

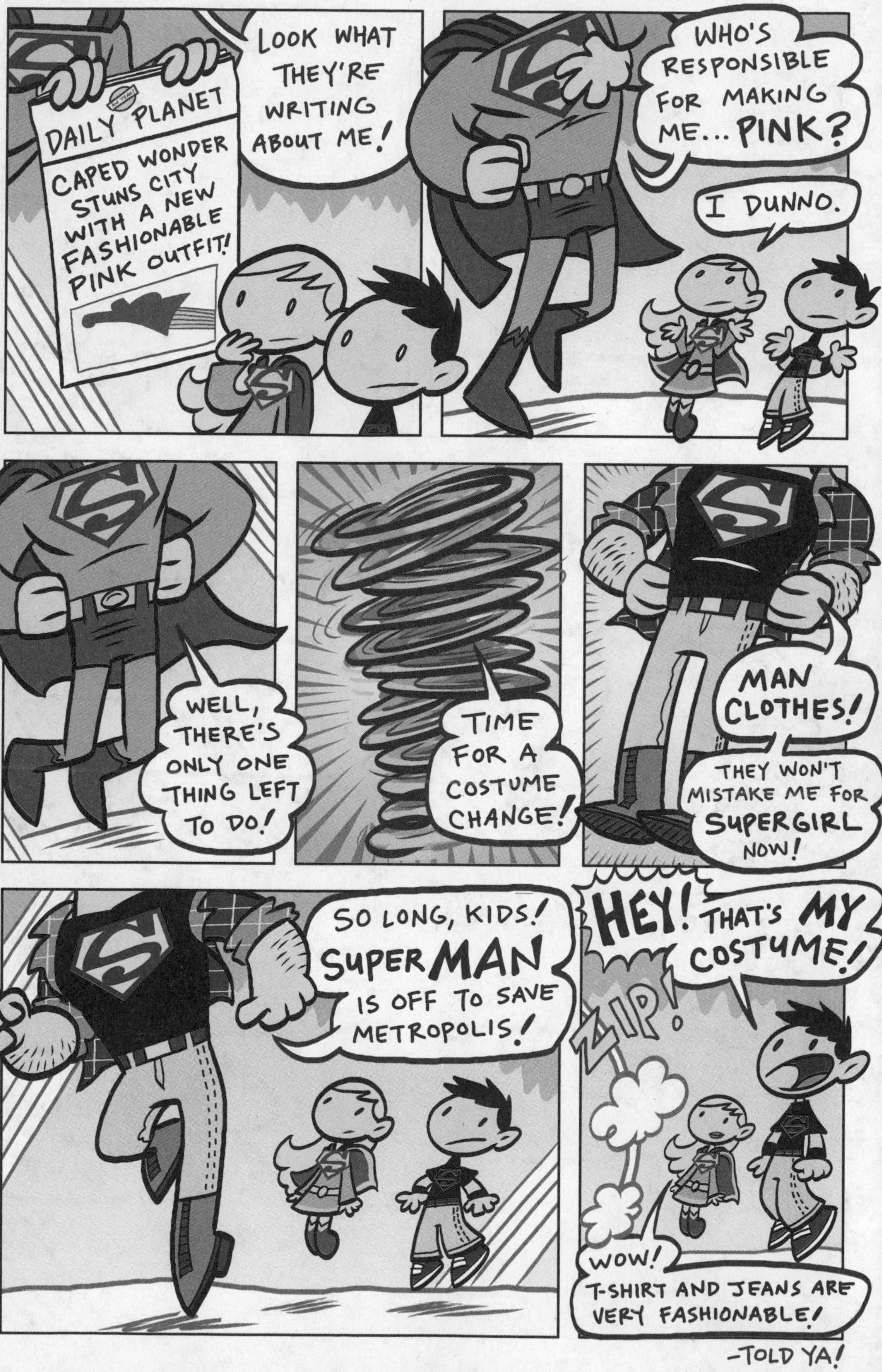
DAILY PLANET
CAPED WONDER STUNS CITY WITH A NEW FASHIONABLE PINK OUTFIT!
LOOK WHAT THEY'RE WRITING ABOUT ME!
WHO'S RESPONSIBLE FOR MAKING ME... PINK?
I DUNNO.
WELL, THERE'S ONLY ONE THING LEFT TO DO!
TIME FOR A COSTUME CHANGE!
MAN CLOTHES!
THEY WON'T MISTAKE ME FOR SUPERGIRL NOW!
SO LONG, KIDS! SUPERMAN IS OFF TO SAVE METROPOLIS!
HEY! THAT'S MY COSTUME!
ZIP!
WOW! T-SHIRT AND JEANS ARE VERY FASHIONABLE!
-TOLD YA!

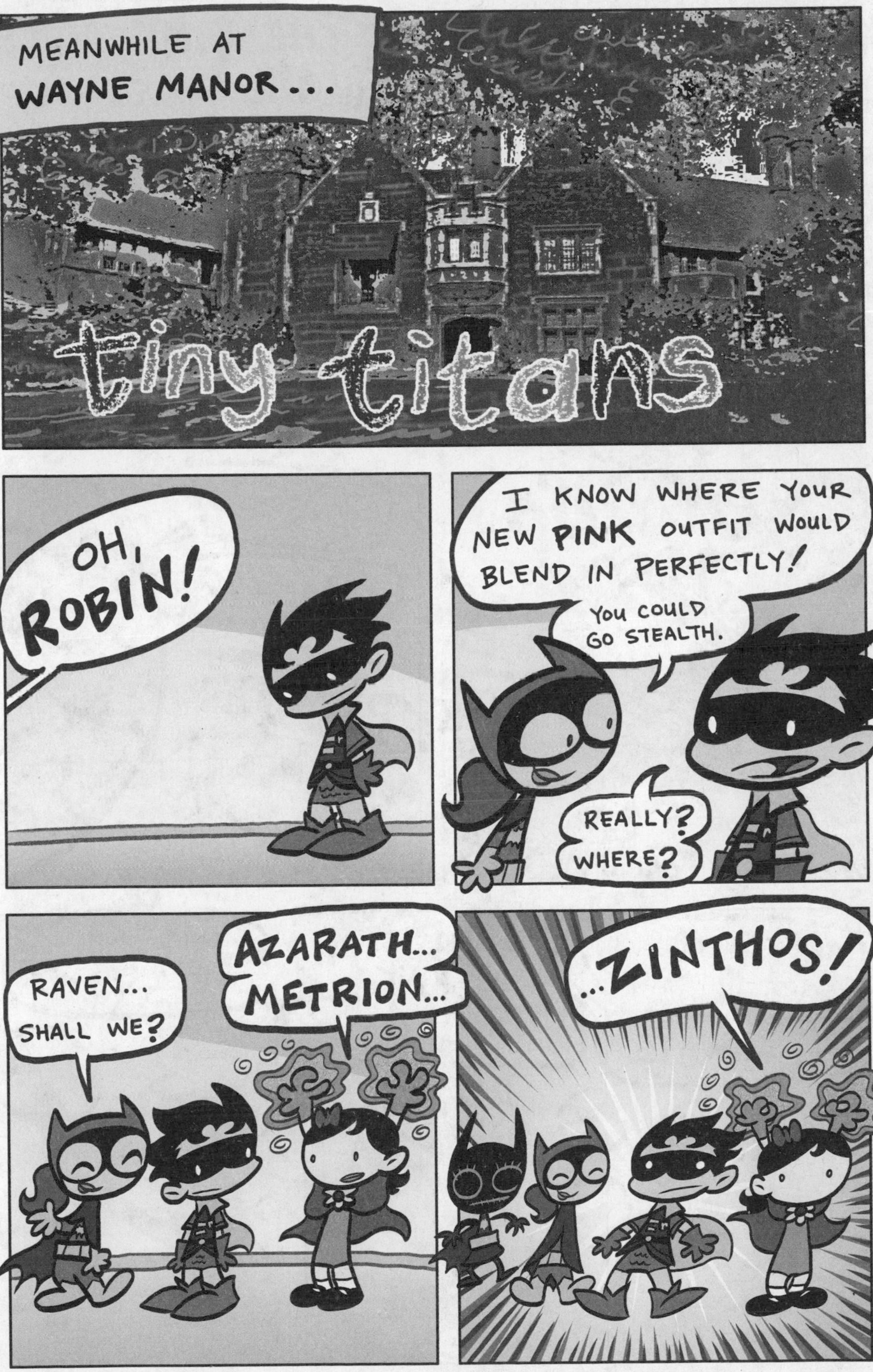

MEANWHILE AT WAYNE MANOR...
tiny titans
OH, ROBIN!
I KNOW WHERE YOUR NEW PINK OUTFIT WOULD BLEND IN PERFECTLY!
YOU COULD GO STEALTH.
REALLY? WHERE?
RAVEN... SHALL WE?
AZARATH... METRION...
...ZINTHOS!

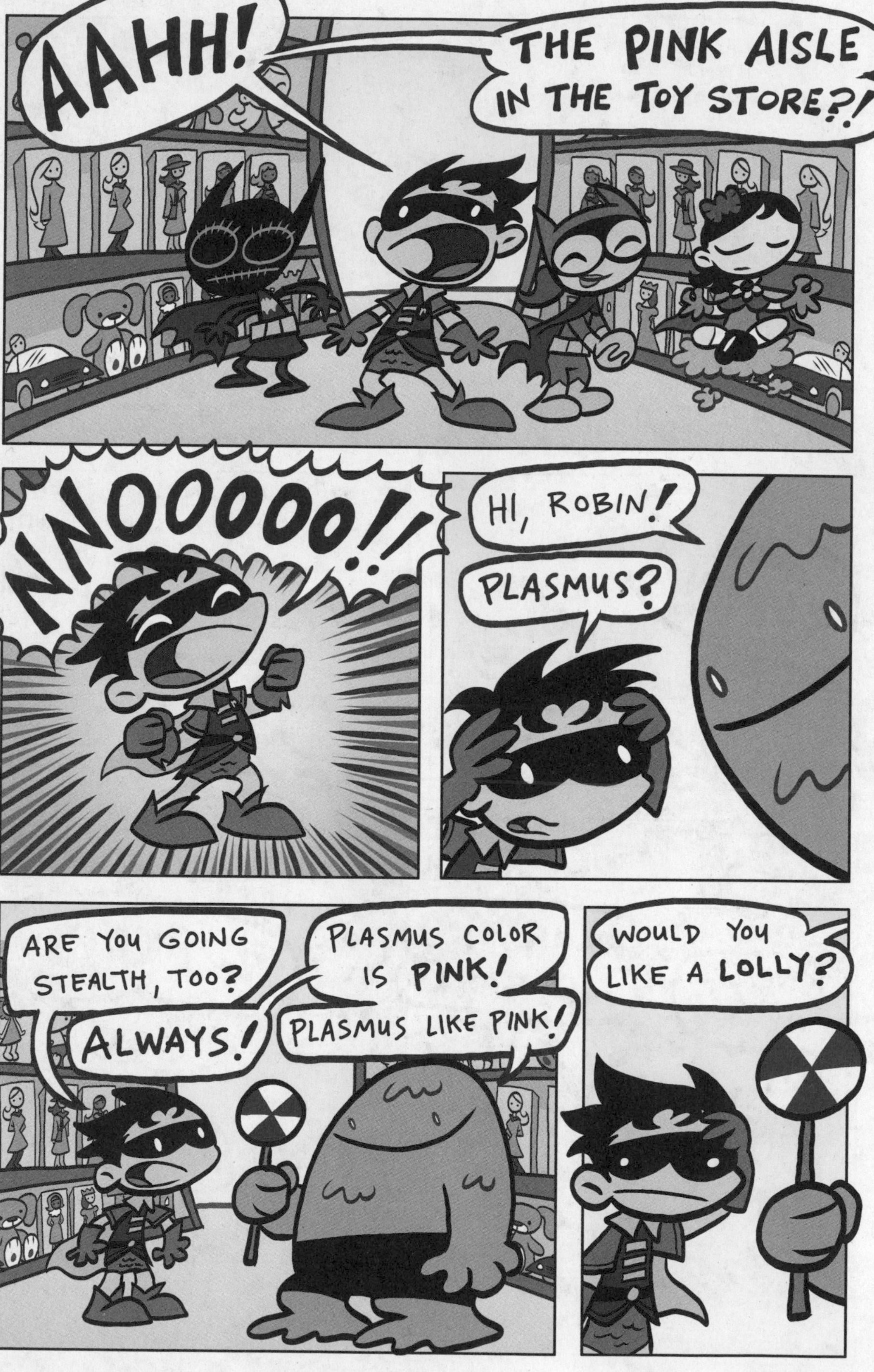
AAHH!
THE PINK AISLE IN THE TOY STORE?!
NNOOOOOO!!
HI, ROBIN!
PLASMUS?
ARE YOU GOING STEALTH, TOO?
ALWAYS!
PLASMUS COLOR IS PINK!
PLASMUS LIKE PINK!
WOULD YOU LIKE A LOLLY?

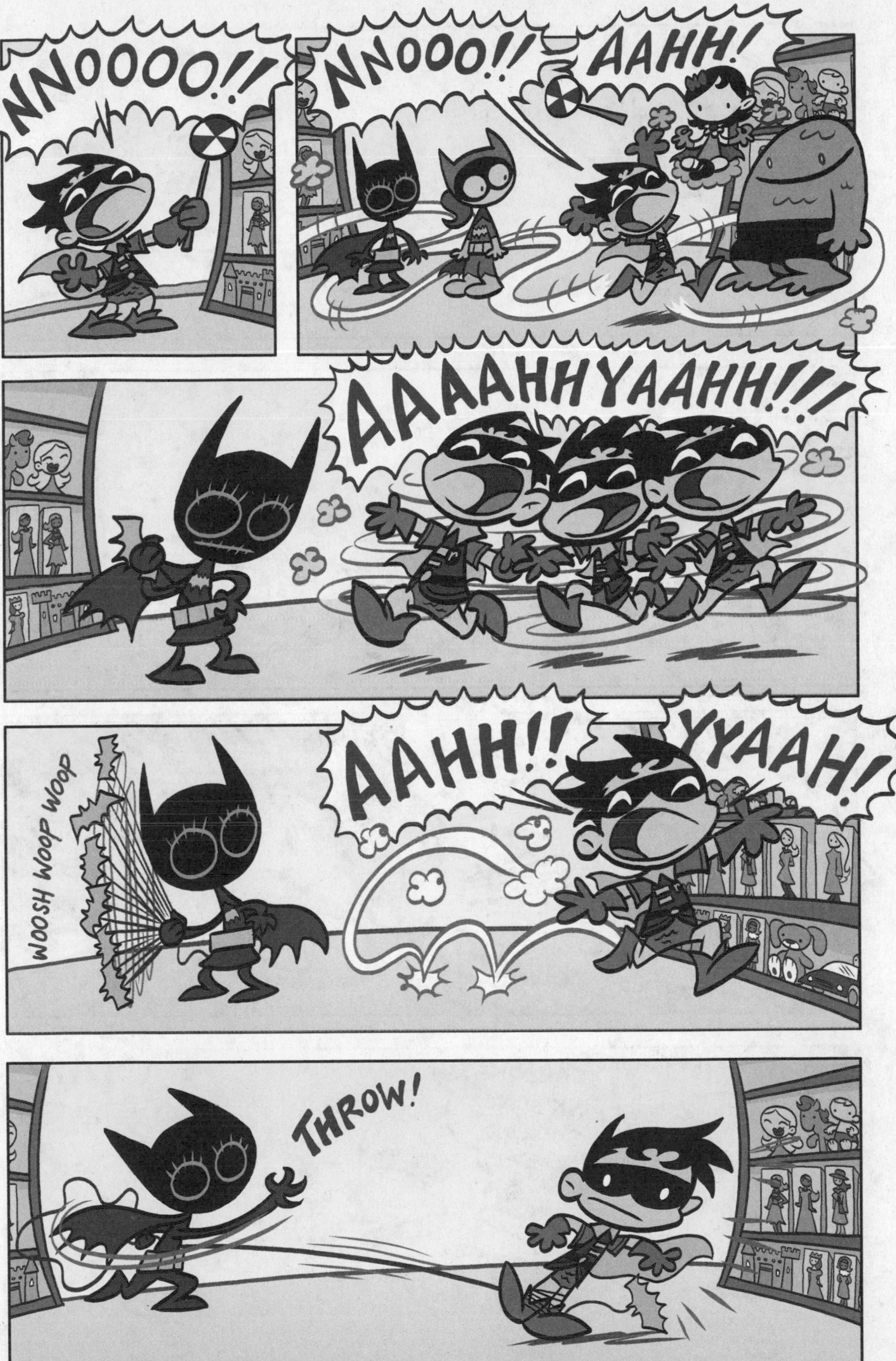
NNOOOO!!
NNOOO!!
AAHH!
AAAAHHYAAHH!!!
AAHH!!
YYAAH!
WOOSH WOOP WOOP
THROW!

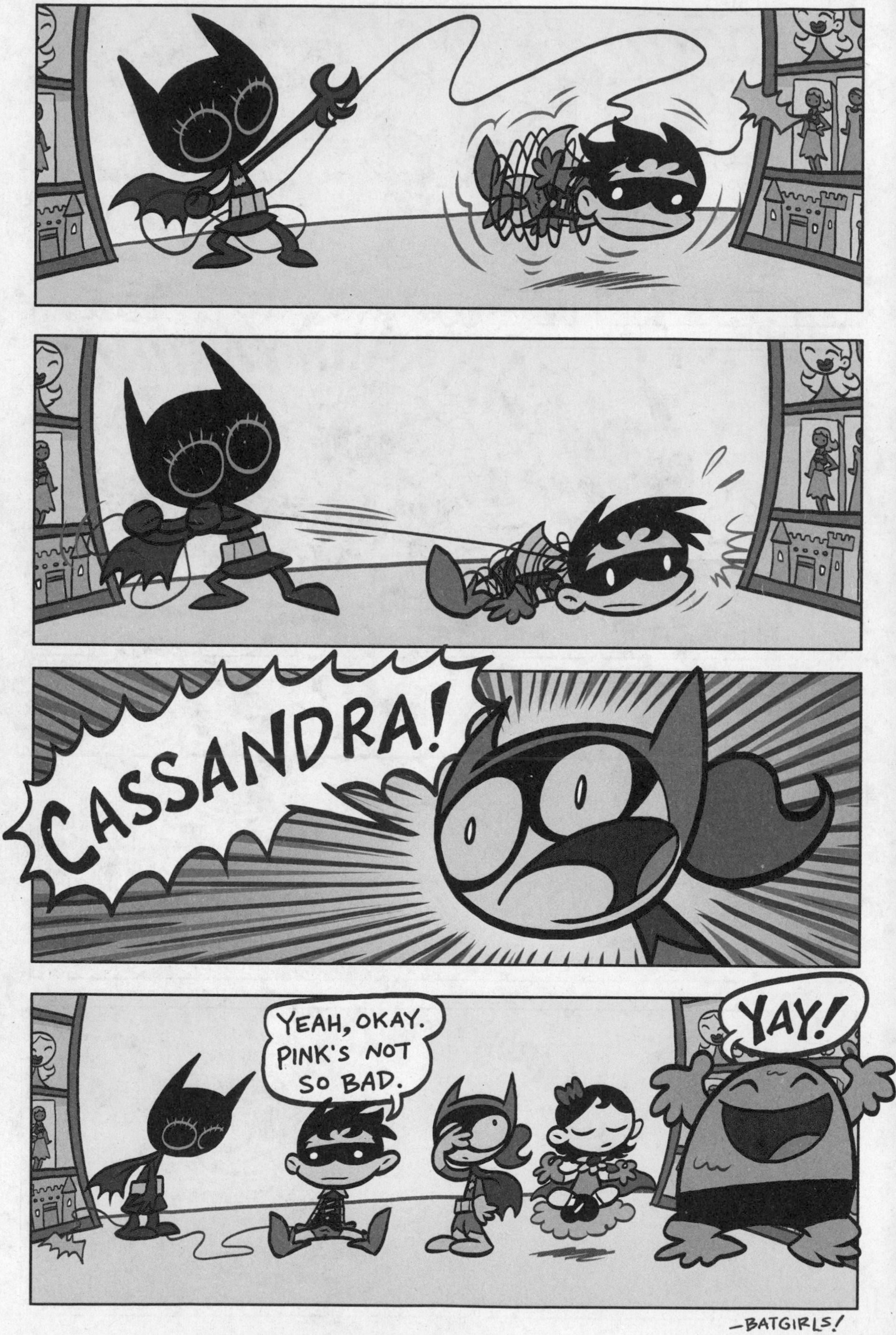
CASSANDRA!
YEAH, OKAY. PINK'S NOT SO BAD.
YAY!
-BATGIRLS!

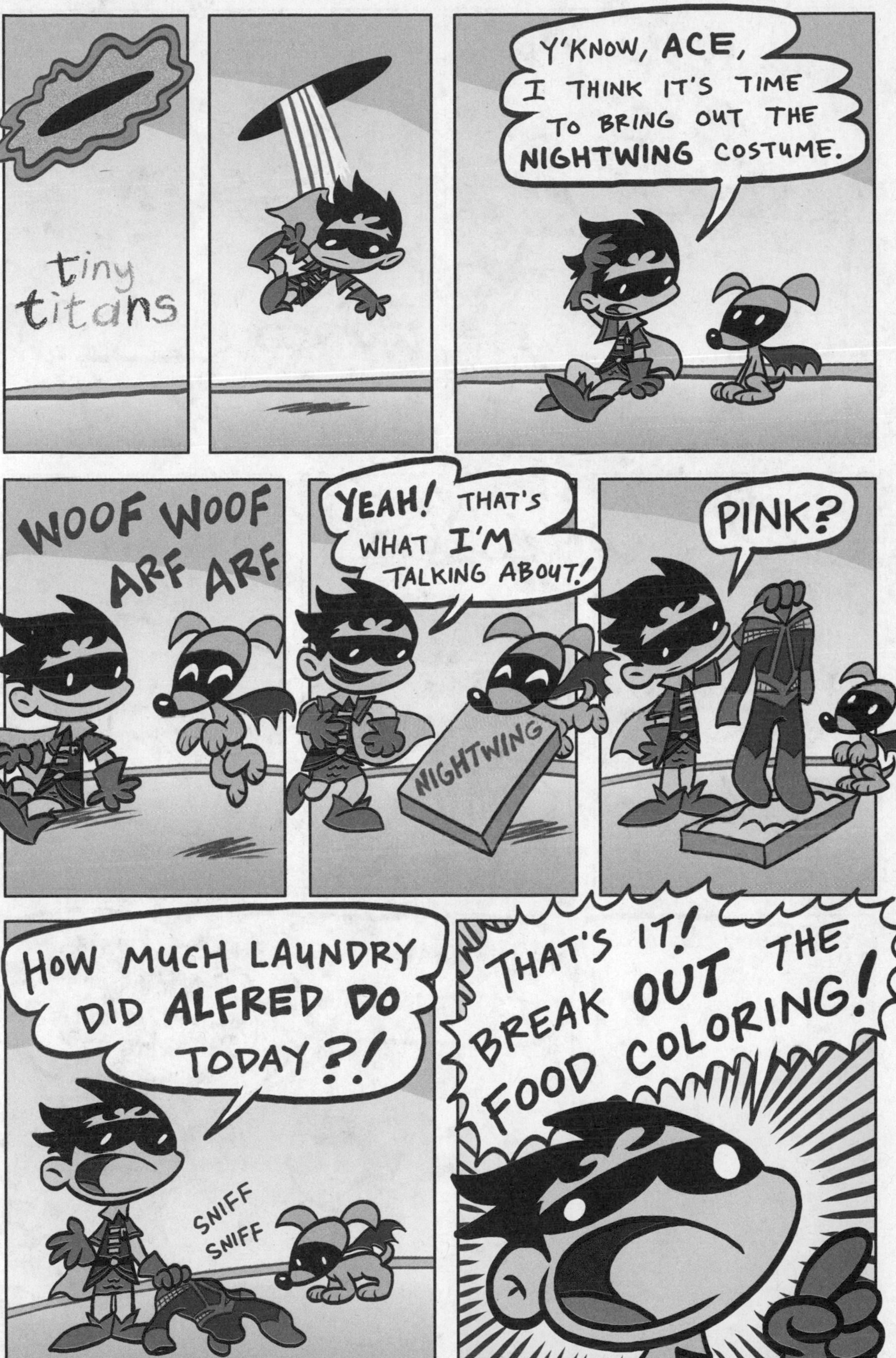
tiny titans
Y'KNOW, ACE, I THINK IT'S TIME TO BRING OUT THE NIGHTWING COSTUME.
WOOF WOOF ARF ARF
YEAH! THAT'S WHAT I'M TALKING ABOUT!
NIGHTWING
PINK?
HOW MUCH LAUNDRY DID ALFRED DO TODAY?!
SNIFF SNIFF
THAT'S IT! BREAK OUT THE FOOD COLORING!

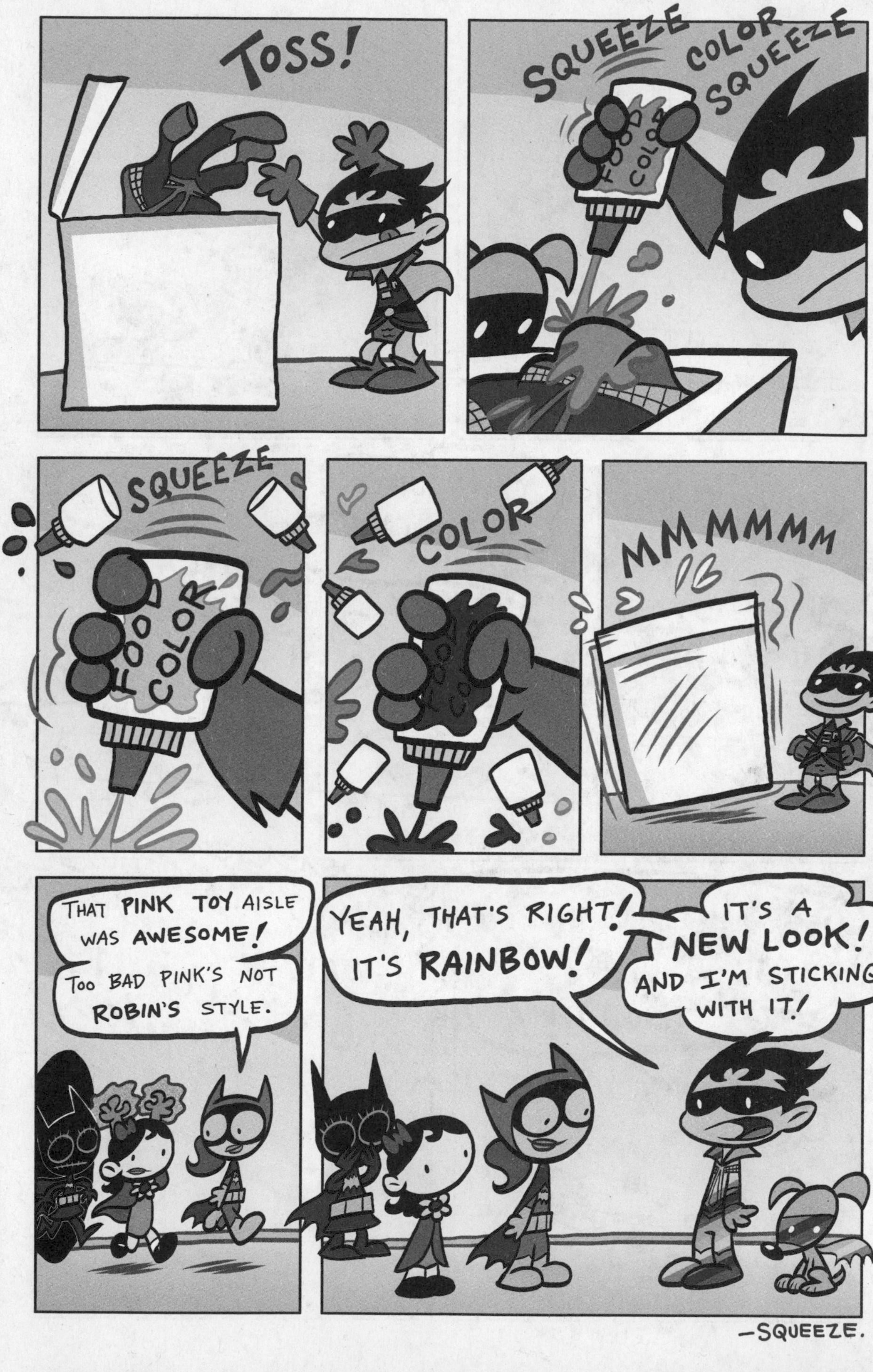

TOSS!
SQUEEZE
COLOR
SQUEEZE
FOOD COLOR
SQUEEZE
FOOD COLOR
COLOR
MMMMMM
THAT PINK TOY AISLE WAS AWESOME!
TOO BAD PINK'S NOT ROBIN'S STYLE.
YEAH, THAT'S RIGHT! IT'S RAINBOW!
IT'S A NEW LOOK! AND I'M STICKING WITH IT!
-SQUEEZE.

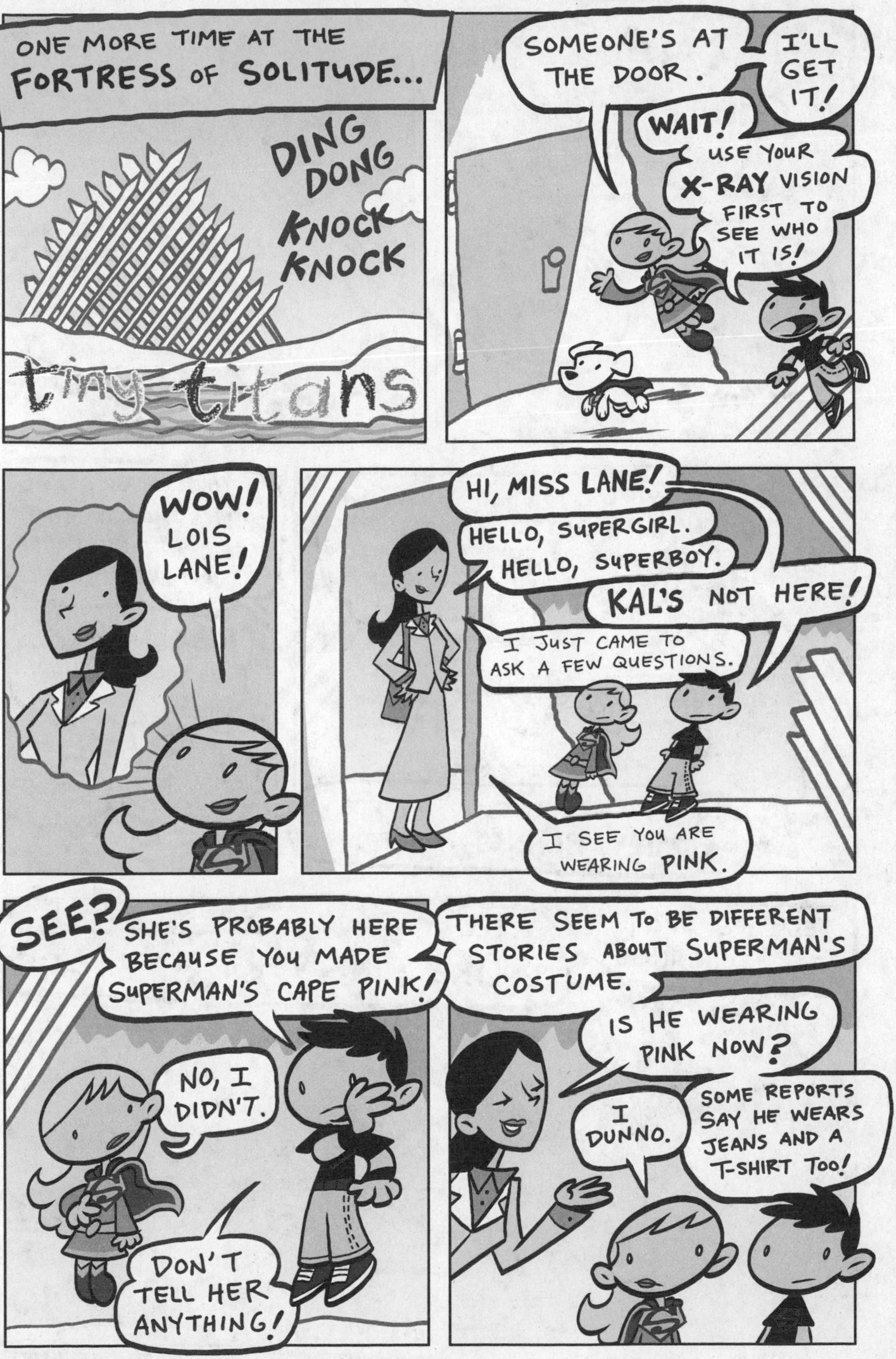
ONE MORE TIME AT THE FORTRESS OF SOLITUDE...
DING DONG
KNOCK KNOCK
tiny titans
SOMEONE'S AT THE DOOR.
I'LL GET IT!
WAIT! USE YOUR X-RAY VISION FIRST TO SEE WHO IT IS!
WOW! LOIS LANE!
HI, MISS LANE!
HELLO, SUPERGIRL. HELLO, SUPERBOY.
KAL'S NOT HERE!
I JUST CAME TO ASK A FEW QUESTIONS.
I SEE YOU ARE WEARING PINK.
SEE?
SHE'S PROBABLY HERE BECAUSE YOU MADE SUPERMAN'S CAPE PINK!
NO, I DIDN'T.
DON'T TELL HER ANYTHING!
THERE SEEM TO BE DIFFERENT STORIES ABOUT SUPERMAN'S COSTUME.
IS HE WEARING PINK NOW?
I DUNNO.
SOME REPORTS SAY HE WEARS JEANS AND A T-SHIRT TOO!

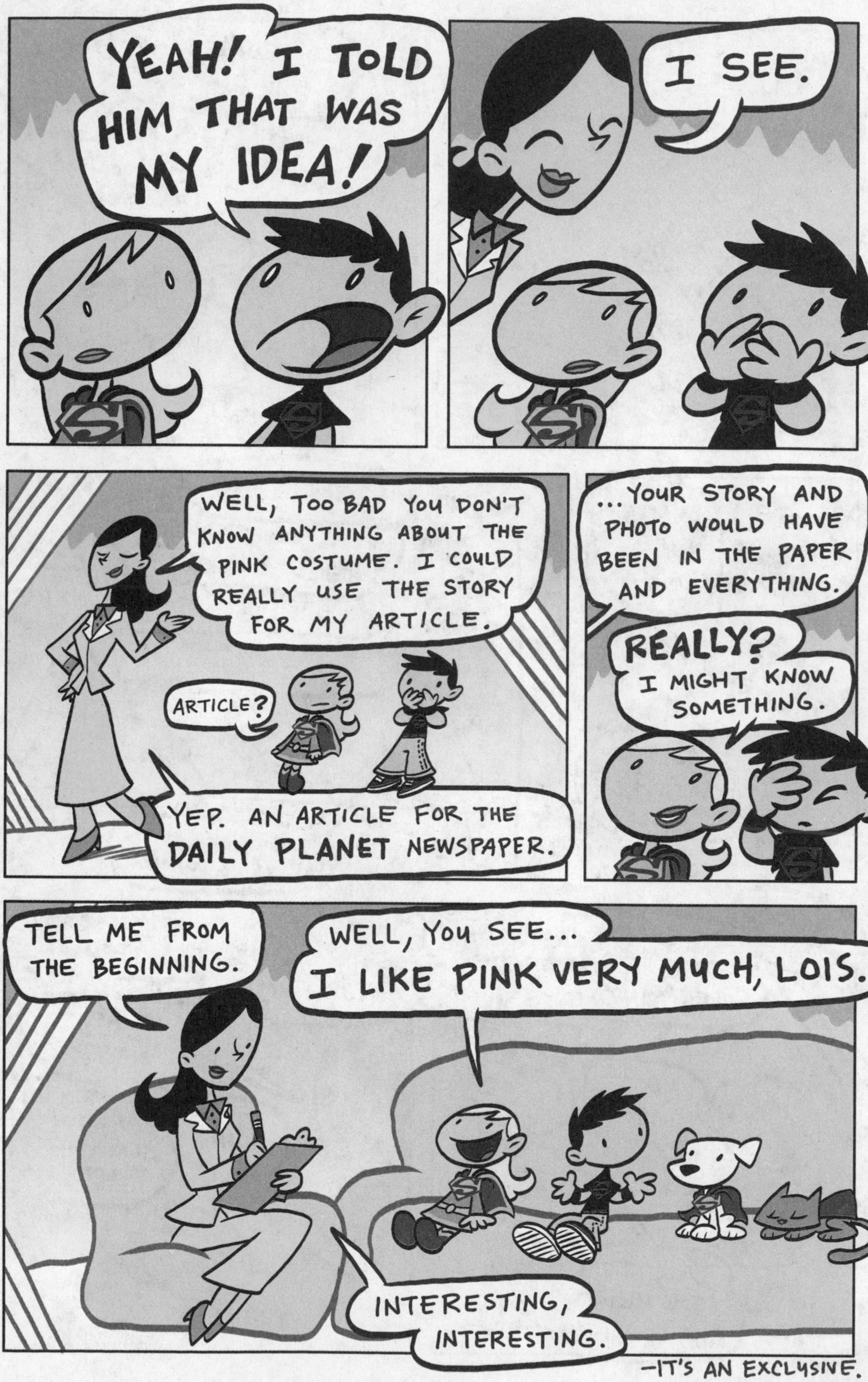
YEAH! I TOLD HIM THAT WAS MY IDEA!
I SEE.
WELL, TOO BAD YOU DON'T KNOW ANYTHING ABOUT THE PINK COSTUME. I COULD REALLY USE THE STORY FOR MY ARTICLE.
ARTICLE?
YEP. AN ARTICLE FOR THE DAILY PLANET NEWSPAPER.
...YOUR STORY AND PHOTO WOULD HAVE BEEN IN THE PAPER AND EVERYTHING.
REALLY? I MIGHT KNOW SOMETHING.
TELL ME FROM THE BEGINNING.
WELL, YOU SEE... I LIKE PINK VERY MUCH, LOIS.
INTERESTING, INTERESTING.
—IT'S AN EXCLUSIVE.

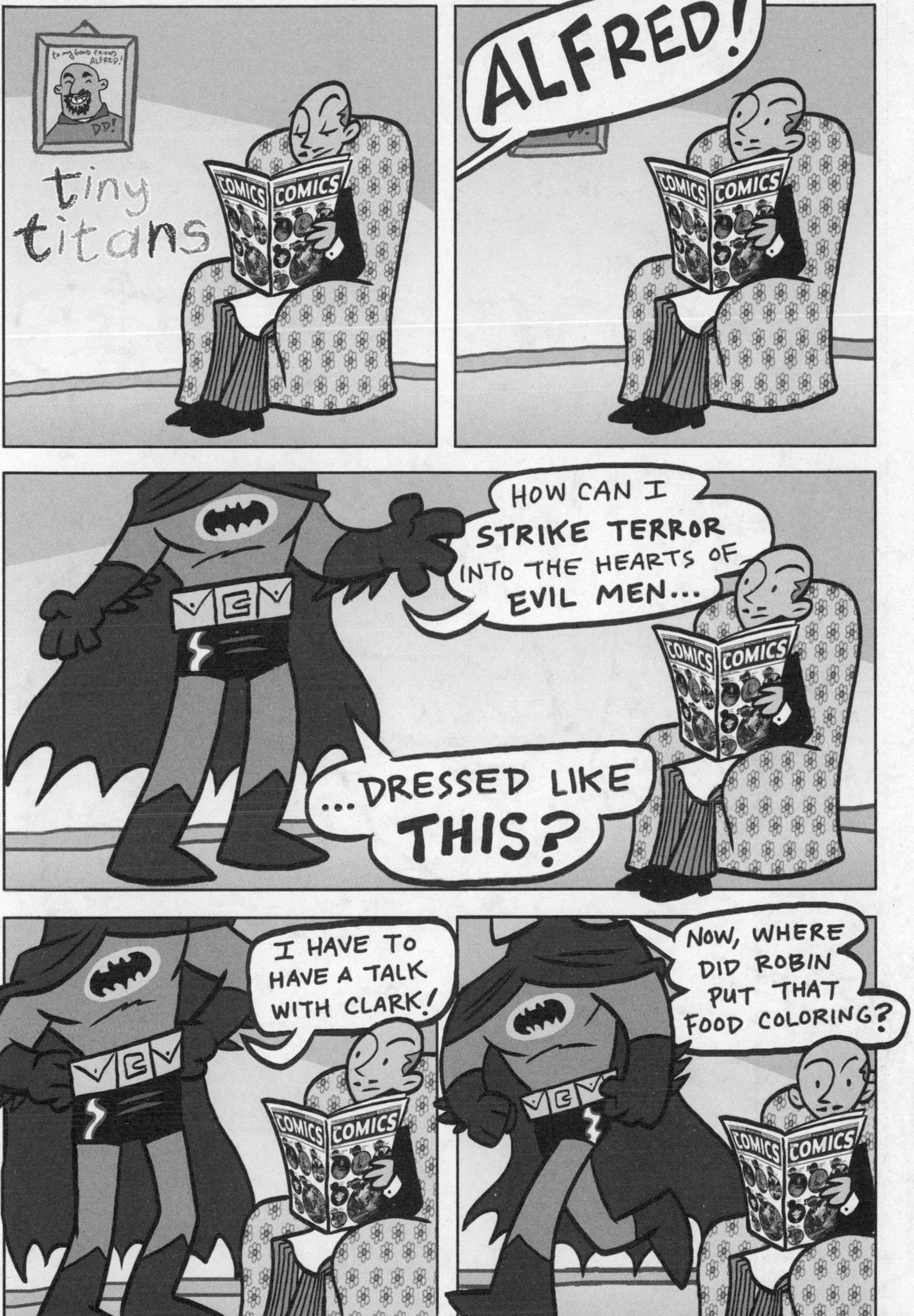
to my GOOD FRIEND ALFRED!
DD!
tiny titans
COMICS
ALFRED!
HOW CAN I STRIKE TERROR INTO THE HEARTS OF EVIL MEN...
...DRESSED LIKE THIS?
I HAVE TO HAVE A TALK WITH CLARK!
NOW, WHERE DID ROBIN PUT THAT FOOD COLORING?

—CALL THE COMMISSIONER!

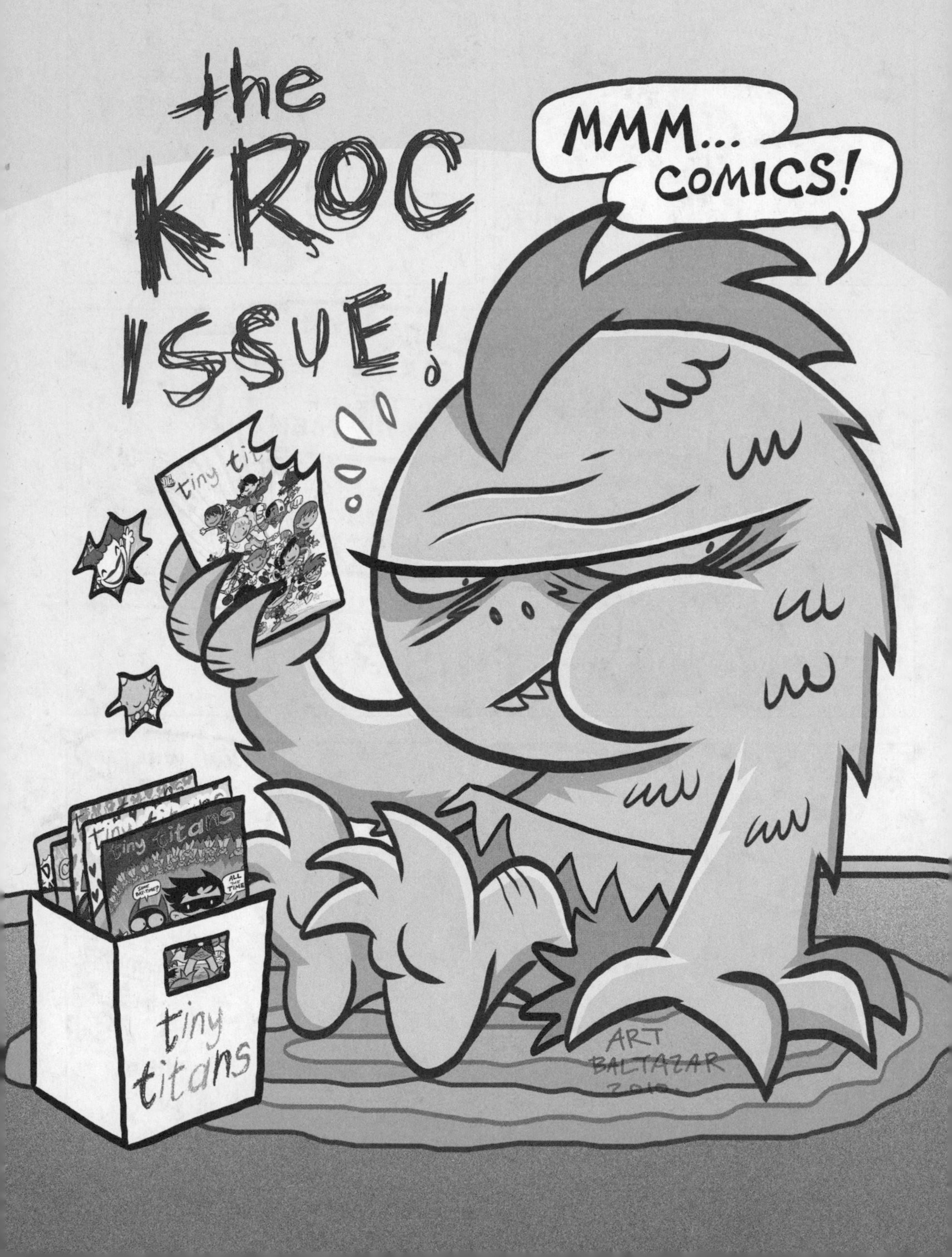
the KROC ISSUE!
MMM... COMICS!
tiny titans
ART BALTAZAR

tiny titans

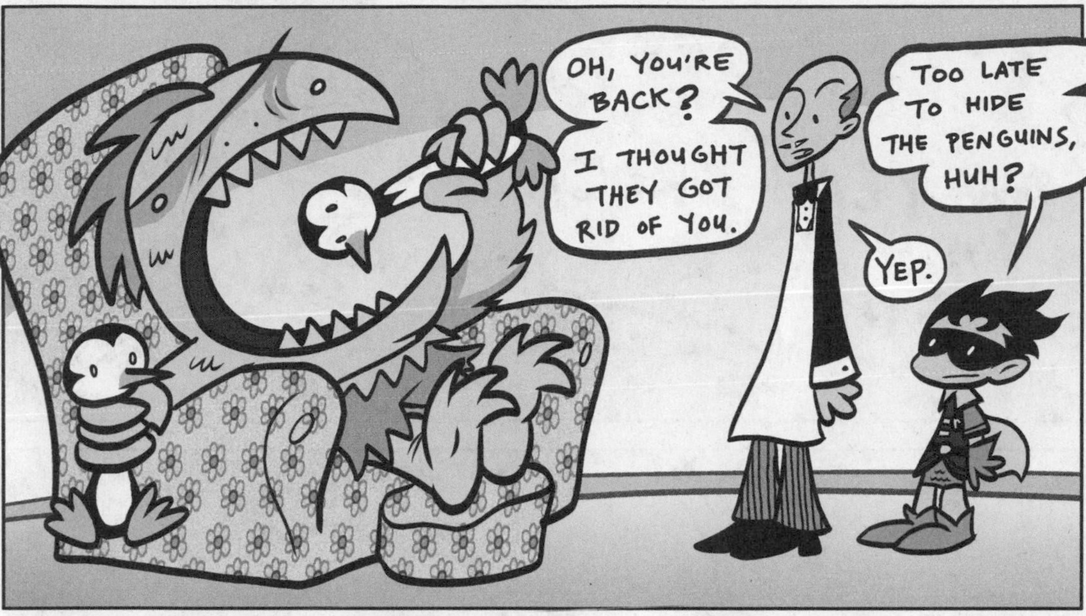
OH, YOU'RE BACK?
I THOUGHT THEY GOT RID OF YOU.
YEP.
TOO LATE TO HIDE THE PENGUINS, HUH?

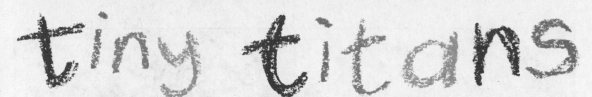

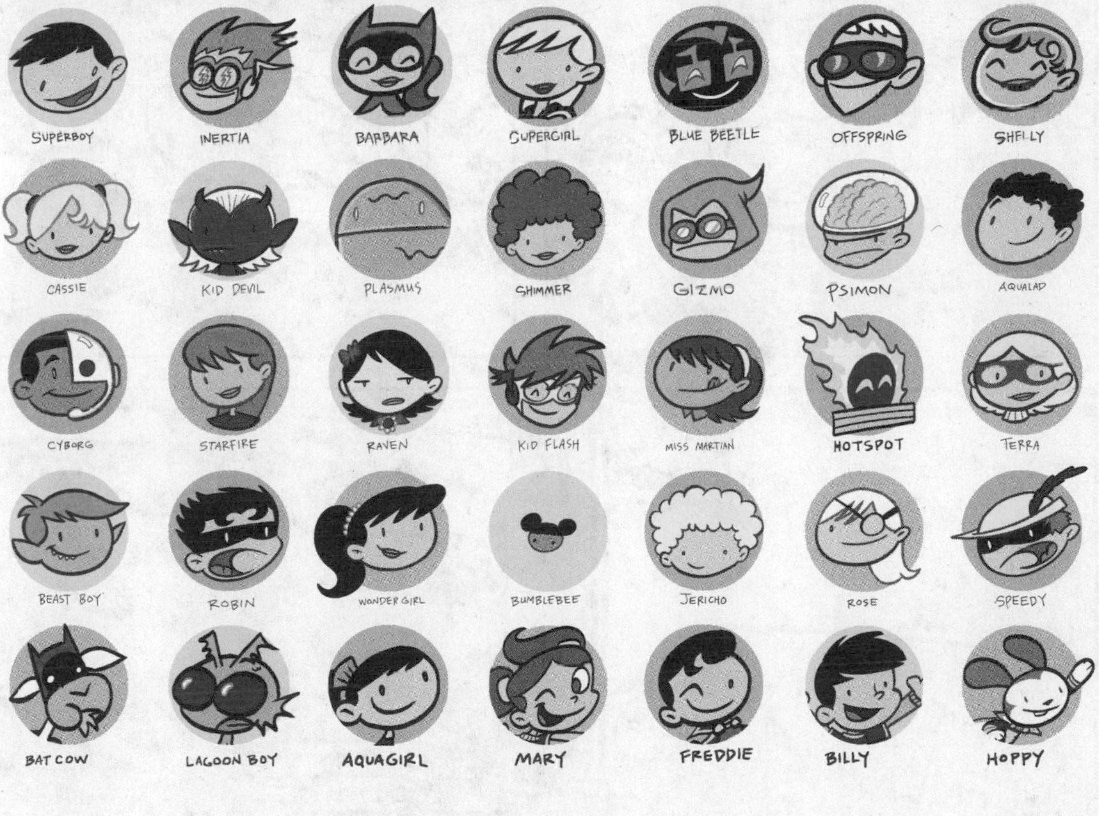
SUPERBOY
INERTIA
BARBARA
SUPERGIRL
BLUE BEETLE
OFFSPRING
SHELLY
CASSIE
KID DEVIL
PLASMUS
SHIMMER
GIZMO
PSIMON
AQUALAD
CYBORG
STARFIRE
RAVEN
KID FLASH
MISS MARTIAN
HOTSPOT
TERRA
BEAST BOY
ROBIN
WONDER GIRL
BUMBLEBEE
JERICHO
ROSE
SPEEDY
BAT COW
LAGOON BOY
AQUAGIRL
MARY
FREDDIE
BILLY
HOPPY

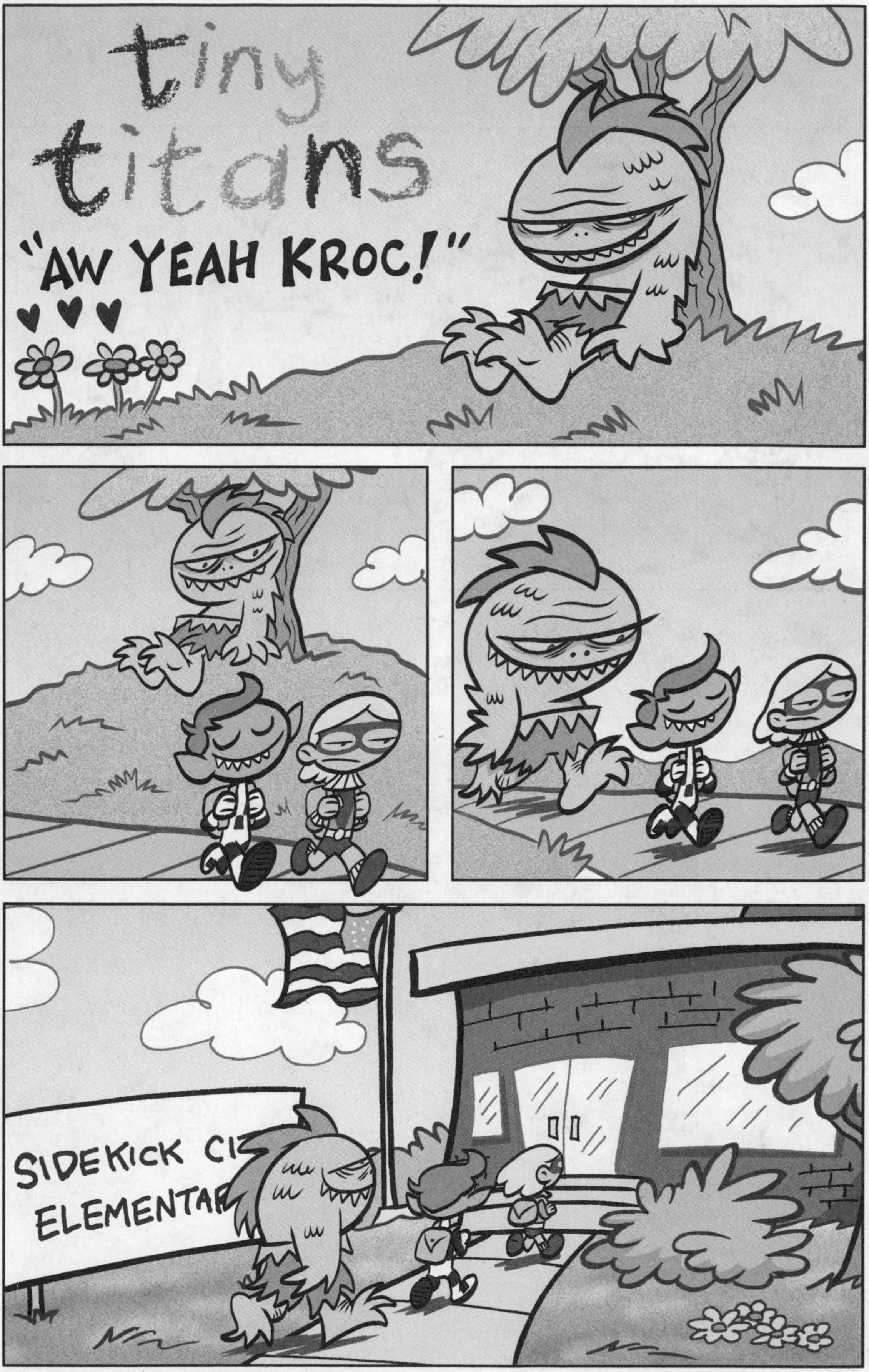
tiny titans
"AW YEAH KROC!"
SIDEKICK CI
ELEMENTAR

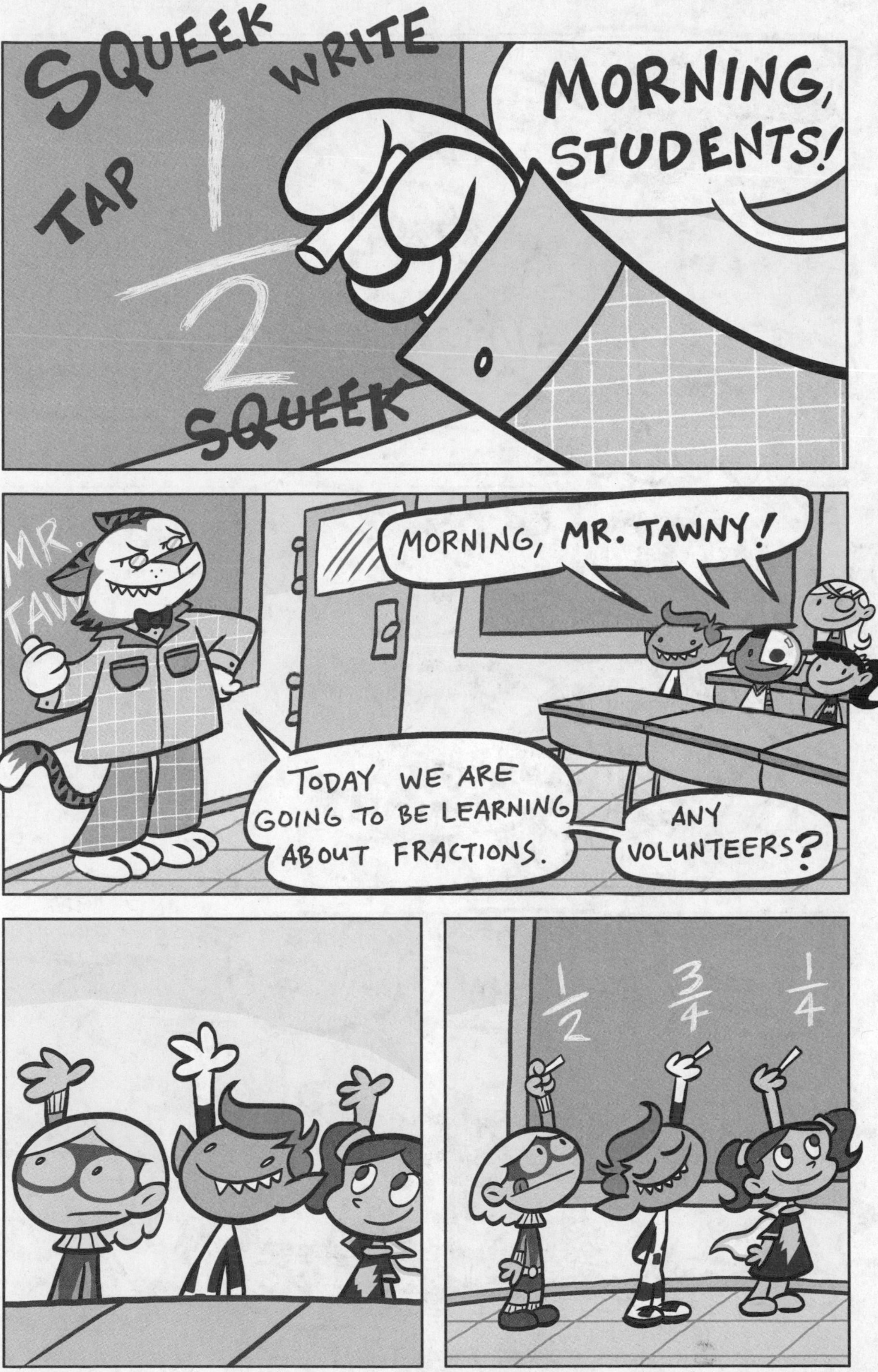
SQUEEK
WRITE
TAP
1/2
SQUEEK
MORNING, STUDENTS!
MR.
MORNING, MR. TAWNY!
TODAY WE ARE GOING TO BE LEARNING ABOUT FRACTIONS.
ANY VOLUNTEERS?
1/2
3/4
1/4

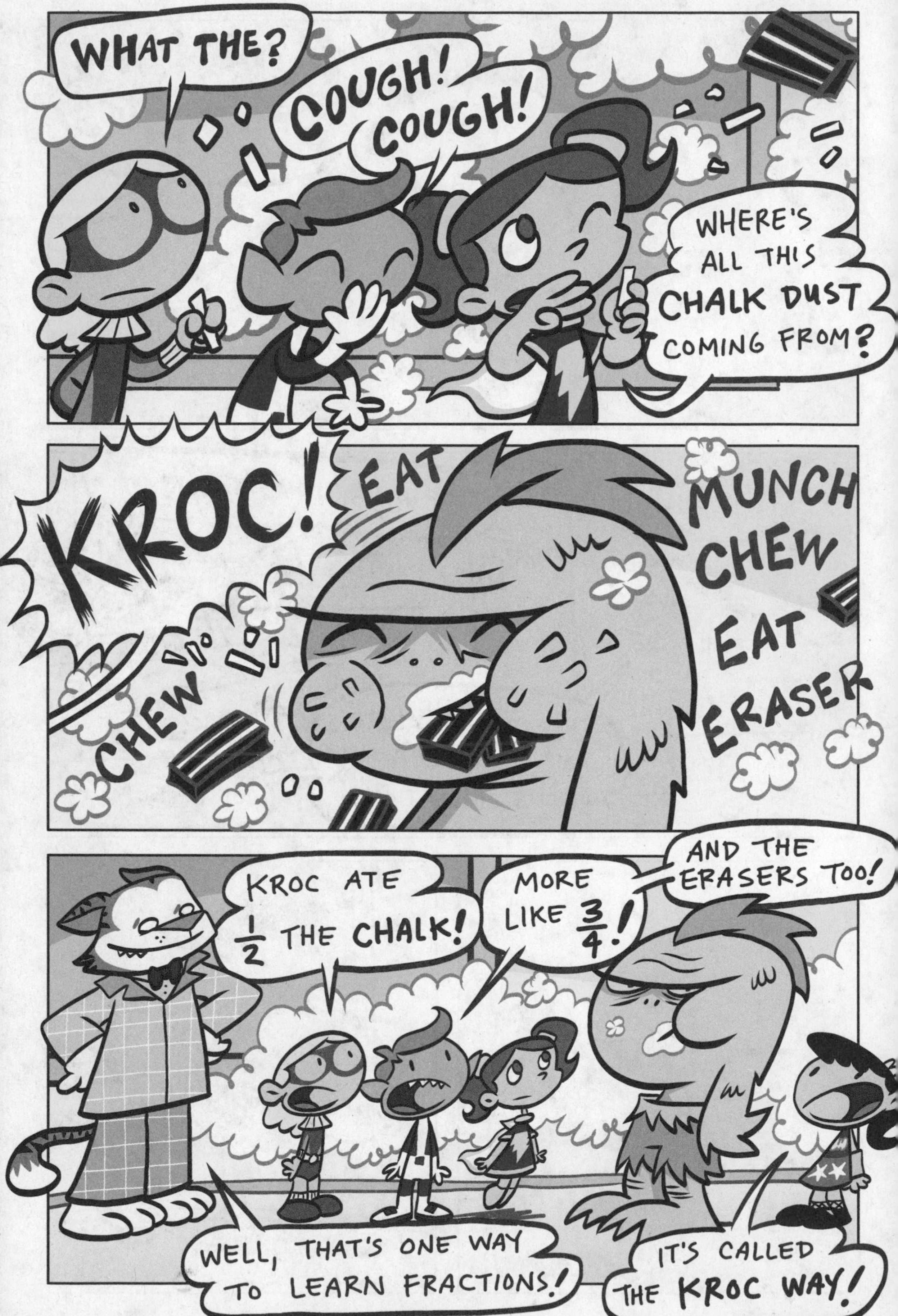
WHAT THE?
COUGH! COUGH!
WHERE'S ALL THIS CHALK DUST COMING FROM?
KROC!
EAT
MUNCH
CHEW
EAT
ERASER
CHEW
KROC ATE 1/2 THE CHALK!
MORE LIKE 3/4!
AND THE ERASERS TOO!
WELL, THAT'S ONE WAY TO LEARN FRACTIONS!
IT'S CALLED THE KROC WAY!

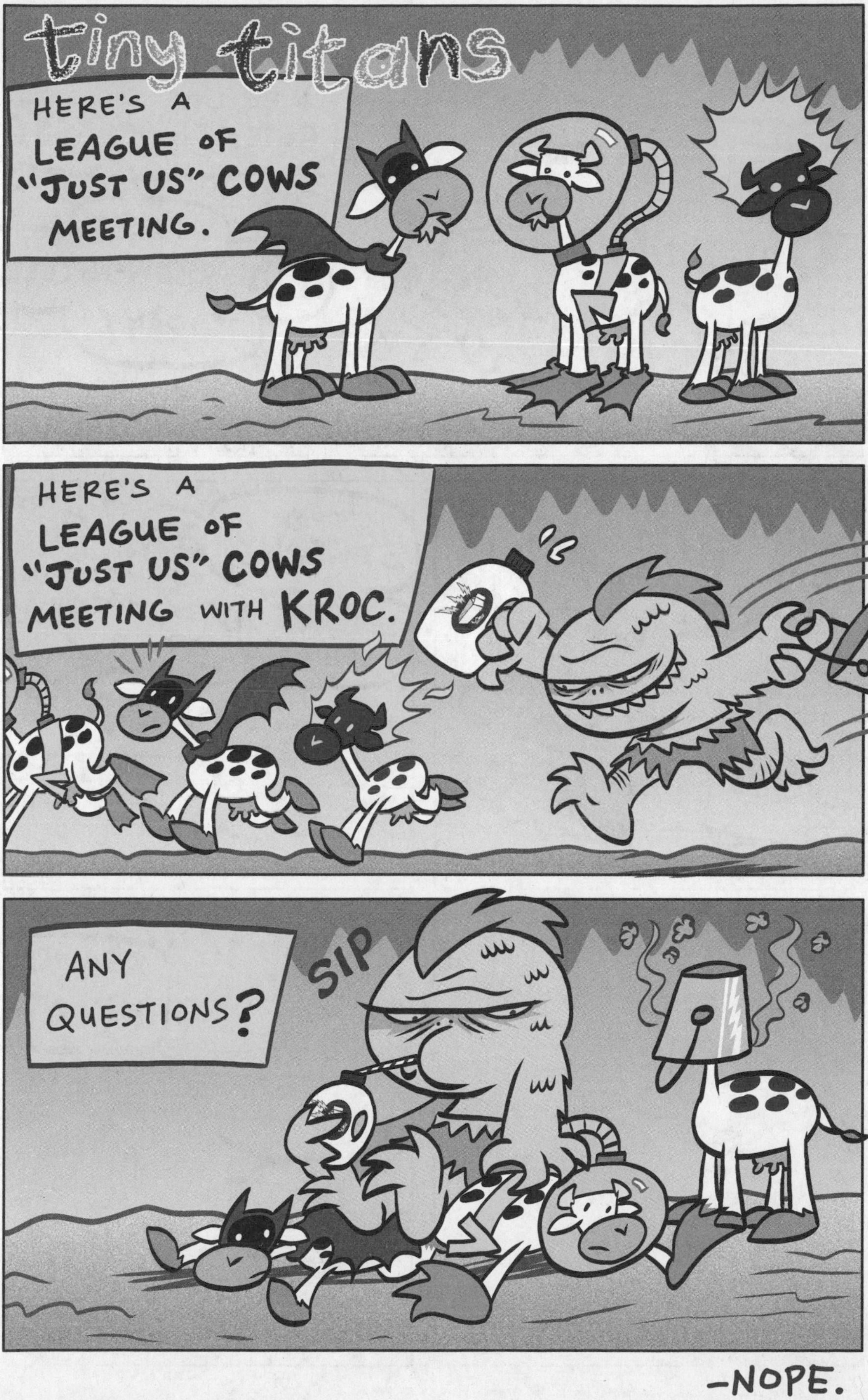
tiny titans
HERE'S A LEAGUE OF "JUST US" COWS MEETING.
HERE'S A LEAGUE OF "JUST US" COWS MEETING WITH KROC.
ANY QUESTIONS?
SIP
-NOPE.

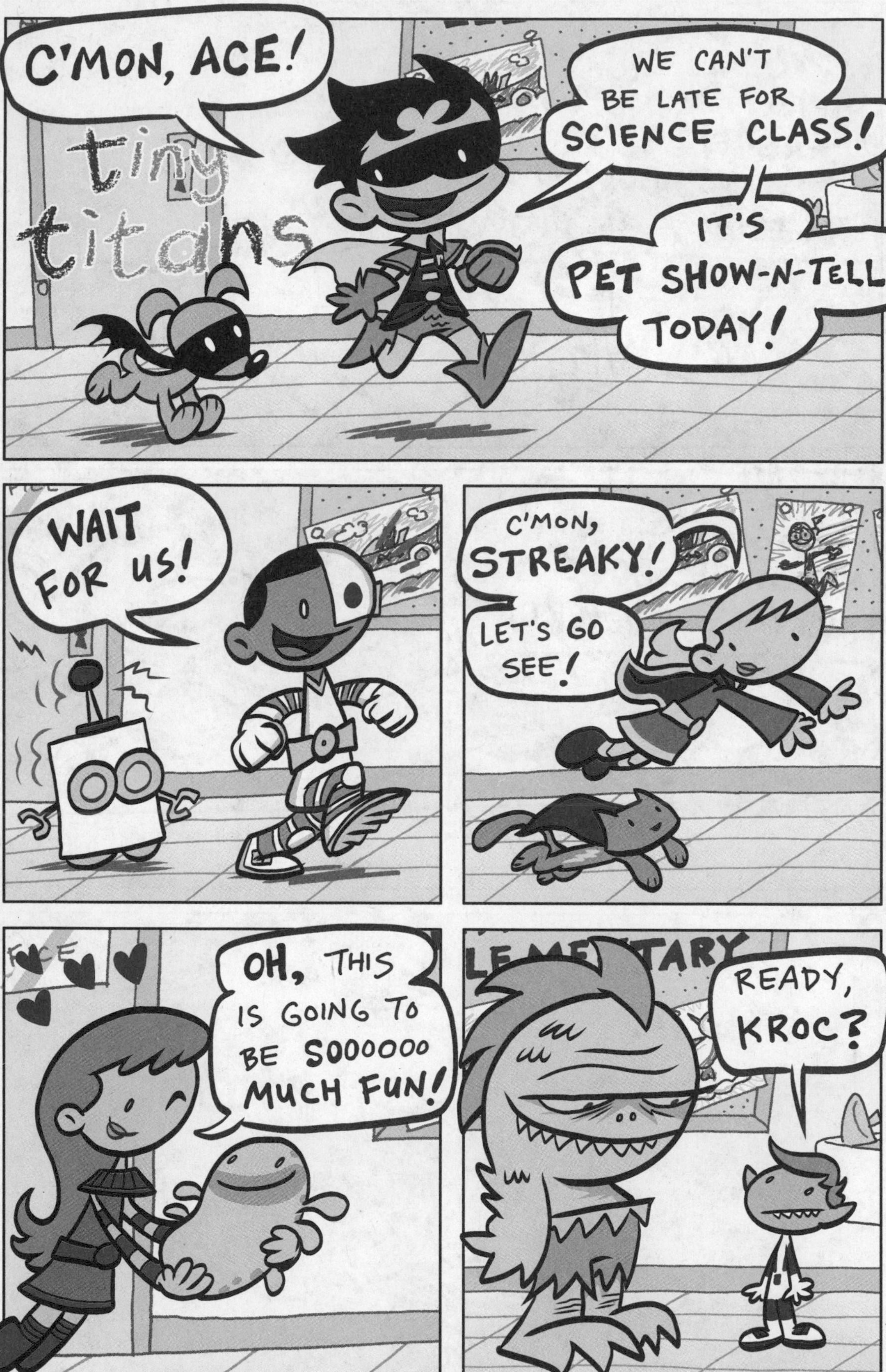
C'MON, ACE!
WE CAN'T BE LATE FOR SCIENCE CLASS!
IT'S PET SHOW-N-TELL TODAY!
tiny titans
WAIT FOR US!
C'MON, STREAKY!
LET'S GO SEE!
OH, THIS IS GOING TO BE SOOOOOO MUCH FUN!
READY, KROC?

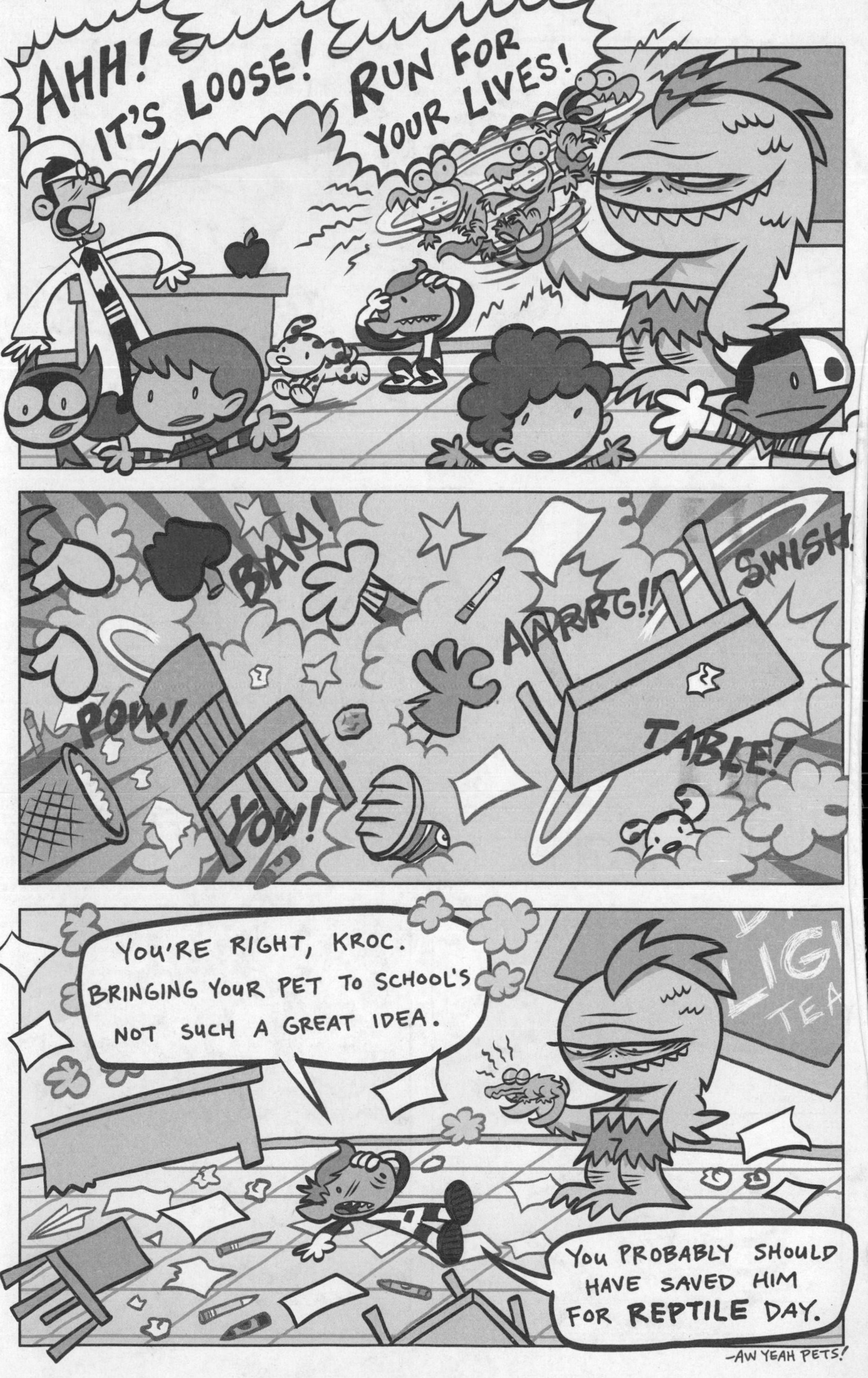
AHH! IT'S LOOSE! RUN FOR YOUR LIVES!
BAM!
SWISH!
AARRG!!
POW!
YOW!
TABLE!
YOU'RE RIGHT, KROC. BRINGING YOUR PET TO SCHOOL'S NOT SUCH A GREAT IDEA.
YOU PROBABLY SHOULD HAVE SAVED HIM FOR REPTILE DAY.
—AW YEAH PETS!

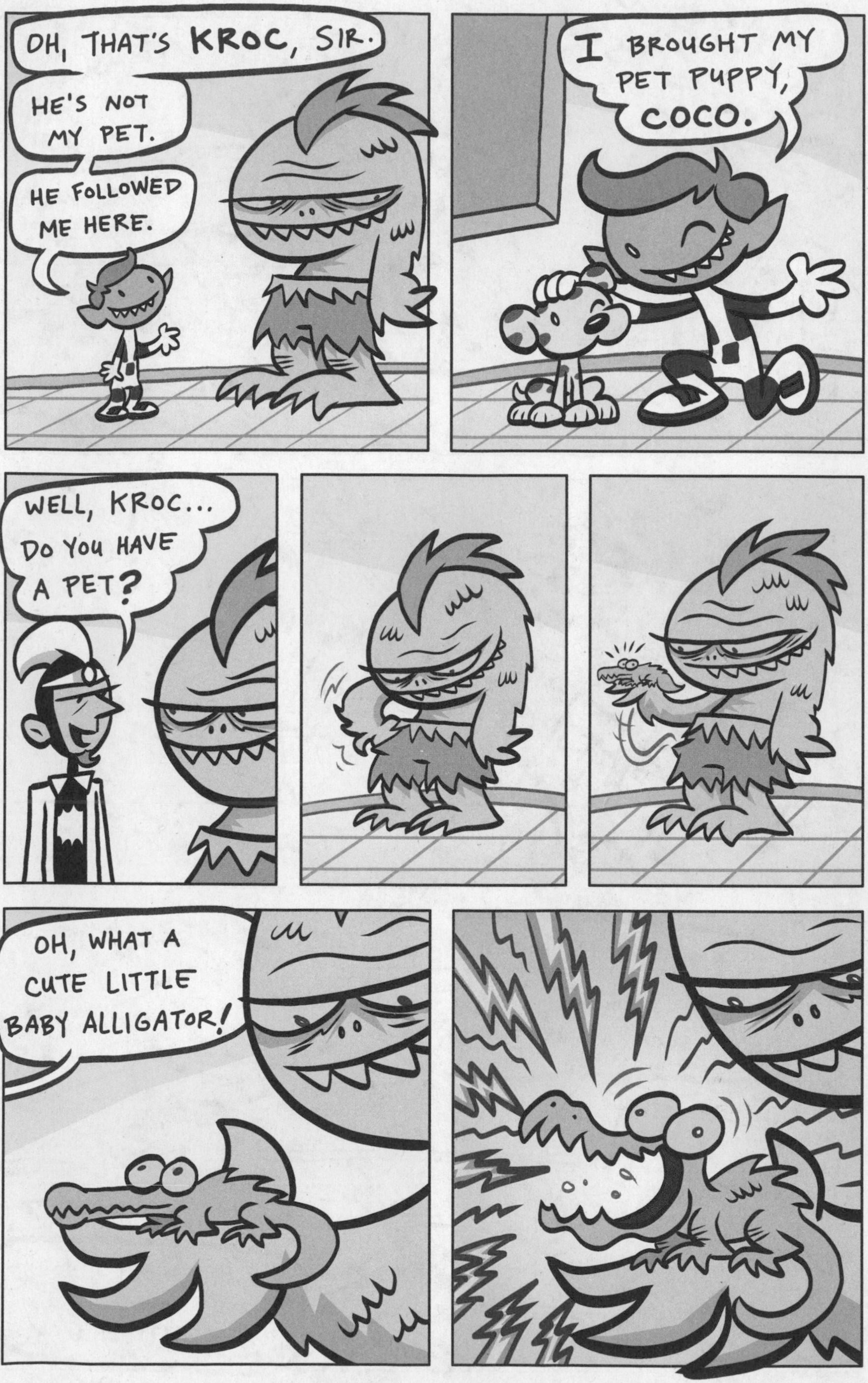
OH, THAT'S KROC, SIR.
HE'S NOT MY PET.
HE FOLLOWED ME HERE.
I BROUGHT MY PET PUPPY, COCO.
WELL, KROC... DO YOU HAVE A PET?
OH, WHAT A CUTE LITTLE BABY ALLIGATOR!

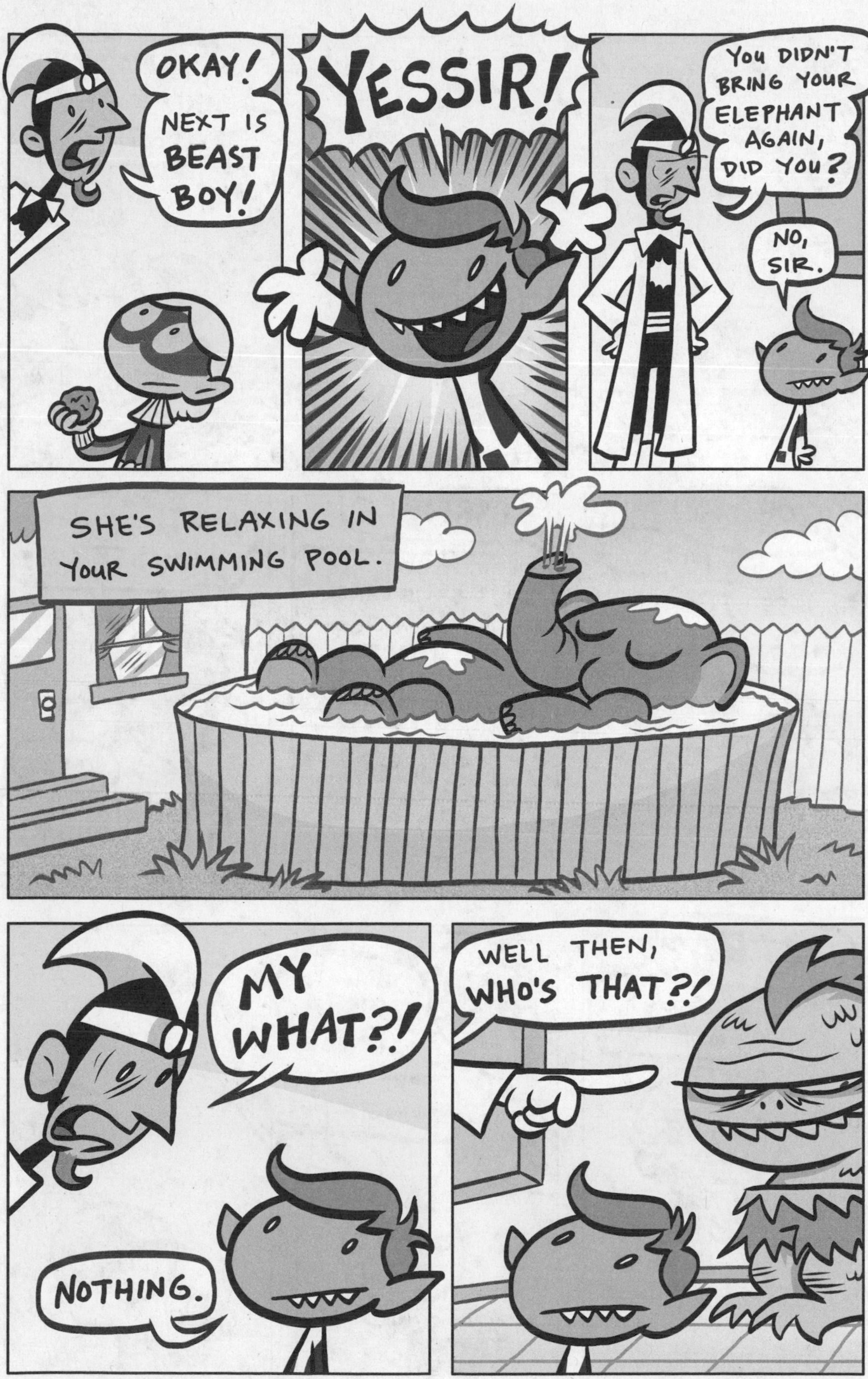
OKAY!
NEXT IS BEAST BOY!
YESSIR!
YOU DIDN'T BRING YOUR ELEPHANT AGAIN, DID YOU?
NO, SIR.
SHE'S RELAXING IN YOUR SWIMMING POOL.
MY WHAT?!
NOTHING.
WELL THEN, WHO'S THAT?!

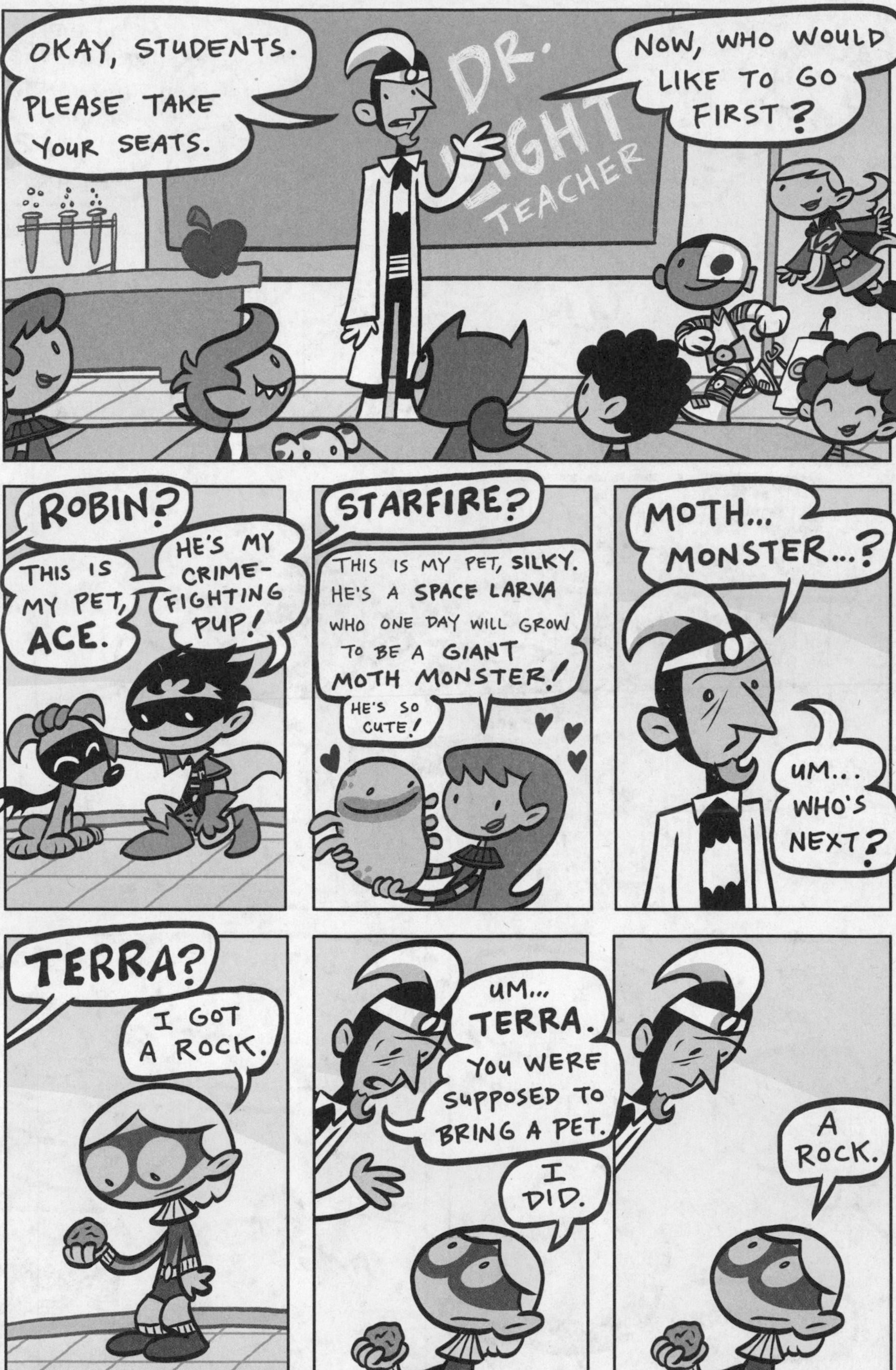
OKAY, STUDENTS. PLEASE TAKE YOUR SEATS.
DR. LIGHT TEACHER
NOW, WHO WOULD LIKE TO GO FIRST?
ROBIN?
THIS IS MY PET, ACE.
HE'S MY CRIME-FIGHTING PUP!
STARFIRE?
THIS IS MY PET, SILKY. HE'S A SPACE LARVA WHO ONE DAY WILL GROW TO BE A GIANT MOTH MONSTER!
HE'S SO CUTE!
MOTH... MONSTER...?
UM... WHO'S NEXT?
TERRA?
I GOT A ROCK.
UM... TERRA. YOU WERE SUPPOSED TO BRING A PET.
I DID.
A ROCK.

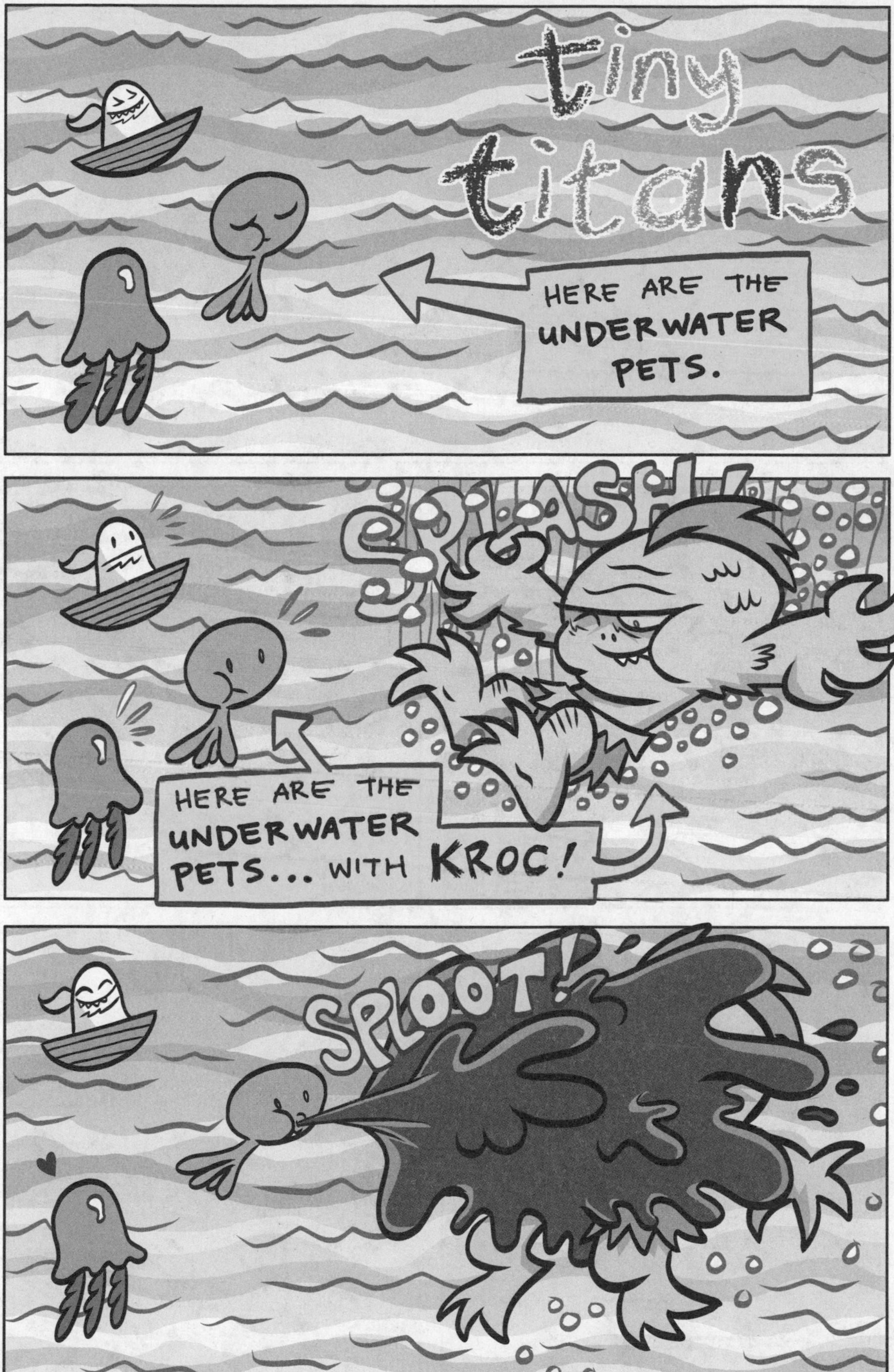
tiny titans
HERE ARE THE UNDERWATER PETS.
SPLASH!
HERE ARE THE UNDERWATER PETS... WITH KROC!
SPLOOT!

-ANY QUESTIONS?

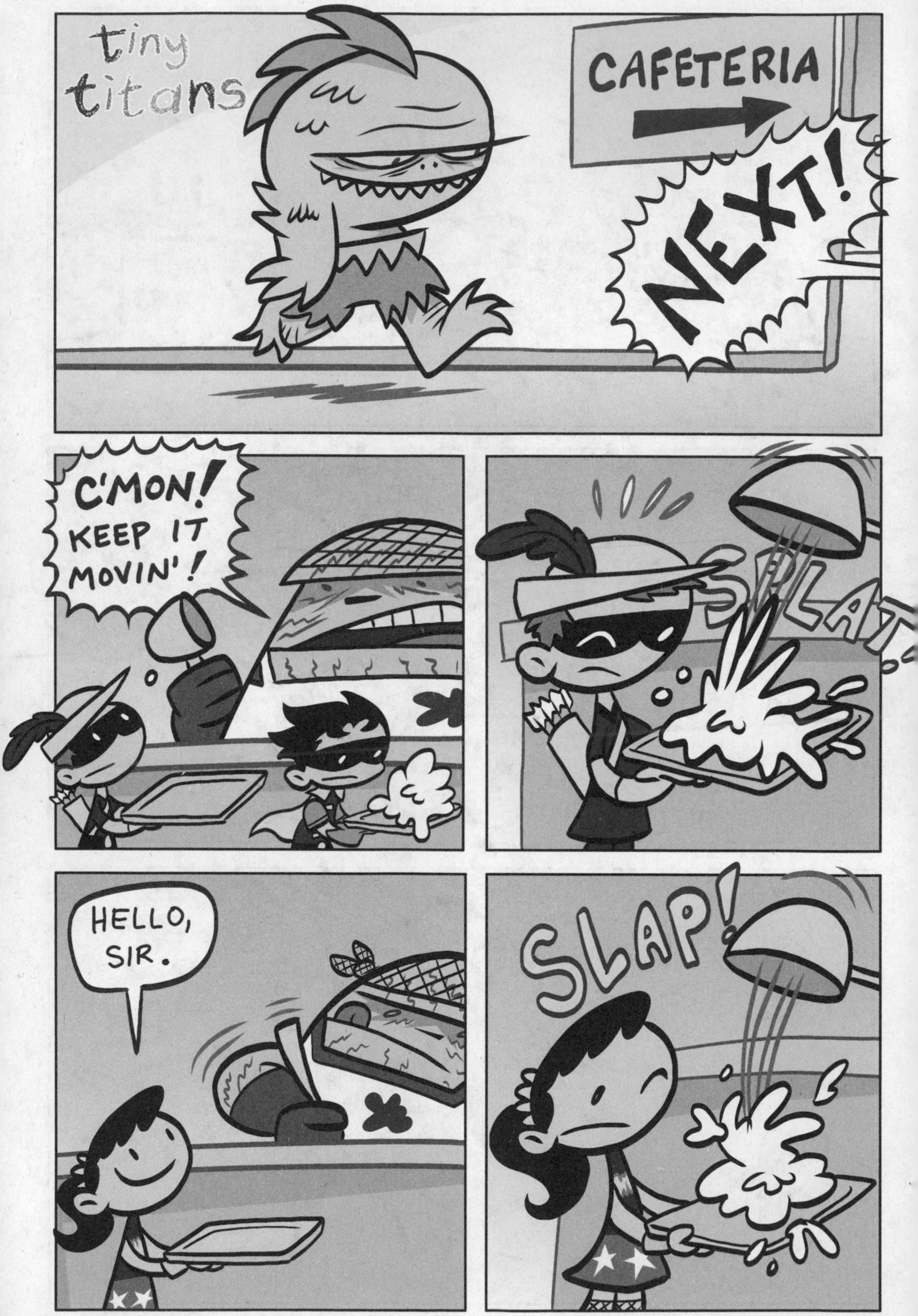
tiny titans
CAFETERIA
NEXT!
C'MON! KEEP IT MOVIN'!
SPLAT
HELLO, SIR.
SLAP!

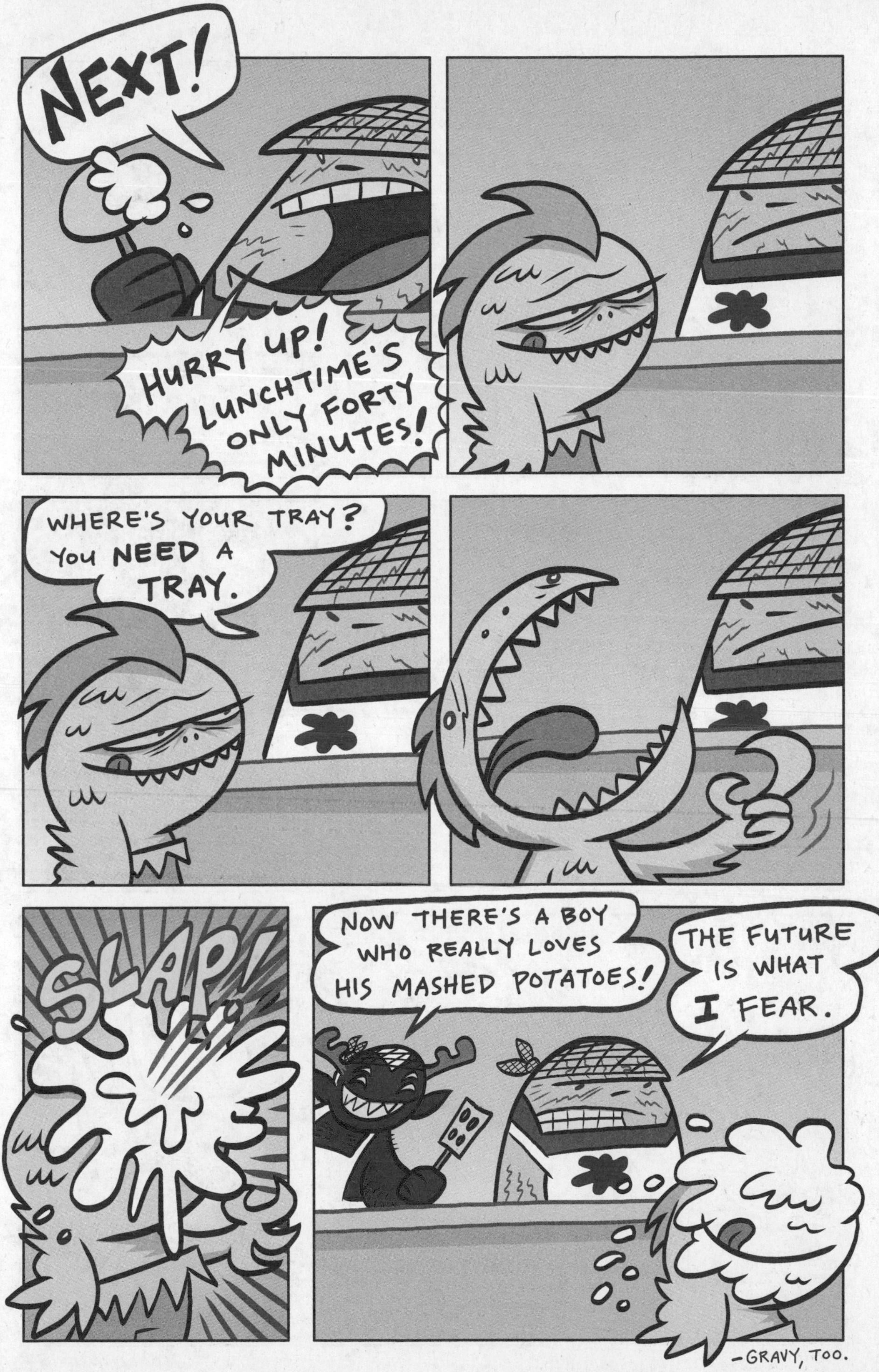
NEXT!
HURRY UP! LUNCHTIME'S ONLY FORTY MINUTES!
WHERE'S YOUR TRAY? YOU NEED A TRAY.
SLAP!
NOW THERE'S A BOY WHO REALLY LOVES HIS MASHED POTATOES!
THE FUTURE IS WHAT I FEAR.
-GRAVY, TOO.

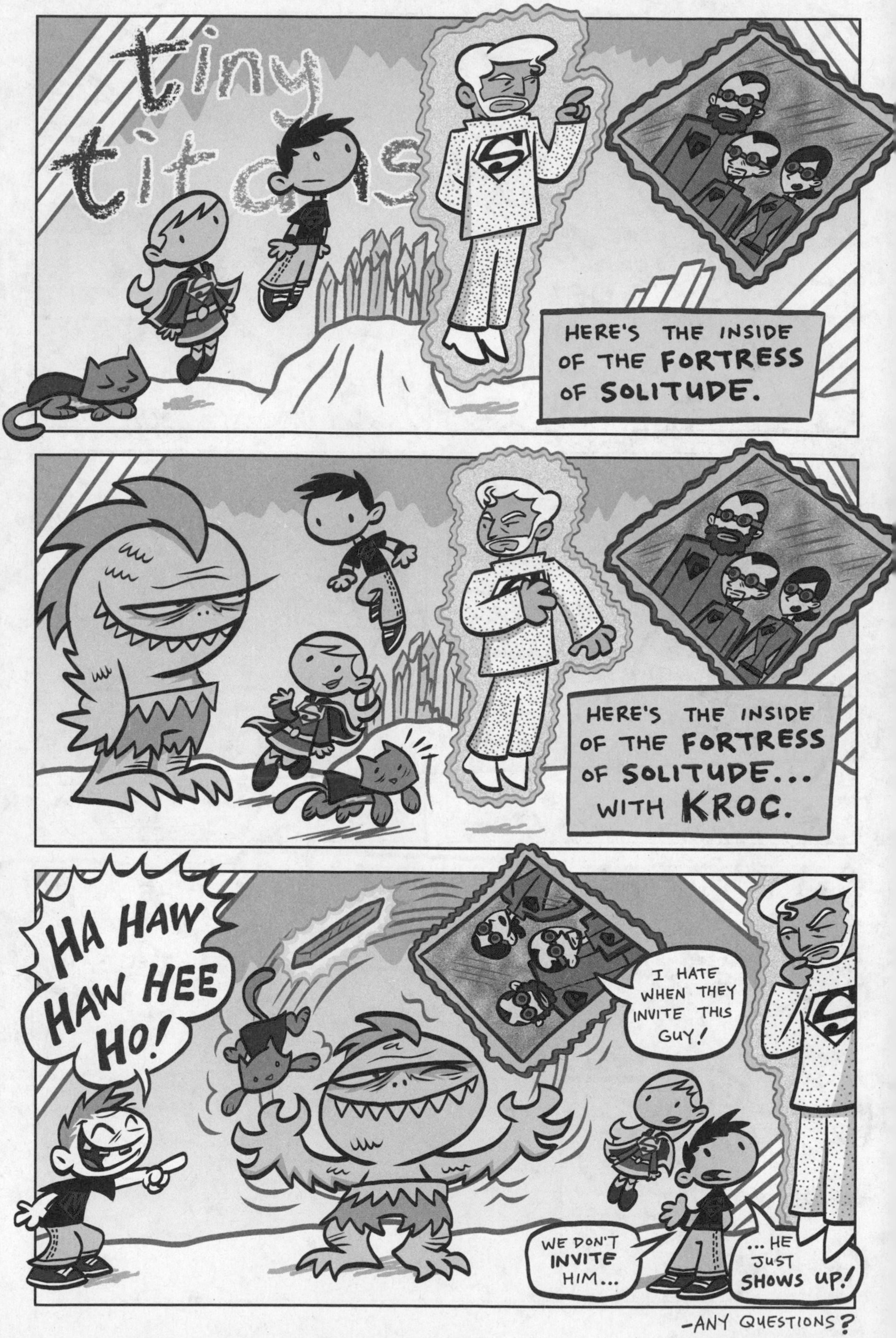
tiny titans
HERE'S THE INSIDE OF THE FORTRESS OF SOLITUDE.
HERE'S THE INSIDE OF THE FORTRESS OF SOLITUDE... WITH KROC.
HA HAW HAW HEE HO!
I HATE WHEN THEY INVITE THIS GUY!
WE DON'T INVITE HIM...
...HE JUST SHOWS UP!
-ANY QUESTIONS?

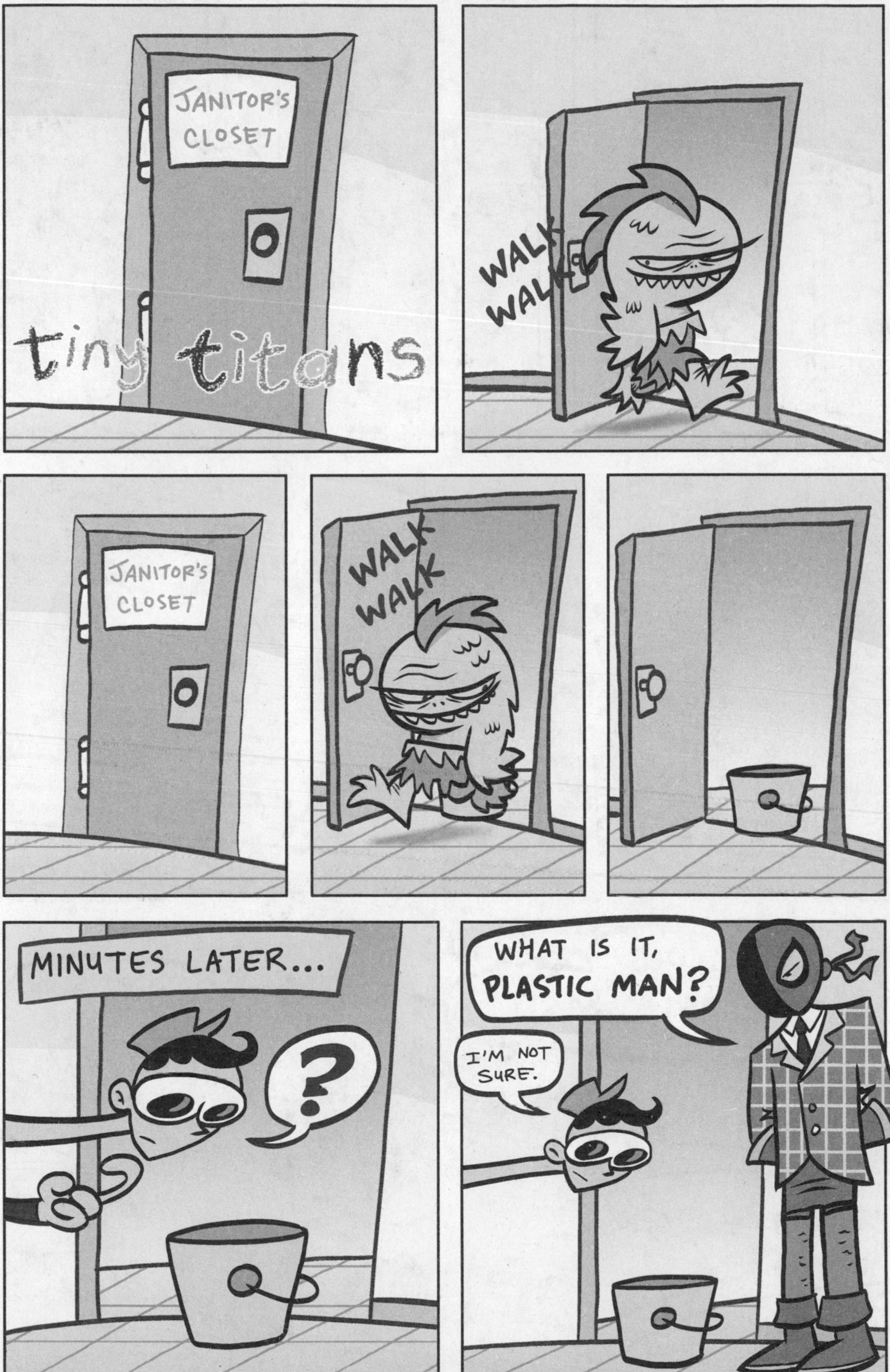
JANITOR'S CLOSET
tiny titans
WALK WALK
JANITOR'S CLOSET
WALK WALK
MINUTES LATER...
?
WHAT IS IT, PLASTIC MAN?
I'M NOT SURE.

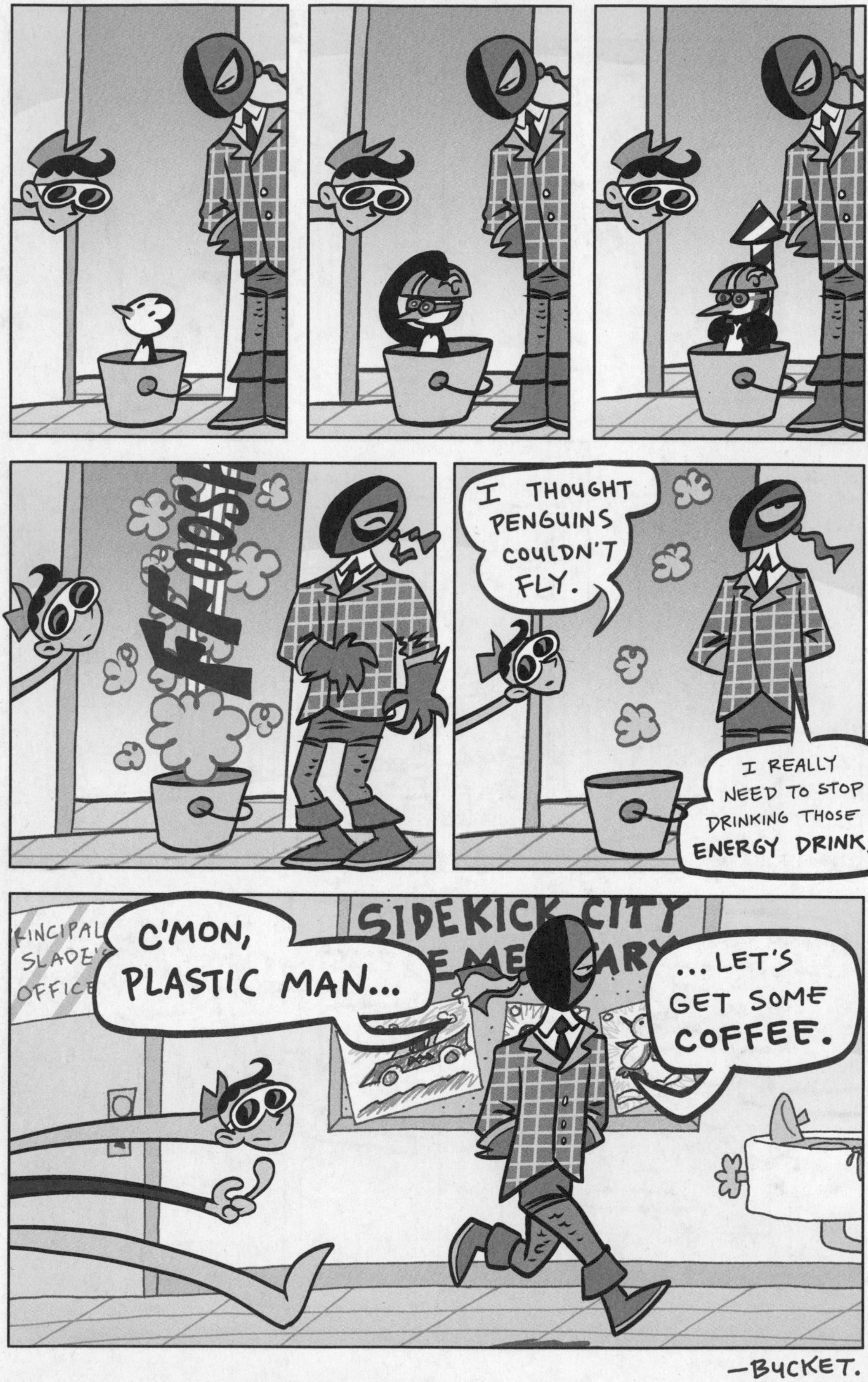
FFOOSH
I THOUGHT PENGUINS COULDN'T FLY.
I REALLY NEED TO STOP DRINKING THOSE ENERGY DRINKS.
PRINCIPAL SLADE'S OFFICE
C'MON, PLASTIC MAN...
SIDEKICK CITY
... LET'S GET SOME COFFEE.

—BUCKET.

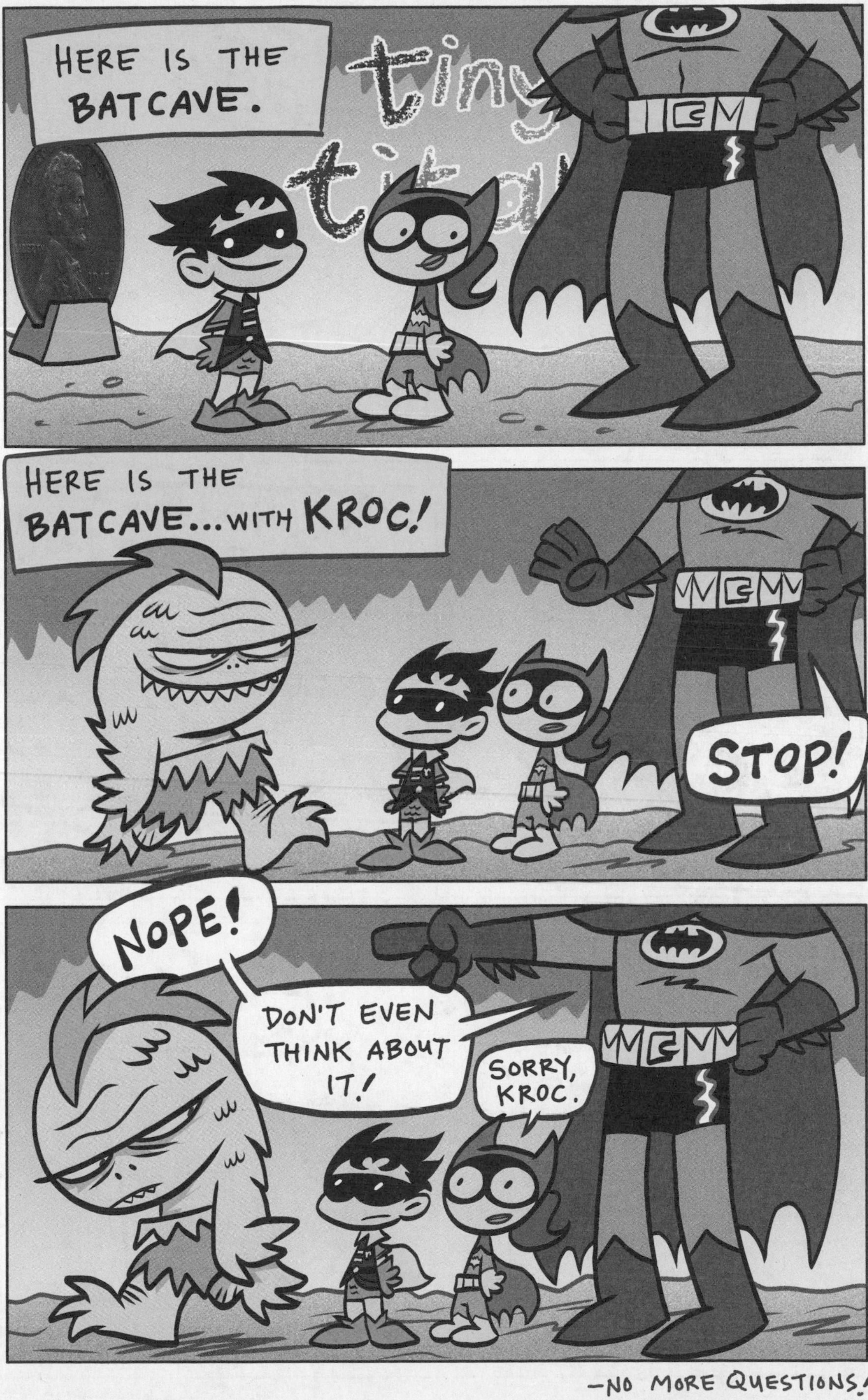
HERE IS THE BATCAVE.
HERE IS THE BATCAVE...WITH KROC!
STOP!
NOPE!
DON'T EVEN THINK ABOUT IT!
SORRY, KROC.

–NO MORE QUESTIONS!

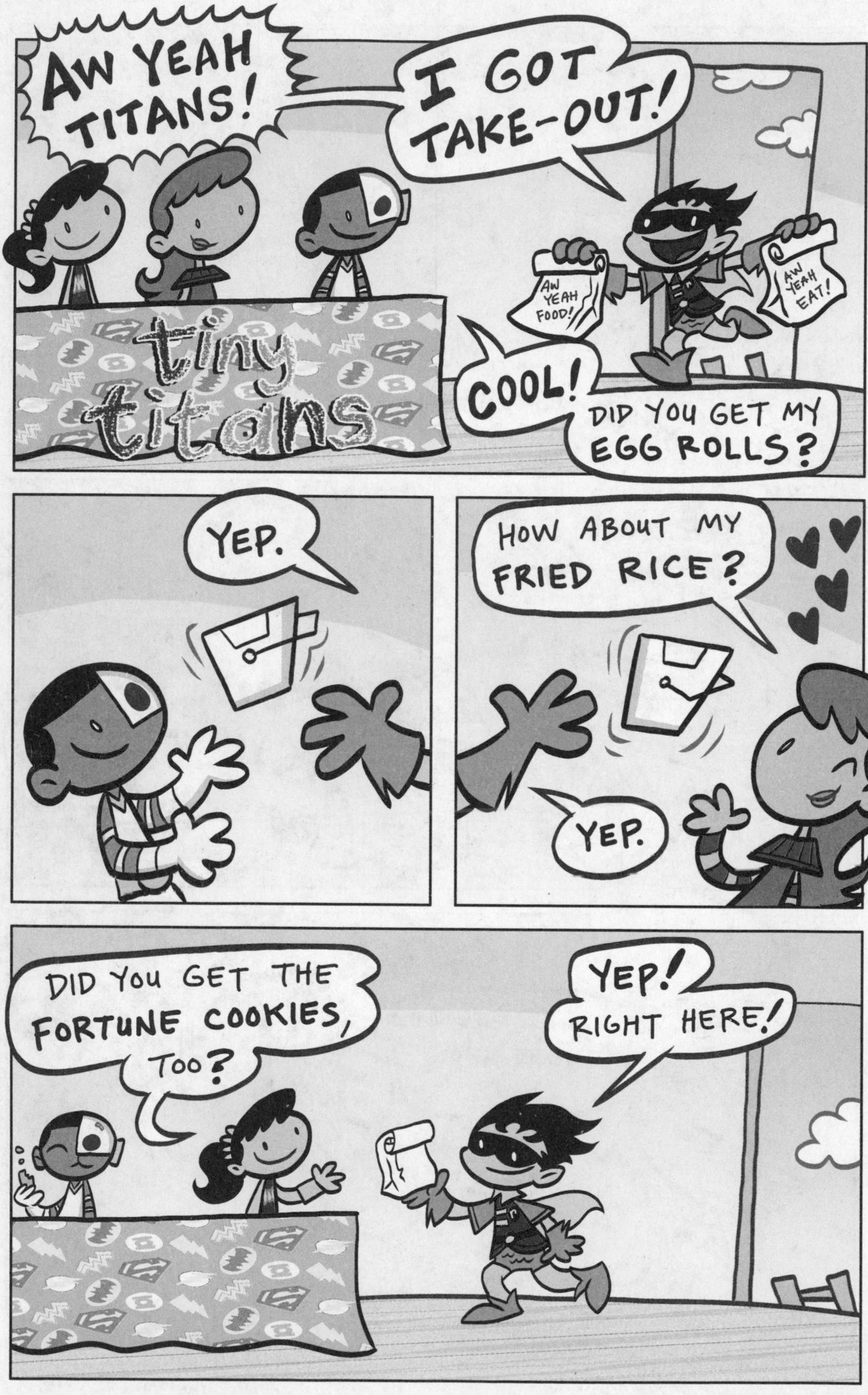
AW YEAH TITANS!
I GOT TAKE-OUT!
AW YEAH FOOD!
AW YEAH EAT!
tiny titans
COOL!
DID YOU GET MY EGG ROLLS?
YEP.
HOW ABOUT MY FRIED RICE?
YEP.
DID YOU GET THE FORTUNE COOKIES, TOO?
YEP! RIGHT HERE!

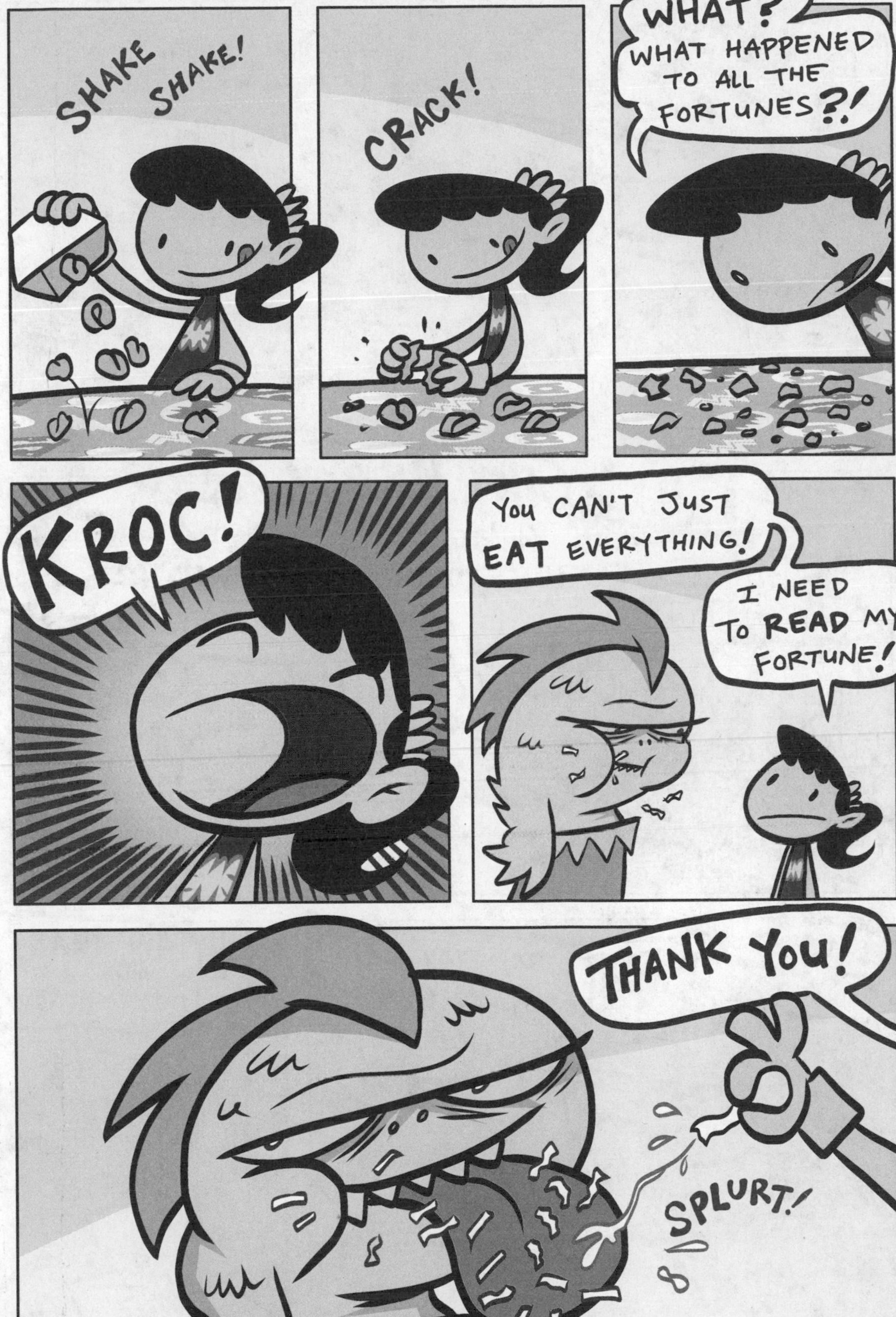
SHAKE SHAKE!
CRACK!
WHAT? WHAT HAPPENED TO ALL THE FORTUNES?!
KROC!
YOU CAN'T JUST EAT EVERYTHING!
I NEED TO READ MY FORTUNE!
THANK YOU!
SPLURT!

–SEND MORE COOKIES!

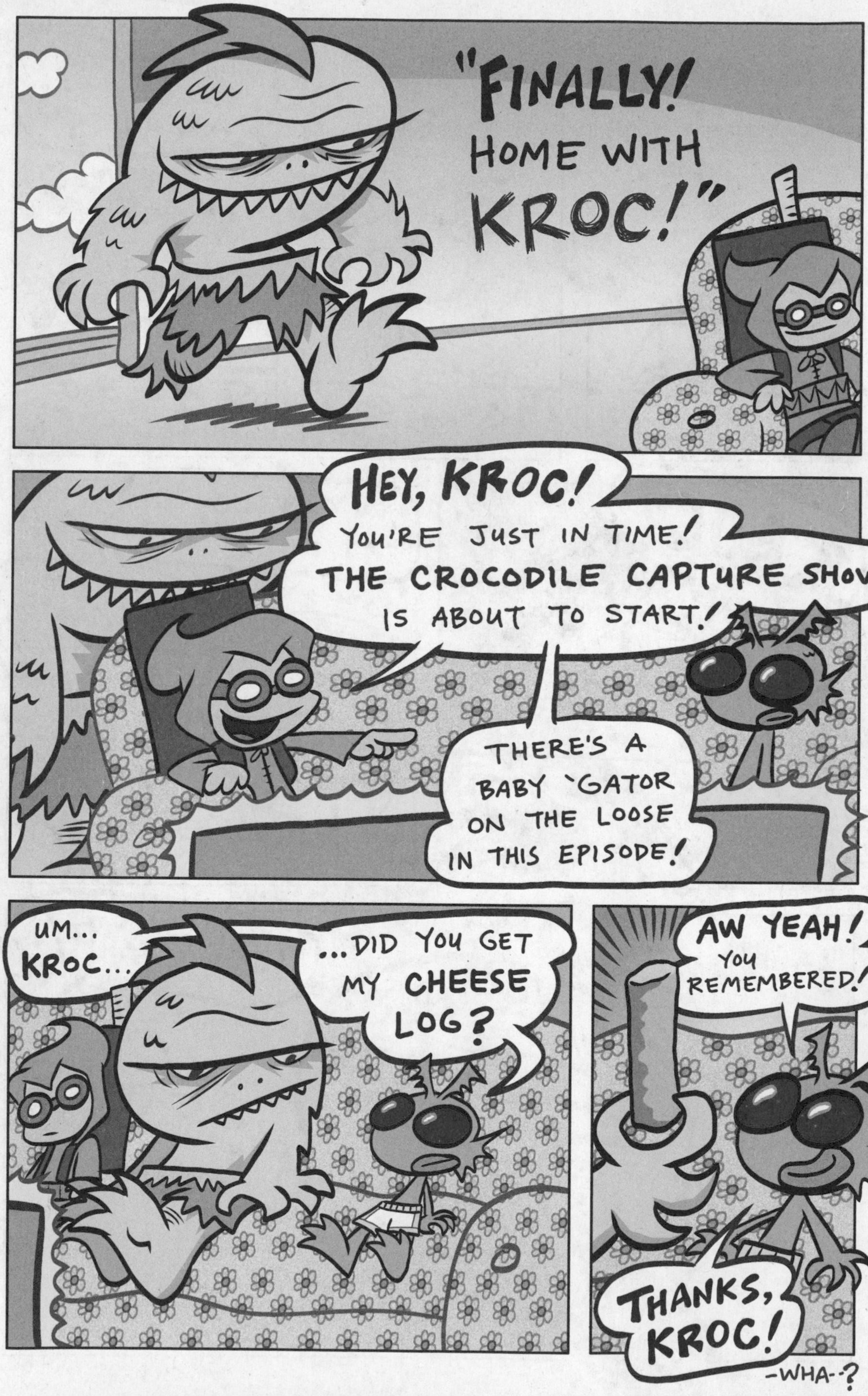
"FINALLY! HOME WITH KROC!"
HEY, KROC! YOU'RE JUST IN TIME! THE CROCODILE CAPTURE SHOW IS ABOUT TO START!
THERE'S A BABY `GATOR ON THE LOOSE IN THIS EPISODE!
UM... KROC...
...DID YOU GET MY CHEESE LOG?
AW YEAH! YOU REMEMBERED!
THANKS, KROC!
-WHA-?

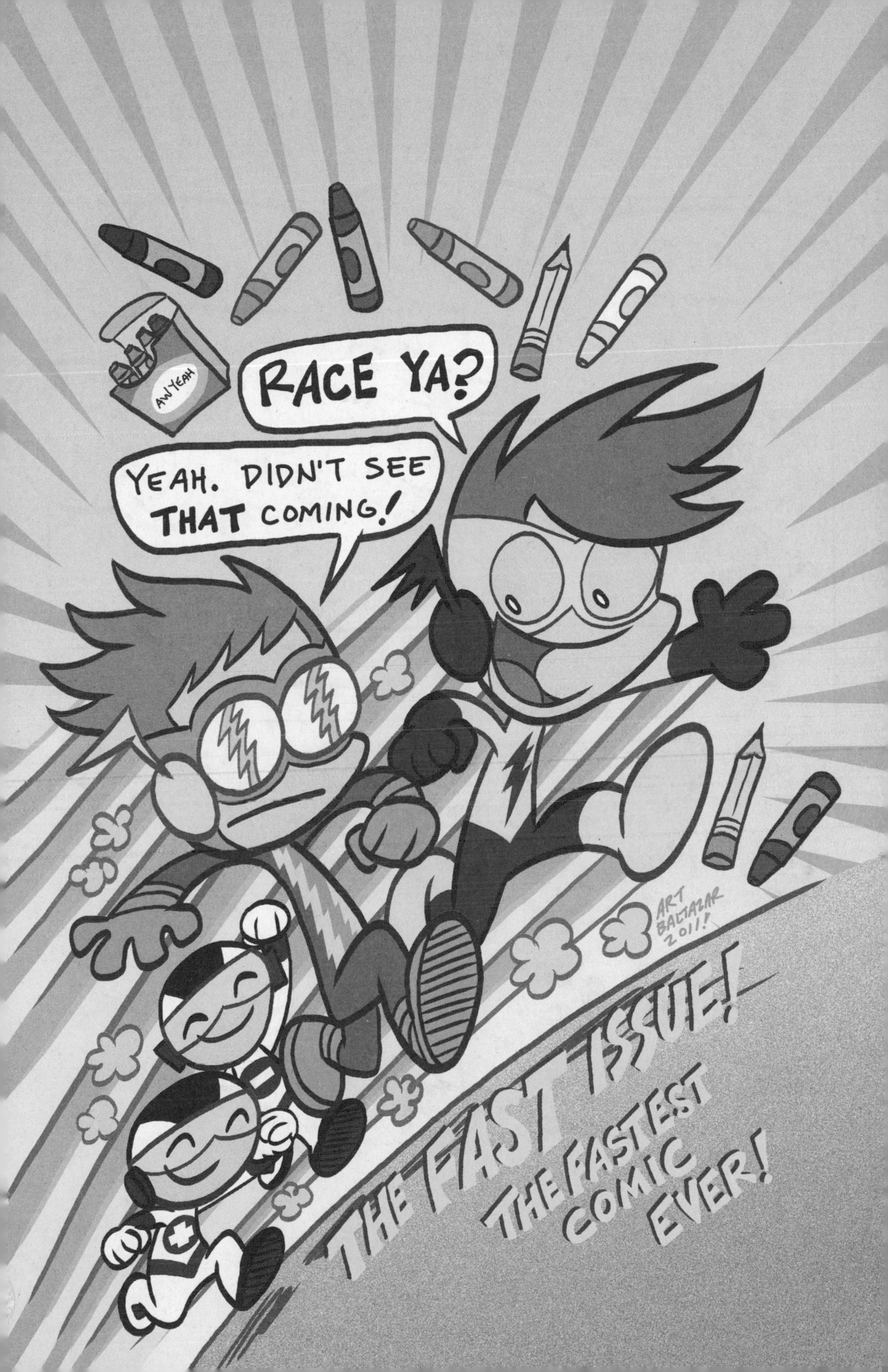
AW YEAH
RACE YA?
YEAH. DIDN'T SEE THAT COMING!
ART BALTAZAR 2011!
THE FAST ISSUE!
THE FASTEST COMIC EVER!

tiny titans

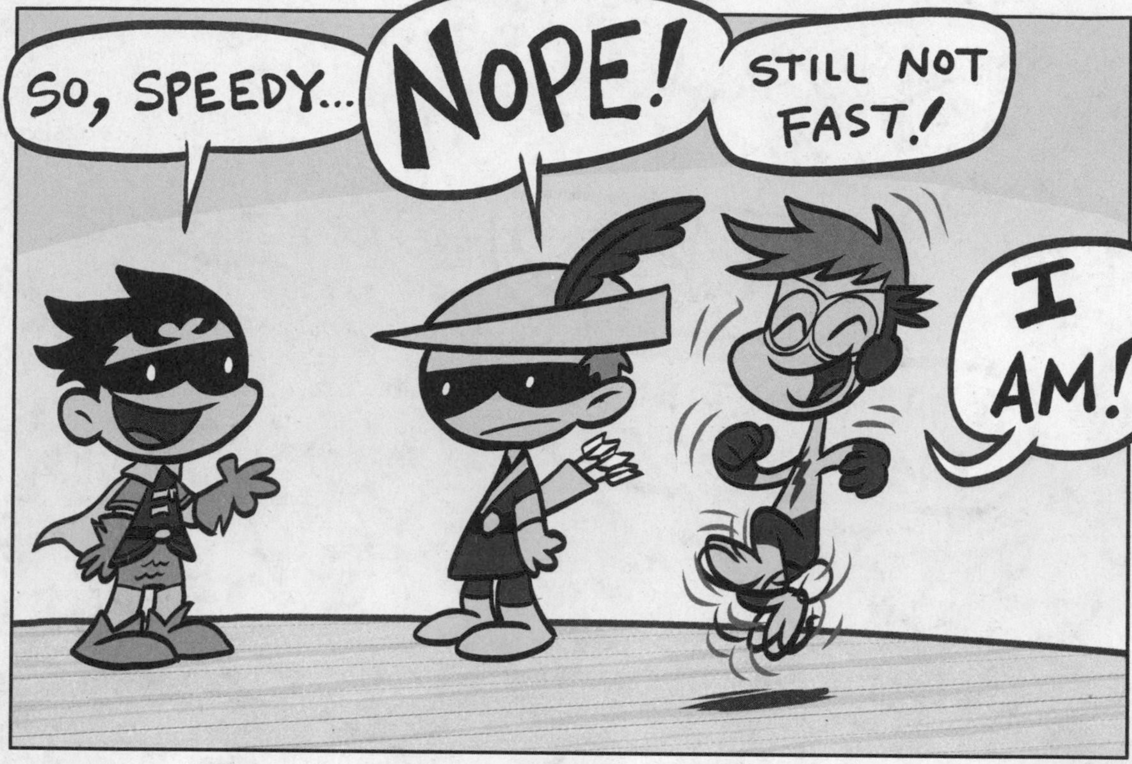
SO, SPEEDY...
NOPE!
STILL NOT FAST!
I AM!

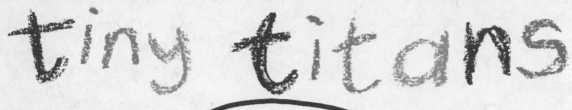

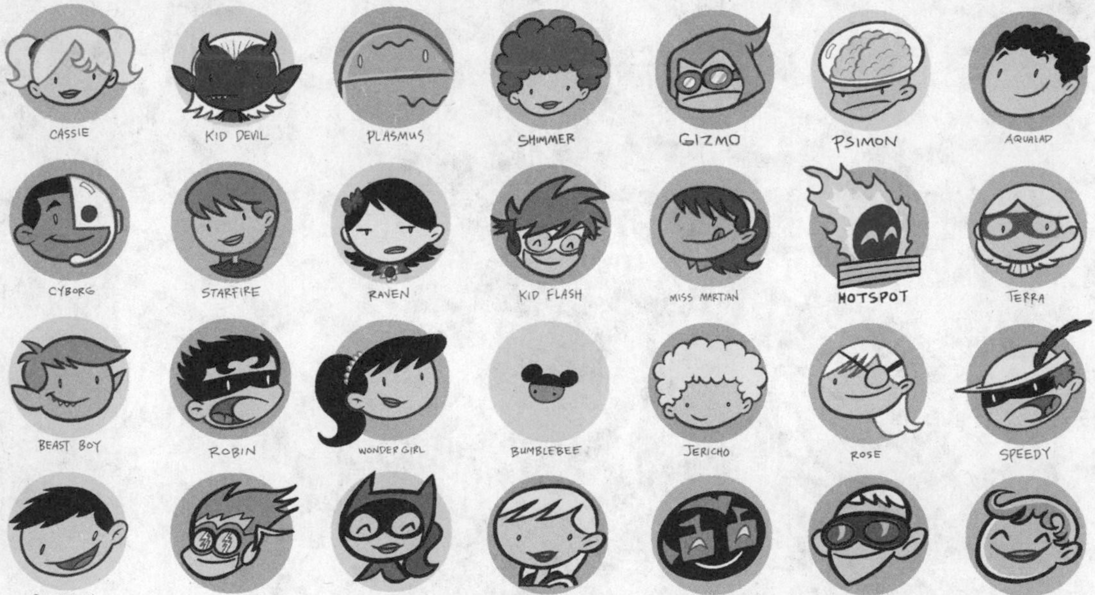
CASSIE
KID DEVIL
PLASMUS
SHIMMER
GIZMO
PSIMON
AQUALAD
CYBORG
STARFIRE
RAVEN
KID FLASH
MISS MARTIAN
HOTSPOT
TERRA
BEAST BOY
ROBIN
WONDER GIRL
BUMBLEBEE
JERICHO
ROSE
SPEEDY
SUPERBOY
INERTIA
BARBARA
SUPERGIRL
BLUE BEETLE
OFFSPRING
SHELLY

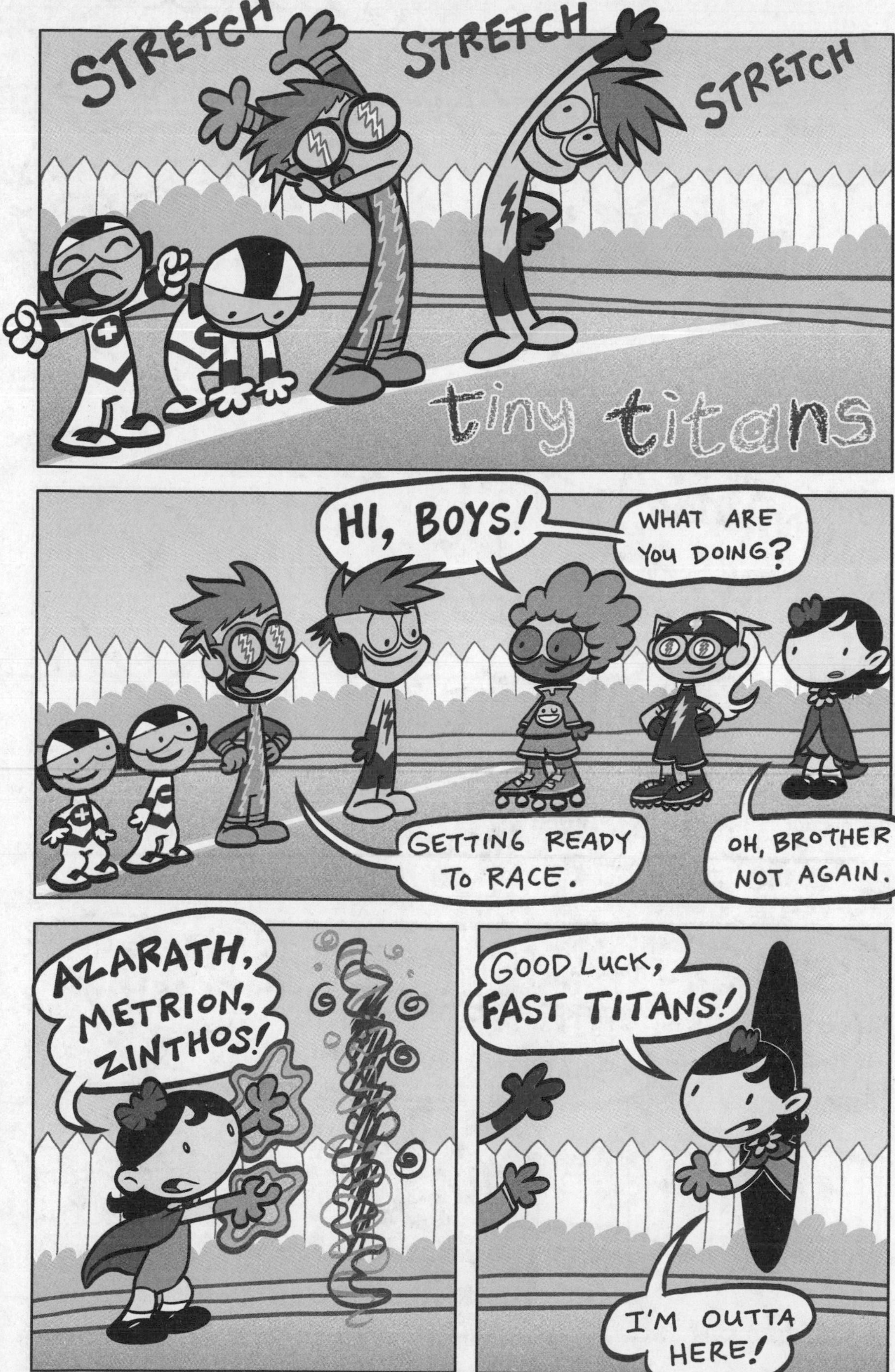
STRETCH
STRETCH
STRETCH
tiny titans
HI, BOYS!
WHAT ARE YOU DOING?
GETTING READY TO RACE.
OH, BROTHER. NOT AGAIN.
AZARATH, METRION, ZINTHOS!
GOOD LUCK, FAST TITANS!
I'M OUTTA HERE!

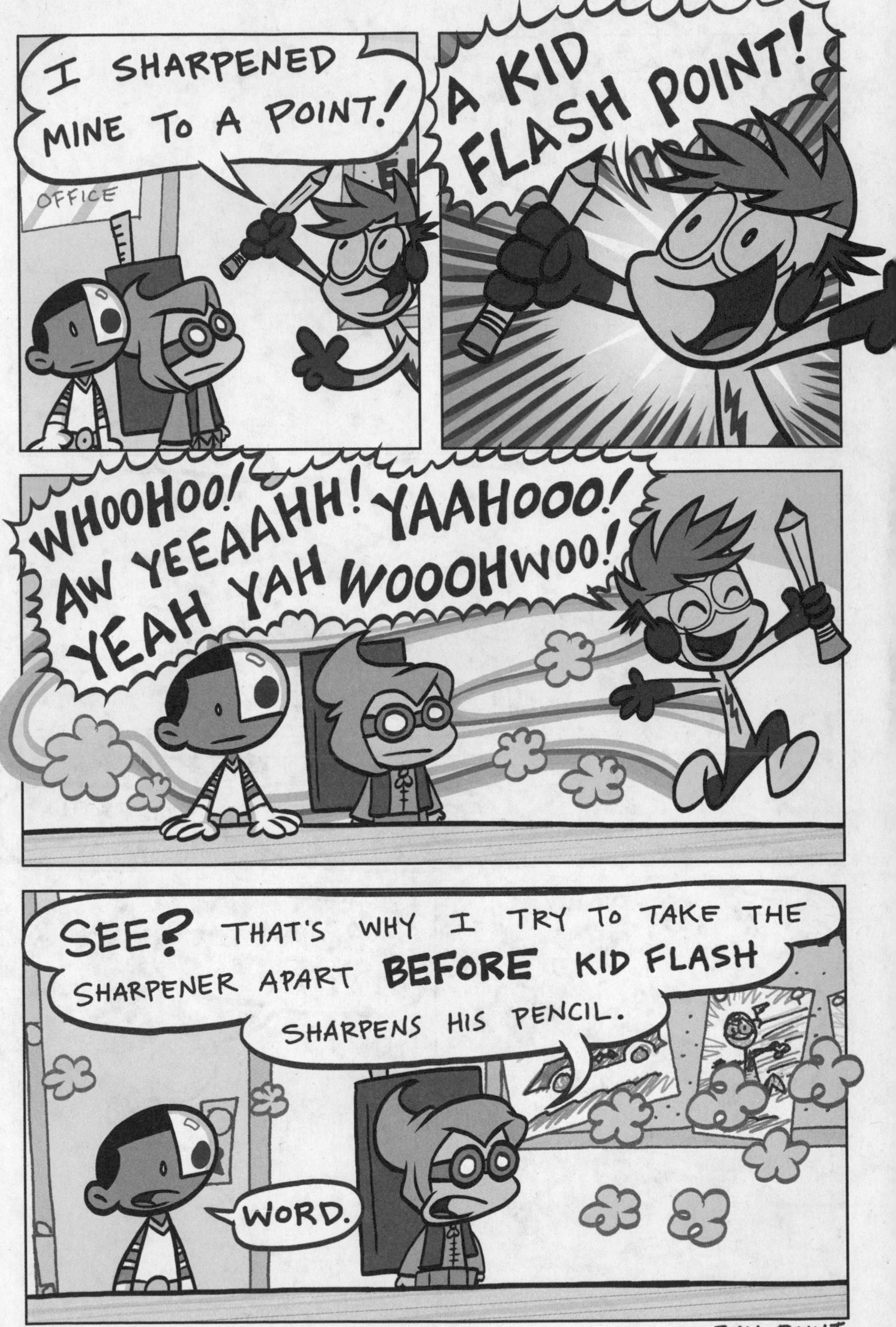
I SHARPENED MINE TO A POINT!
OFFICE
A KID FLASH POINT!
WHOOHOO! AW YEEAAHH! YAAHOOO! YEAH YAH WOOOHWOO!
SEE? THAT'S WHY I TRY TO TAKE THE SHARPENER APART BEFORE KID FLASH SHARPENS HIS PENCIL.
WORD.

—BALL POINT.

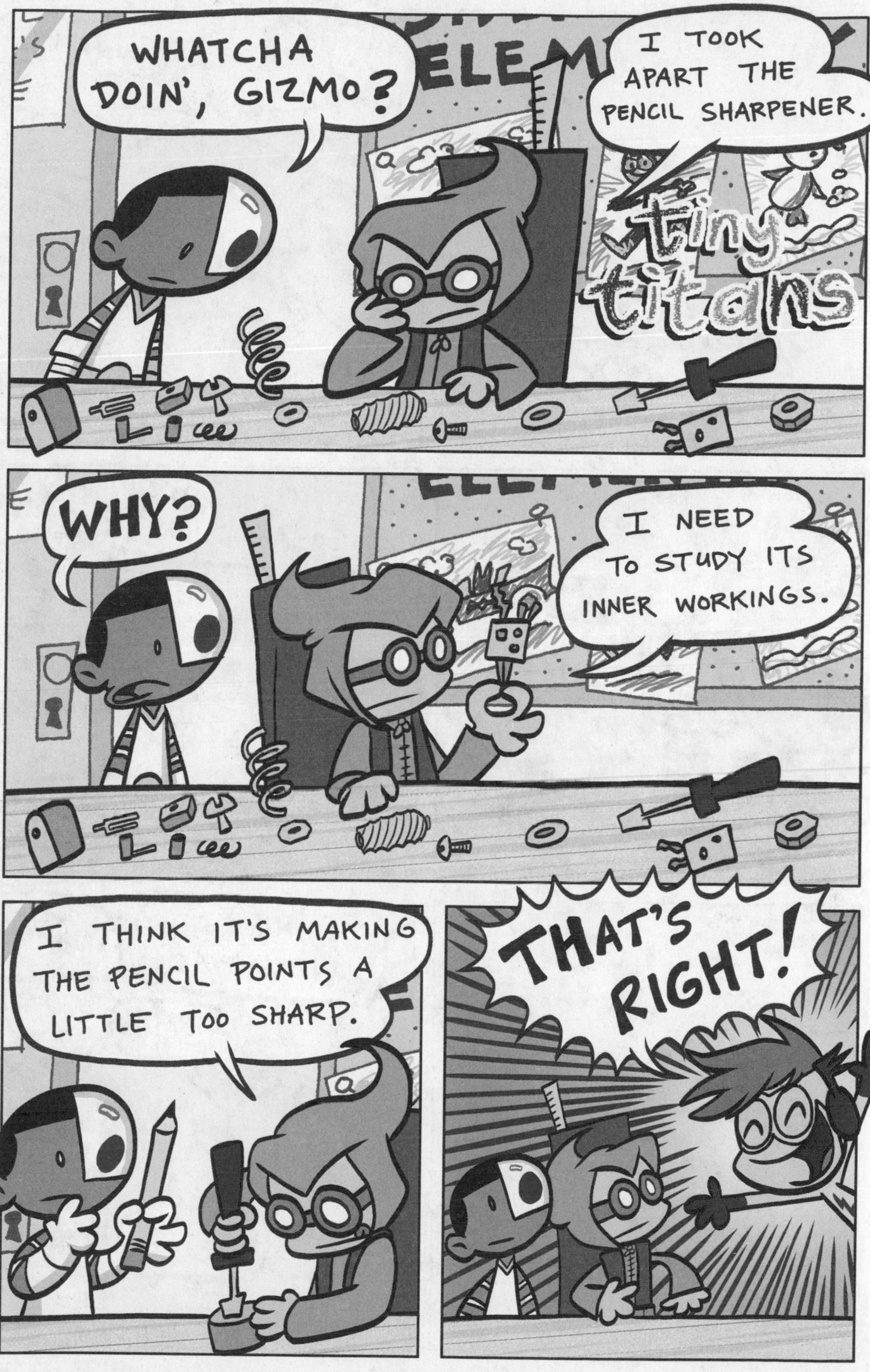
WHATCHA DOIN', GIZMO?
I TOOK APART THE PENCIL SHARPENER.
tiny titans
WHY?
I NEED TO STUDY ITS INNER WORKINGS.
I THINK IT'S MAKING THE PENCIL POINTS A LITTLE TOO SHARP.
THAT'S RIGHT!

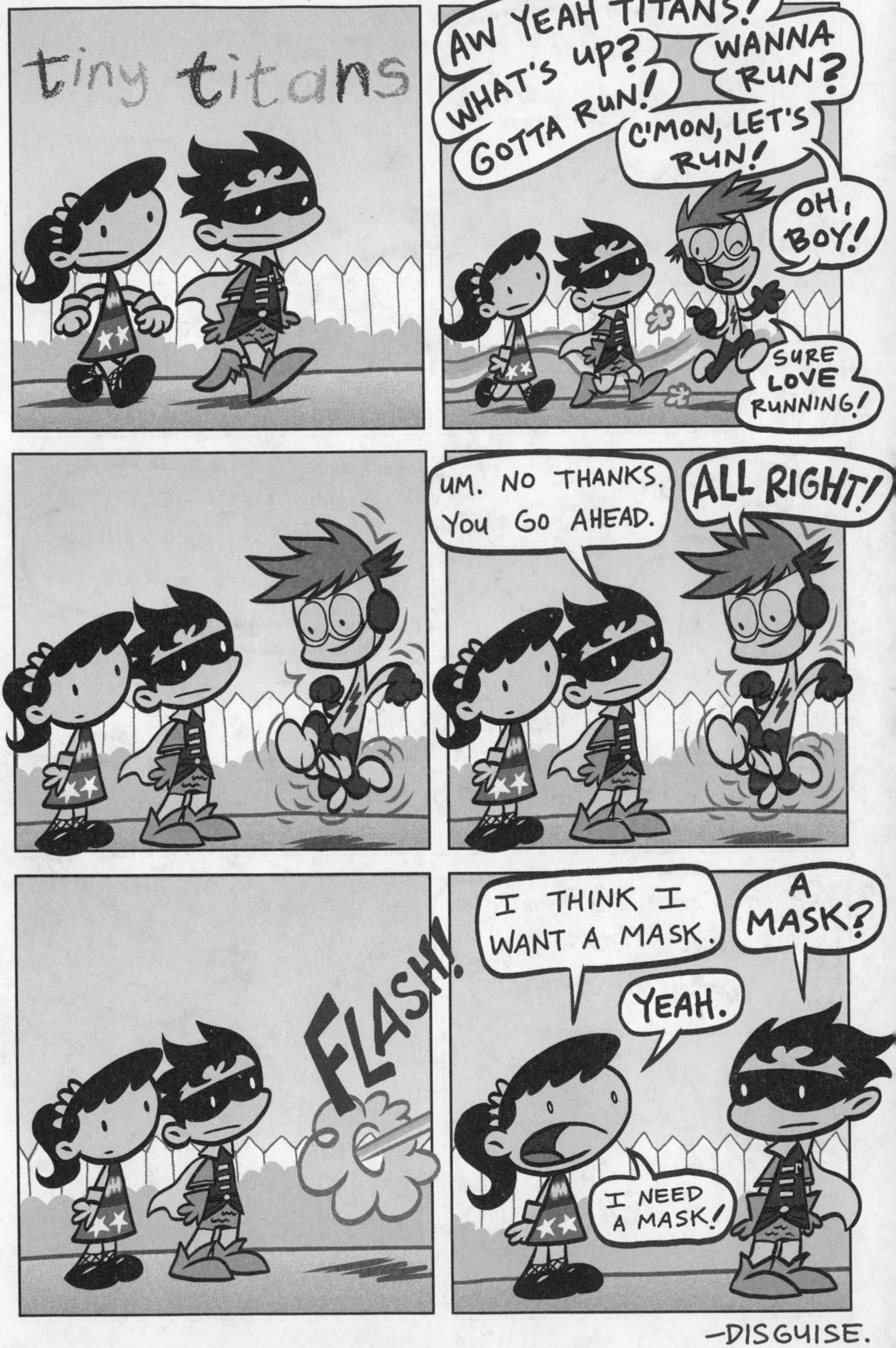
tiny titans
AW YEAH TITANS! WHAT'S UP? GOTTA RUN!
WANNA RUN?
C'MON, LET'S RUN!
OH, BOY!
SURE LOVE RUNNING!
UM. NO THANKS. YOU GO AHEAD.
ALL RIGHT!
FLASH!
I THINK I WANT A MASK.
A MASK?
YEAH.
I NEED A MASK!
-DISGUISE.

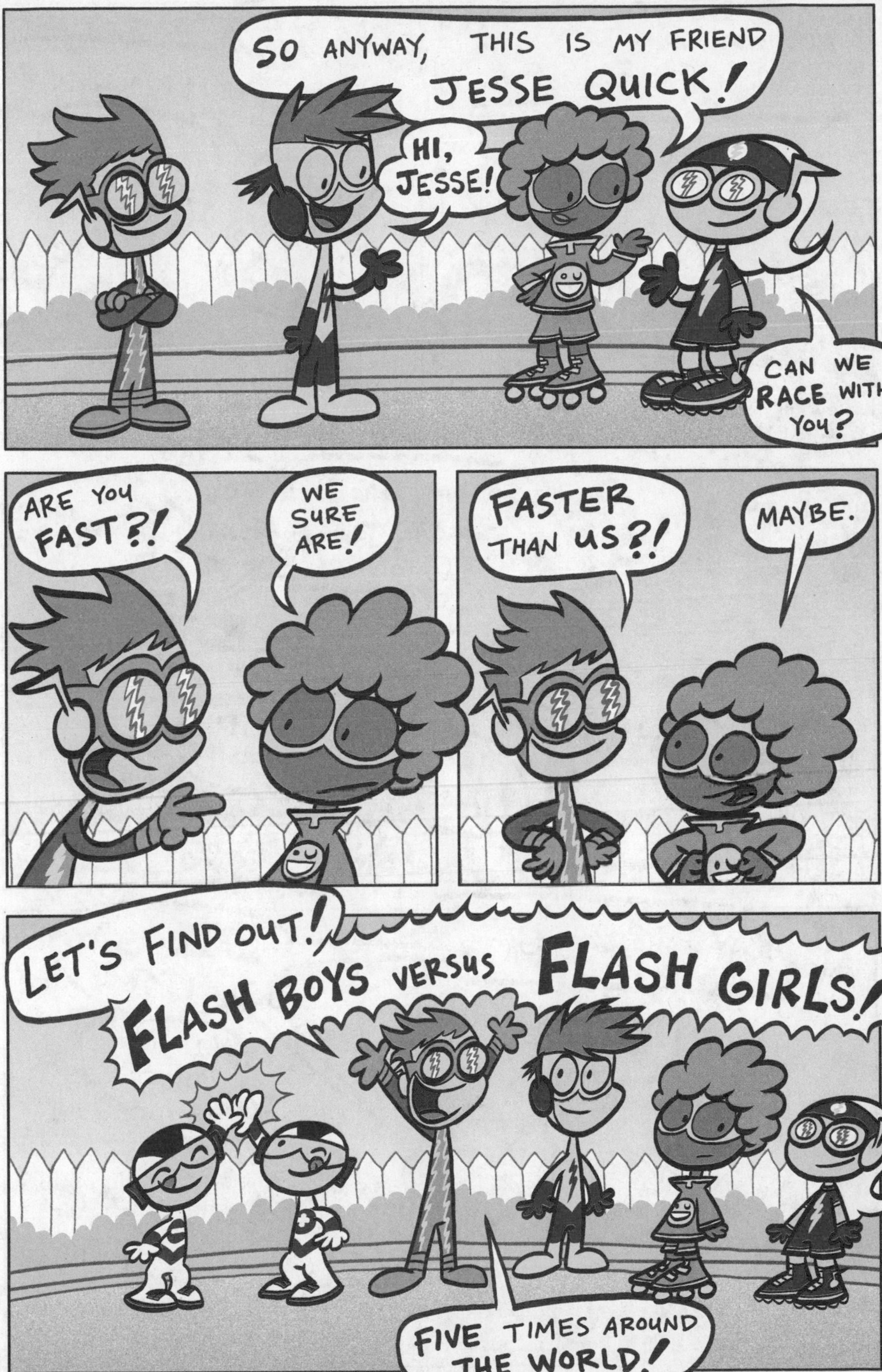
SO ANYWAY, THIS IS MY FRIEND JESSE QUICK!
HI, JESSE!
CAN WE RACE WITH YOU?
ARE YOU FAST?!
WE SURE ARE!
FASTER THAN US?!
MAYBE.
LET'S FIND OUT!
FLASH BOYS VERSUS FLASH GIRLS!
FIVE TIMES AROUND THE WORLD!

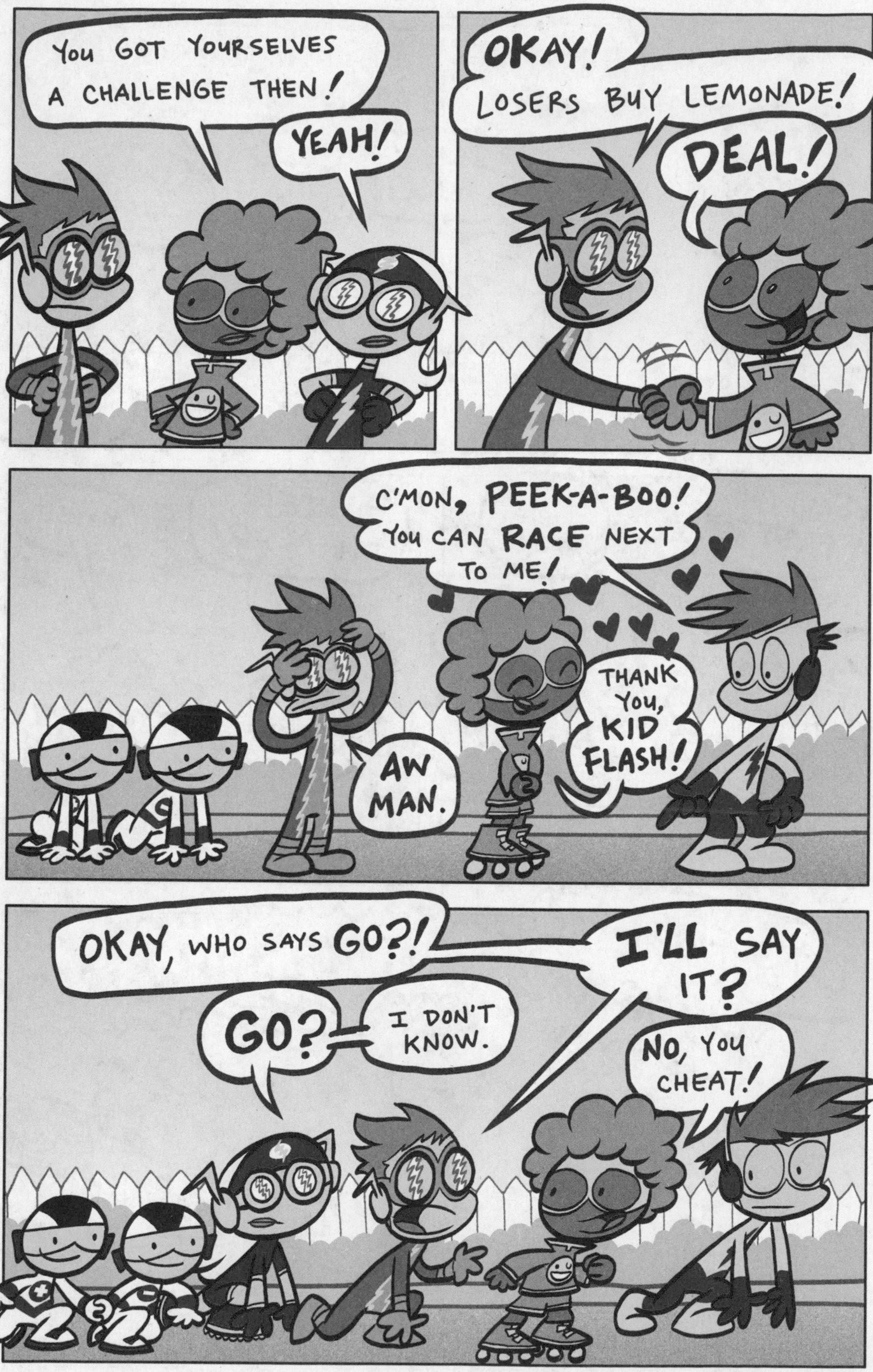

You GOT YOURSELVES A CHALLENGE THEN!
YEAH!
OKAY! LOSERS BUY LEMONADE!
DEAL!
C'MON, PEEK-A-BOO! You CAN RACE NEXT TO ME!
AW MAN.
THANK You, KID FLASH!
OKAY, WHO SAYS GO?!
GO?
I DON'T KNOW.
I'LL SAY IT?
NO, You CHEAT!

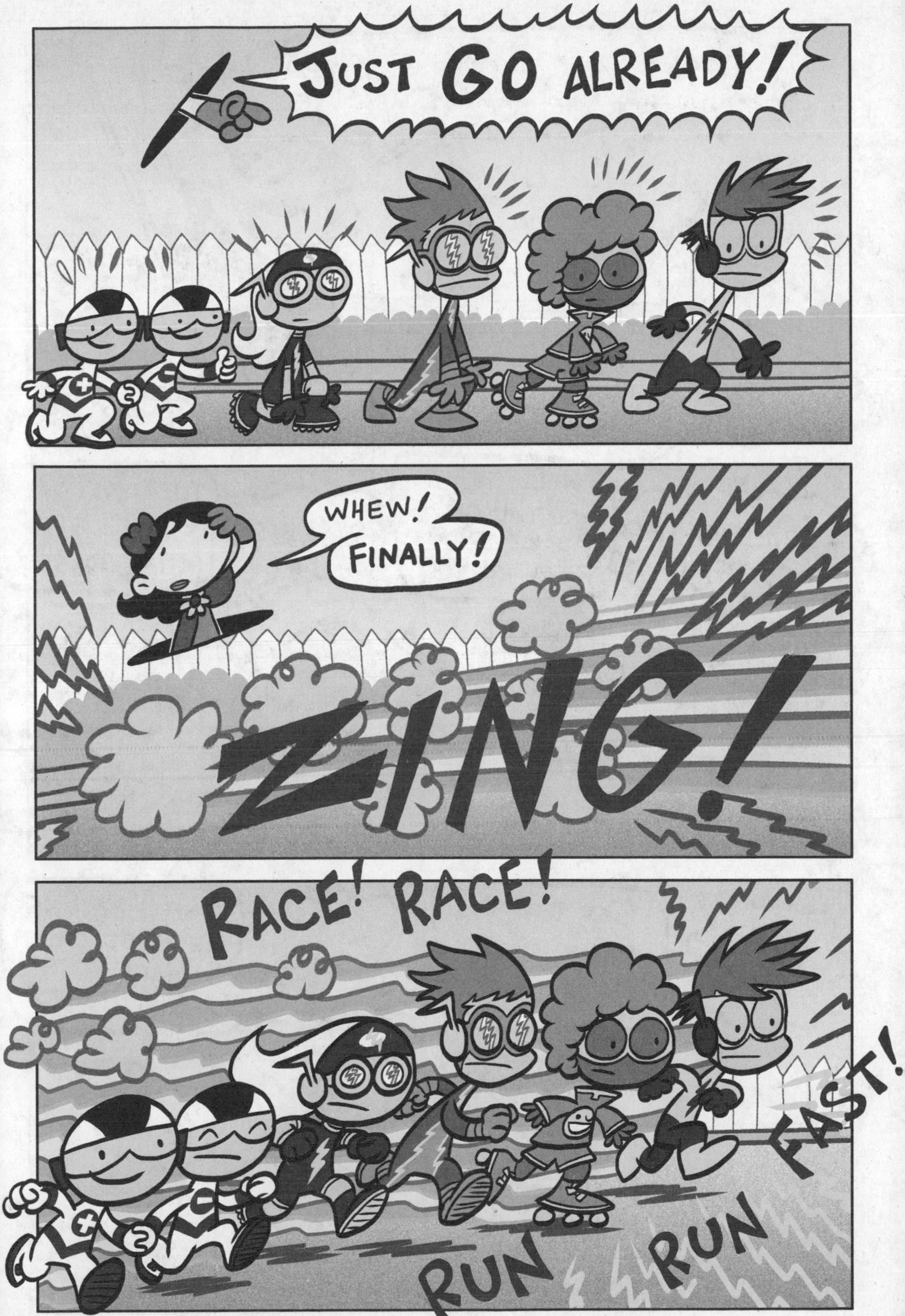

JUST GO ALREADY!
WHEW! FINALLY!
ZING!
RACE! RACE!
RUN RUN FAST!

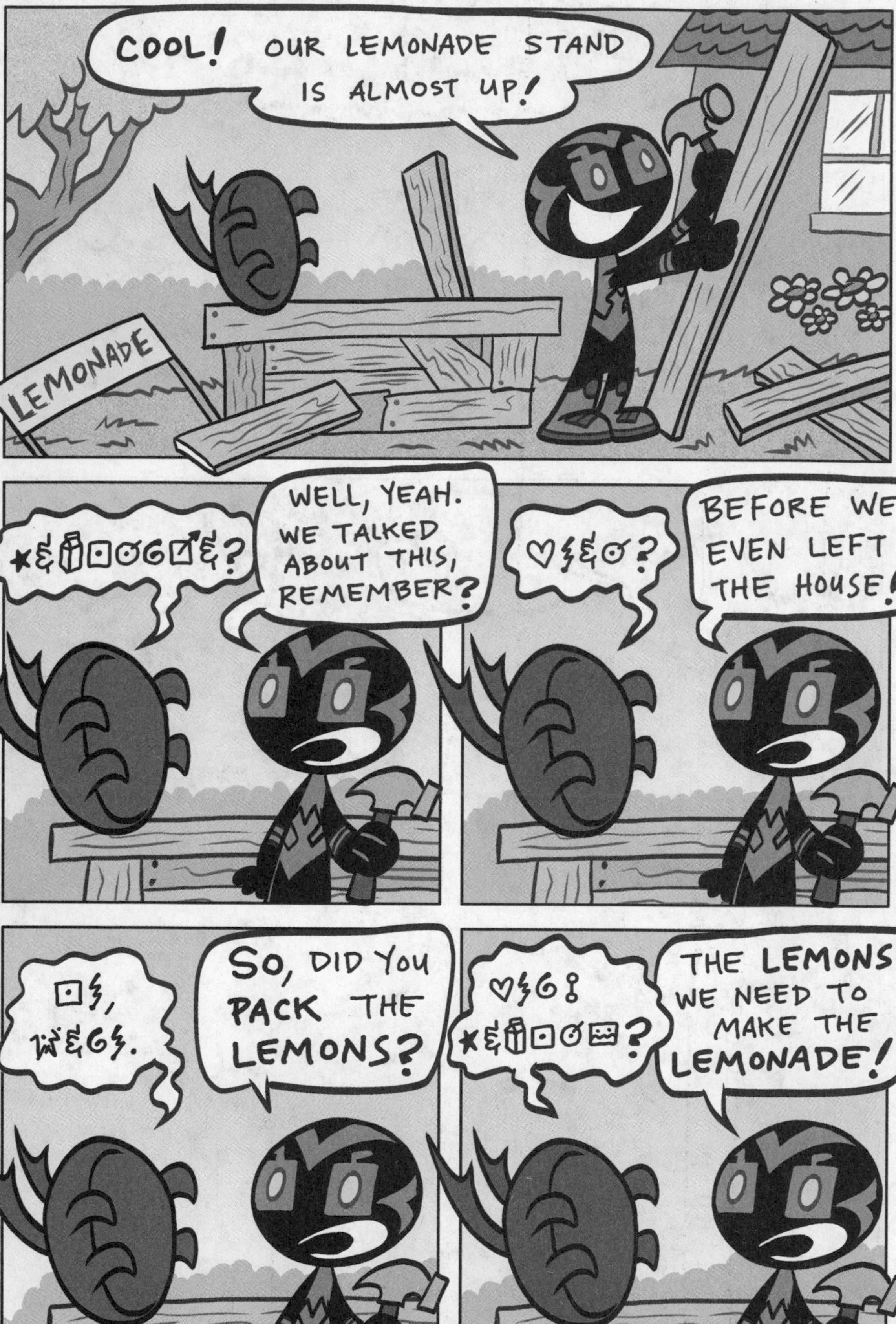
COOL! OUR LEMONADE STAND IS ALMOST UP!
LEMONADE
WELL, YEAH. WE TALKED ABOUT THIS, REMEMBER?
BEFORE WE EVEN LEFT THE HOUSE!
SO, DID YOU PACK THE LEMONS?
THE LEMONS WE NEED TO MAKE THE LEMONADE!

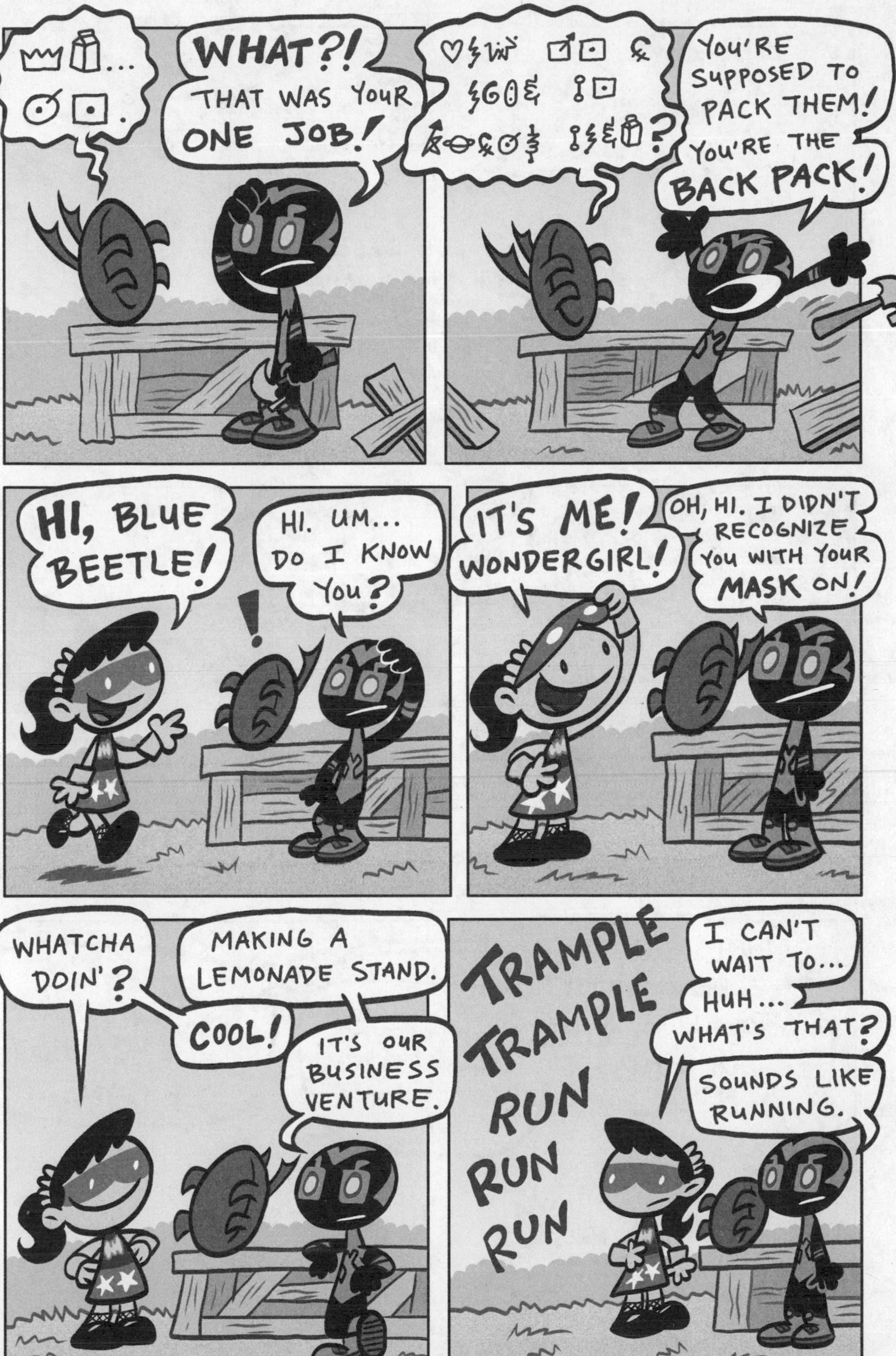
WHAT?! THAT WAS YOUR ONE JOB!
YOU'RE SUPPOSED TO PACK THEM! YOU'RE THE BACK PACK!
HI, BLUE BEETLE!
HI. UM... DO I KNOW YOU?
!
IT'S ME! WONDERGIRL!
OH, HI. I DIDN'T RECOGNIZE YOU WITH YOUR MASK ON!
WHATCHA DOIN'?
MAKING A LEMONADE STAND.
COOL!
IT'S OUR BUSINESS VENTURE.
TRAMPLE TRAMPLE RUN RUN RUN
I CAN'T WAIT TO... HUH... WHAT'S THAT?
SOUNDS LIKE RUNNING.

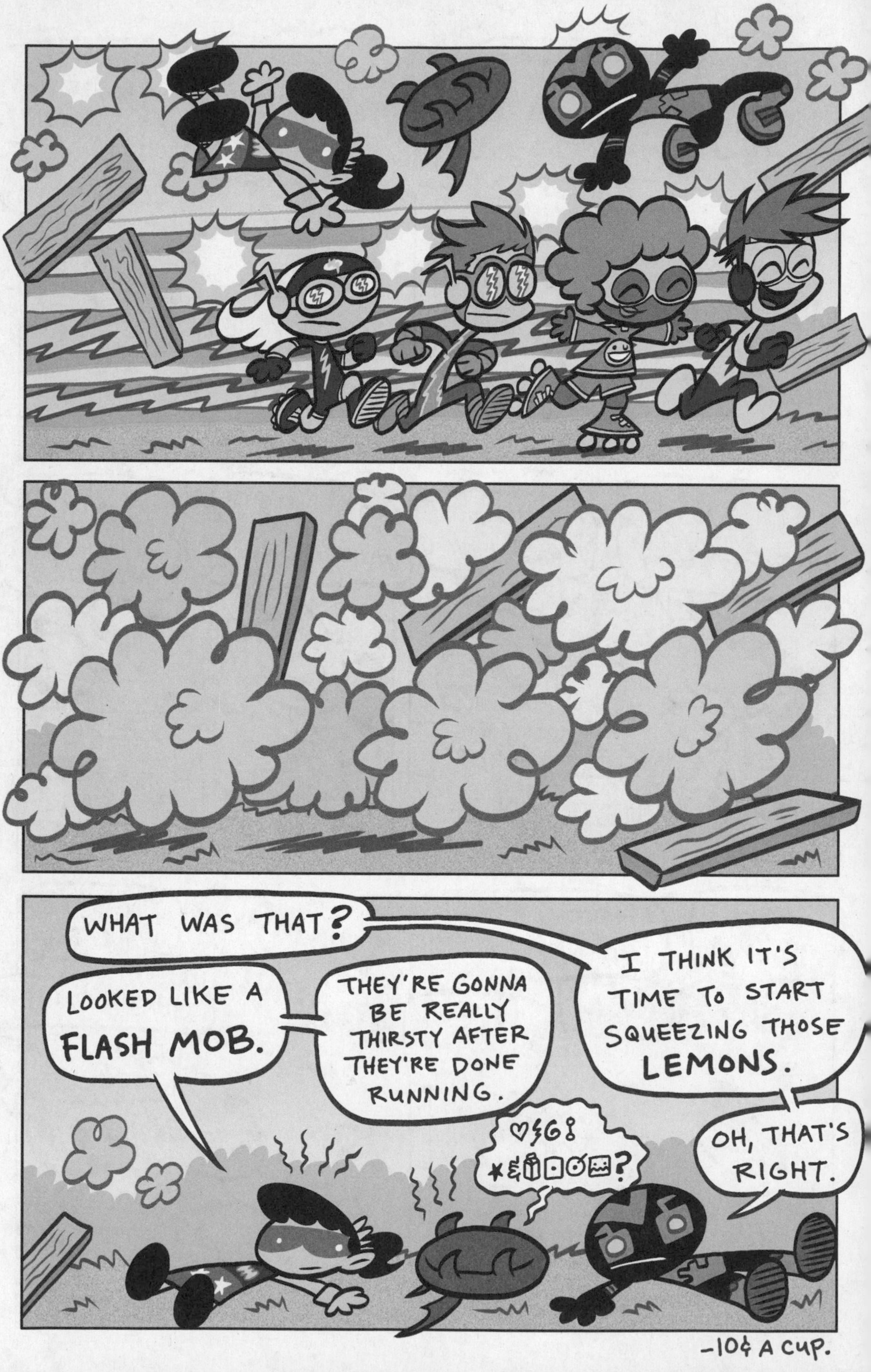
WHAT WAS THAT?
LOOKED LIKE A FLASH MOB.
THEY'RE GONNA BE REALLY THIRSTY AFTER THEY'RE DONE RUNNING.
I THINK IT'S TIME TO START SQUEEZING THOSE LEMONS.
OH, THAT'S RIGHT.
-10¢ A CUP.

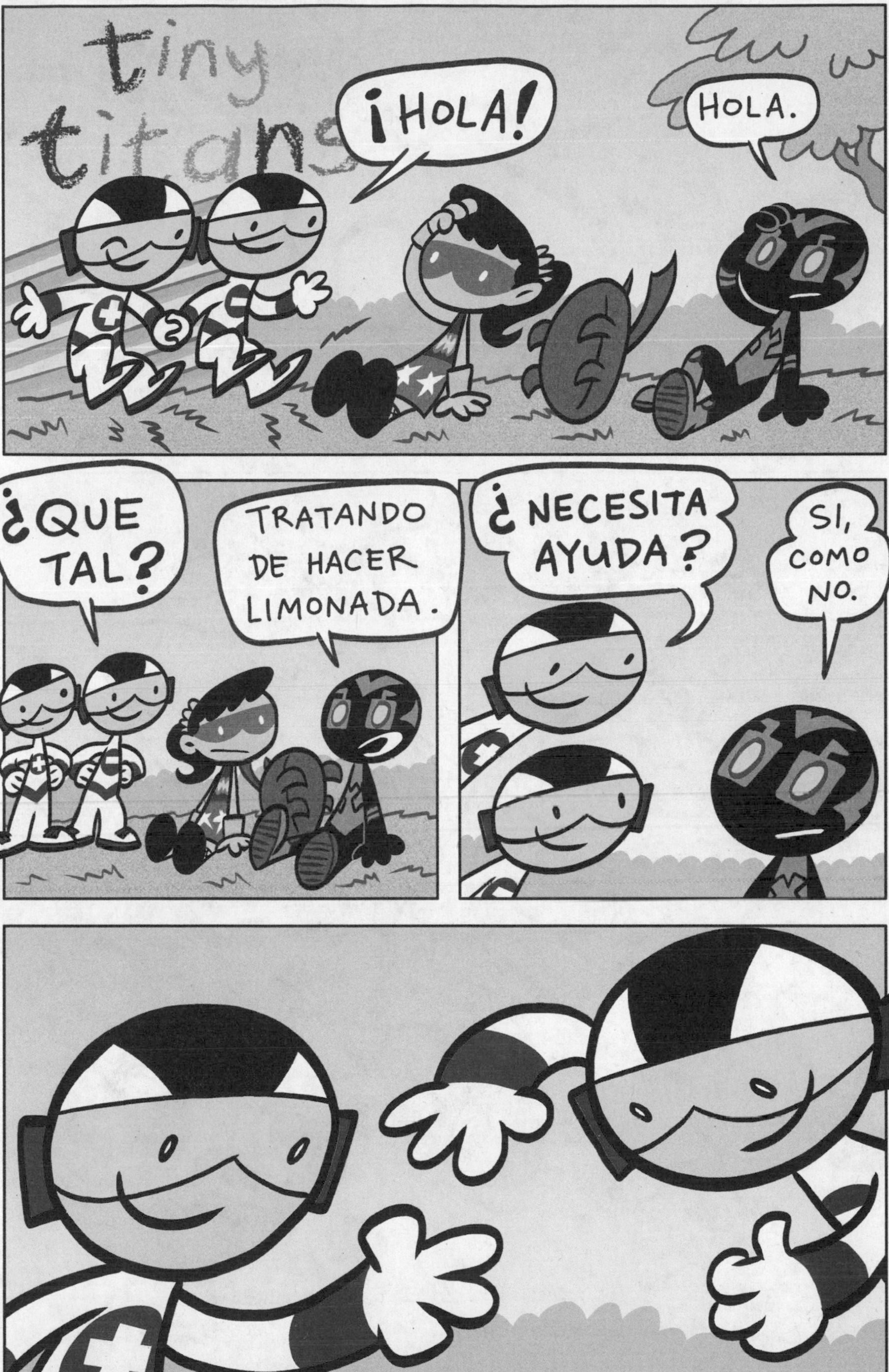
tiny titans
¡HOLA!
HOLA.
¿QUE TAL?
TRATANDO DE HACER LIMONADA.
¿NECESITA AYUDA?
SI, COMO NO.

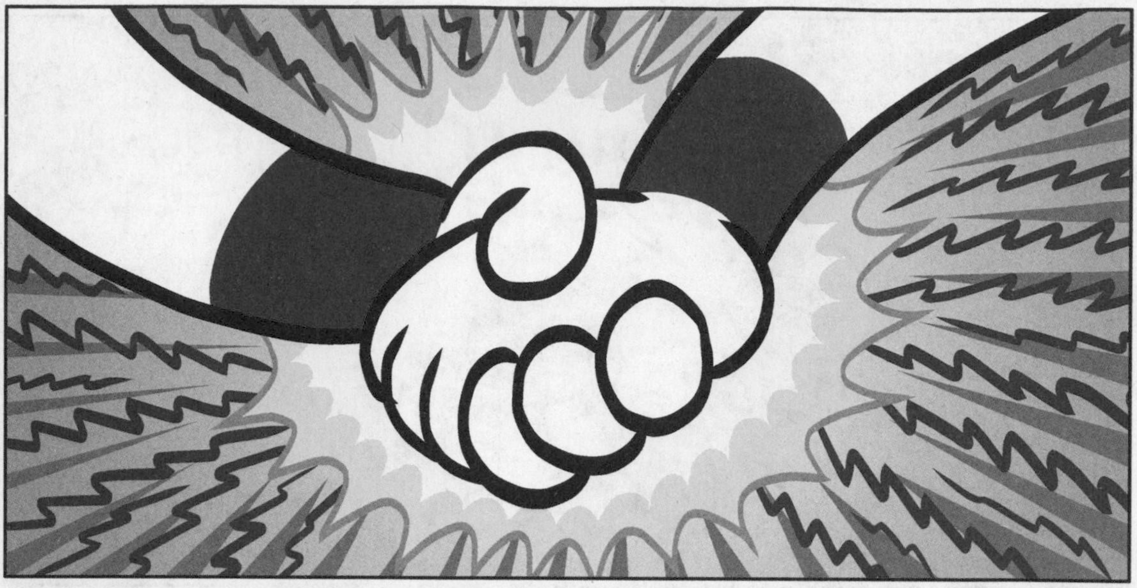

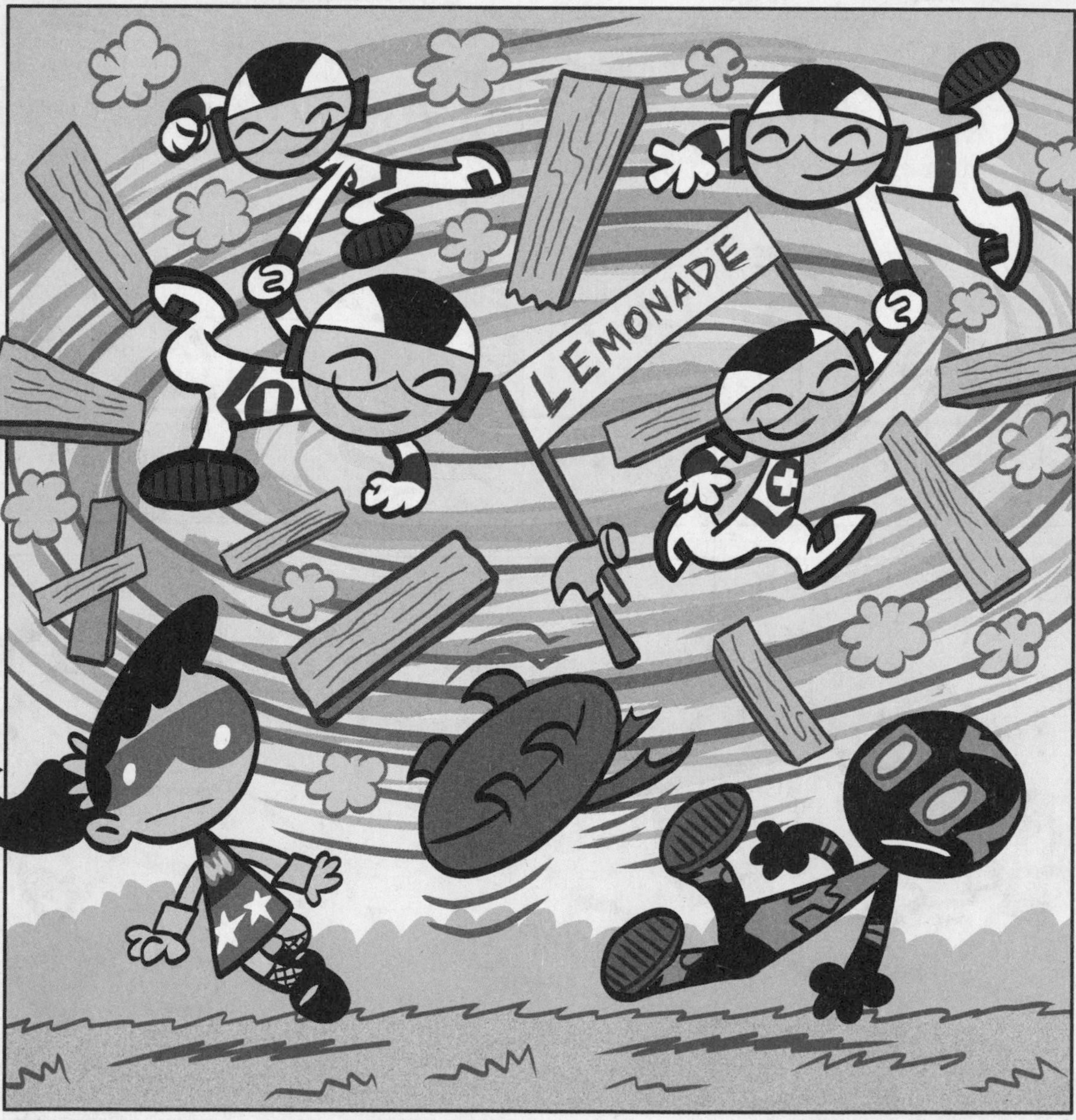
LEMONADE

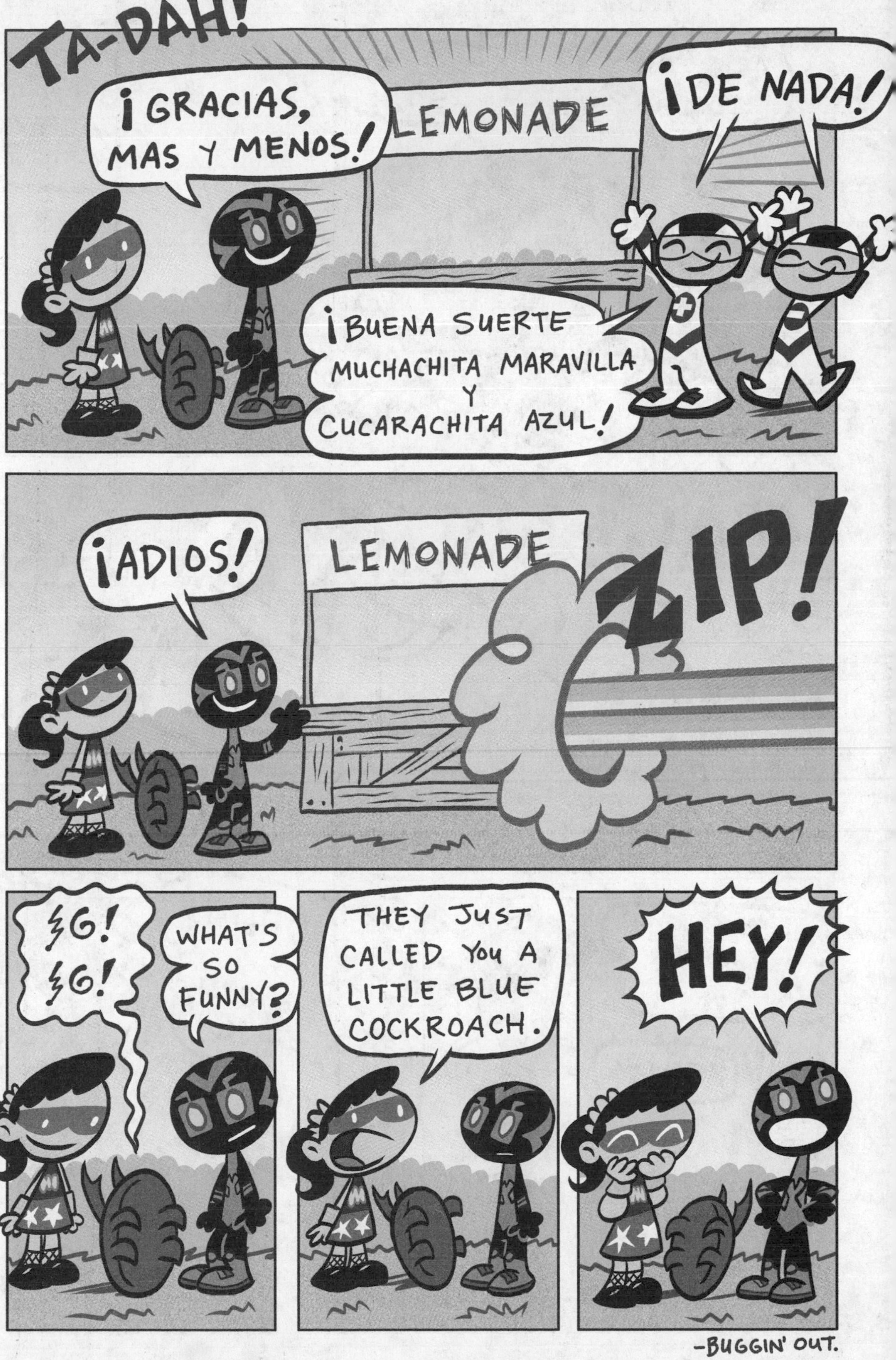
TA-DAH!
¡GRACIAS, MAS Y MENOS!
LEMONADE
¡DE NADA!
¡BUENA SUERTE MUCHACHITA MARAVILLA Y CUCARACHITA AZUL!
¡ADIOS!
LEMONADE
ZIP!
¡G! ¡G!
WHAT'S SO FUNNY?
THEY JUST CALLED YOU A LITTLE BLUE COCKROACH.
HEY!

–BUGGIN' OUT.

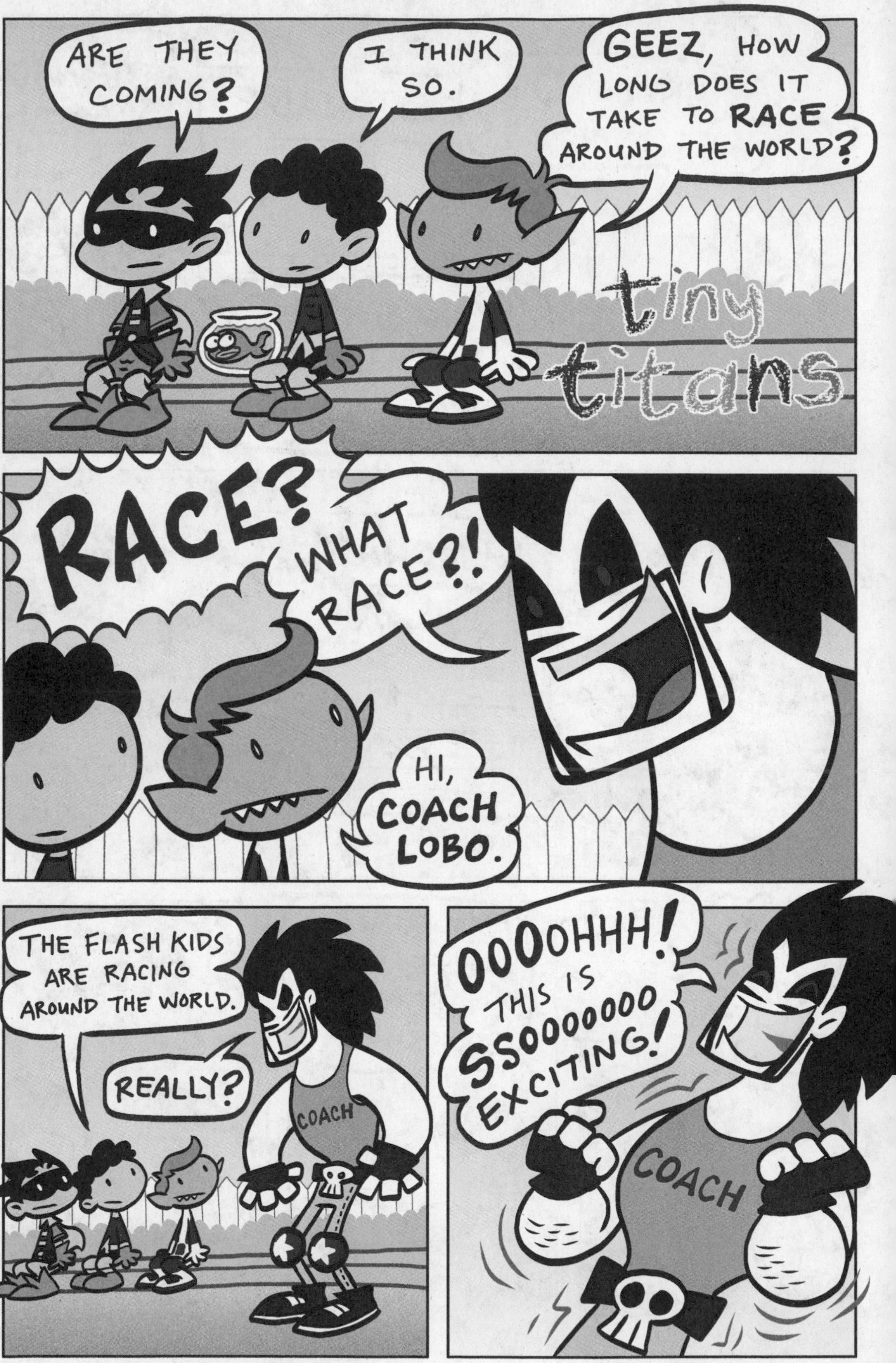
ARE THEY COMING?
I THINK SO.
GEEZ, HOW LONG DOES IT TAKE TO RACE AROUND THE WORLD?
tiny titans
RACE?
WHAT RACE?!
HI, COACH LOBO.
THE FLASH KIDS ARE RACING AROUND THE WORLD.
REALLY?
COACH
OOOOHHH! THIS IS SSOOOOOOO EXCITING!
COACH

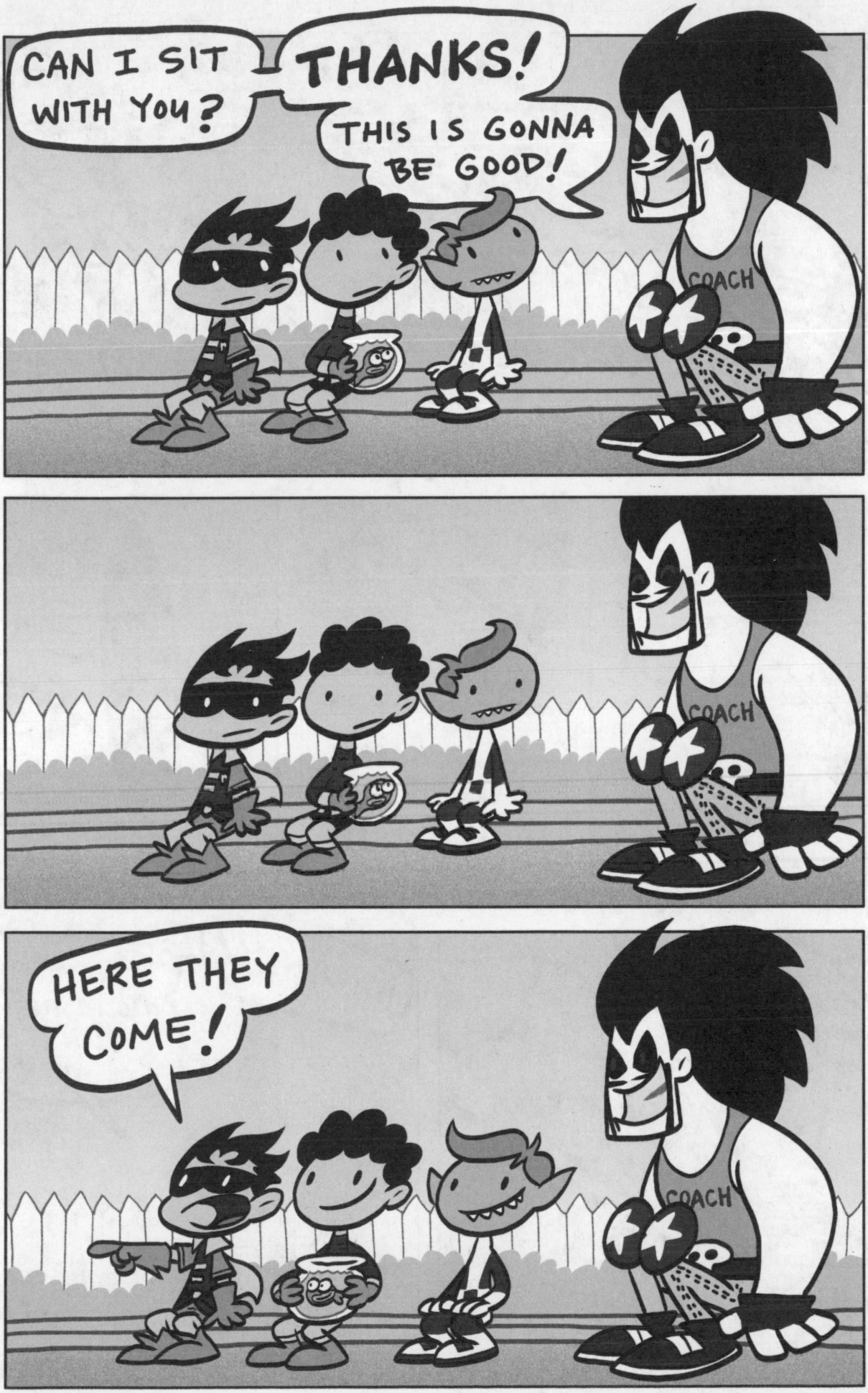
CAN I SIT WITH YOU?
THANKS!
THIS IS GONNA BE GOOD!
COACH
COACH
HERE THEY COME!
COACH

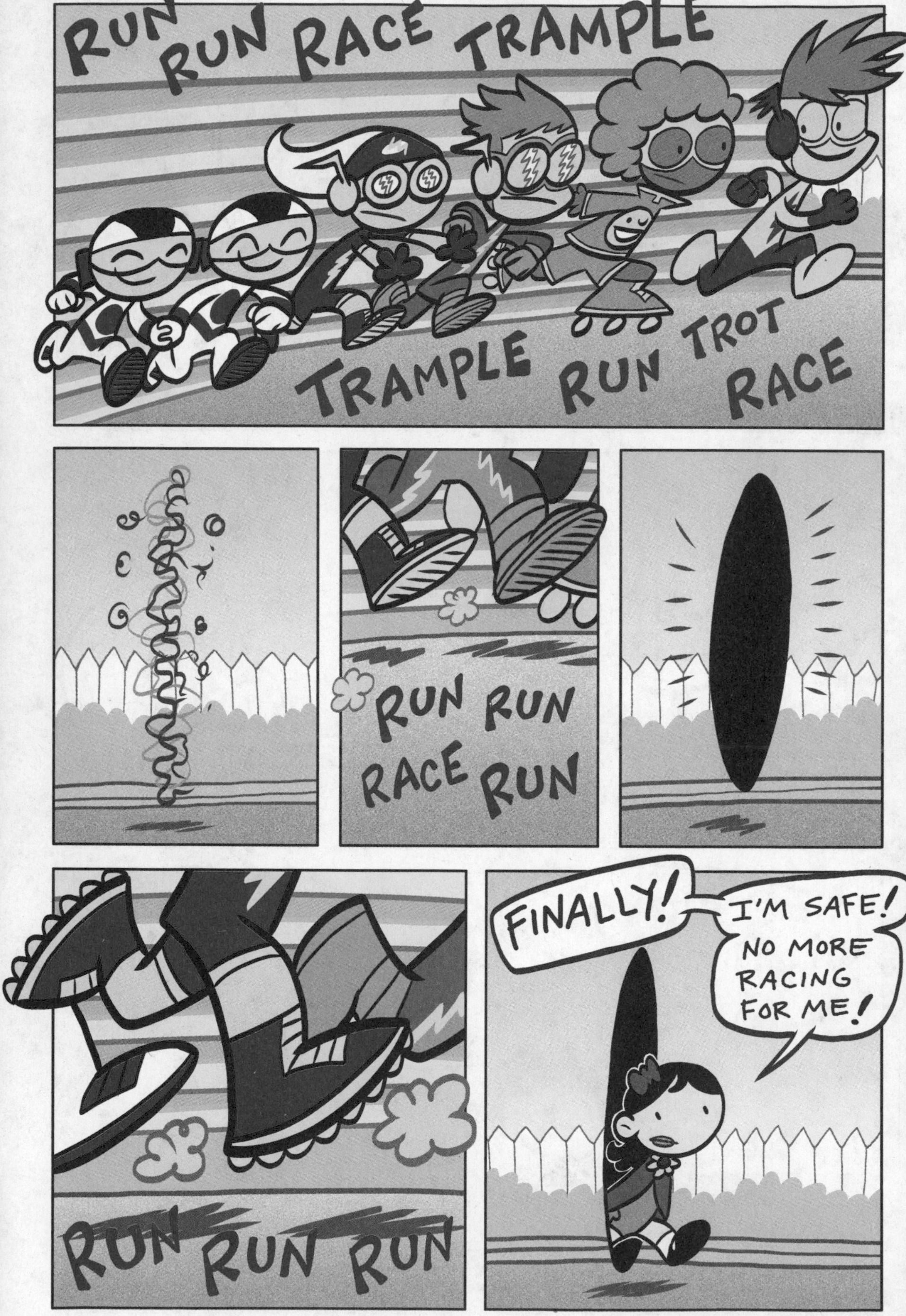
RUN RUN RACE TRAMPLE
TRAMPLE RUN TROT RACE
RUN RUN RACE RUN
RUN RUN RUN
FINALLY!
I'M SAFE! NO MORE RACING FOR ME!

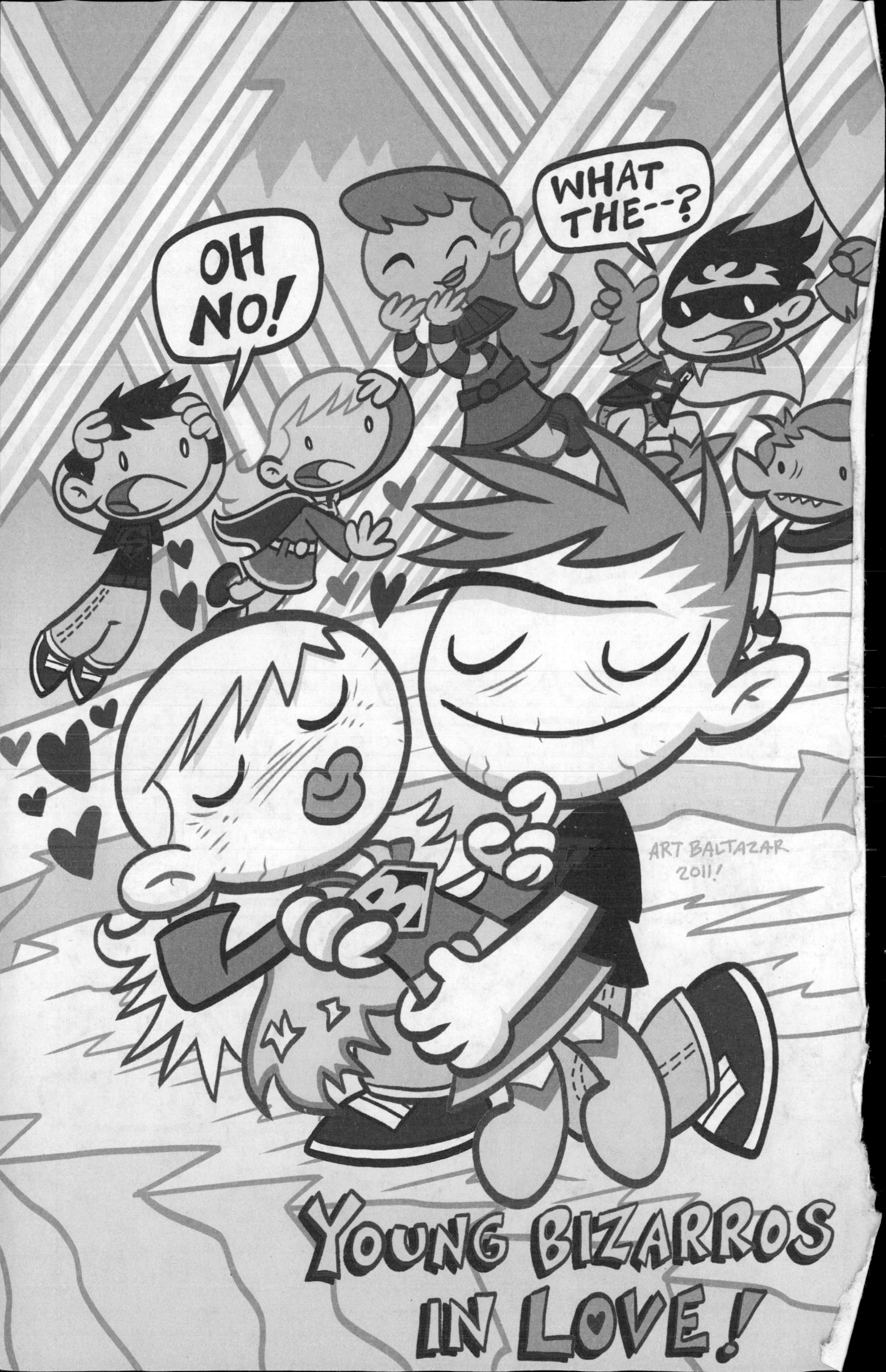
OH NO!
WHAT THE--?
ART BALTAZAR 2011!
YOUNG BIZARROS IN LOVE!

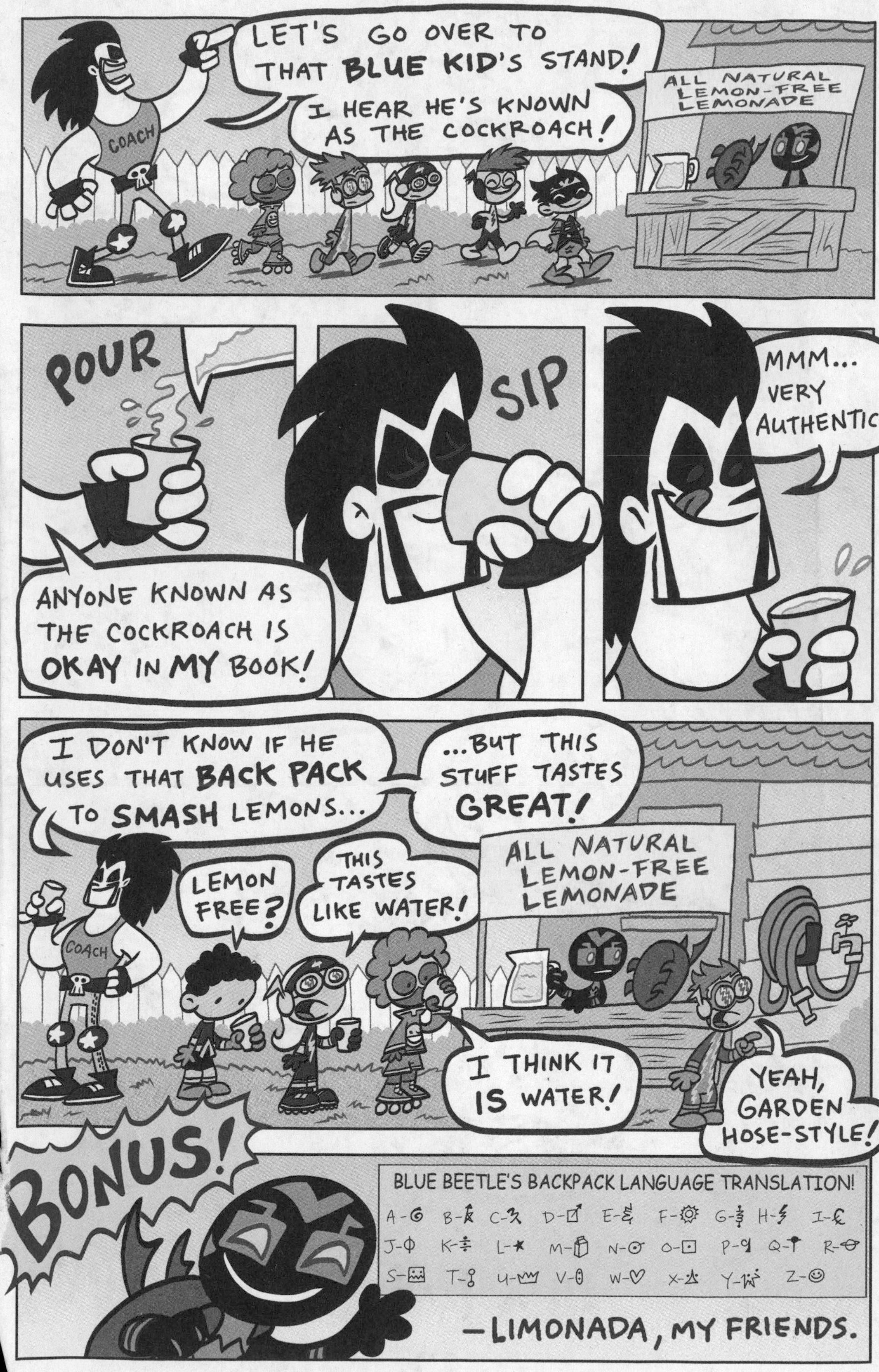

LET'S GO OVER TO THAT BLUE KID'S STAND!
I HEAR HE'S KNOWN AS THE COCKROACH!
ALL NATURAL LEMON-FREE LEMONADE
COACH
POUR
ANYONE KNOWN AS THE COCKROACH IS OKAY IN MY BOOK!
SIP
MMM... VERY AUTHENTIC!
I DON'T KNOW IF HE USES THAT BACK PACK TO SMASH LEMONS...
...BUT THIS STUFF TASTES GREAT!
LEMON FREE?
THIS TASTES LIKE WATER!
ALL NATURAL LEMON-FREE LEMONADE
COACH
I THINK IT IS WATER!
YEAH, GARDEN HOSE-STYLE!
BONUS!
BLUE BEETLE'S BACKPACK LANGUAGE TRANSLATION!
—LIMONADA, MY FRIENDS.

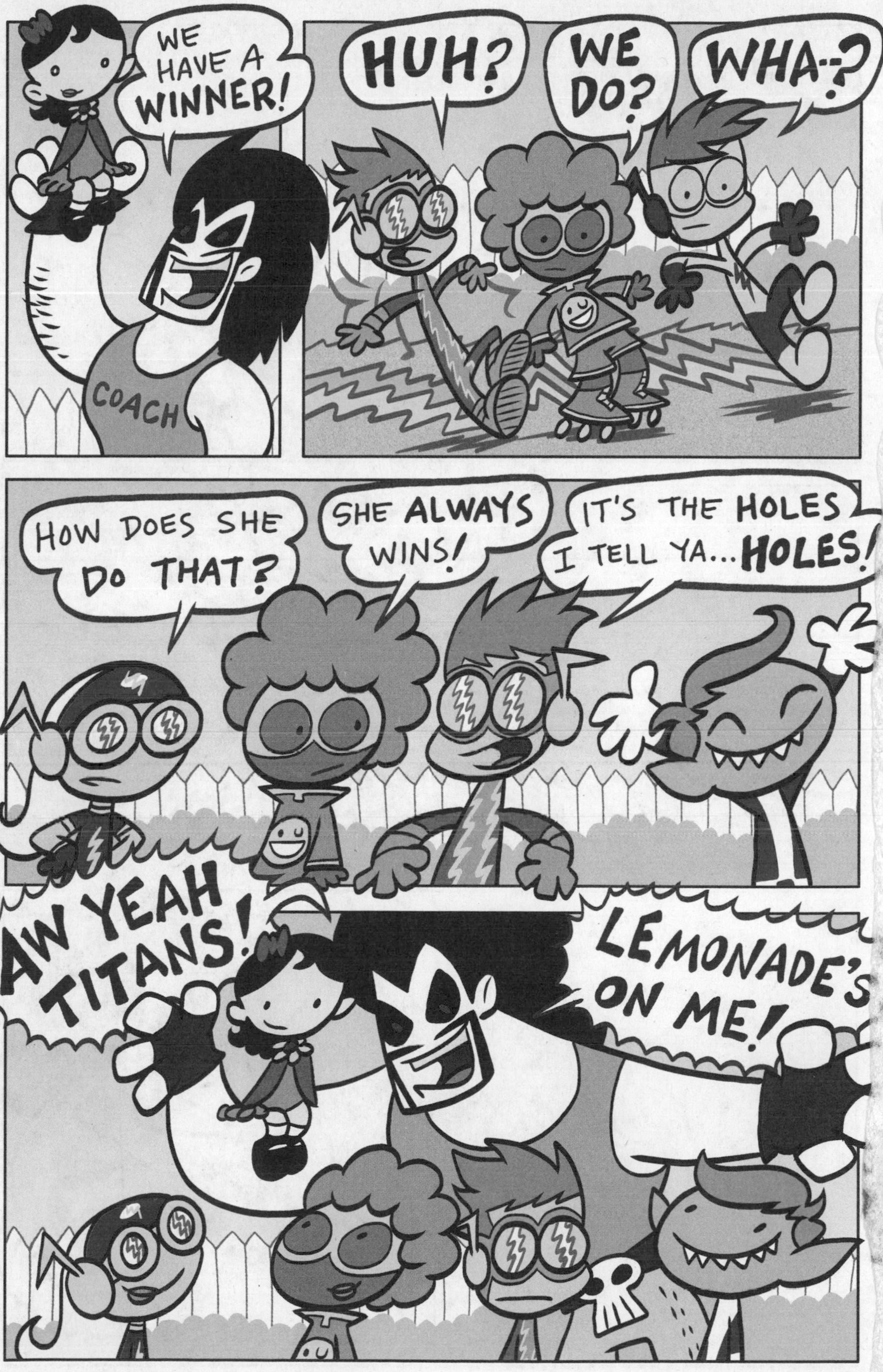
WE HAVE A WINNER!
HUH?
WE DO?
WHA--?
HOW DOES SHE DO THAT?
SHE ALWAYS WINS!
IT'S THE HOLES I TELL YA... HOLES!
AW YEAH TITANS!
LEMONADE'S ON ME!
COACH

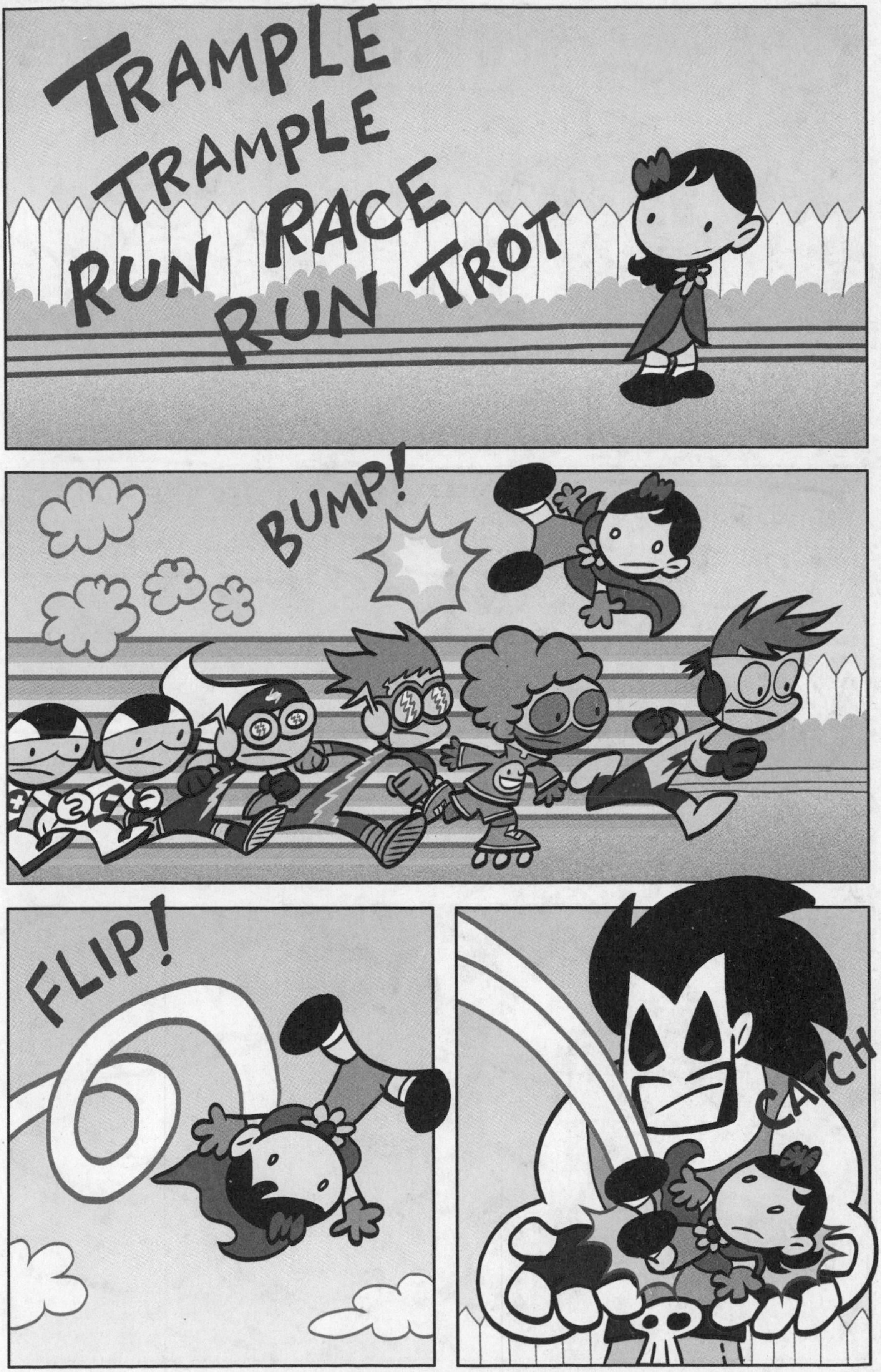
TRAMPLE
TRAMPLE
RUN RACE
RUN TROT
BUMP!
FLIP!
CATCH

tiny titans

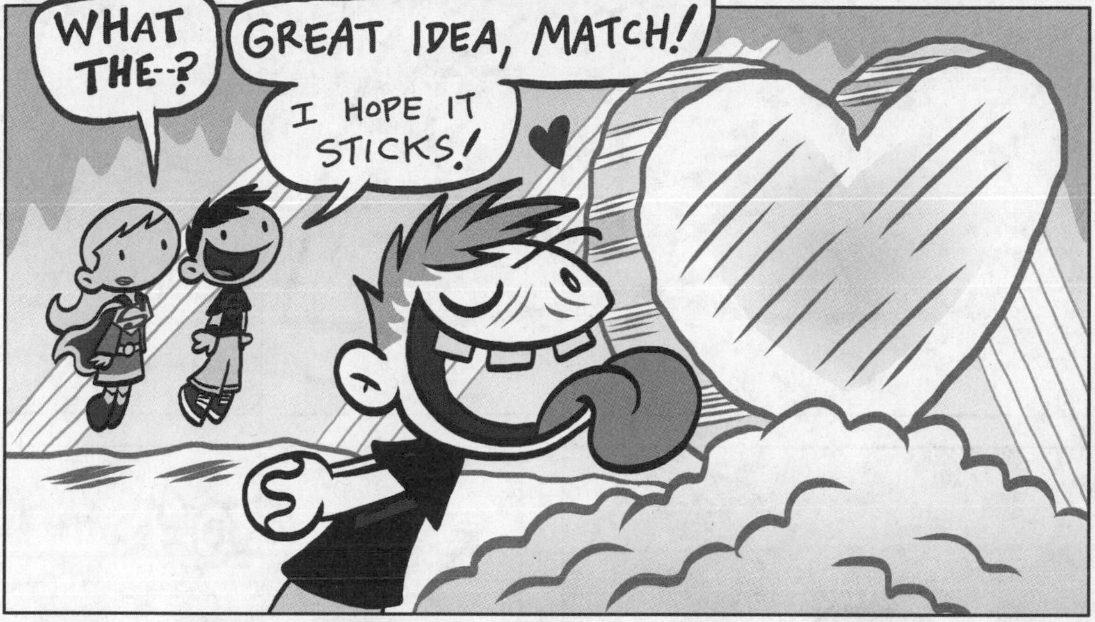
WHAT THE--?
GREAT IDEA, MATCH!
I HOPE IT STICKS!

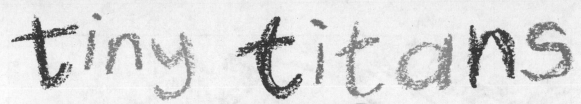

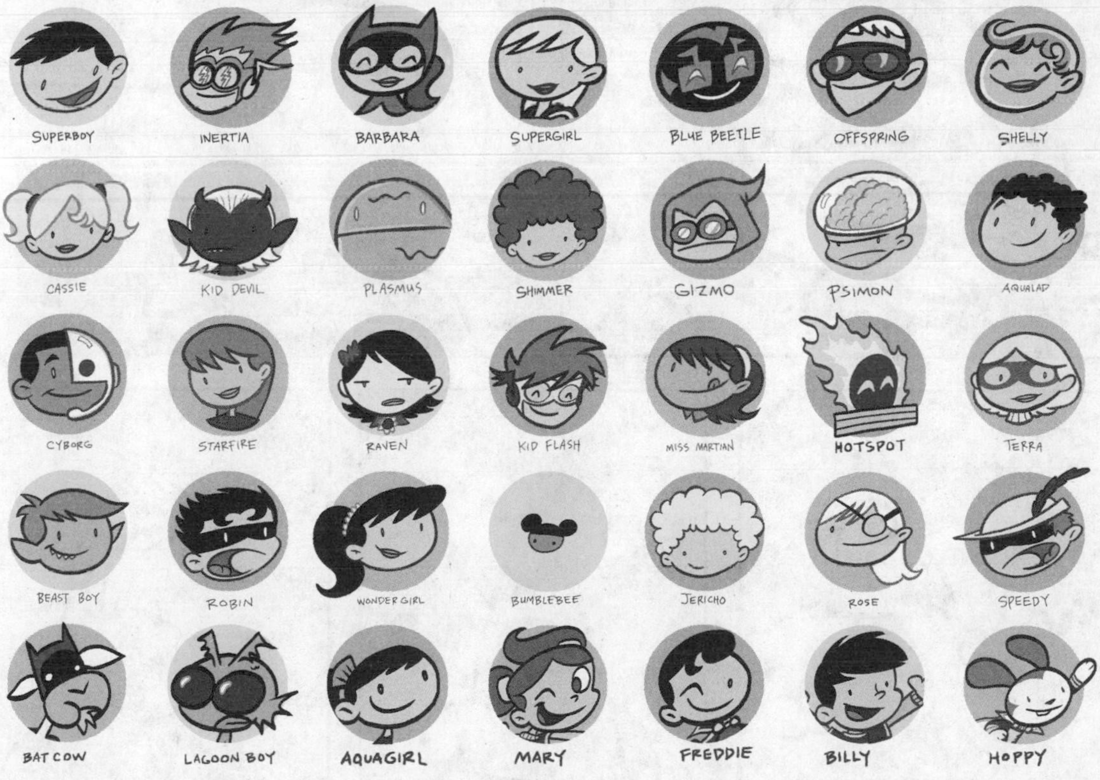
SUPERBOY
INERTIA
BARBARA
SUPERGIRL
BLUE BEETLE
OFFSPRING
SHELLY
CASSIE
KID DEVIL
PLASMUS
SHIMMER
GIZMO
PSIMON
AQUALAD
CYBORG
STARFIRE
RAVEN
KID FLASH
MISS MARTIAN
HOTSPOT
TERRA
BEAST BOY
ROBIN
WONDER GIRL
BUMBLEBEE
JERICHO
ROSE
SPEEDY
BAT COW
LAGOON BOY
AQUAGIRL
MARY
FREDDIE
BILLY
HOPPY

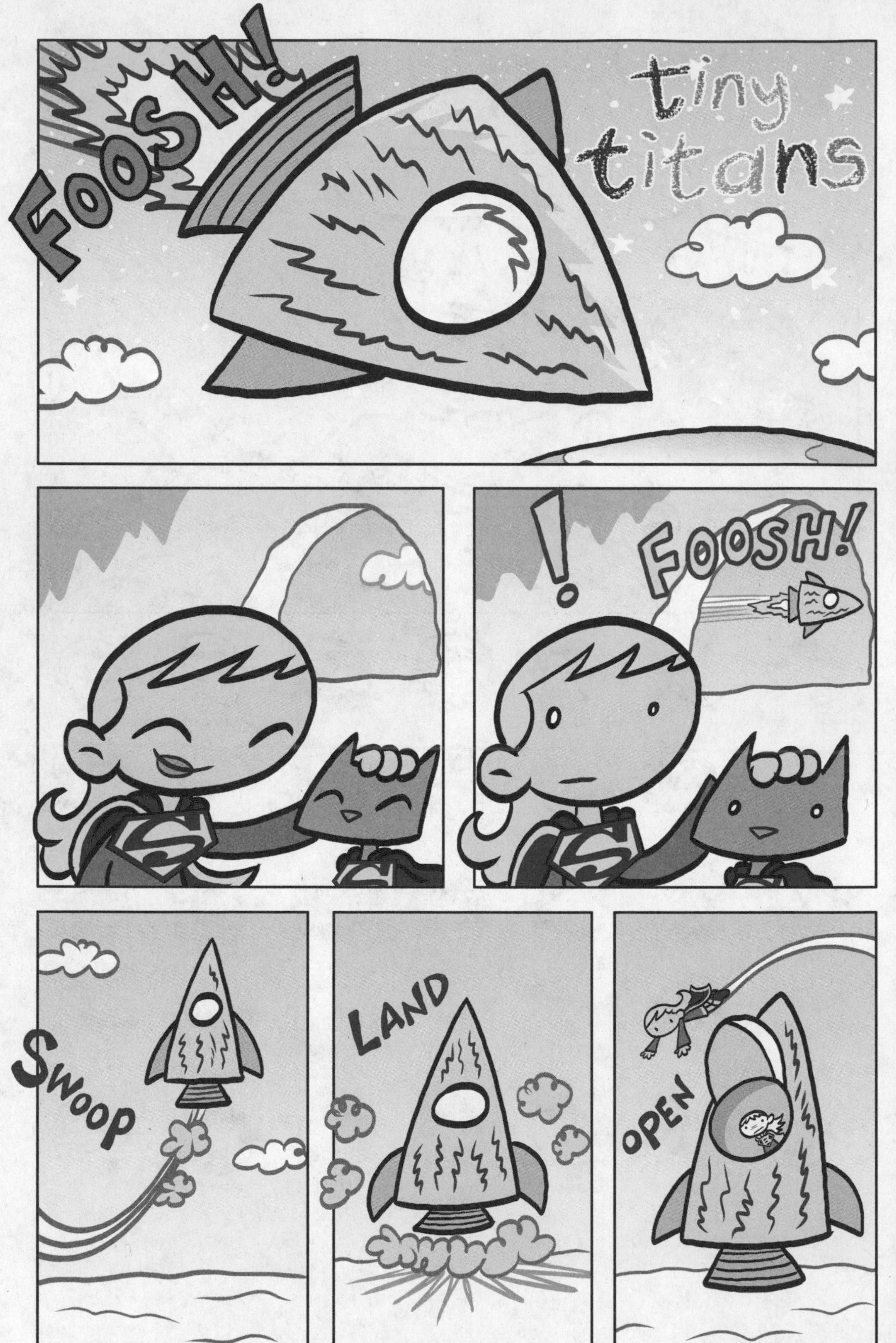
FOOSH!
tiny titans
!
FOOSH!
SWOOP
LAND
OPEN

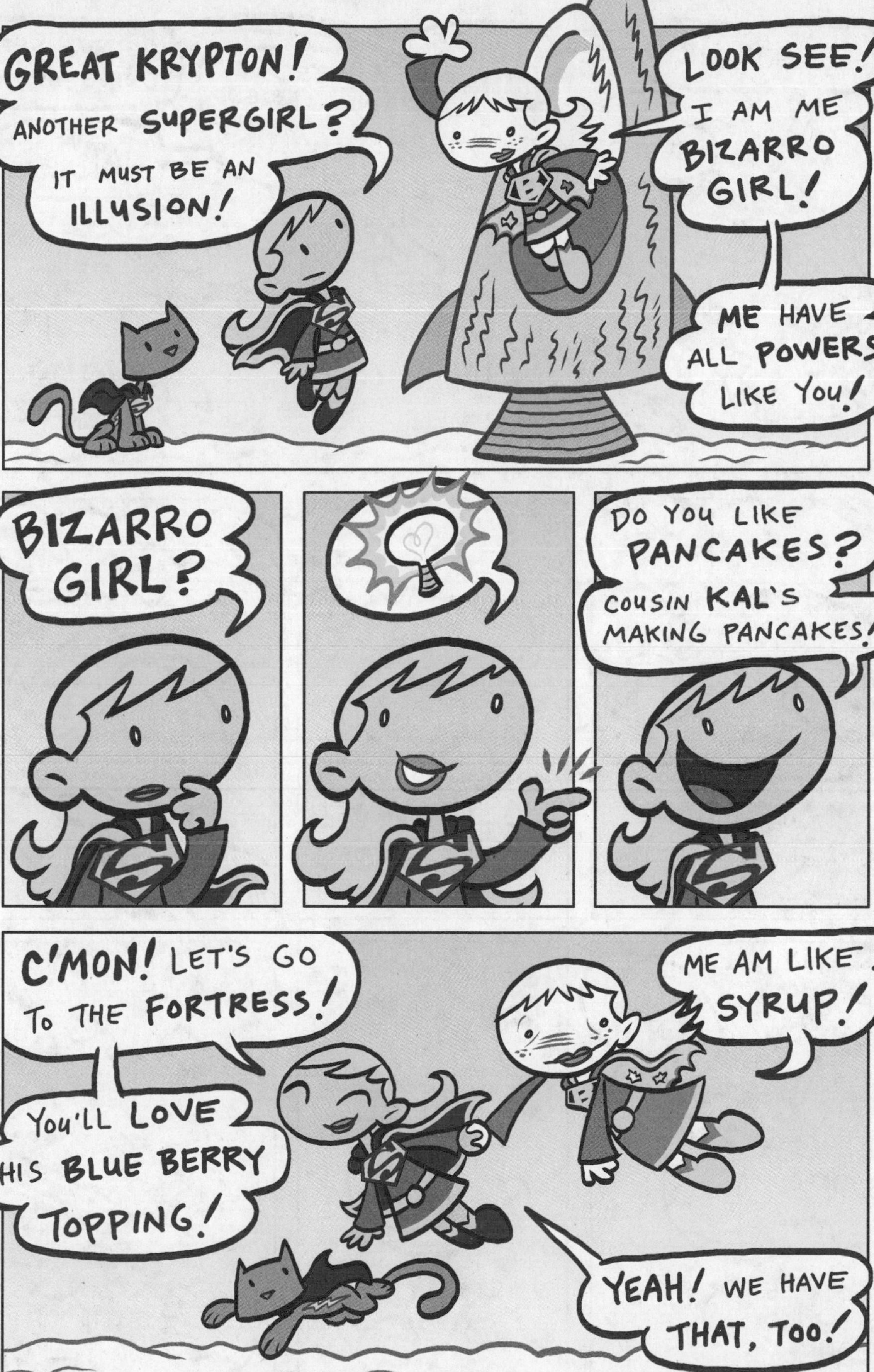
GREAT KRYPTON! ANOTHER SUPERGIRL? IT MUST BE AN ILLUSION!
LOOK SEE! I AM ME BIZARRO GIRL!
ME HAVE ALL POWERS LIKE YOU!
BIZARRO GIRL?
DO YOU LIKE PANCAKES? COUSIN KAL'S MAKING PANCAKES!
C'MON! LET'S GO TO THE FORTRESS!
YOU'LL LOVE HIS BLUE BERRY TOPPING!
ME AM LIKE SYRUP!
YEAH! WE HAVE THAT, TOO!

—TIME FOR BREAKFAST!

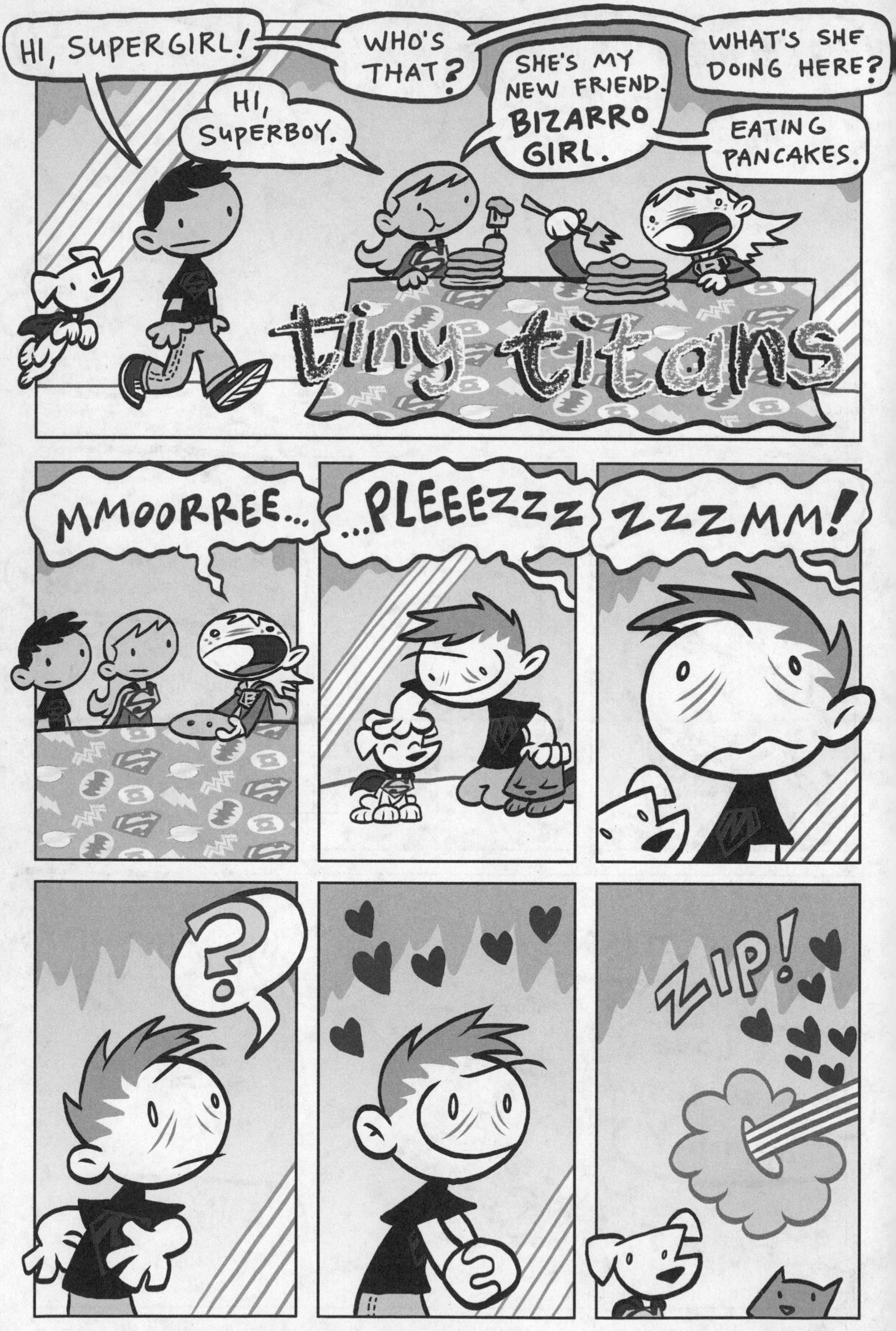
HI, SUPERGIRL!
WHO'S THAT?
WHAT'S SHE DOING HERE?
HI, SUPERBOY.
SHE'S MY NEW FRIEND. BIZARRO GIRL.
EATING PANCAKES.
tiny titans
MMOORREE...
...PLEEEZZZ
ZZZMM!
?
ZIP!

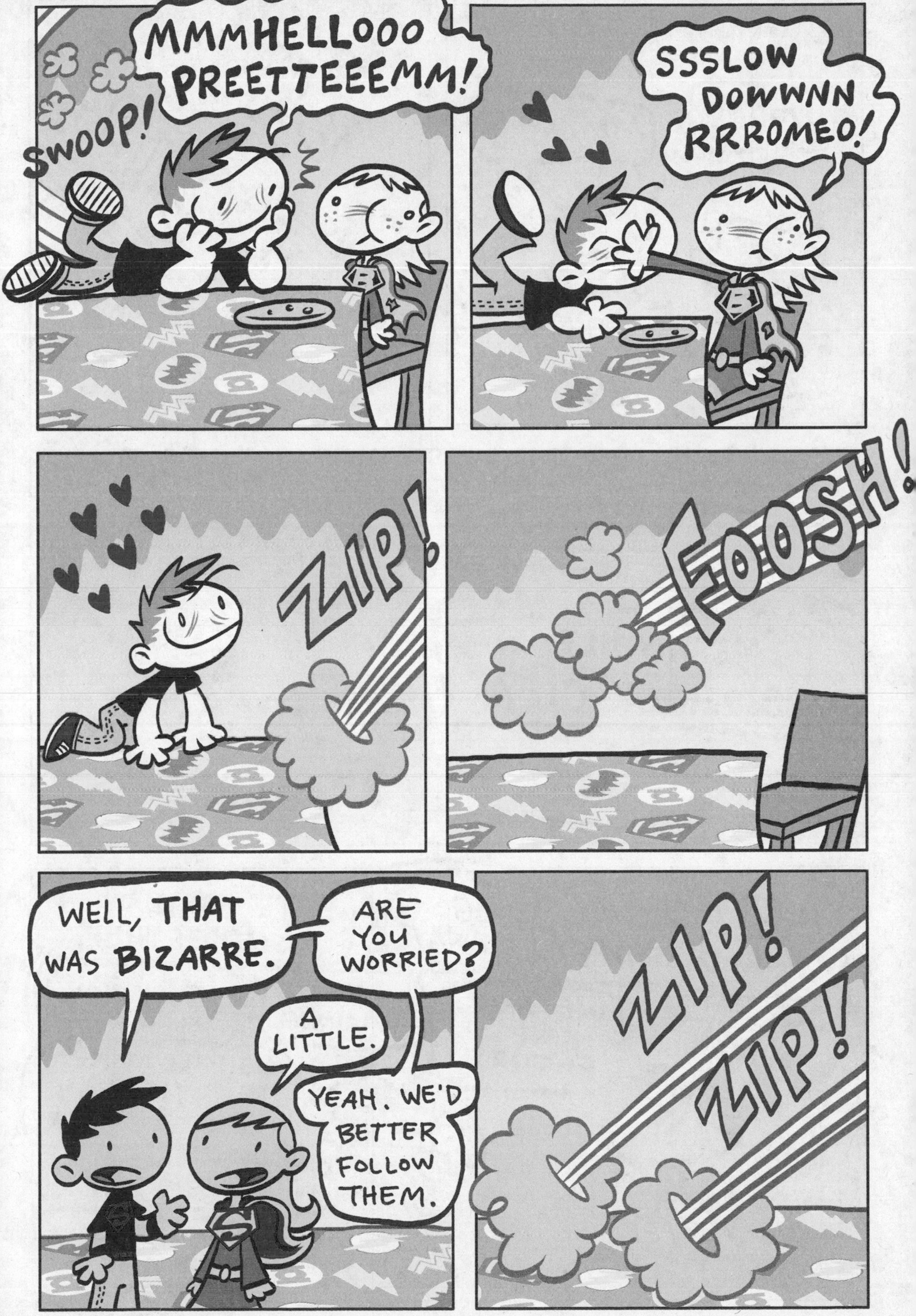

MMMHELLOOO PREETTEEEMM!
SWOOP!
SSSLOW DOWWNN RRROMEO!
ZIP!
FOOSH!
WELL, THAT WAS BIZARRE.
ARE YOU WORRIED?
A LITTLE.
YEAH. WE'D BETTER FOLLOW THEM.
ZIP!
ZIP!

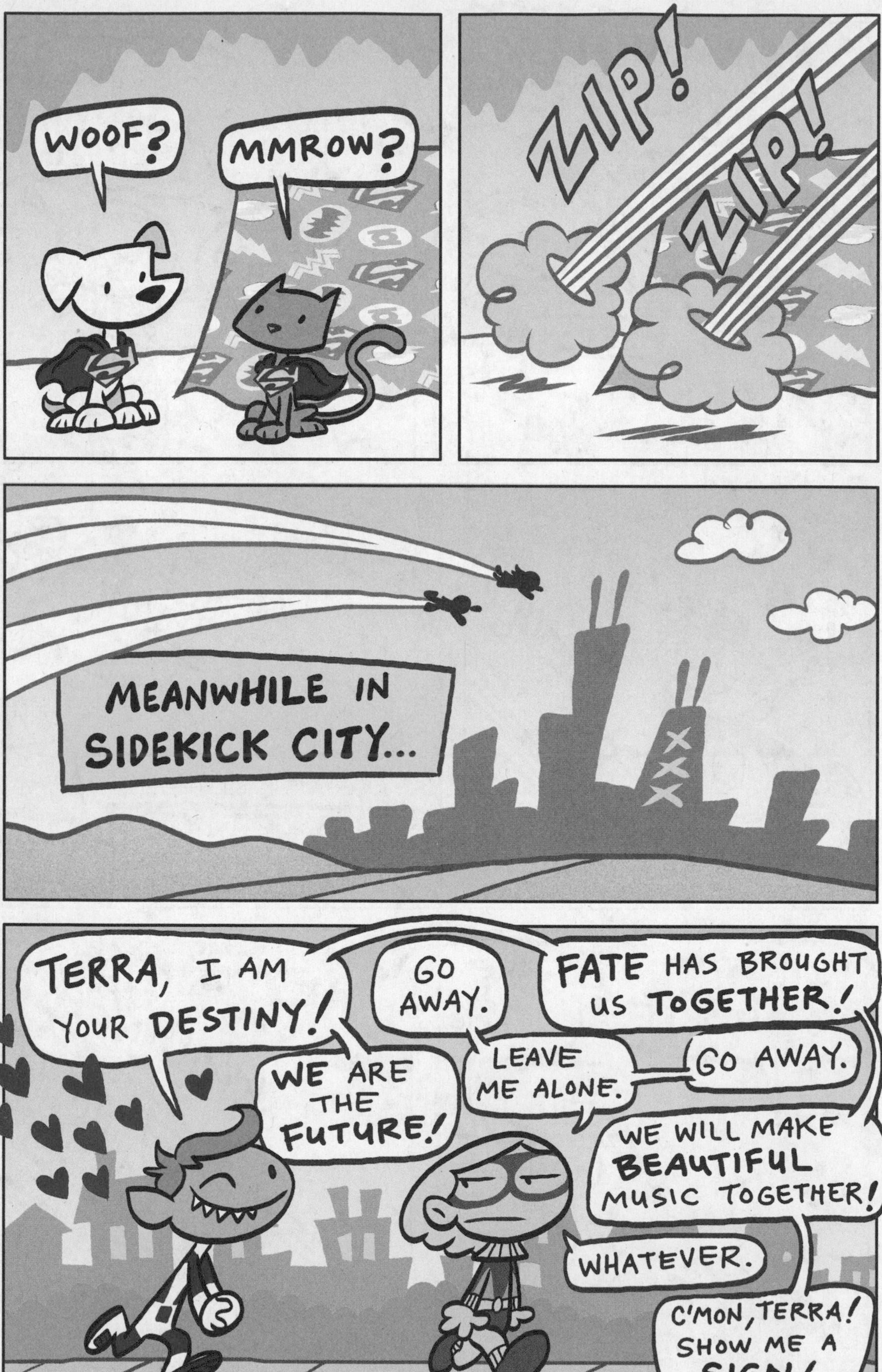
WOOF?
MMROW?
ZIP!
ZIP!
MEANWHILE IN SIDEKICK CITY...
TERRA, I AM YOUR DESTINY!
GO AWAY.
FATE HAS BROUGHT US TOGETHER!
WE ARE THE FUTURE!
LEAVE ME ALONE.
GO AWAY.
WE WILL MAKE BEAUTIFUL MUSIC TOGETHER!
WHATEVER.
C'MON, TERRA! SHOW ME A SIGN!

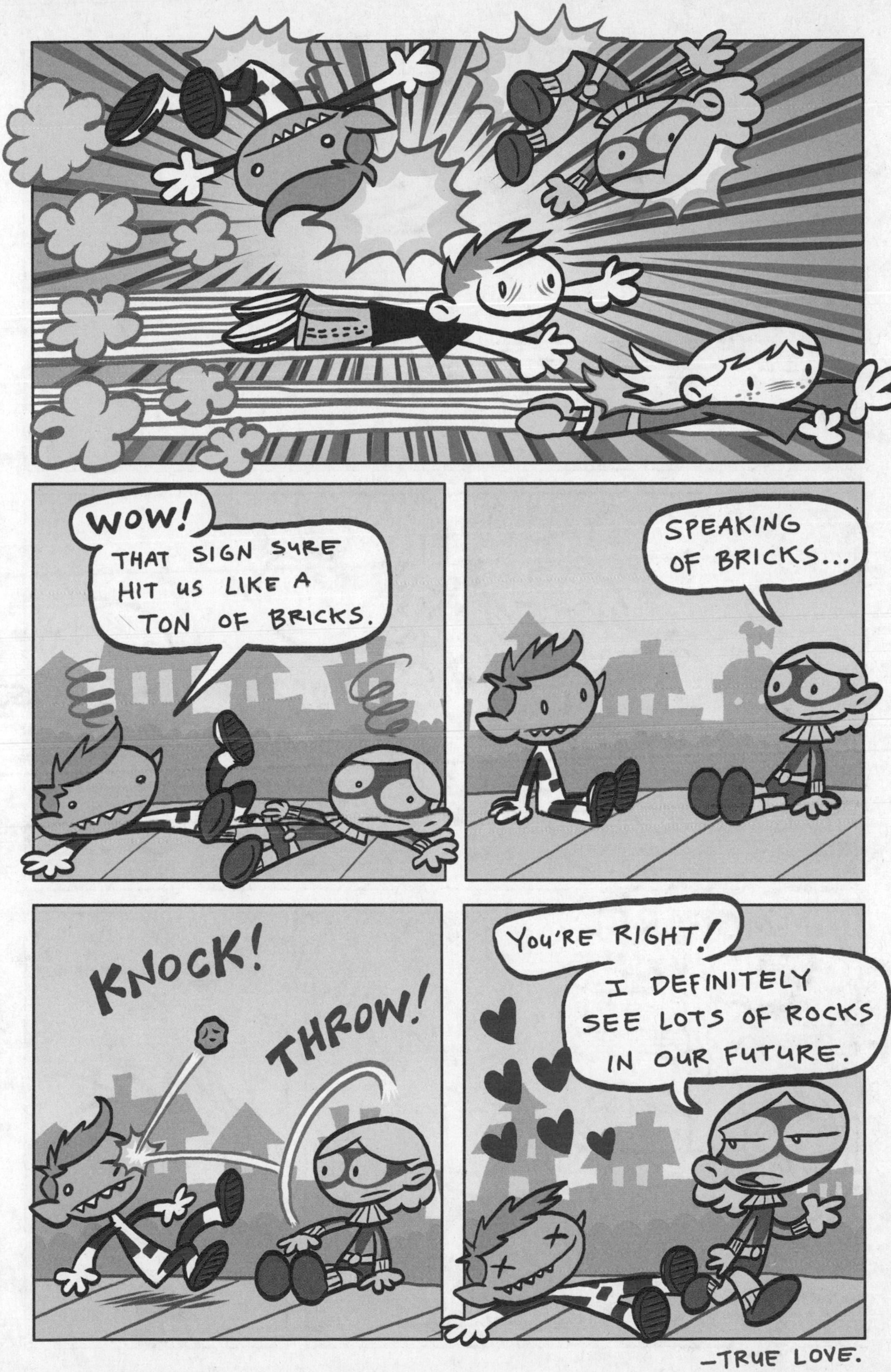
WOW!
THAT SIGN SURE HIT US LIKE A TON OF BRICKS.
SPEAKING OF BRICKS...
KNOCK!
THROW!
YOU'RE RIGHT!
I DEFINITELY SEE LOTS OF ROCKS IN OUR FUTURE.
-TRUE LOVE.

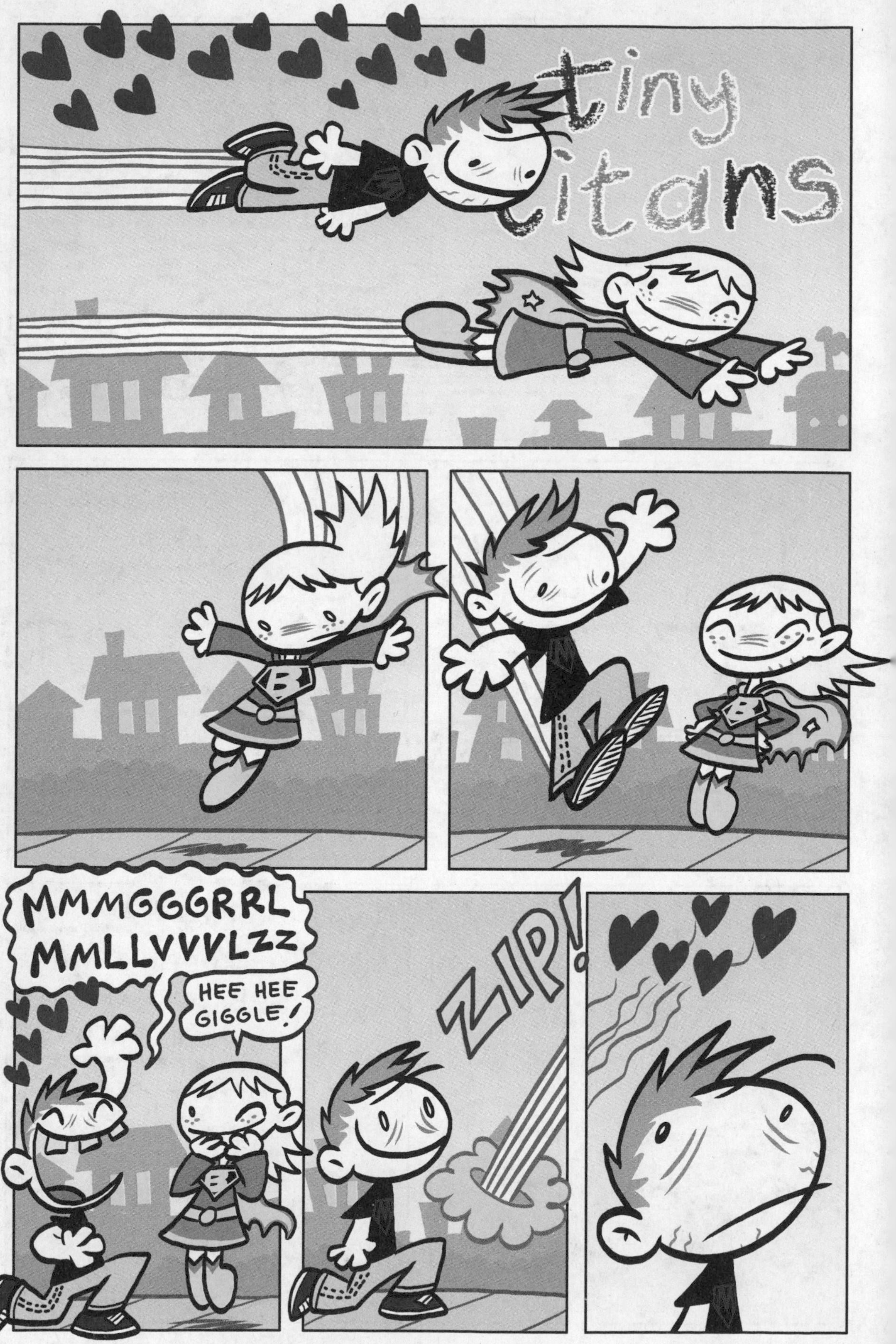
tiny titans
MMMGGGRRL MMLLVVVLZZ
HEE HEE GIGGLE!
ZIP!

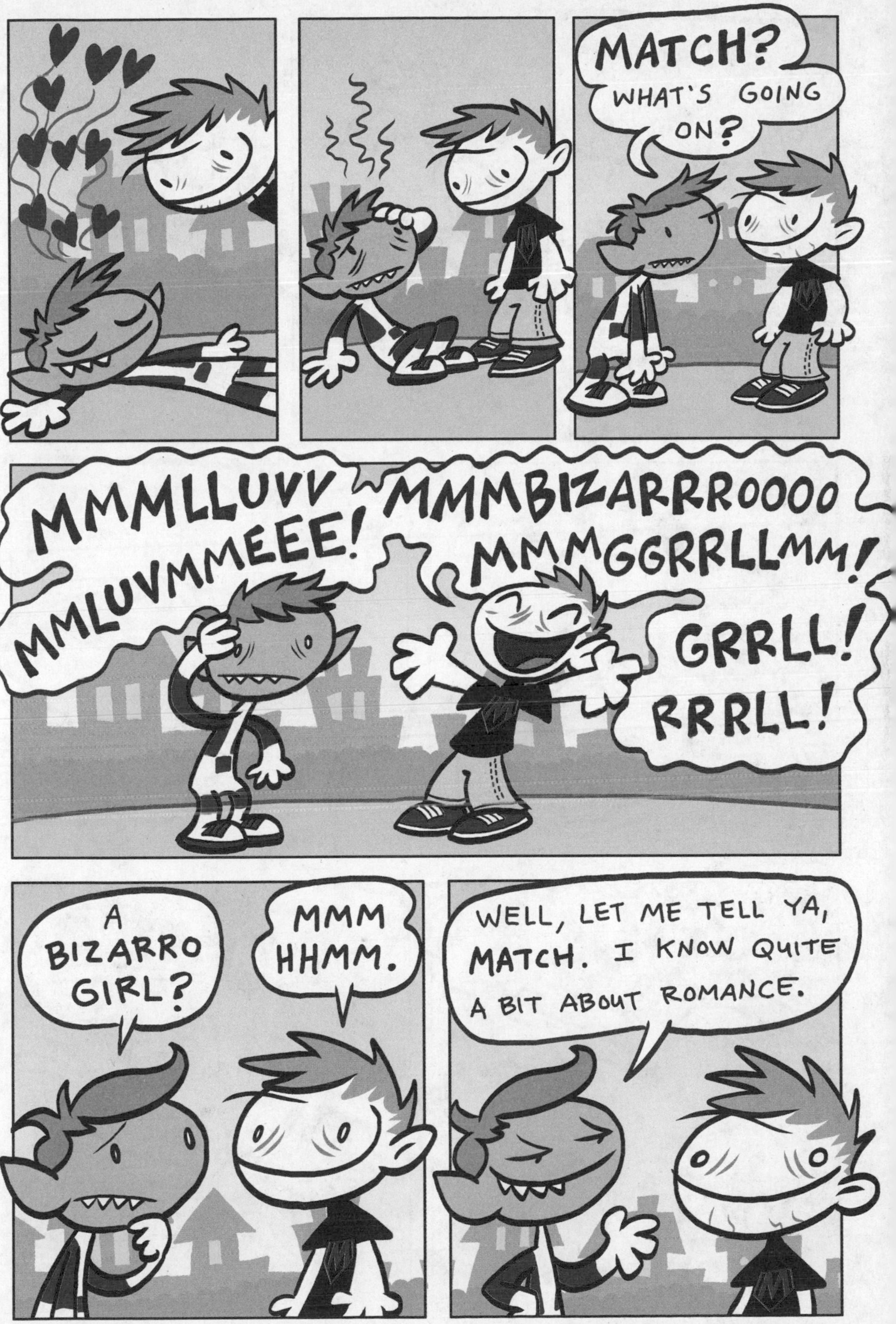
MATCH? WHAT'S GOING ON?
MMMLLUVV MMLUVMMEEE!
MMMBIZARRROOOO MMMGGRRLLMM!
GRRLL! RRRLL!
A BIZARRO GIRL?
MMM HHMM.
WELL, LET ME TELL YA, MATCH. I KNOW QUITE A BIT ABOUT ROMANCE.

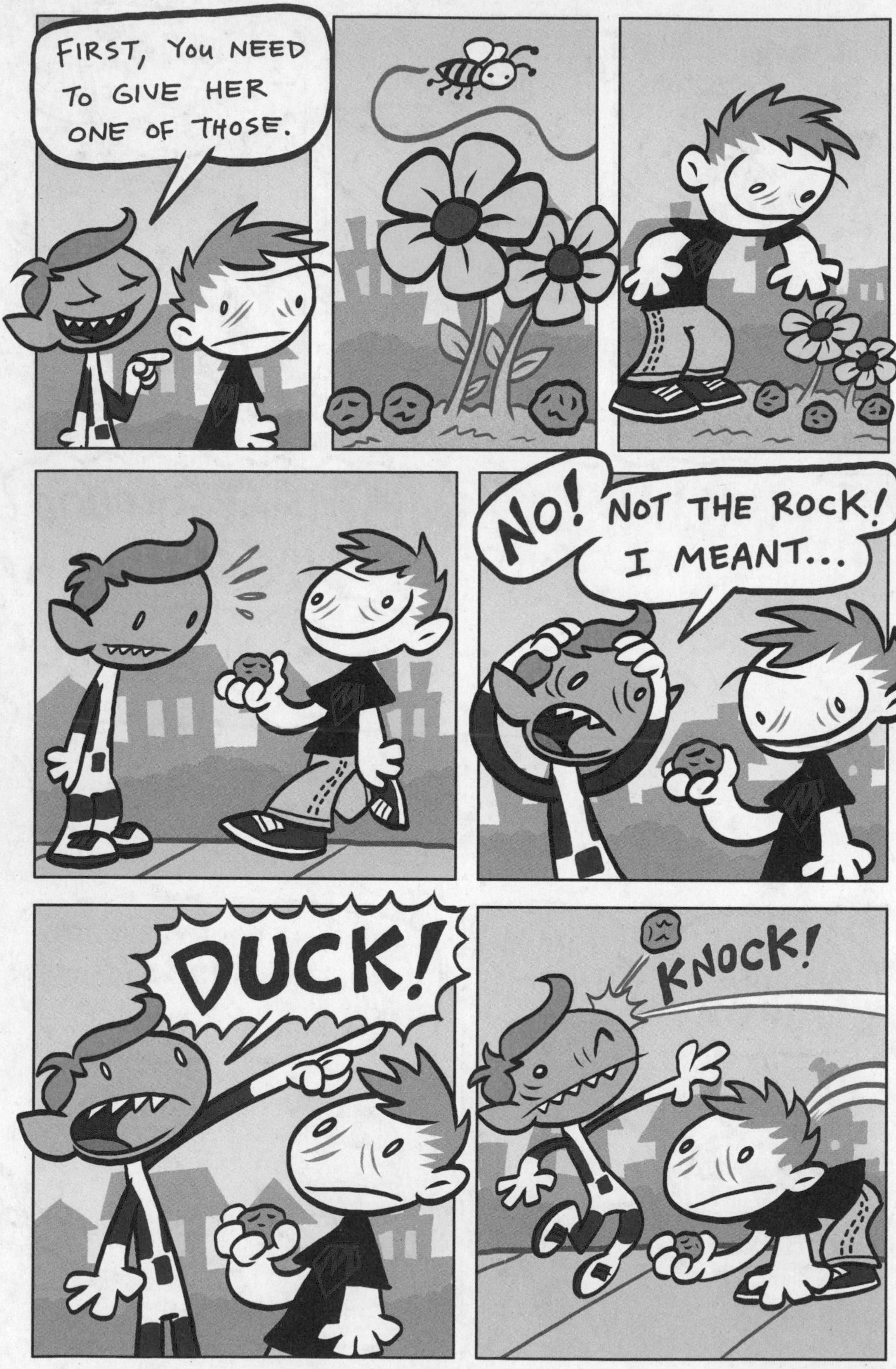
FIRST, YOU NEED TO GIVE HER ONE OF THOSE.
NO! NOT THE ROCK! I MEANT...
DUCK!
KNOCK!

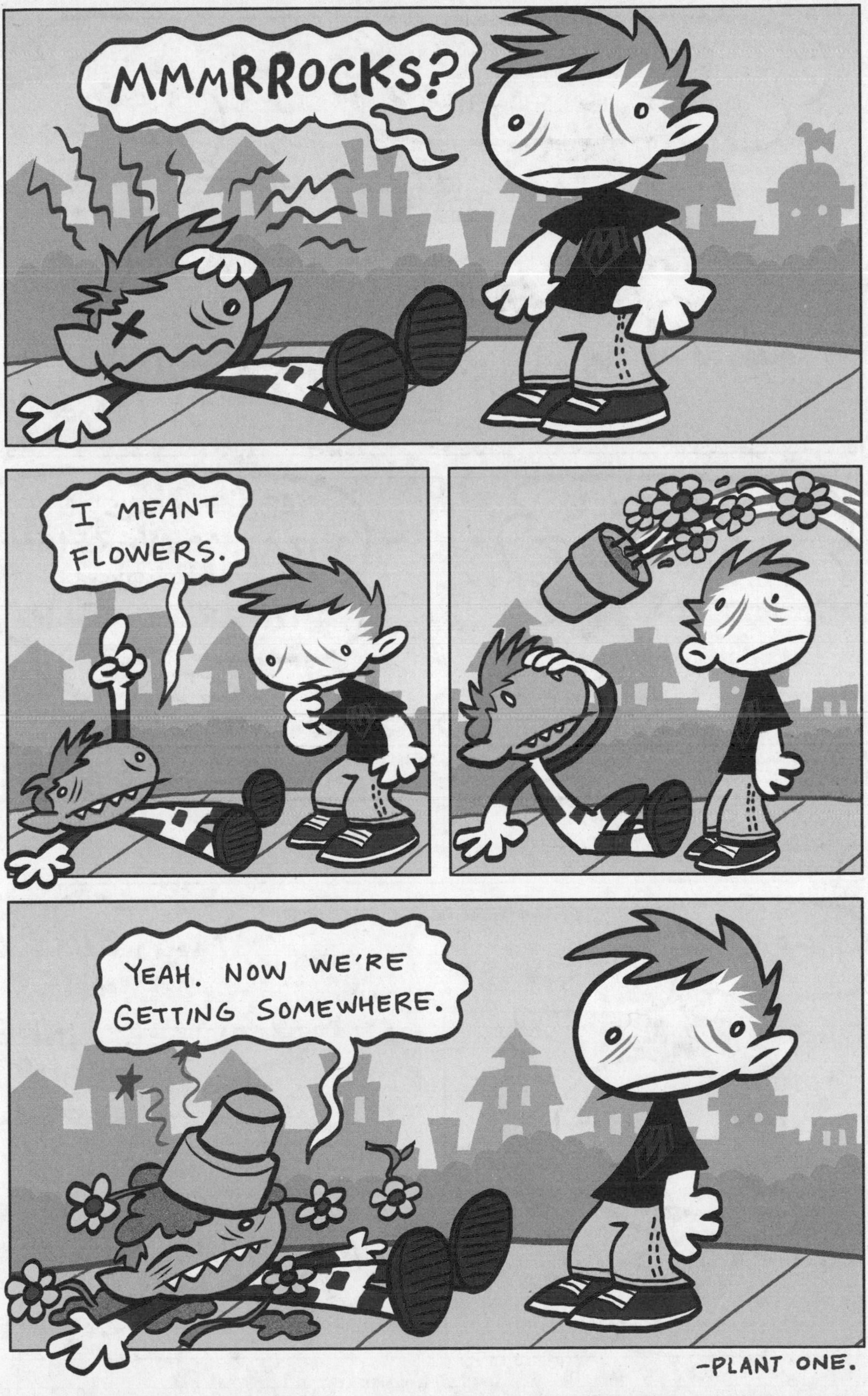
MMMRROCKS?
I MEANT FLOWERS.
YEAH. NOW WE'RE GETTING SOMEWHERE.

-PLANT ONE.

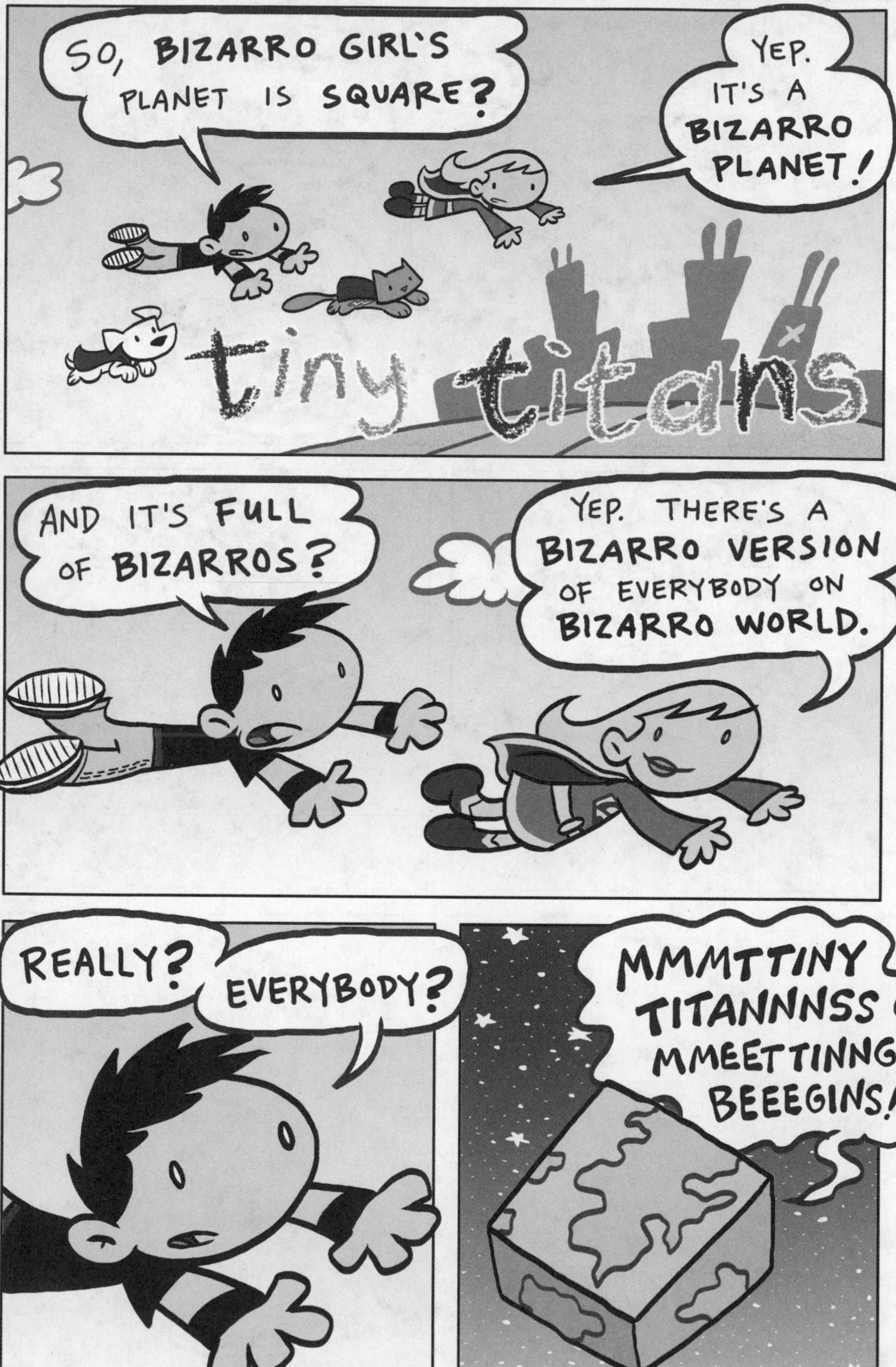
SO, BIZARRO GIRL'S PLANET IS SQUARE?
YEP. IT'S A BIZARRO PLANET!
tiny titans
AND IT'S FULL OF BIZARROS?
YEP. THERE'S A BIZARRO VERSION OF EVERYBODY ON BIZARRO WORLD.
REALLY?
EVERYBODY?
MMMTTINY TITANNNSS MMEETTINNG BEEEGINS!

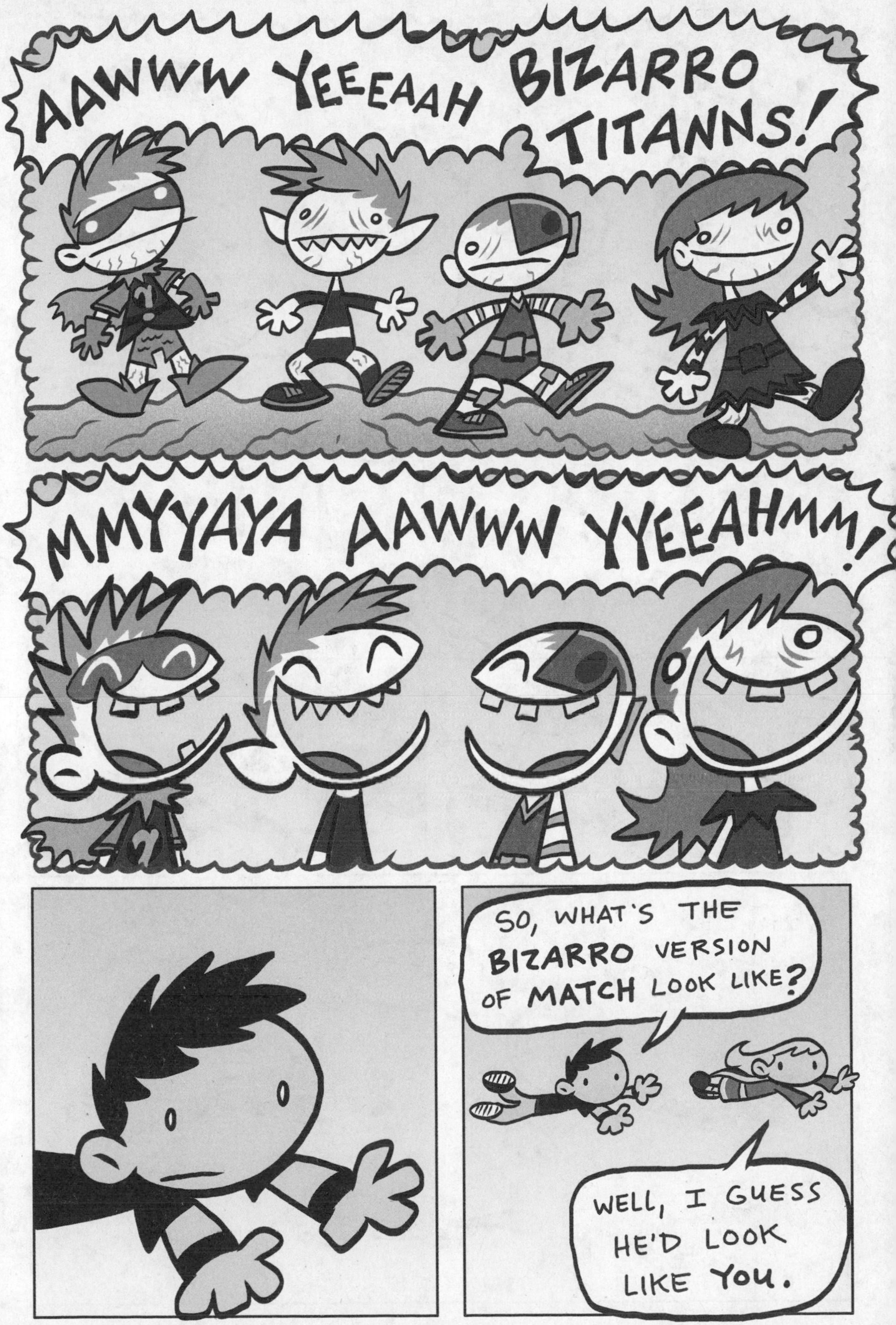
AAWWW YEEEAAH BIZARRO TITANNS!
MMYYAYA AAWWW YYEEAHMM!
SO, WHAT'S THE BIZARRO VERSION OF MATCH LOOK LIKE?
WELL, I GUESS HE'D LOOK LIKE YOU.

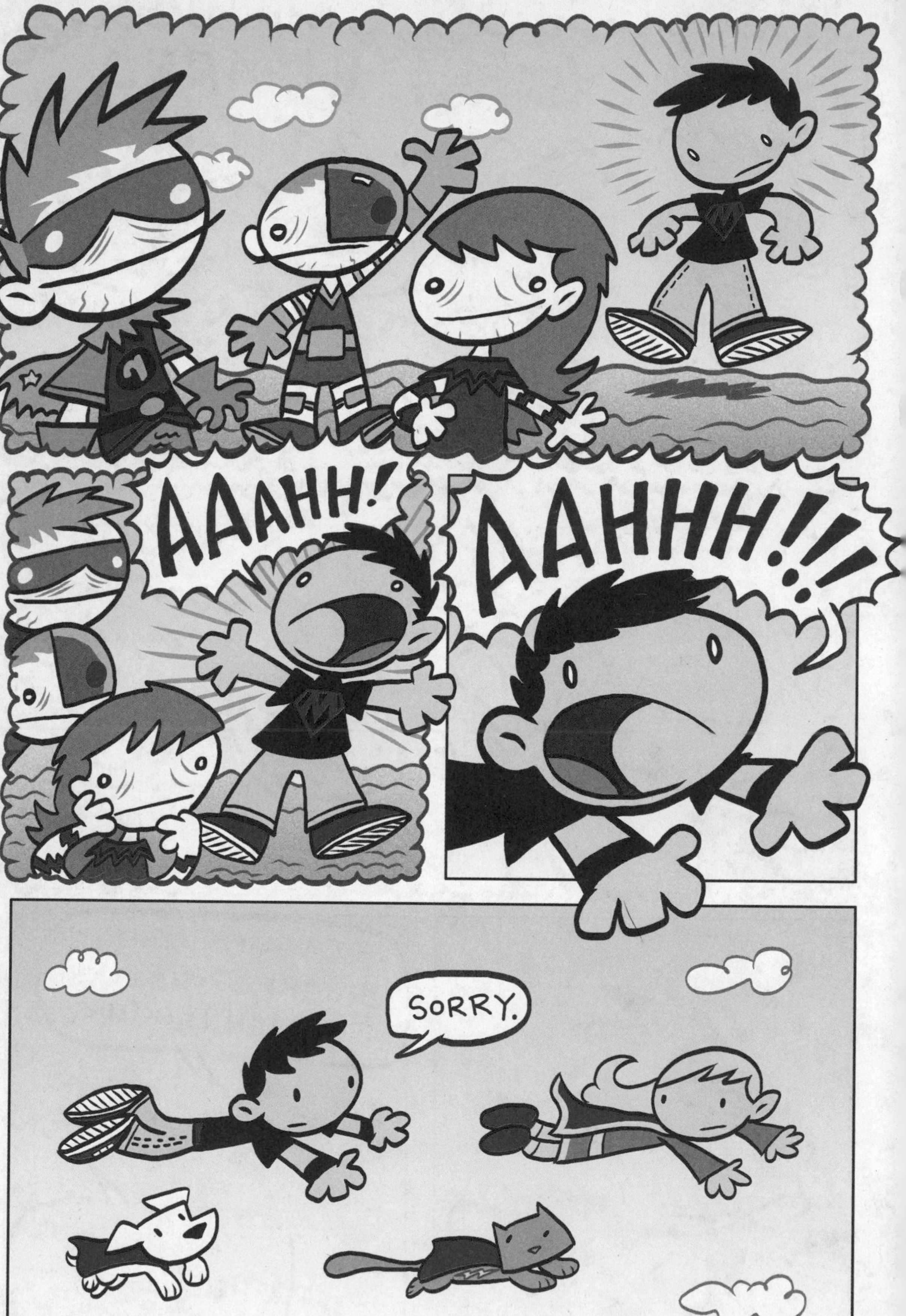
AAAHH!
AAHHH!!!
SORRY.

-BIZARRE OH!

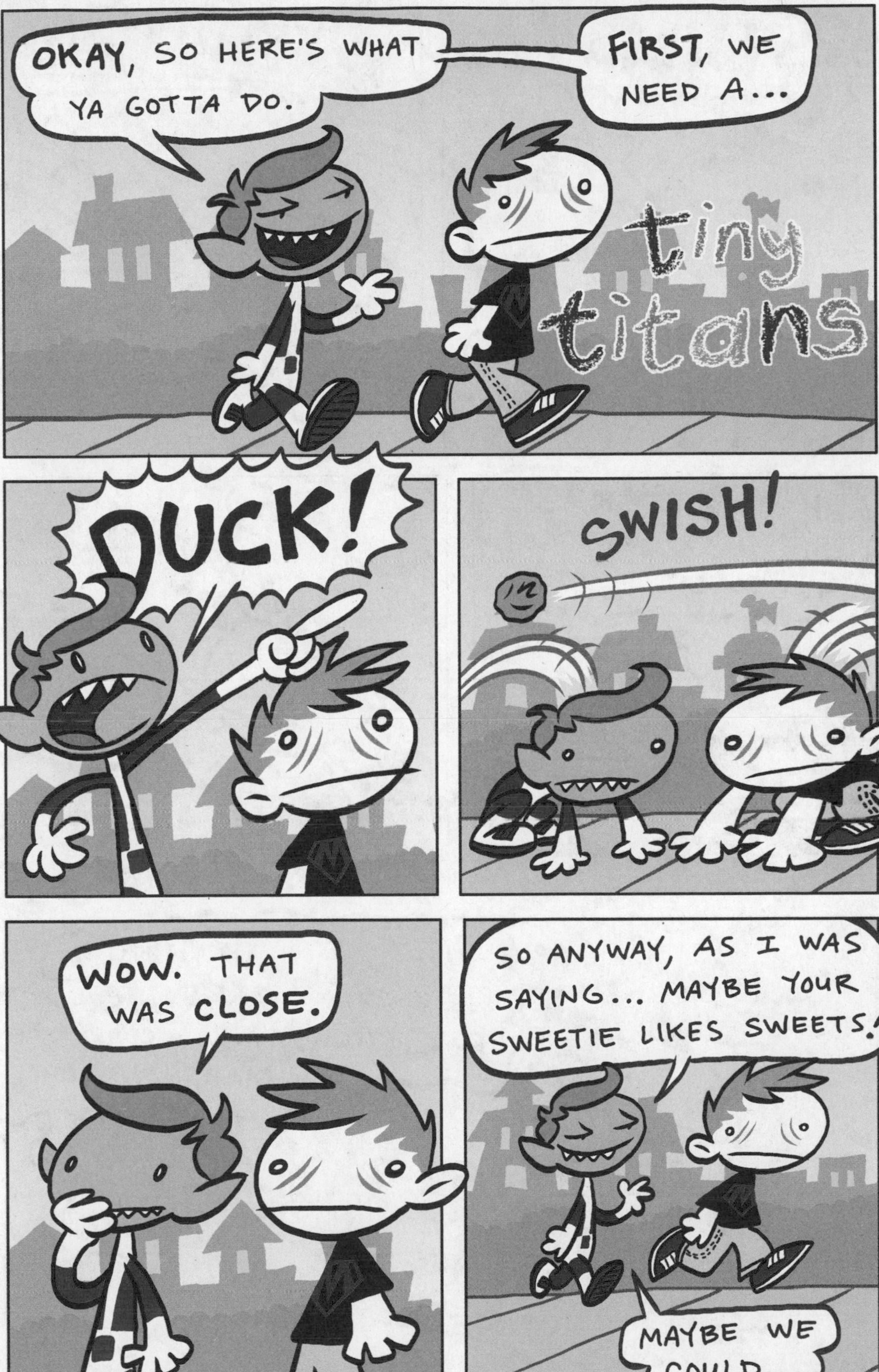
OKAY, SO HERE'S WHAT YA GOTTA DO.
FIRST, WE NEED A...
tiny titans
DUCK!
SWISH!
WOW. THAT WAS CLOSE.
SO ANYWAY, AS I WAS SAYING... MAYBE YOUR SWEETIE LIKES SWEETS!
MAYBE WE COULD...

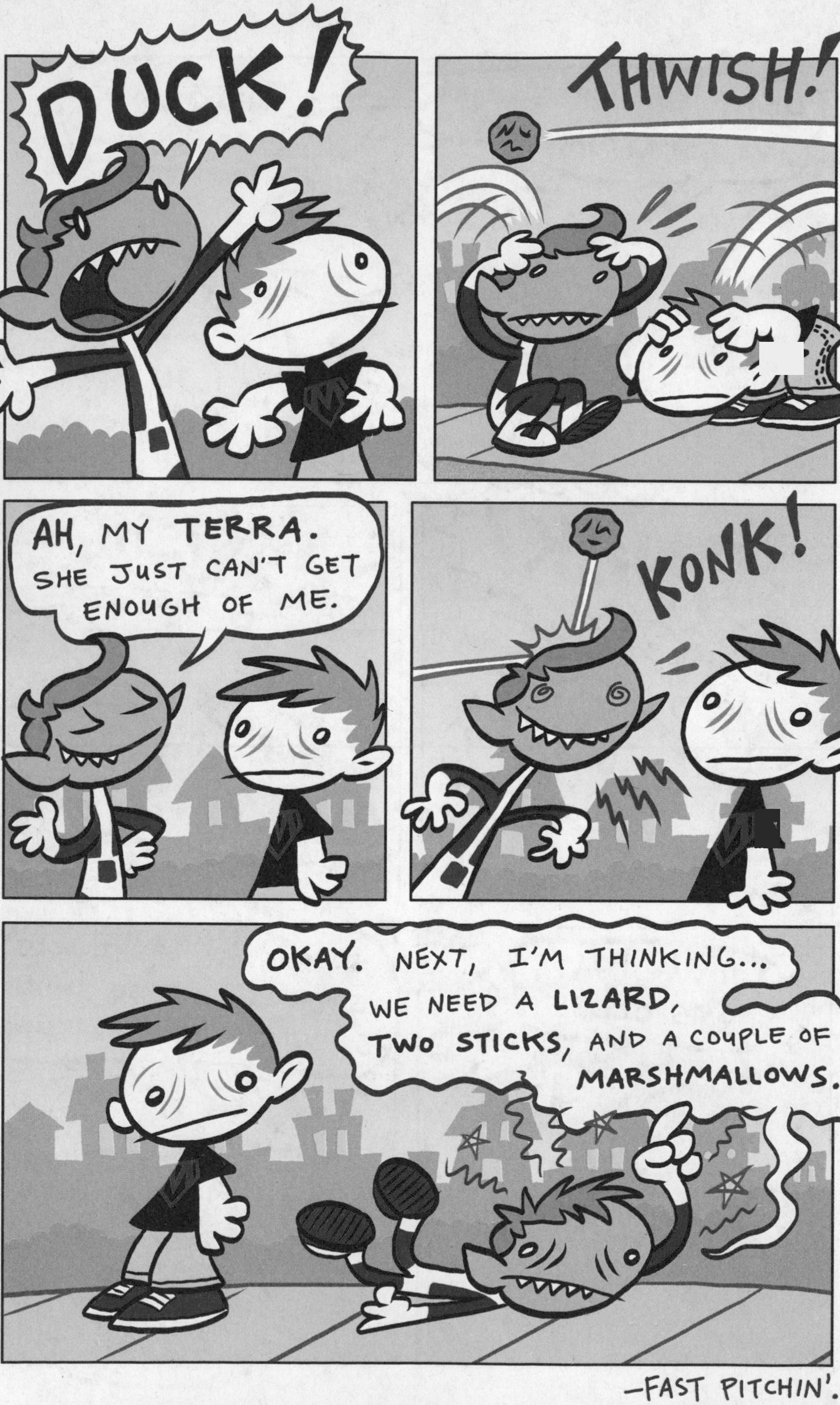
DUCK!
THWISH!
AH, MY TERRA. SHE JUST CAN'T GET ENOUGH OF ME.
KONK!
OKAY. NEXT, I'M THINKING... WE NEED A LIZARD, TWO STICKS, AND A COUPLE OF MARSHMALLOWS.

—FAST PITCHIN'.

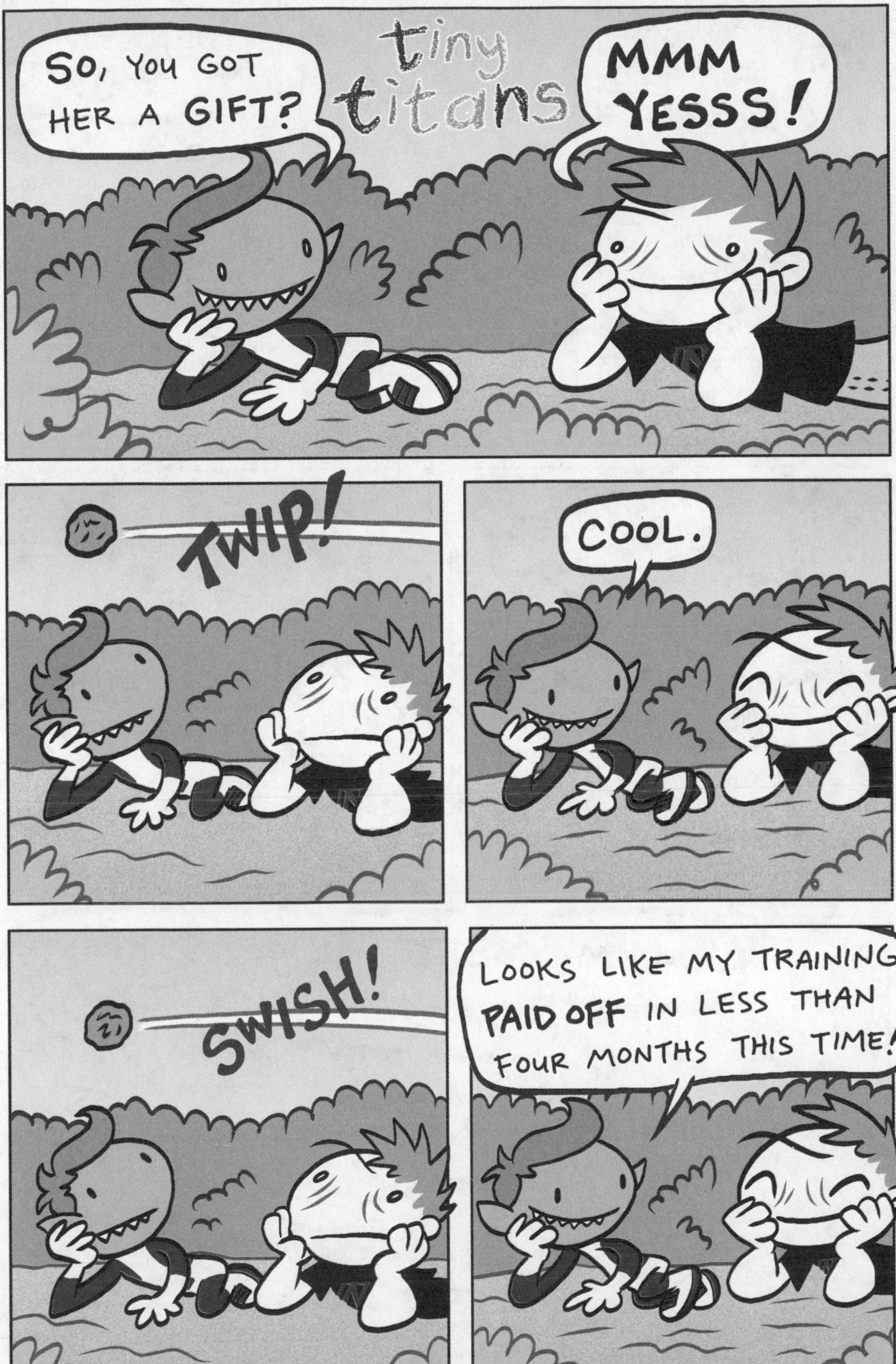
SO, YOU GOT HER A GIFT?
tiny titans
MMM YESSS!
TWIP!
COOL.
SWISH!
LOOKS LIKE MY TRAINING PAID OFF IN LESS THAN FOUR MONTHS THIS TIME!

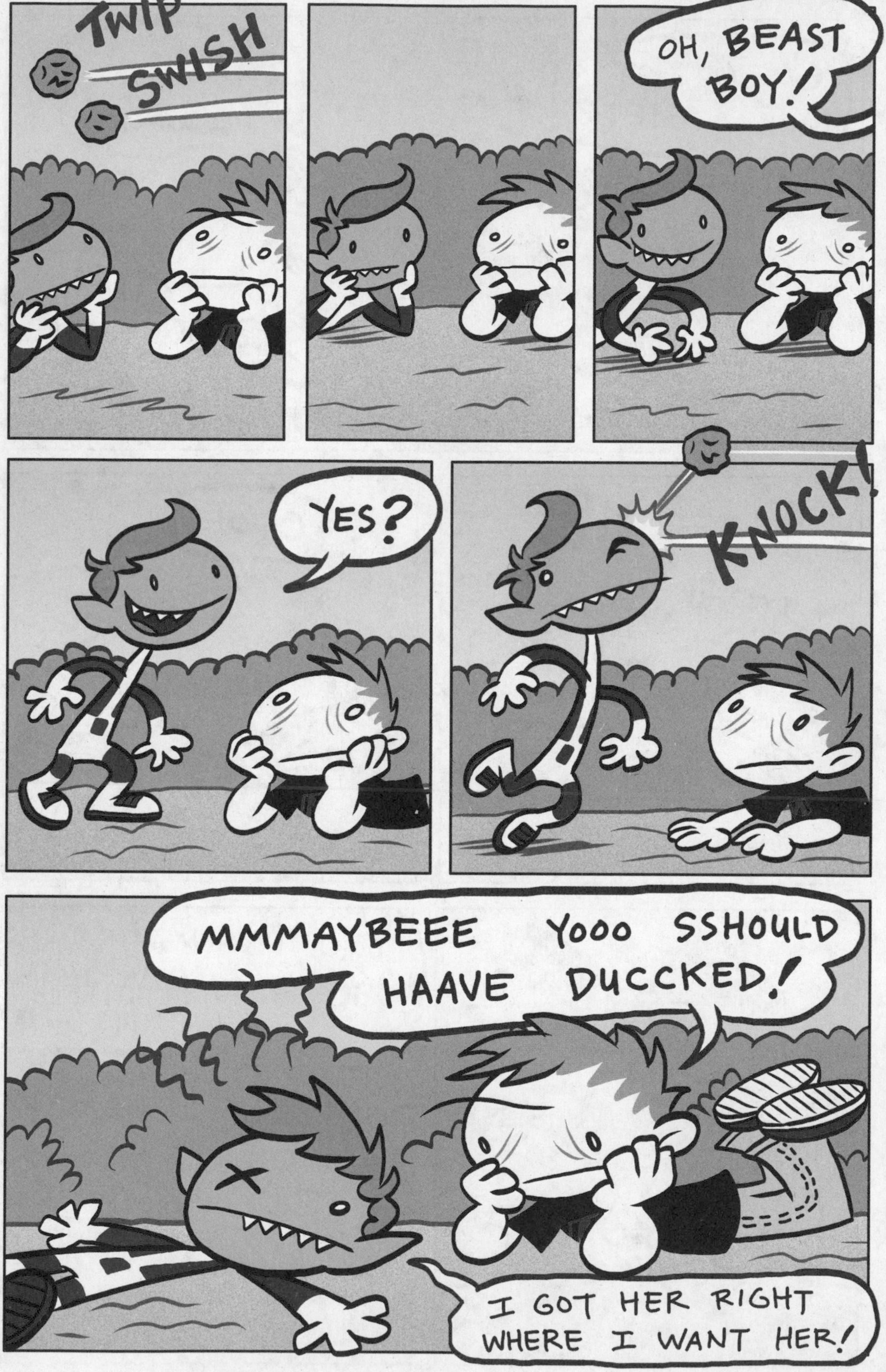
TWIP
SWISH
OH, BEAST BOY!
YES?
KNOCK!
MMMAYBEEE YOOO SSHOULD HAAVE DUCCKED!
I GOT HER RIGHT WHERE I WANT HER!
-ROCKIN' THE STONE.

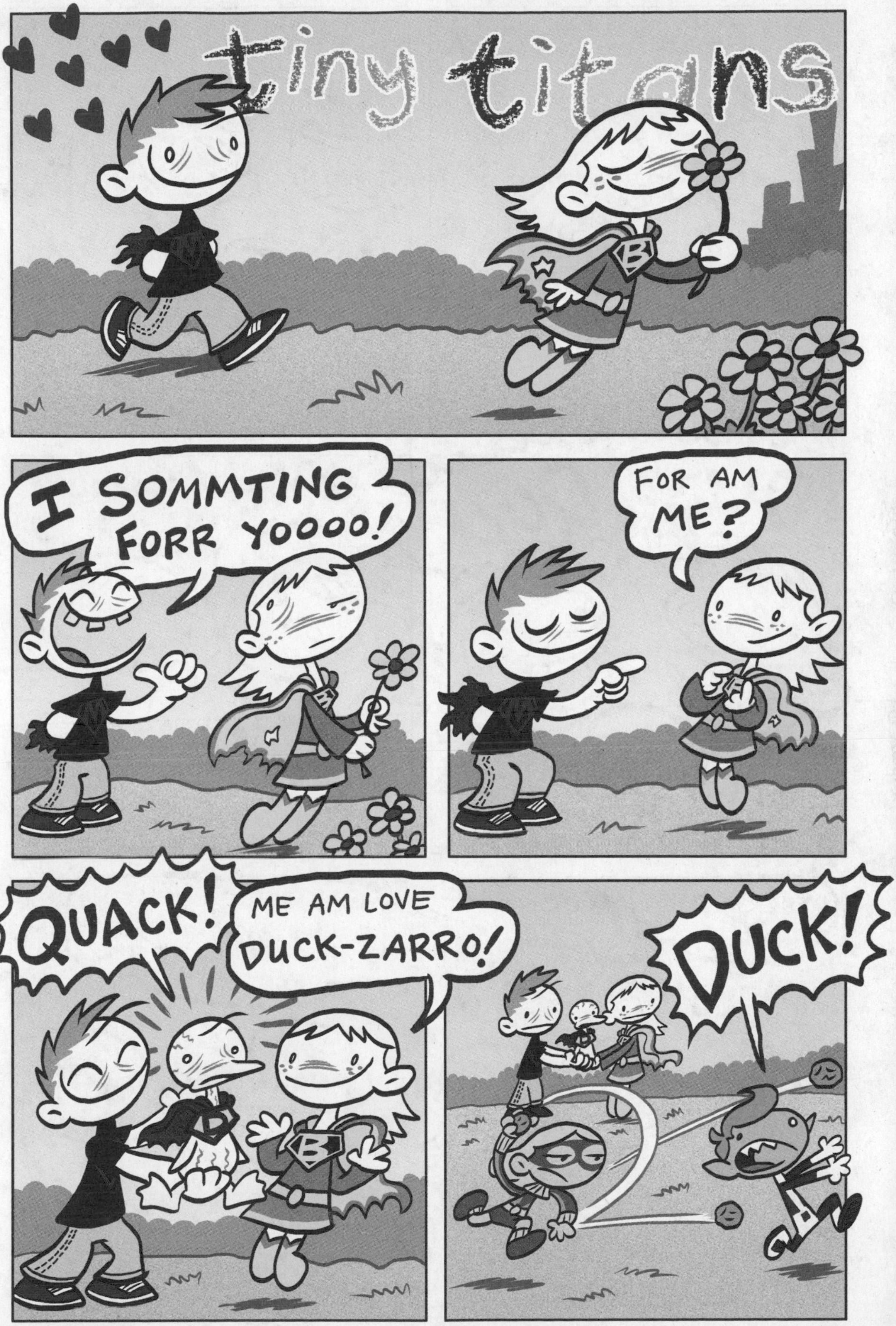
tiny titans
I SOMMTING FORR YOOOO!
FOR AM ME?
QUACK!
ME AM LOVE DUCK-ZARRO!
DUCK!

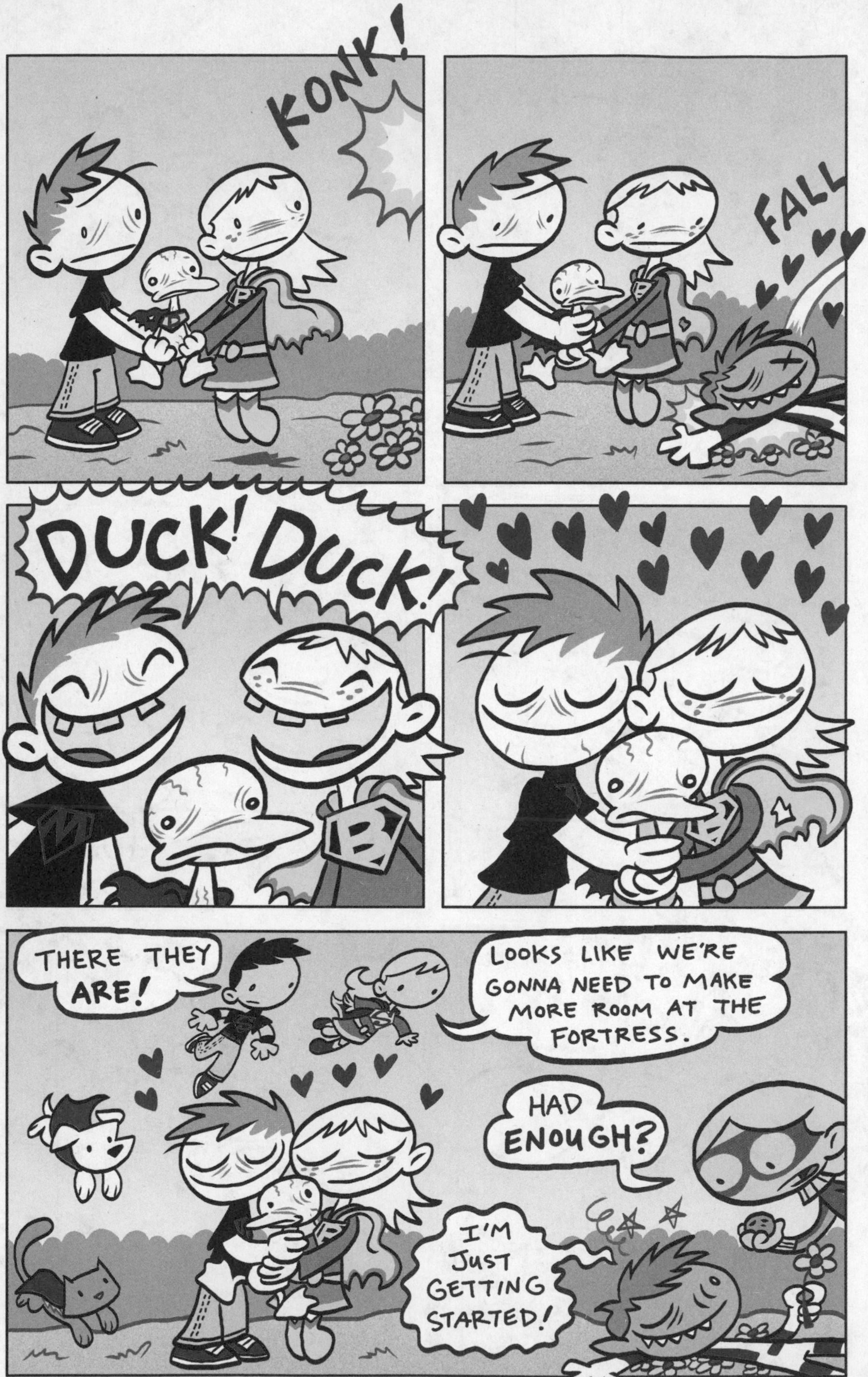
KONK!
FALL
DUCK! DUCK!
THERE THEY ARE!
LOOKS LIKE WE'RE GONNA NEED TO MAKE MORE ROOM AT THE FORTRESS.
HAD ENOUGH?
I'M JUST GETTING STARTED!
-ROCKIN' PLANETS!

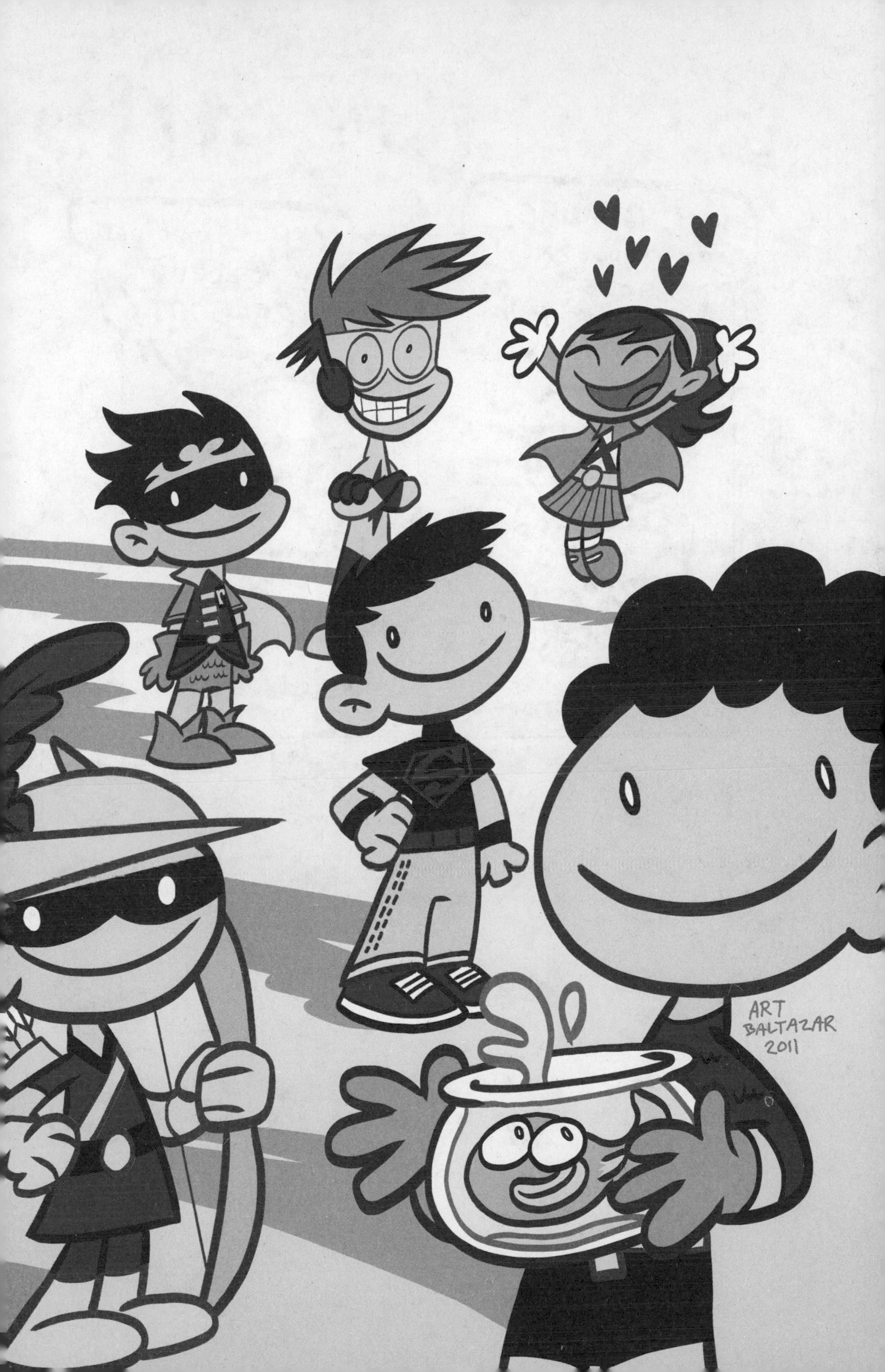
ART BALTAZAR 2011

tiny titans

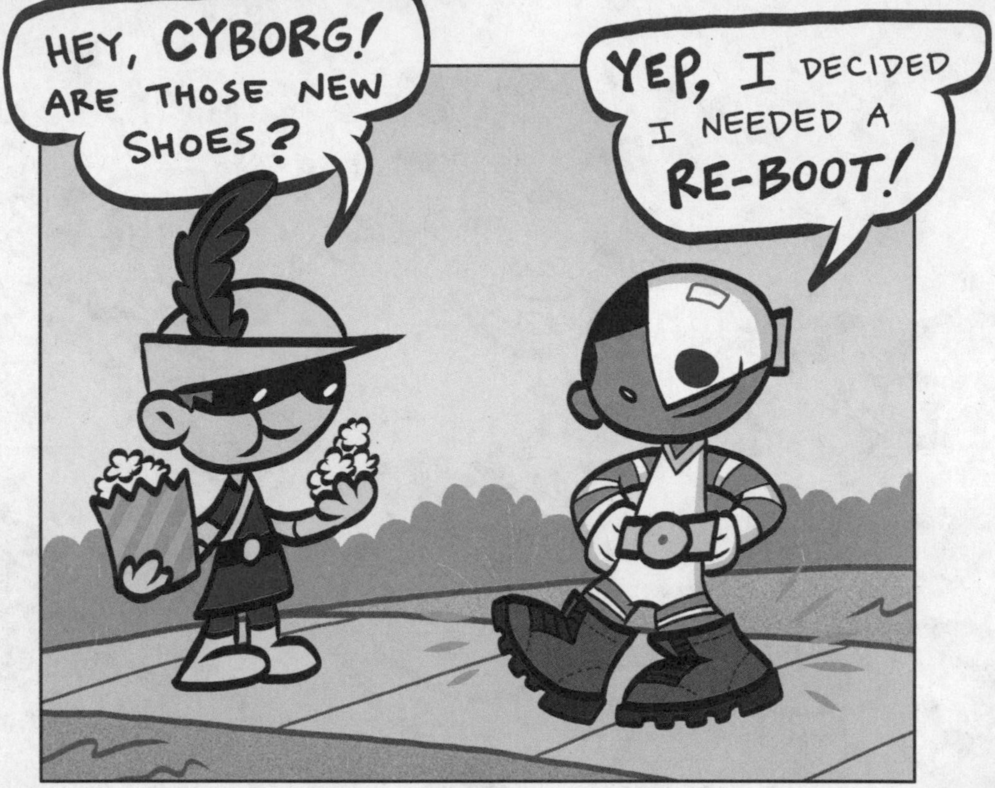
HEY, CYBORG! ARE THOSE NEW SHOES?
YEP, I DECIDED I NEEDED A RE-BOOT!

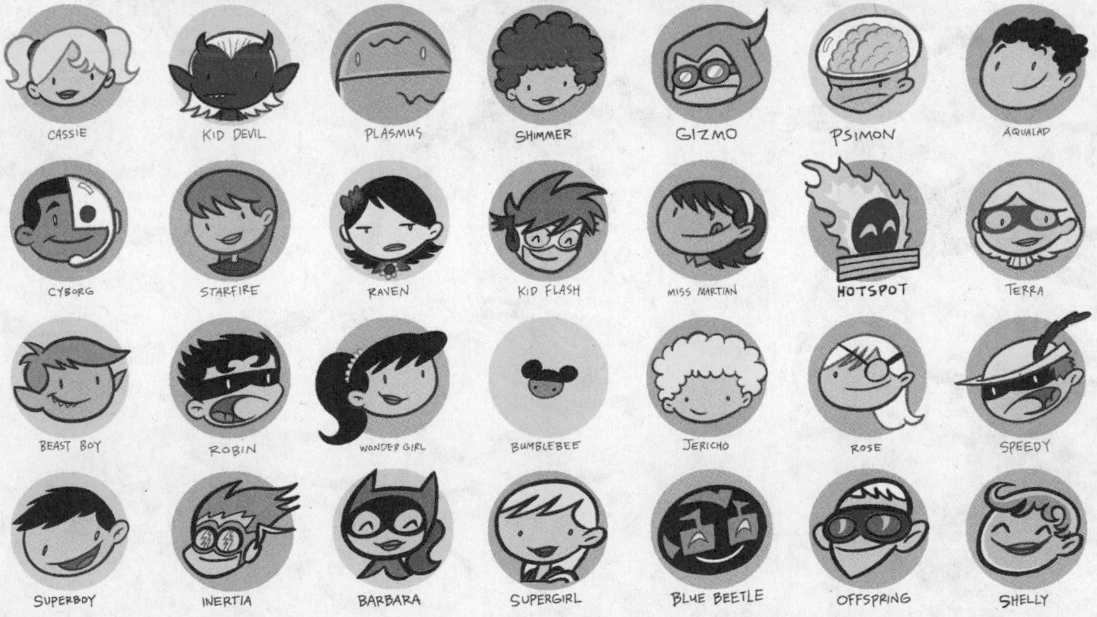
CASSIE
KID DEVIL
PLASMUS
SHIMMER
GIZMO
PSIMON
AQUALAD
CYBORG
STARFIRE
RAVEN
KID FLASH
MISS MARTIAN
HOTSPOT
TERRA
BEAST BOY
ROBIN
WONDER GIRL
BUMBLEBEE
JERICHO
ROSE
SPEEDY
SUPERBOY
INERTIA
BARBARA
SUPERGIRL
BLUE BEETLE
OFFSPRING
SHELLY

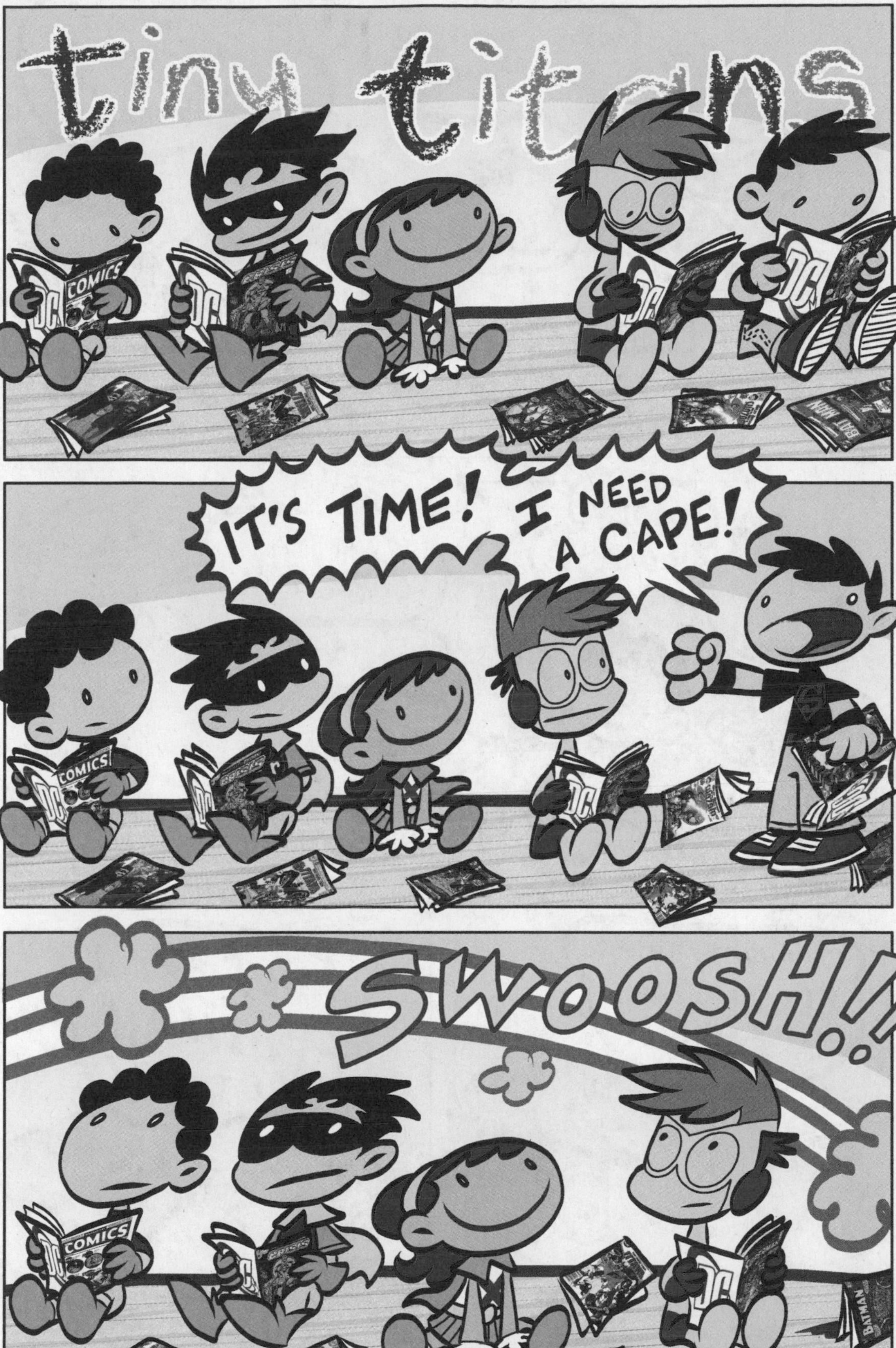
tiny titans
COMICS
IT'S TIME! I NEED A CAPE!
COMICS
SWOOSH!!
COMICS
BATMAN

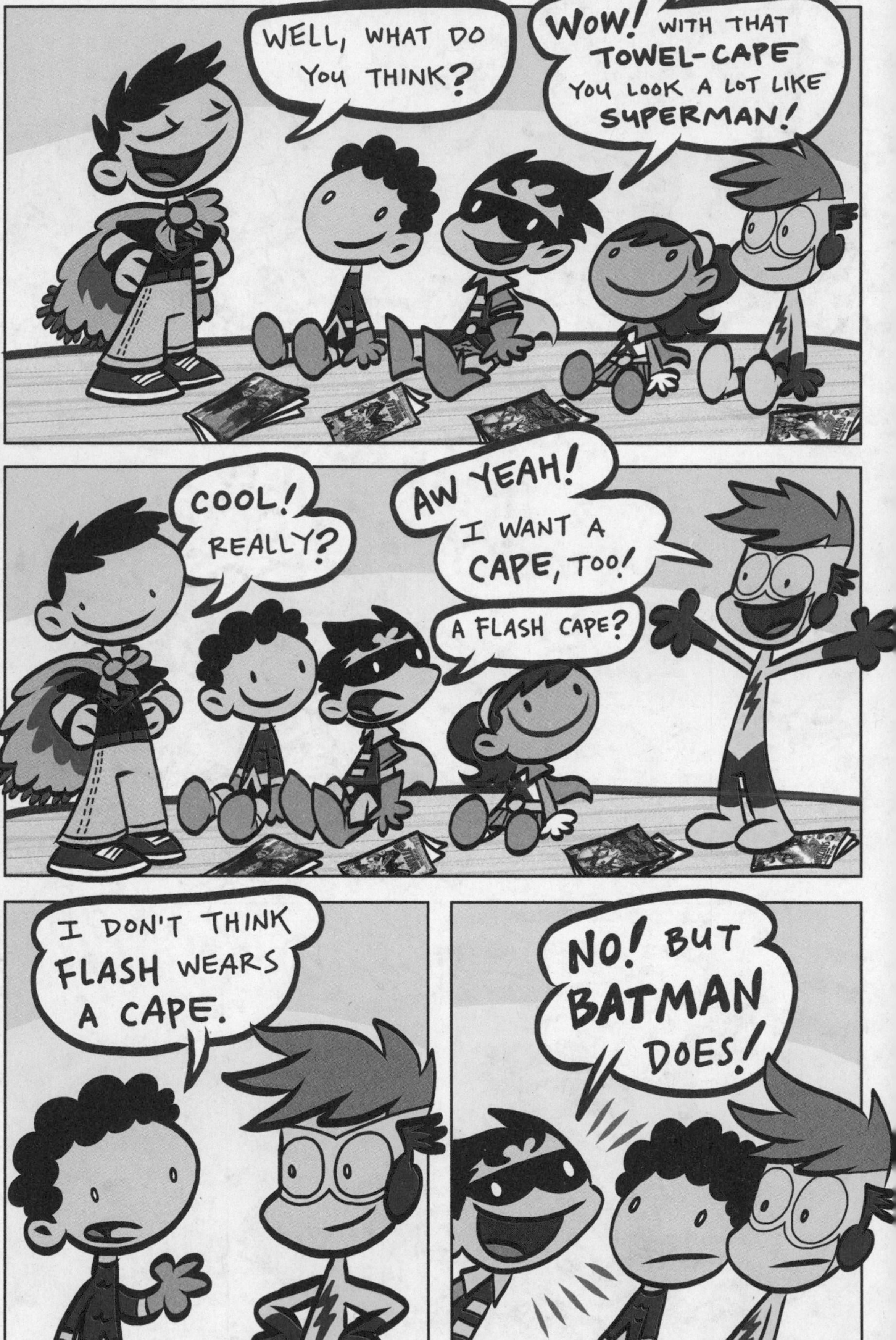
WELL, WHAT DO YOU THINK?
WOW! WITH THAT TOWEL-CAPE YOU LOOK A LOT LIKE SUPERMAN!
COOL! REALLY?
AW YEAH! I WANT A CAPE, TOO!
A FLASH CAPE?
I DON'T THINK FLASH WEARS A CAPE.
NO! BUT BATMAN DOES!

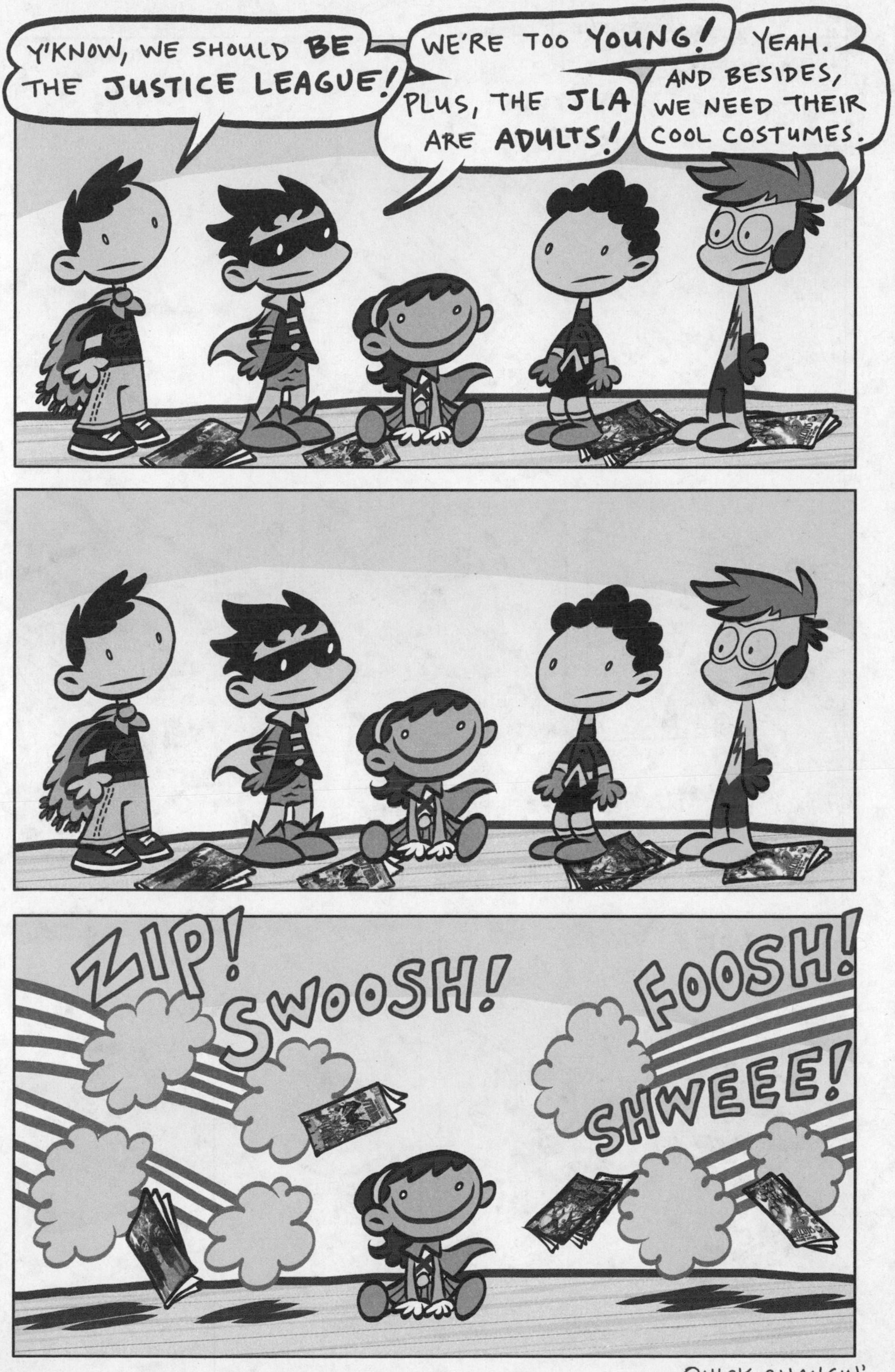
Y'KNOW, WE SHOULD BE THE JUSTICE LEAGUE!
WE'RE TOO YOUNG!
PLUS, THE JLA ARE ADULTS!
YEAH.
AND BESIDES, WE NEED THEIR COOL COSTUMES.
ZIP!
SWOOSH!
FOOSH!
SHWEEE!

—QUICK CHANGIN'.

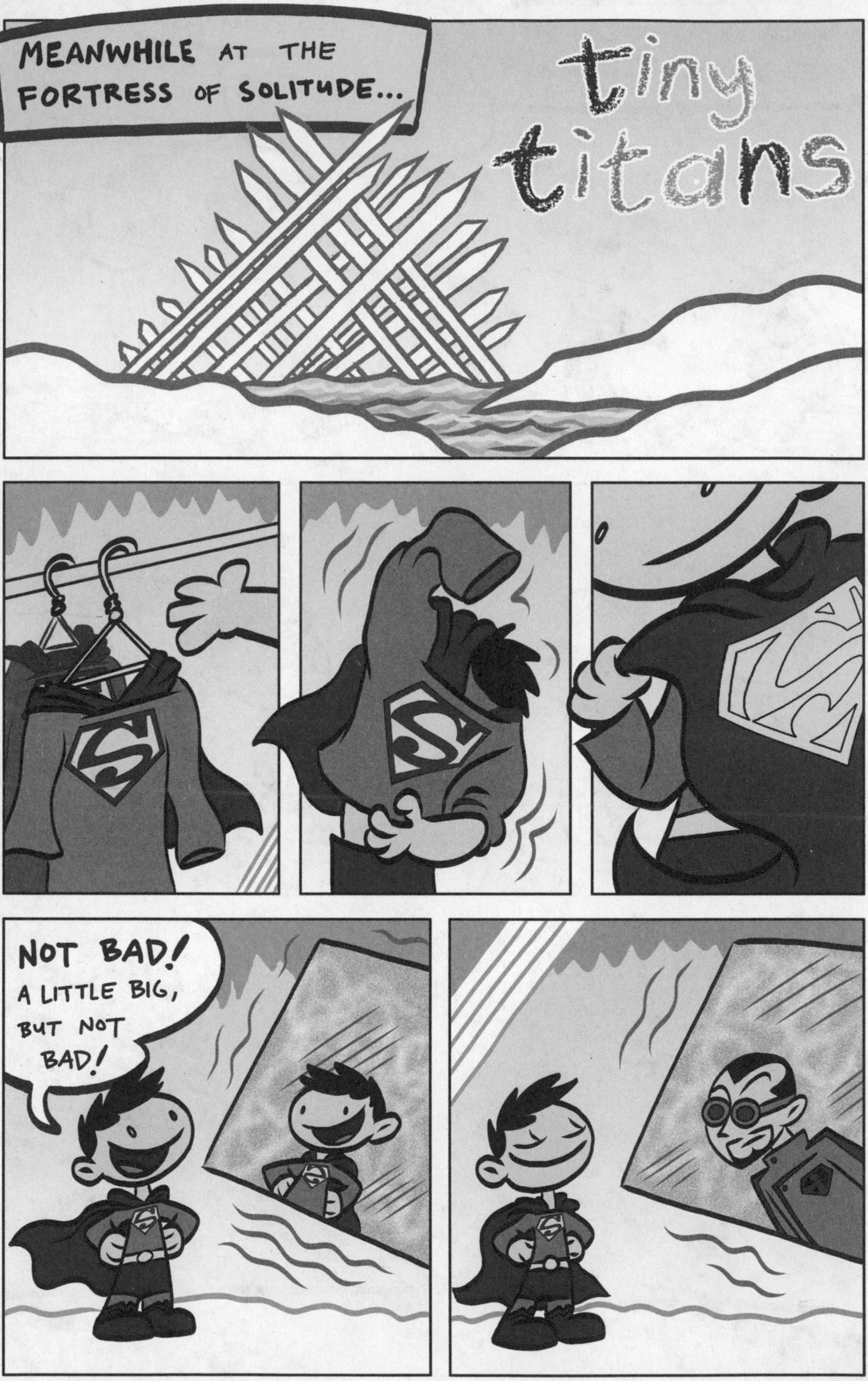
MEANWHILE AT THE FORTRESS OF SOLITUDE...
tiny titans
NOT BAD! A LITTLE BIG, BUT NOT BAD!

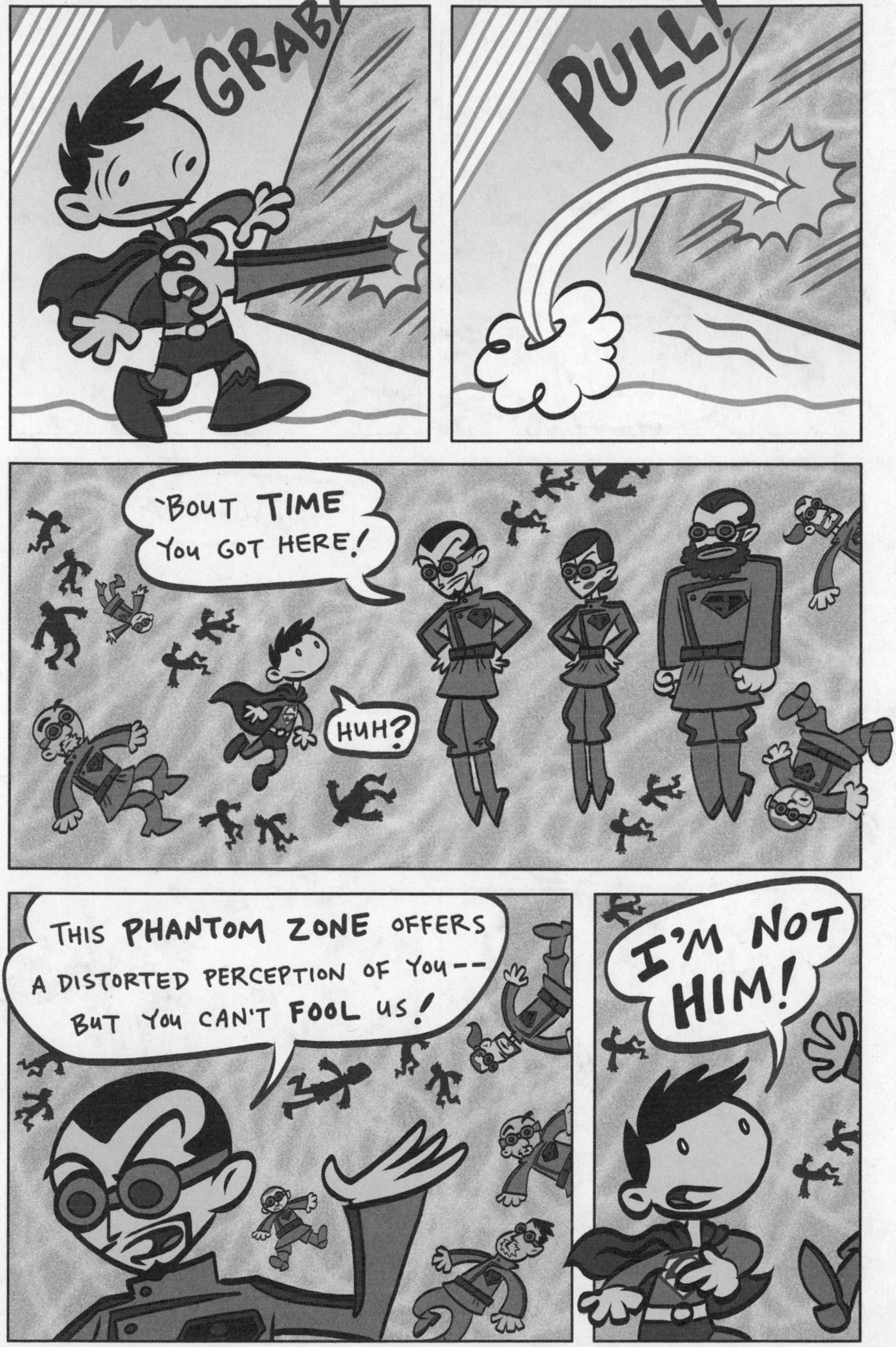
GRAB!
PULL!
`BOUT TIME YOU GOT HERE!
HUH?
THIS PHANTOM ZONE OFFERS A DISTORTED PERCEPTION OF YOU-- BUT YOU CAN'T FOOL US!
I'M NOT HIM!

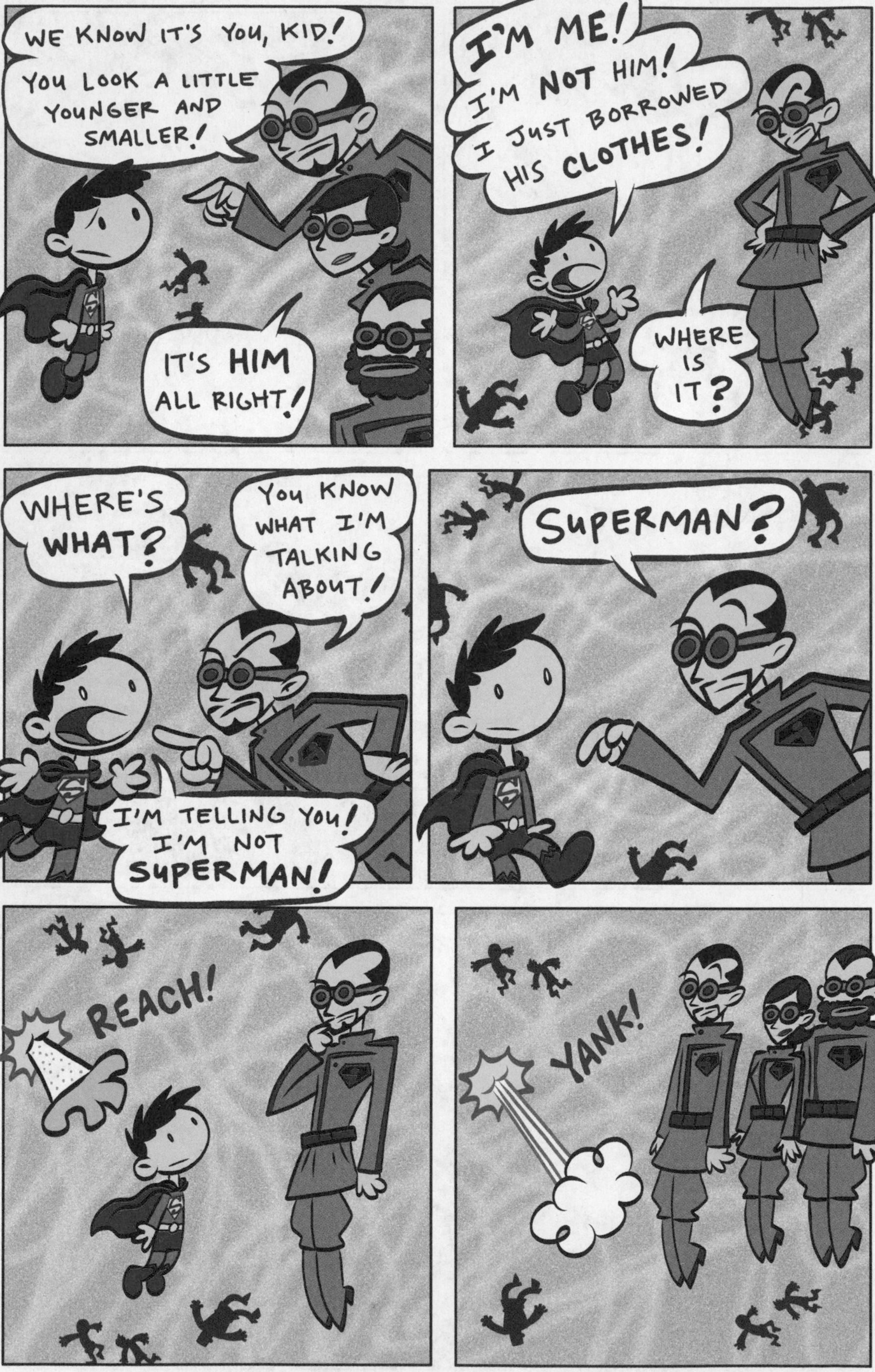
WE KNOW IT'S YOU, KID!
YOU LOOK A LITTLE YOUNGER AND SMALLER!
IT'S HIM ALL RIGHT!
I'M ME!
I'M NOT HIM! I JUST BORROWED HIS CLOTHES!
WHERE IS IT?
WHERE'S WHAT?
YOU KNOW WHAT I'M TALKING ABOUT!
I'M TELLING YOU! I'M NOT SUPERMAN!
SUPERMAN?
REACH!
YANK!

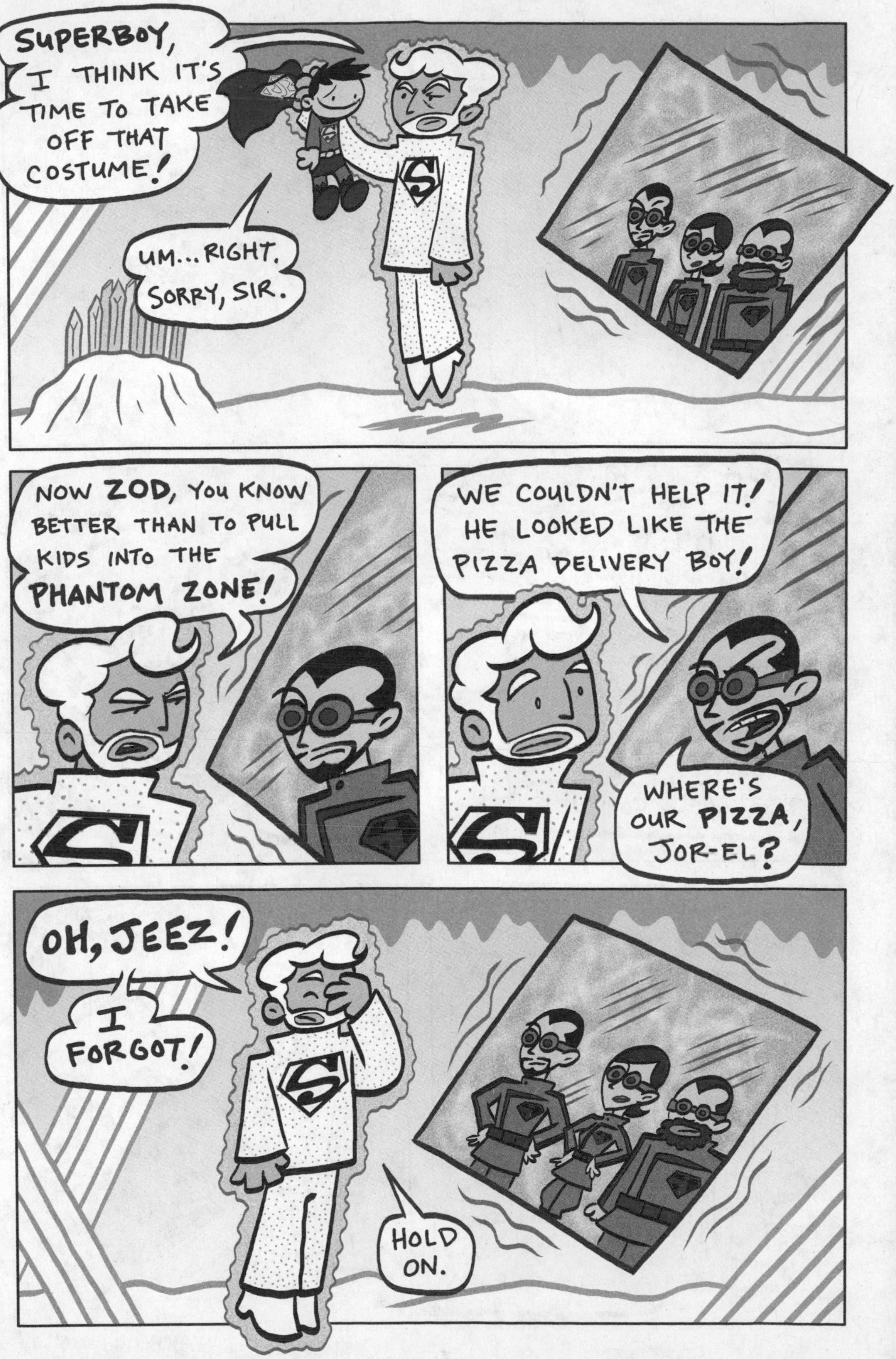
SUPERBOY, I THINK IT'S TIME TO TAKE OFF THAT COSTUME!
UM... RIGHT. SORRY, SIR.
NOW ZOD, YOU KNOW BETTER THAN TO PULL KIDS INTO THE PHANTOM ZONE!
WE COULDN'T HELP IT! HE LOOKED LIKE THE PIZZA DELIVERY BOY!
WHERE'S OUR PIZZA, JOR-EL?
OH, JEEZ!
I FORGOT!
HOLD ON.

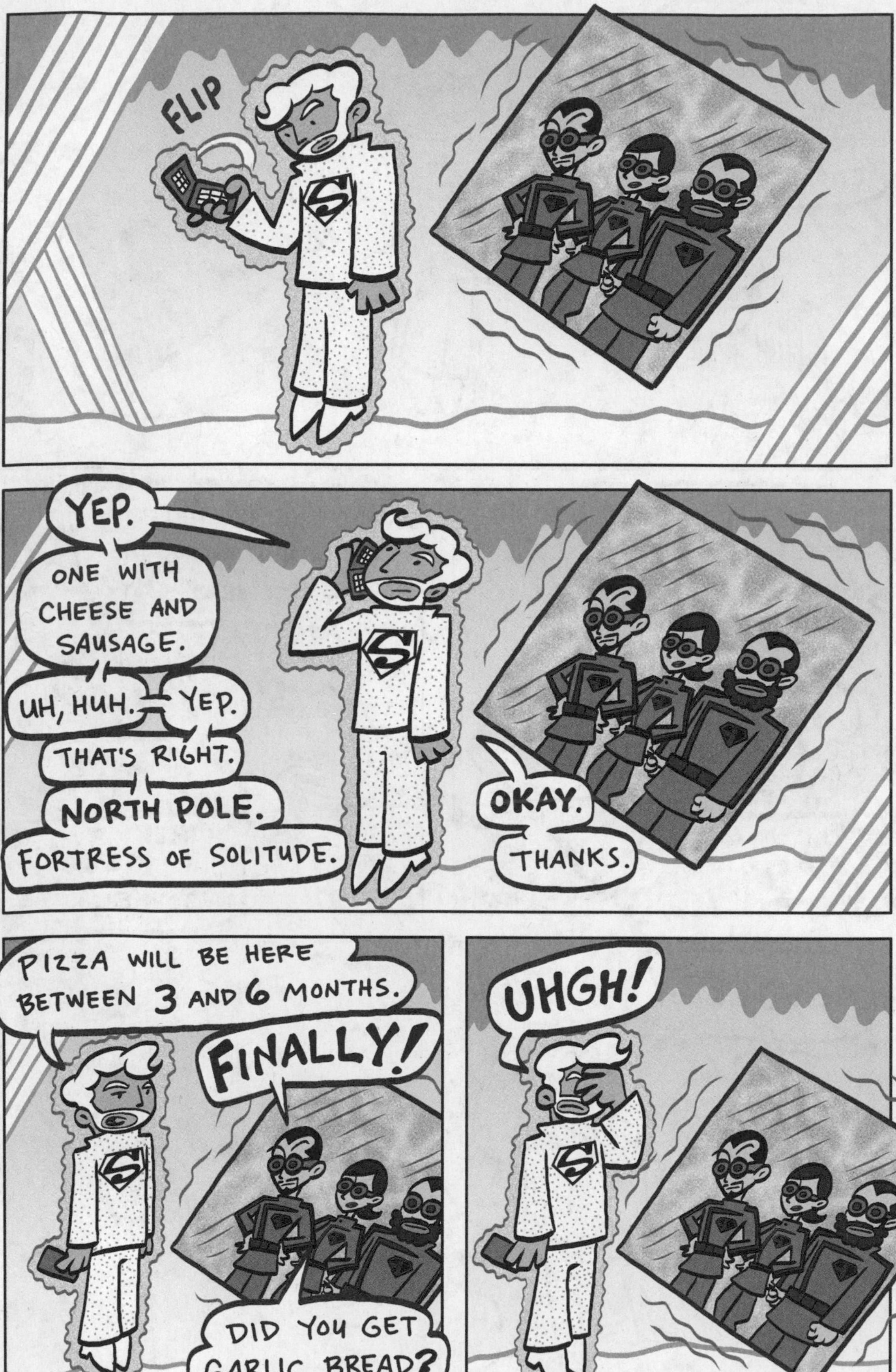
FLIP
YEP.
ONE WITH CHEESE AND SAUSAGE.
UH, HUH.
YEP.
THAT'S RIGHT.
NORTH POLE.
FORTRESS OF SOLITUDE.
OKAY.
THANKS.
PIZZA WILL BE HERE BETWEEN 3 AND 6 MONTHS.
FINALLY!
DID YOU GET GARLIC BREAD?
UHGH!

-TAKE OUT ONLY!

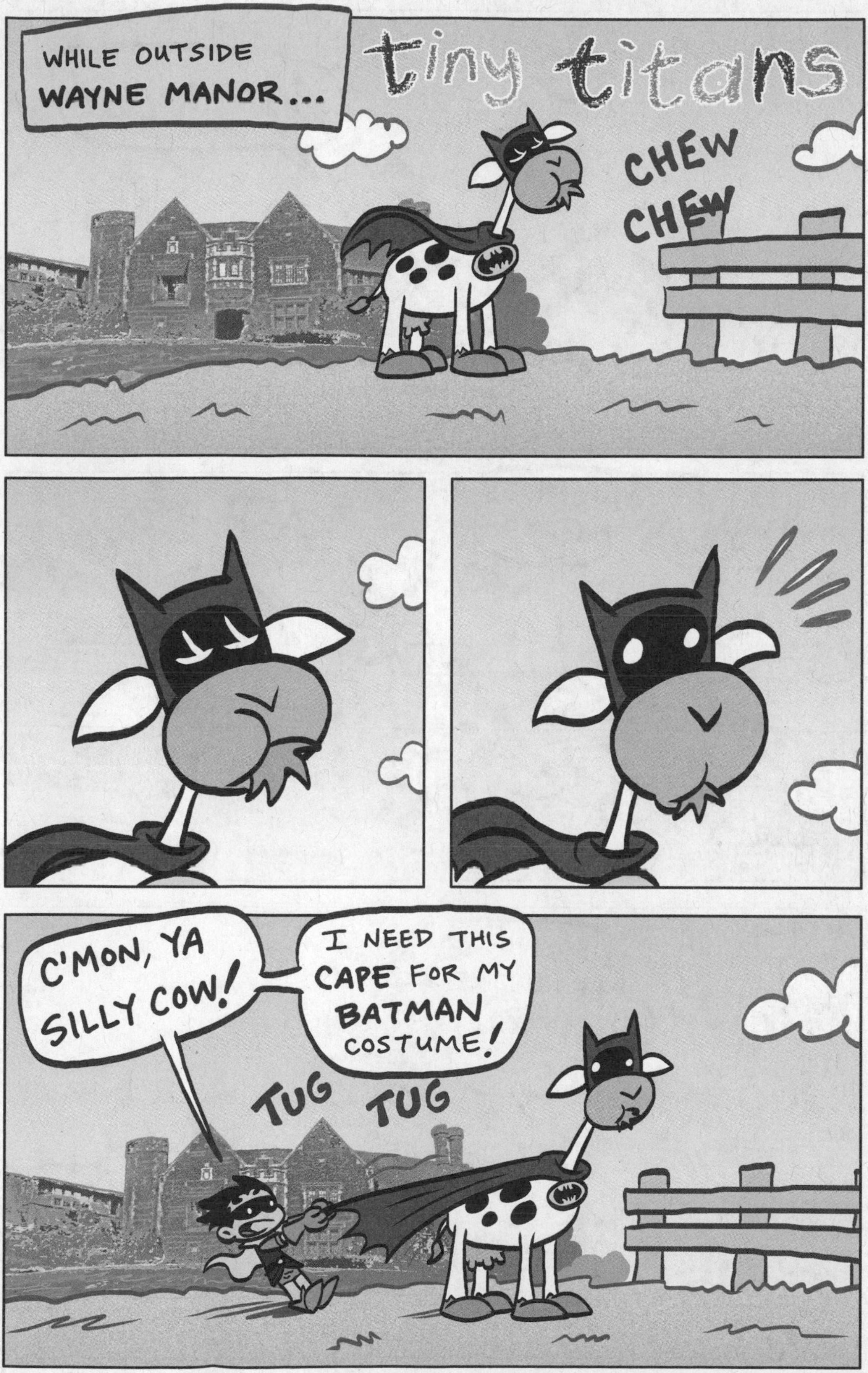
WHILE OUTSIDE WAYNE MANOR...
tiny titans
CHEW
CHEW
C'MON, YA SILLY COW!
I NEED THIS CAPE FOR MY BATMAN COSTUME!
TUG
TUG

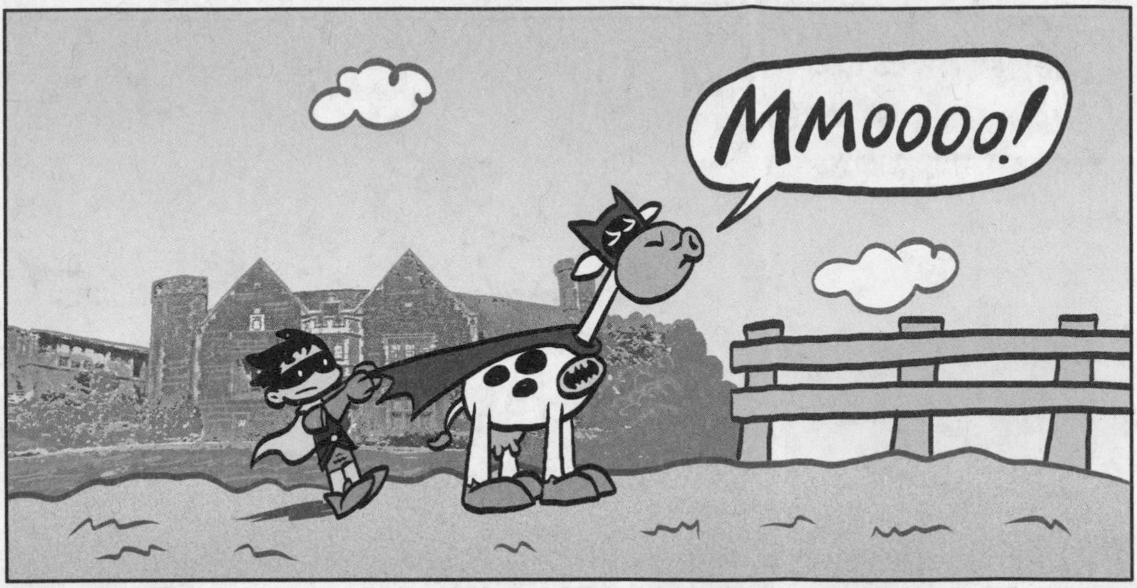
MMOOOO!

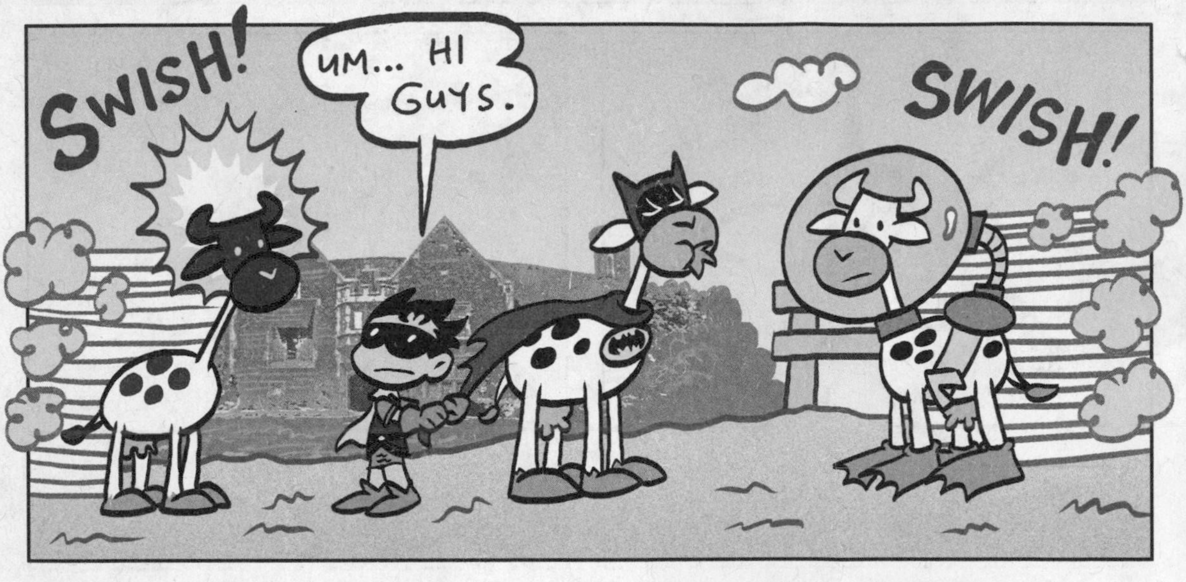
SWISH!
UM... HI GUYS.
SWISH!

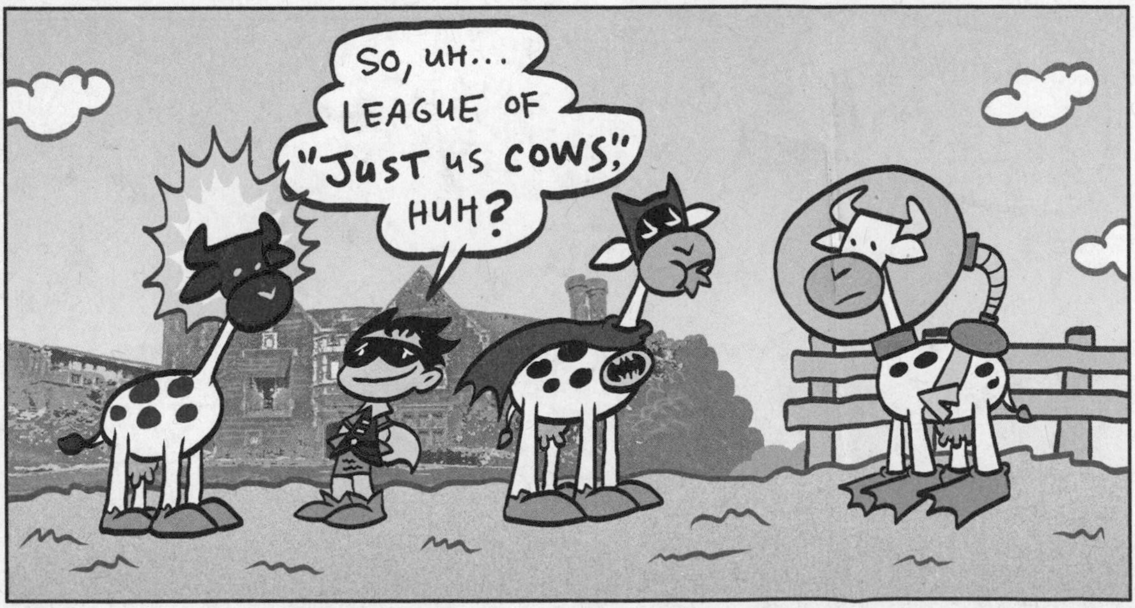
SO, UH... LEAGUE OF "JUST US COWS," HUH?

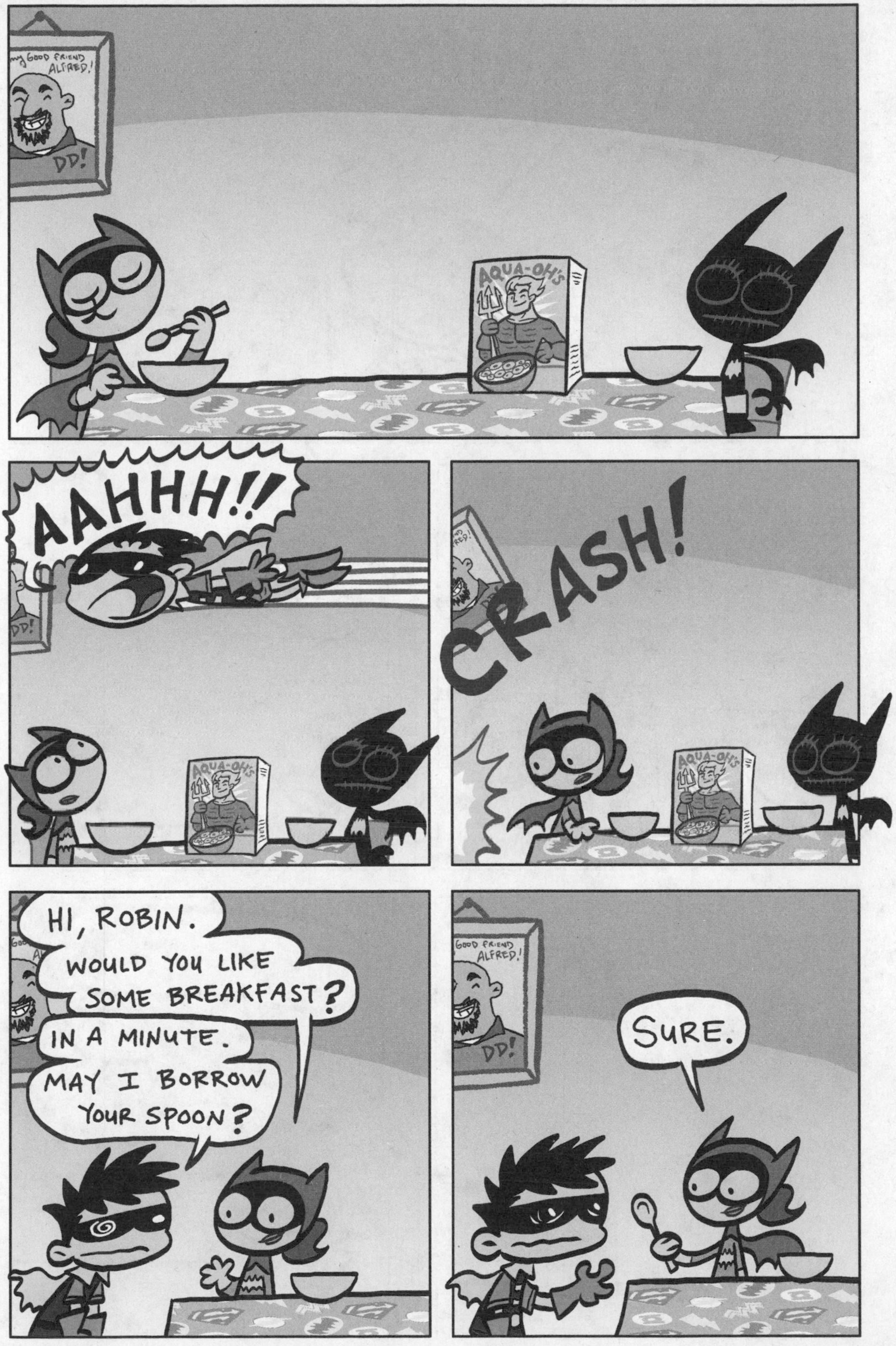

GOOD FRIEND ALFRED!
DD!
AQUA-OH'S
AAHHH!!
CRASH!
HI, ROBIN.
WOULD YOU LIKE SOME BREAKFAST?
IN A MINUTE.
MAY I BORROW YOUR SPOON?
GOOD FRIEND ALFRED!
DD!
SURE.

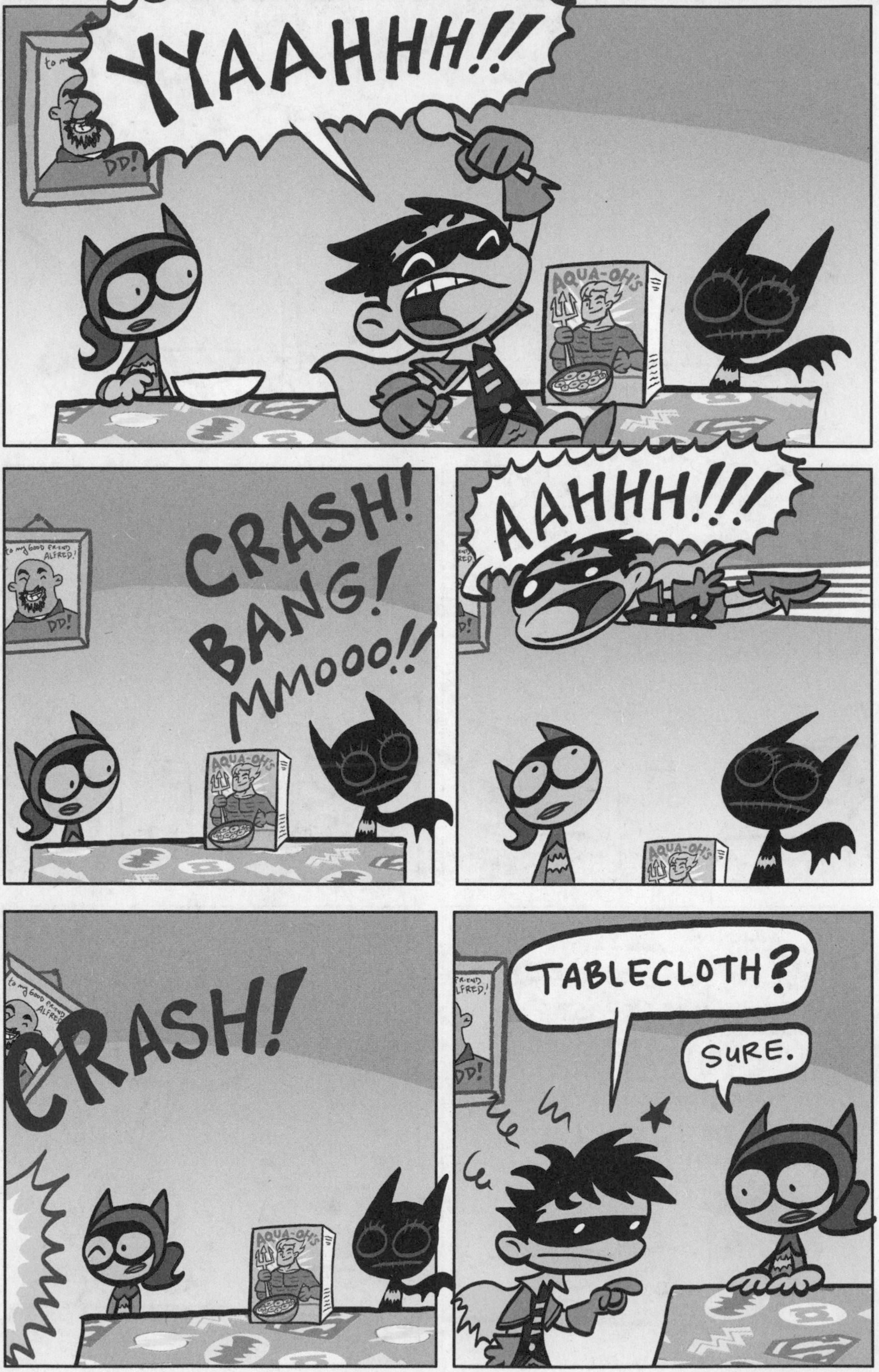
YYAAHHH!!!
AQUA-OH'S
CRASH!
BANG!
MMOOO!!
to my GOOD FRIEND ALFRED!
DD!
AQUA-OH'S
AAHHH!!!
CRASH!
TABLECLOTH?
SURE.

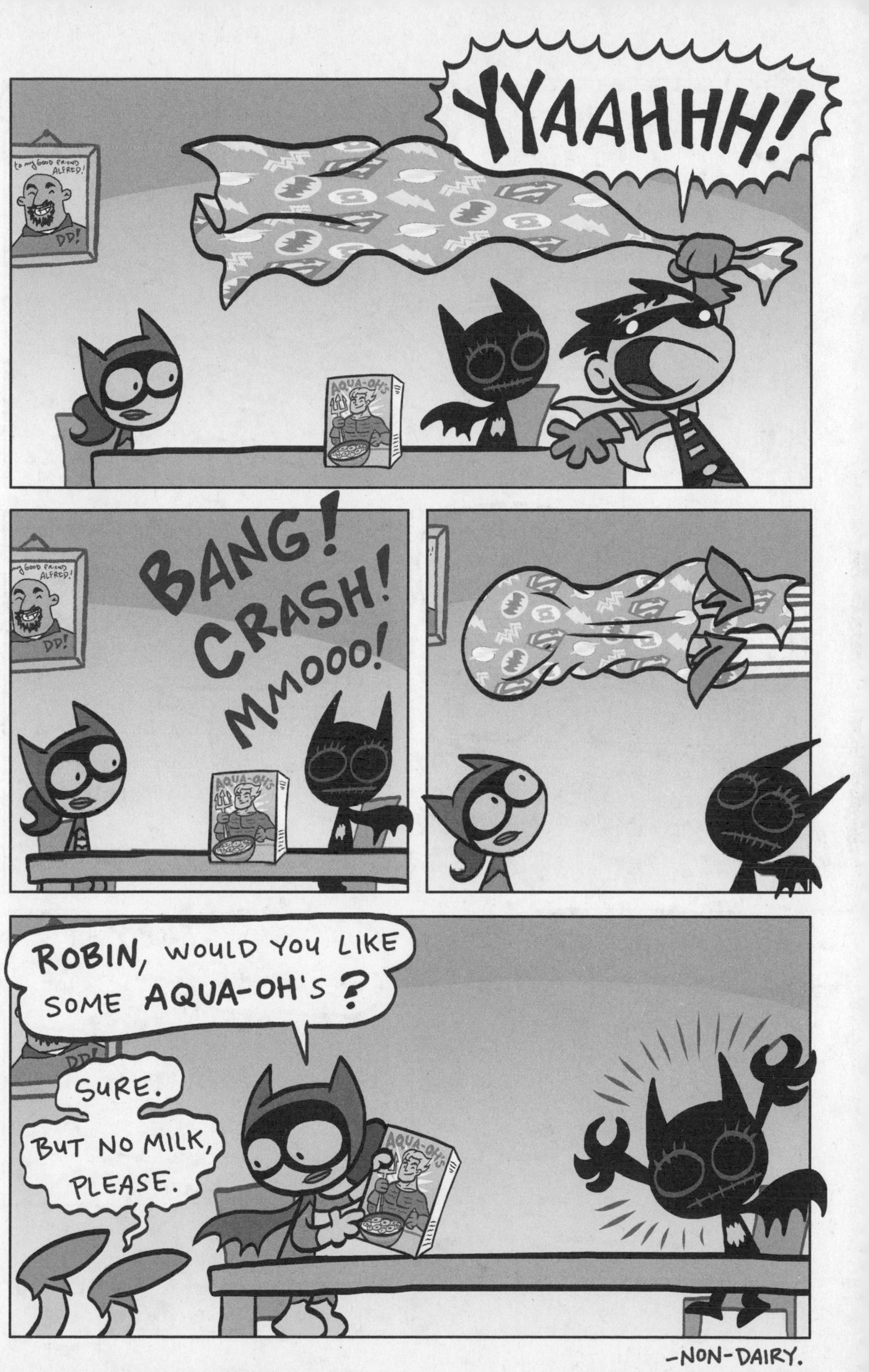
YYAAHHH!
to my GOOD FRIEND ALFRED!
DD!
AQUA-OH'S
BANG! CRASH! MMOOO!
ROBIN, WOULD YOU LIKE SOME AQUA-OH'S?
SURE.
BUT NO MILK, PLEASE.

-NON-DAIRY.

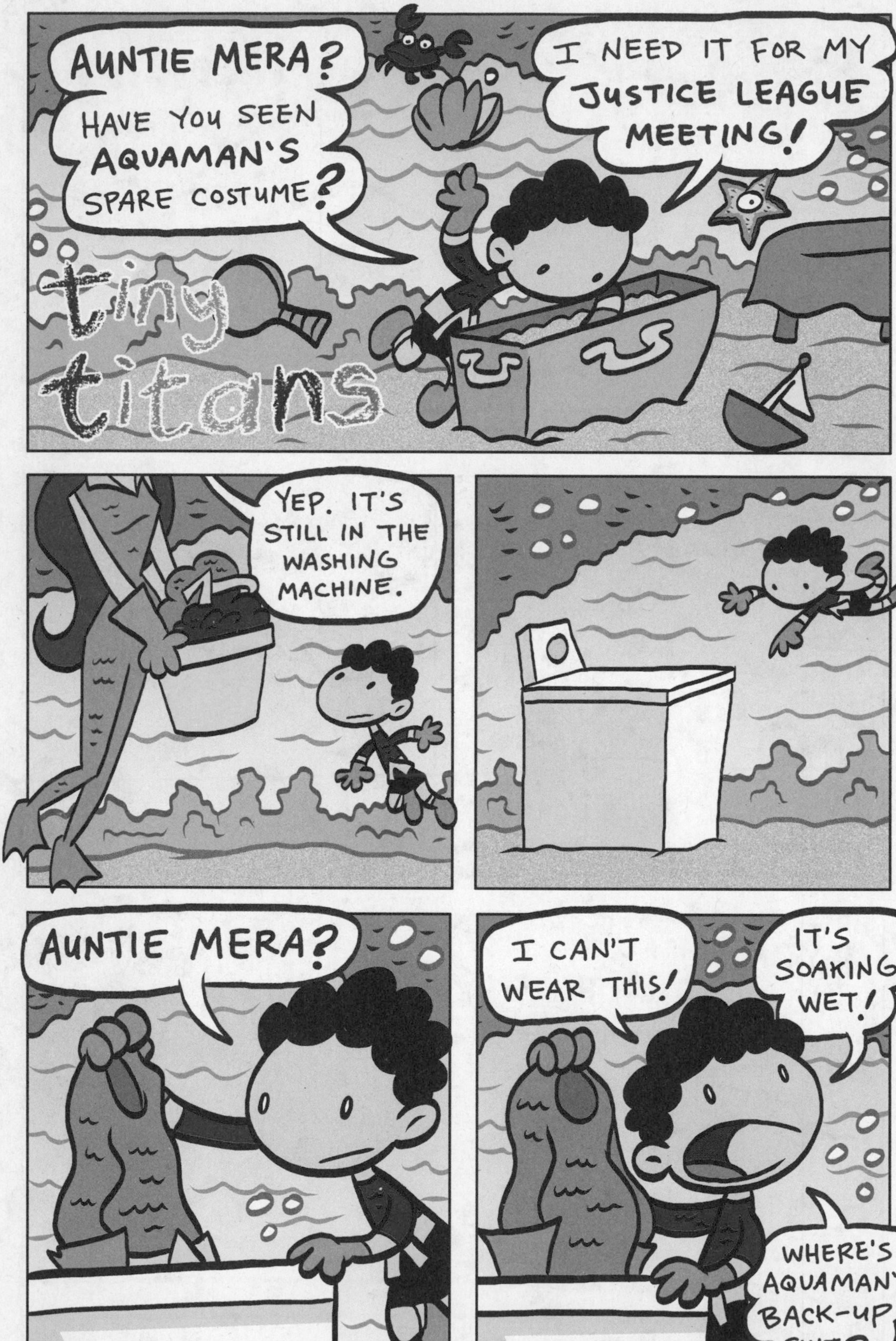
tiny titans
AUNTIE MERA?
HAVE YOU SEEN AQUAMAN'S SPARE COSTUME?
I NEED IT FOR MY JUSTICE LEAGUE MEETING!
YEP. IT'S STILL IN THE WASHING MACHINE.
AUNTIE MERA?
I CAN'T WEAR THIS!
IT'S SOAKING WET!
WHERE'S AQUAMAN'S BACK-UP SUIT?

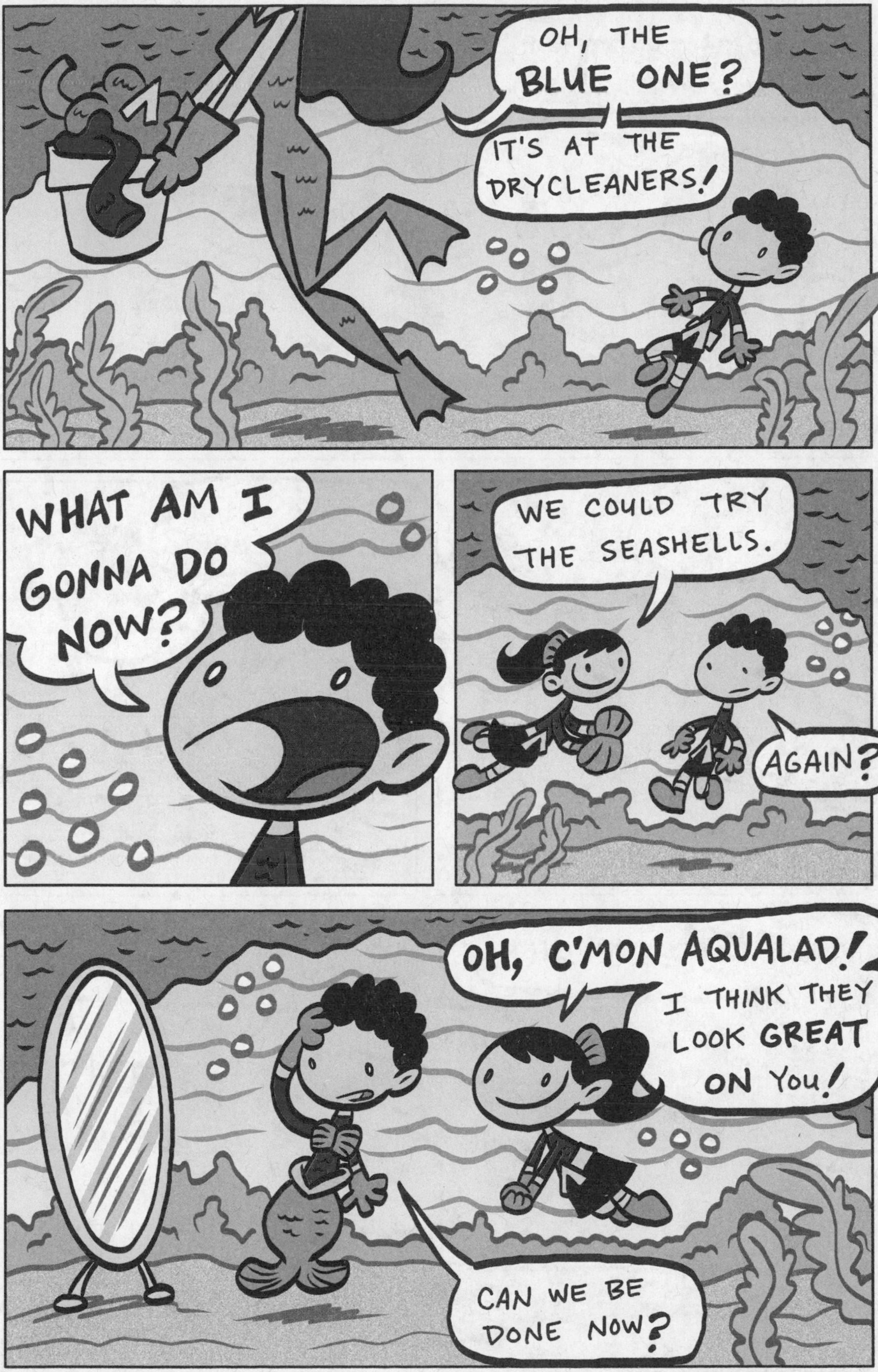
OH, THE BLUE ONE?
IT'S AT THE DRYCLEANERS!
WHAT AM I GONNA DO NOW?
WE COULD TRY THE SEASHELLS.
AGAIN?
OH, C'MON AQUALAD! I THINK THEY LOOK GREAT ON YOU!
CAN WE BE DONE NOW?

-UNDER the SEA!

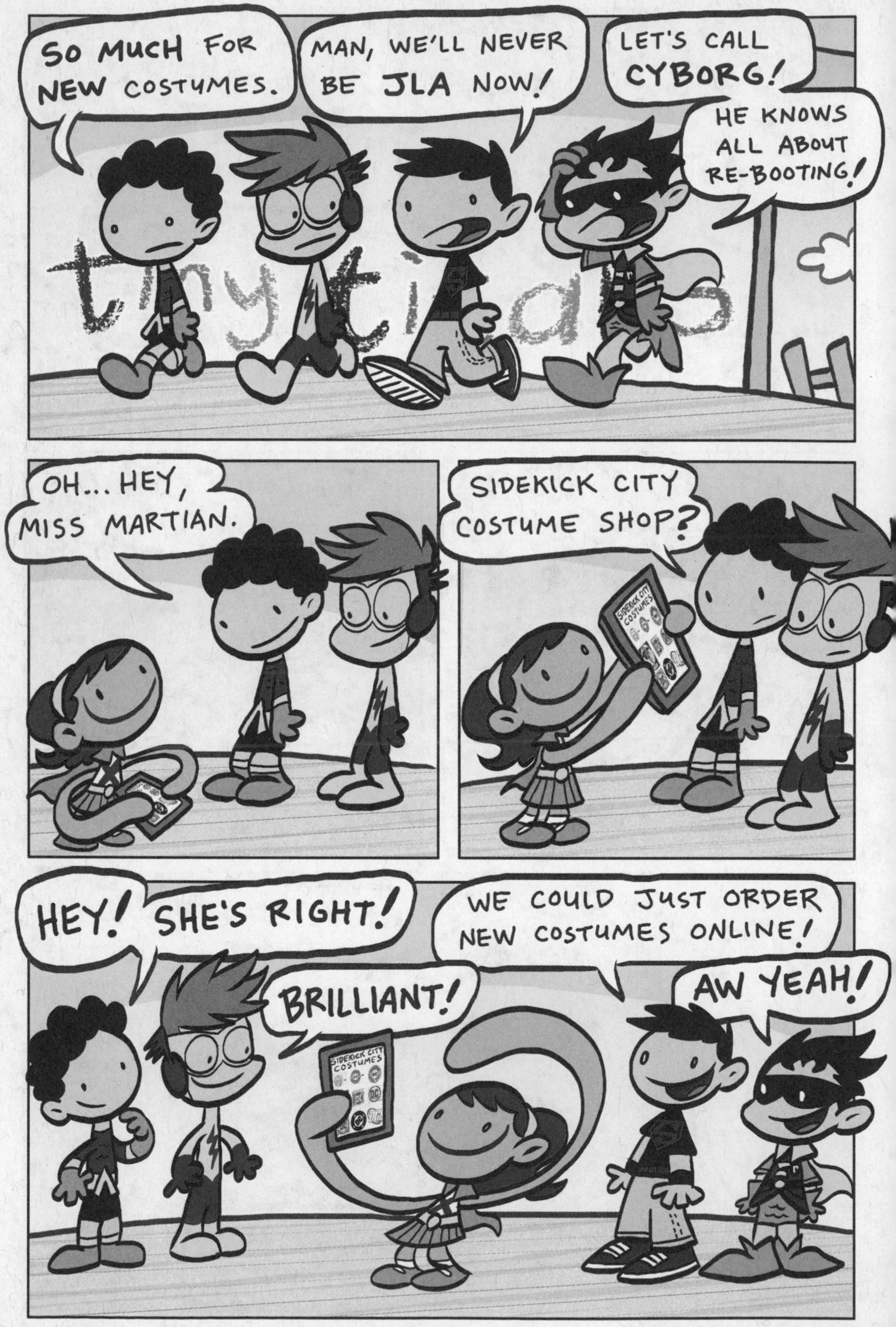
SO MUCH FOR NEW COSTUMES.
MAN, WE'LL NEVER BE JLA NOW!
LET'S CALL CYBORG!
HE KNOWS ALL ABOUT RE-BOOTING!
OH... HEY, MISS MARTIAN.
SIDEKICK CITY COSTUME SHOP?
SIDEKICK CITY COSTUMES
HEY! SHE'S RIGHT!
WE COULD JUST ORDER NEW COSTUMES ONLINE!
BRILLIANT!
SIDEKICK CITY COSTUMES
AW YEAH!

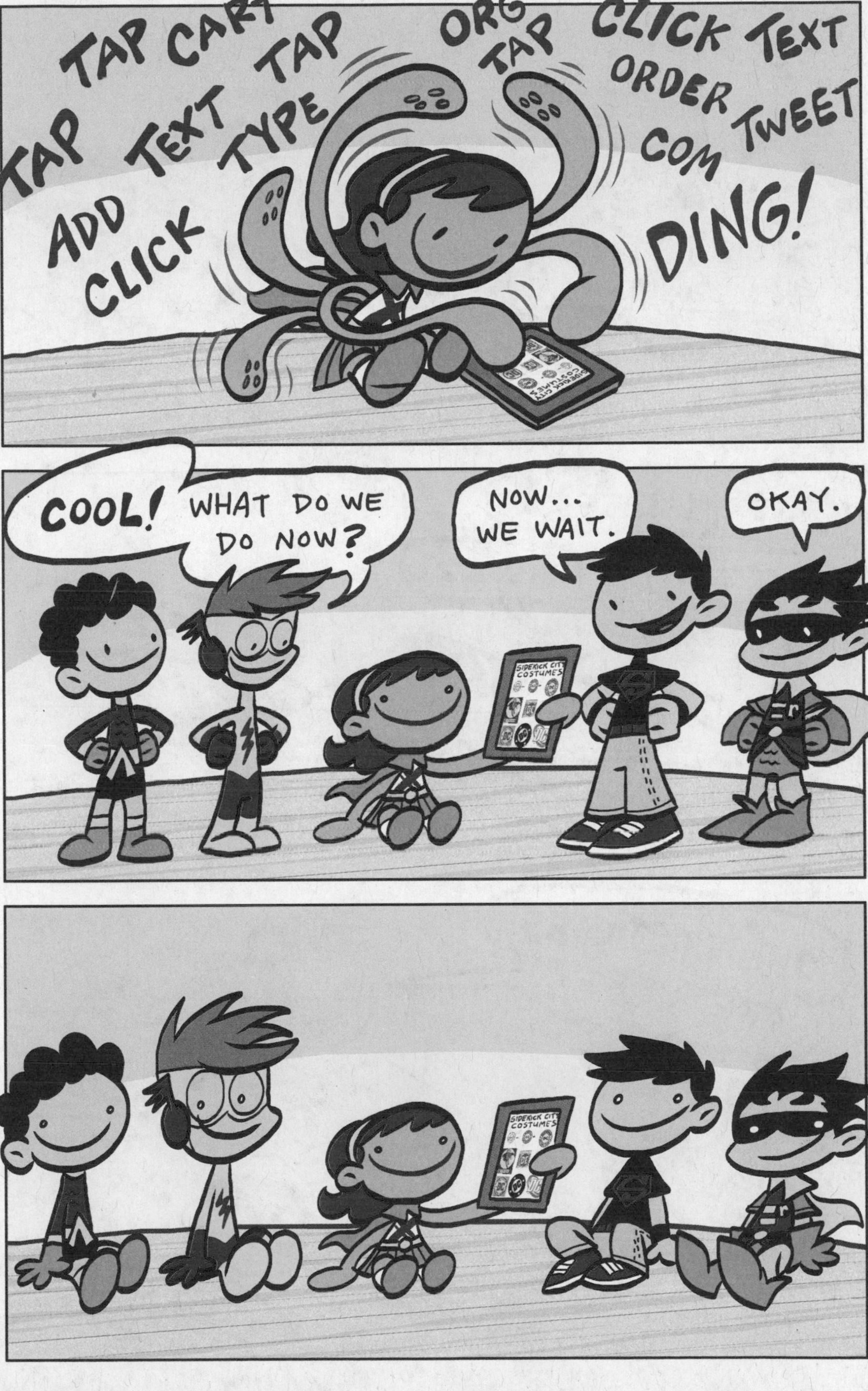
TAP TAP CART
ADD TEXT TAP
CLICK TYPE
ORG TAP
CLICK TEXT
ORDER TWEET
COM
DING!
SIDEKICK CITY COSTUMES
COOL!
WHAT DO WE DO NOW?
NOW... WE WAIT.
OKAY.
SIDEKICK CITY COSTUMES
SIDEKICK CITY COSTUMES

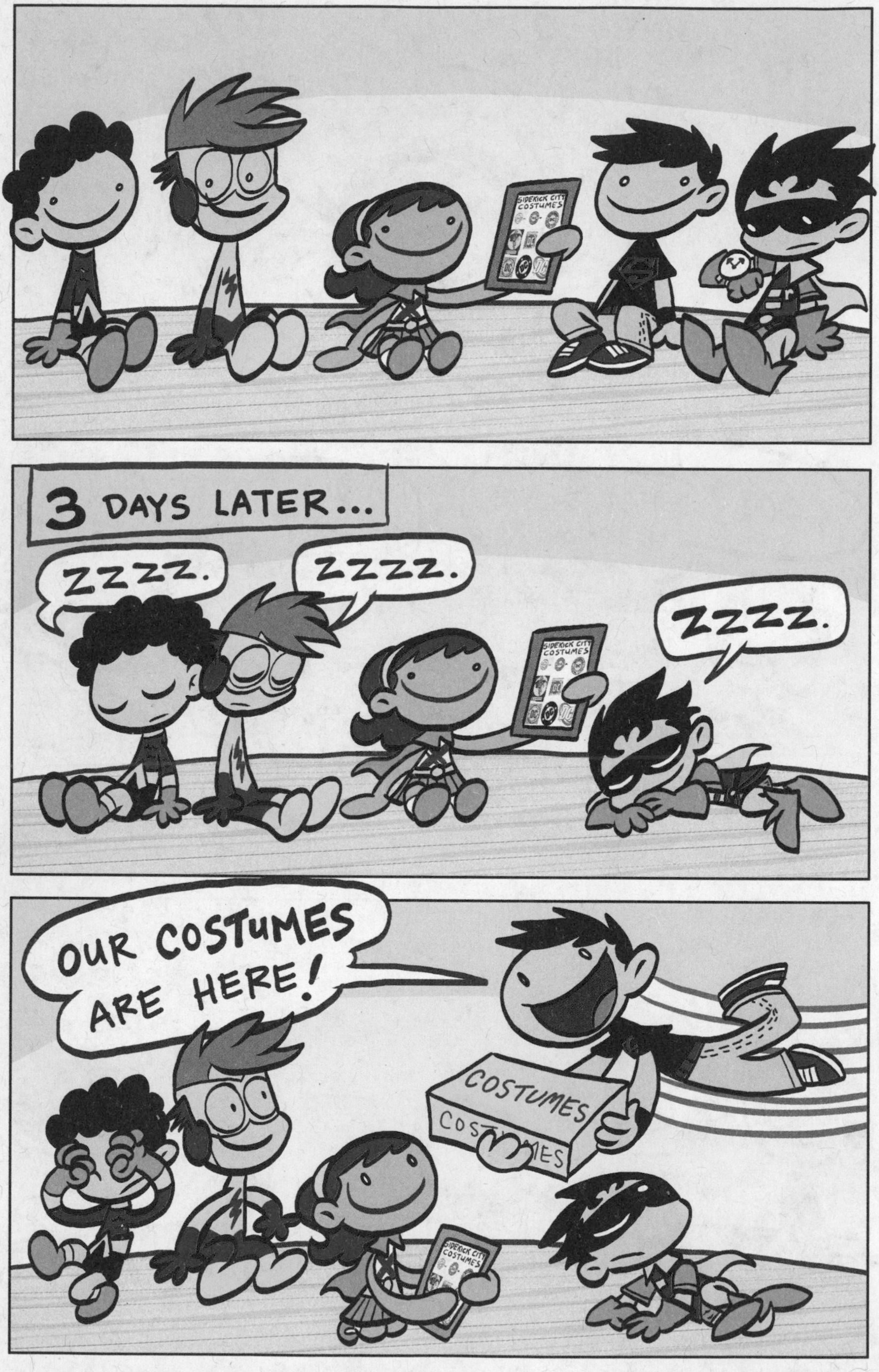
SIDEKICK CITY COSTUMES
3 DAYS LATER...
ZZZZ.
ZZZZ.
SIDEKICK CITY COSTUMES
ZZZZ.
OUR COSTUMES ARE HERE!
COSTUMES
SIDEKICK CITY COSTUMES

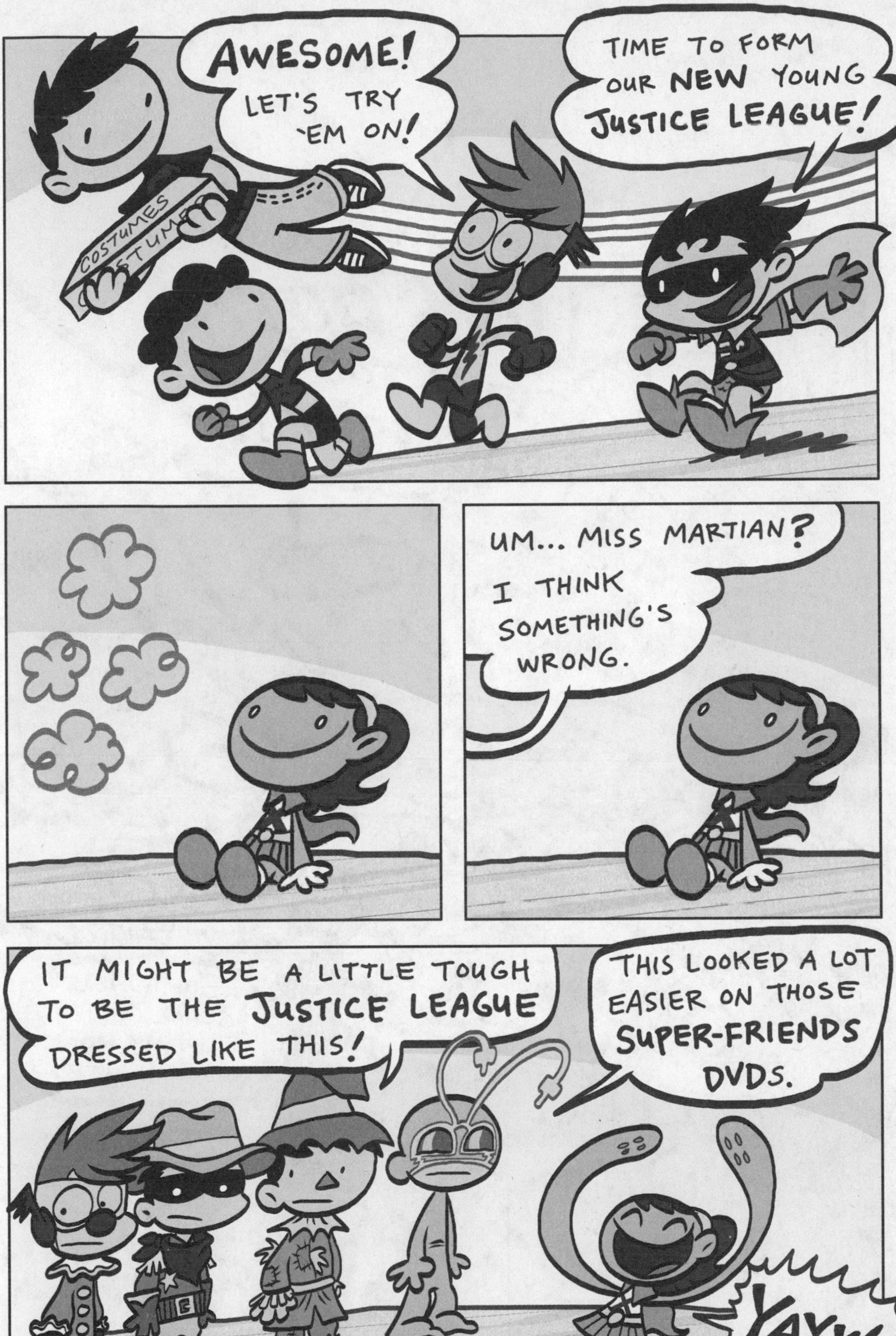
AWESOME! LET'S TRY 'EM ON!
COSTUMES
TIME TO FORM OUR NEW YOUNG JUSTICE LEAGUE!
UM... MISS MARTIAN? I THINK SOMETHING'S WRONG.
IT MIGHT BE A LITTLE TOUGH TO BE THE JUSTICE LEAGUE DRESSED LIKE THIS!
THIS LOOKED A LOT EASIER ON THOSE SUPER-FRIENDS DVDS.
YAYY!!

—GET ANIMATED!

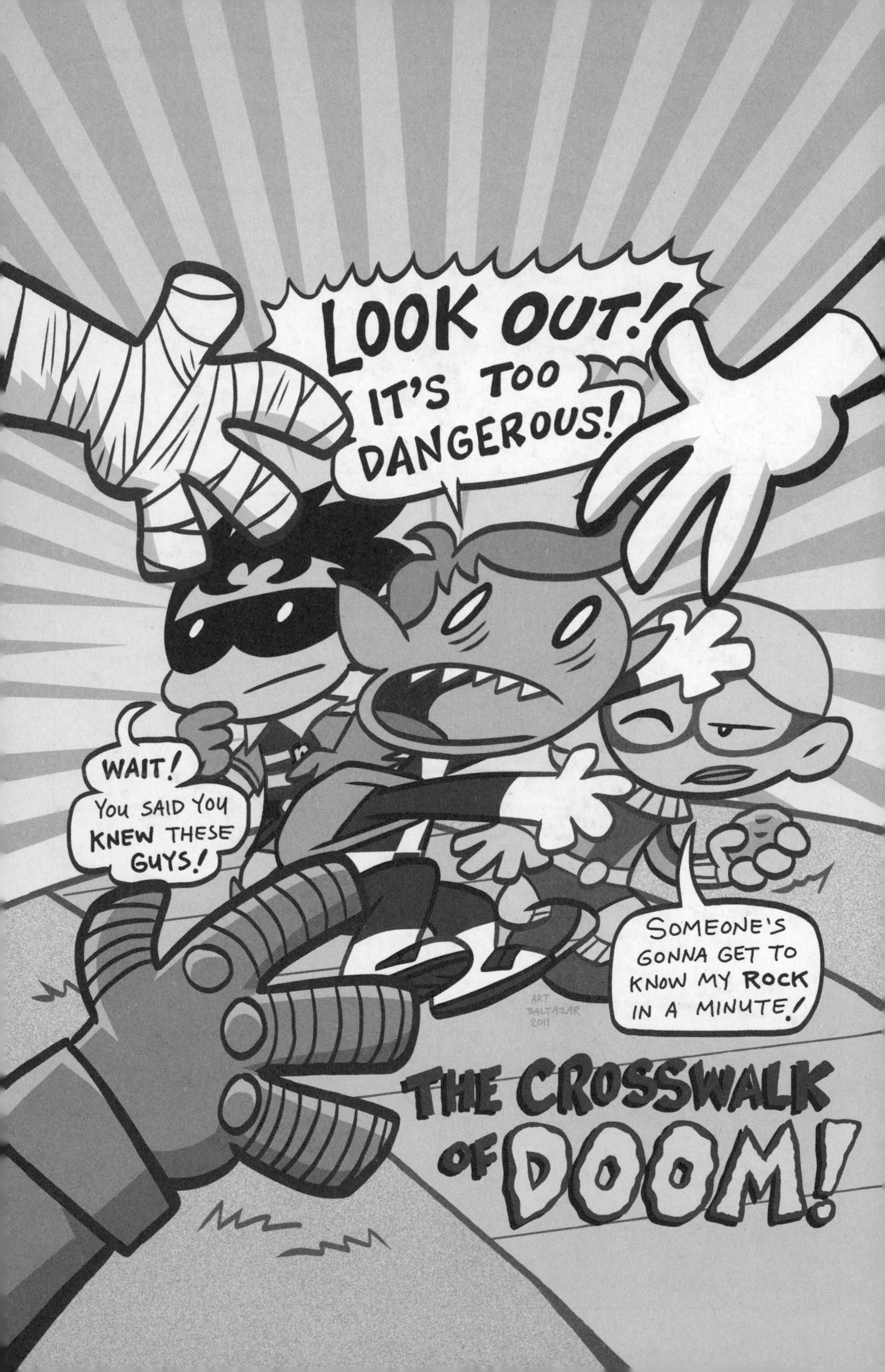
LOOK OUT! IT'S TOO DANGEROUS!
WAIT! You SAID You KNEW THESE GUYS!
SOMEONE'S GONNA GET TO KNOW MY ROCK IN A MINUTE!
ART BALTAZAR 2011
THE CROSSWALK OF DOOM!

tiny titans

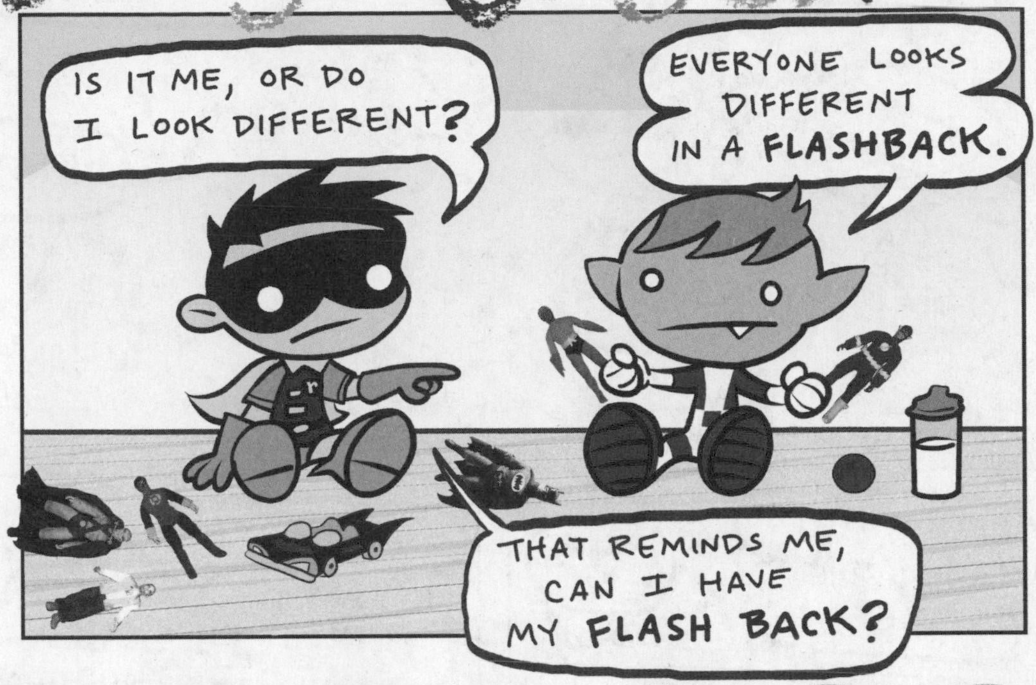
IS IT ME, OR DO I LOOK DIFFERENT?
EVERYONE LOOKS DIFFERENT IN A FLASHBACK.
THAT REMINDS ME, CAN I HAVE MY FLASH BACK?

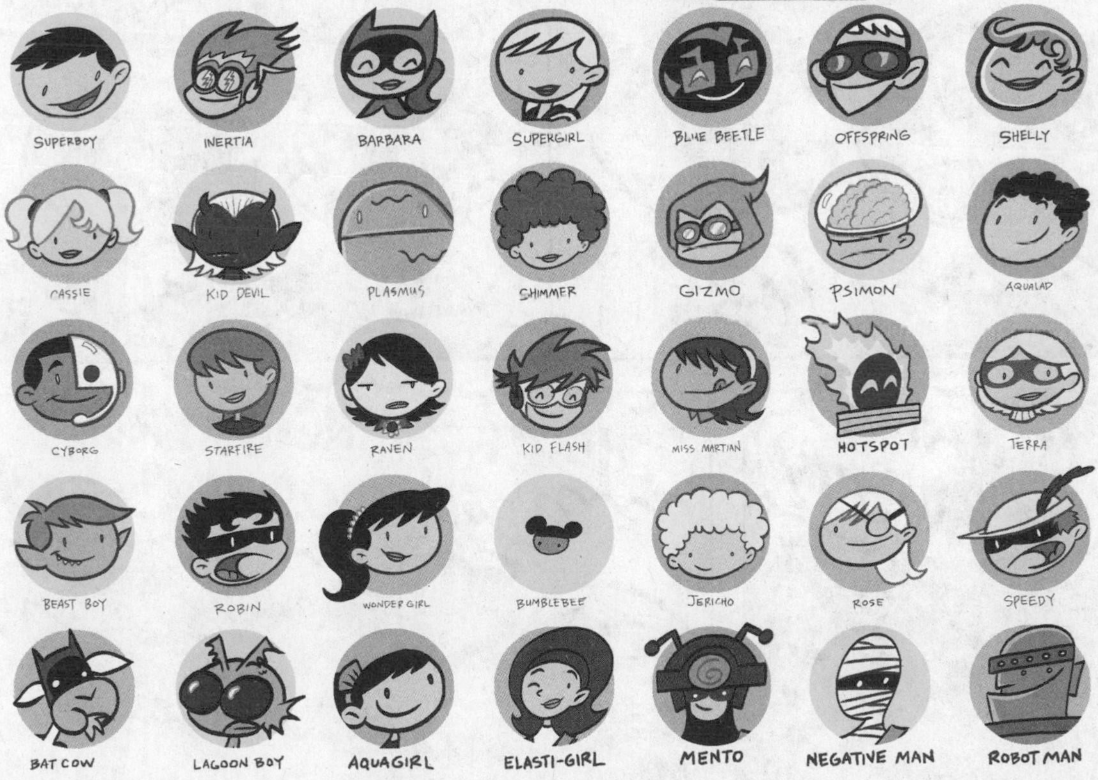
SUPERBOY
INERTIA
BARBARA
SUPERGIRL
BLUE BEETLE
OFFSPRING
SHELLY
CASSIE
KID DEVIL
PLASMUS
SHIMMER
GIZMO
PSIMON
AQUALAD
CYBORG
STARFIRE
RAVEN
KID FLASH
MISS MARTIAN
HOTSPOT
TERRA
BEAST BOY
ROBIN
WONDER GIRL
BUMBLEBEE
JERICHO
ROSE
SPEEDY
BAT COW
LAGOON BOY
AQUAGIRL
ELASTI-GIRL
MENTO
NEGATIVE MAN
ROBOT MAN

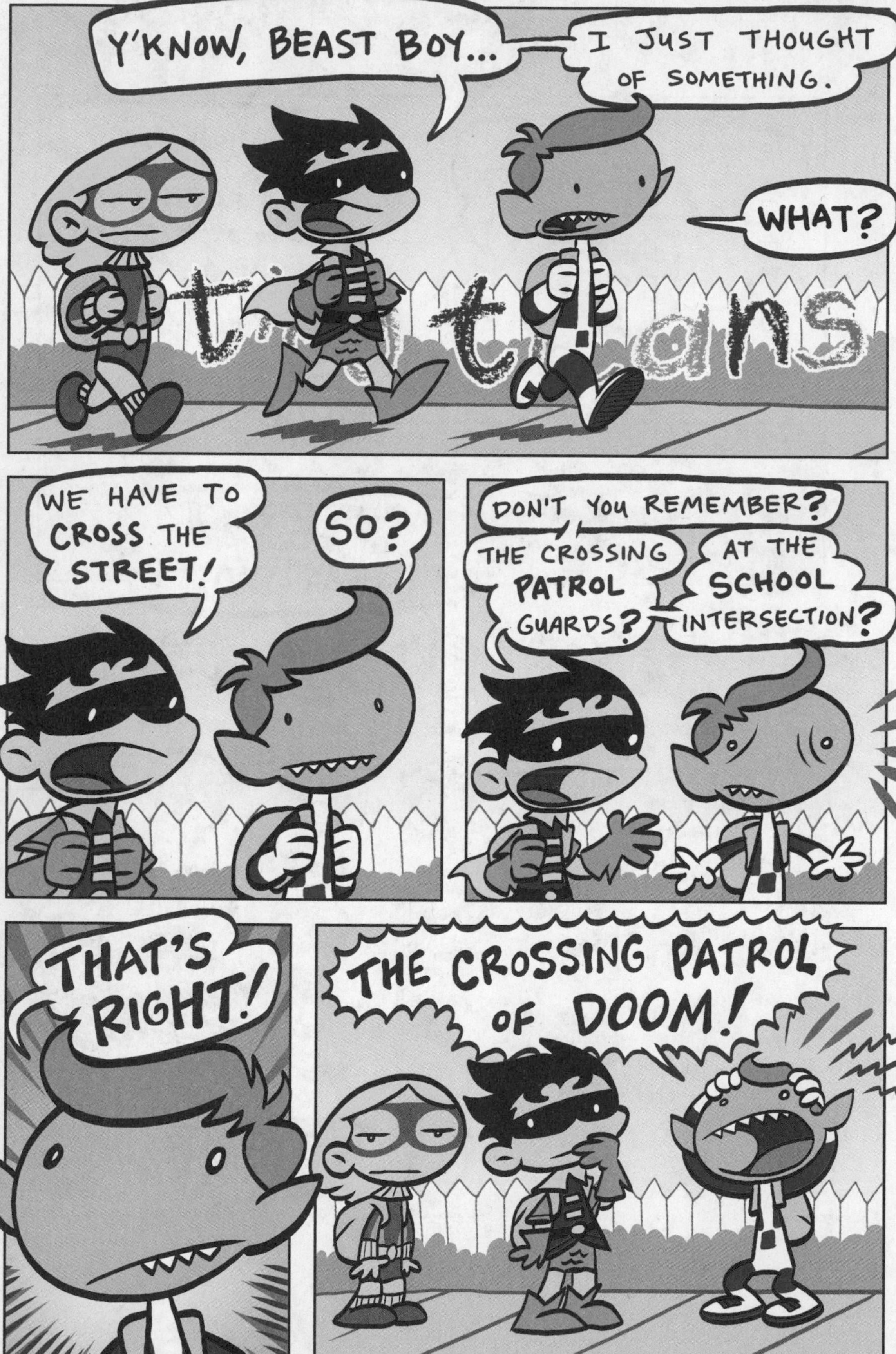
Y'KNOW, BEAST BOY...
I JUST THOUGHT OF SOMETHING.
WHAT?
WE HAVE TO CROSS THE STREET!
SO?
DON'T YOU REMEMBER?
THE CROSSING PATROL GUARDS?
AT THE SCHOOL INTERSECTION?
THAT'S RIGHT!
THE CROSSING PATROL OF DOOM!

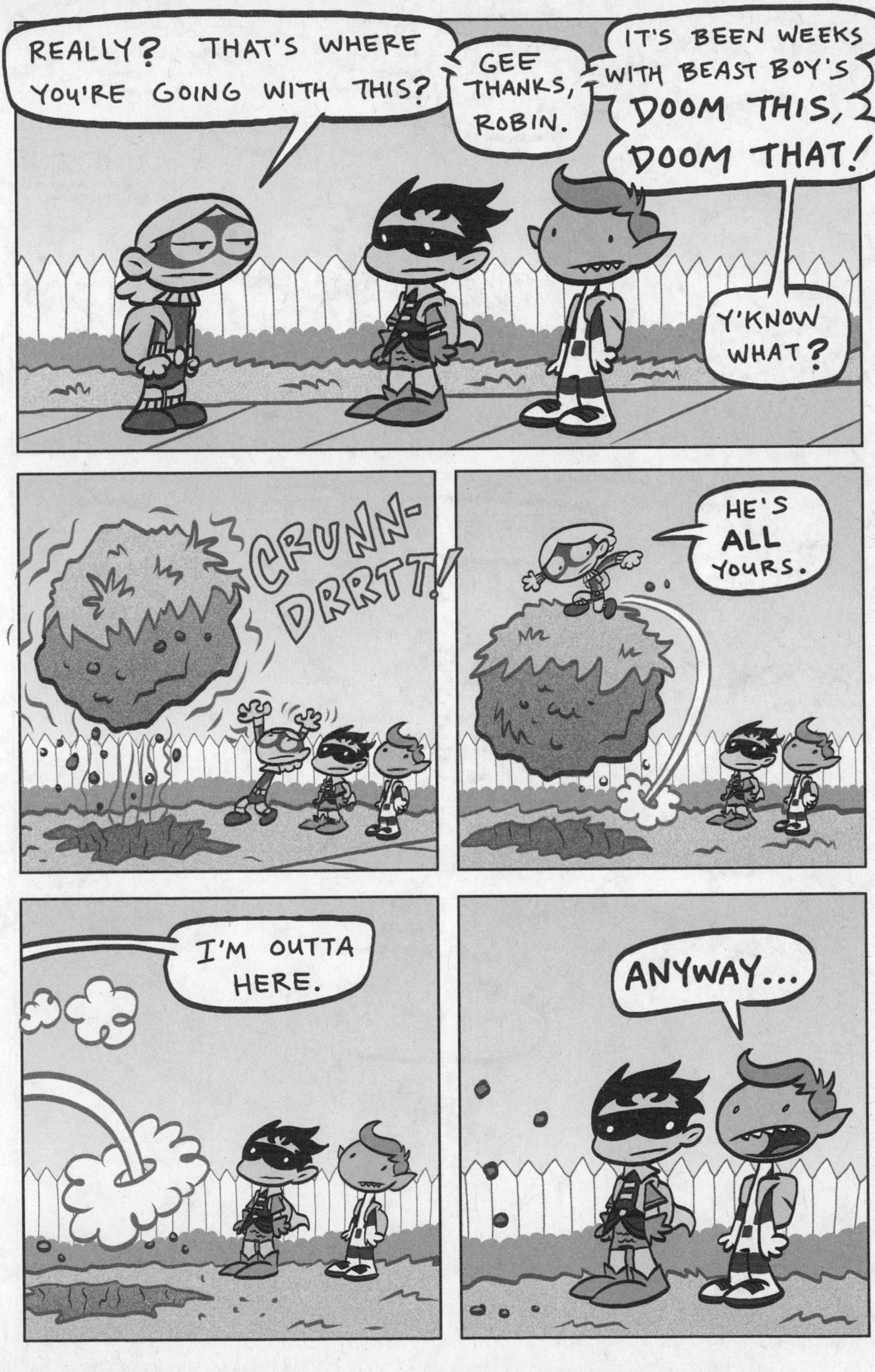
REALLY? THAT'S WHERE YOU'RE GOING WITH THIS?
GEE THANKS, ROBIN.
IT'S BEEN WEEKS WITH BEAST BOY'S DOOM THIS, DOOM THAT!
Y'KNOW WHAT?
CRUNN-DRRTT!
HE'S ALL YOURS.
I'M OUTTA HERE.
ANYWAY...

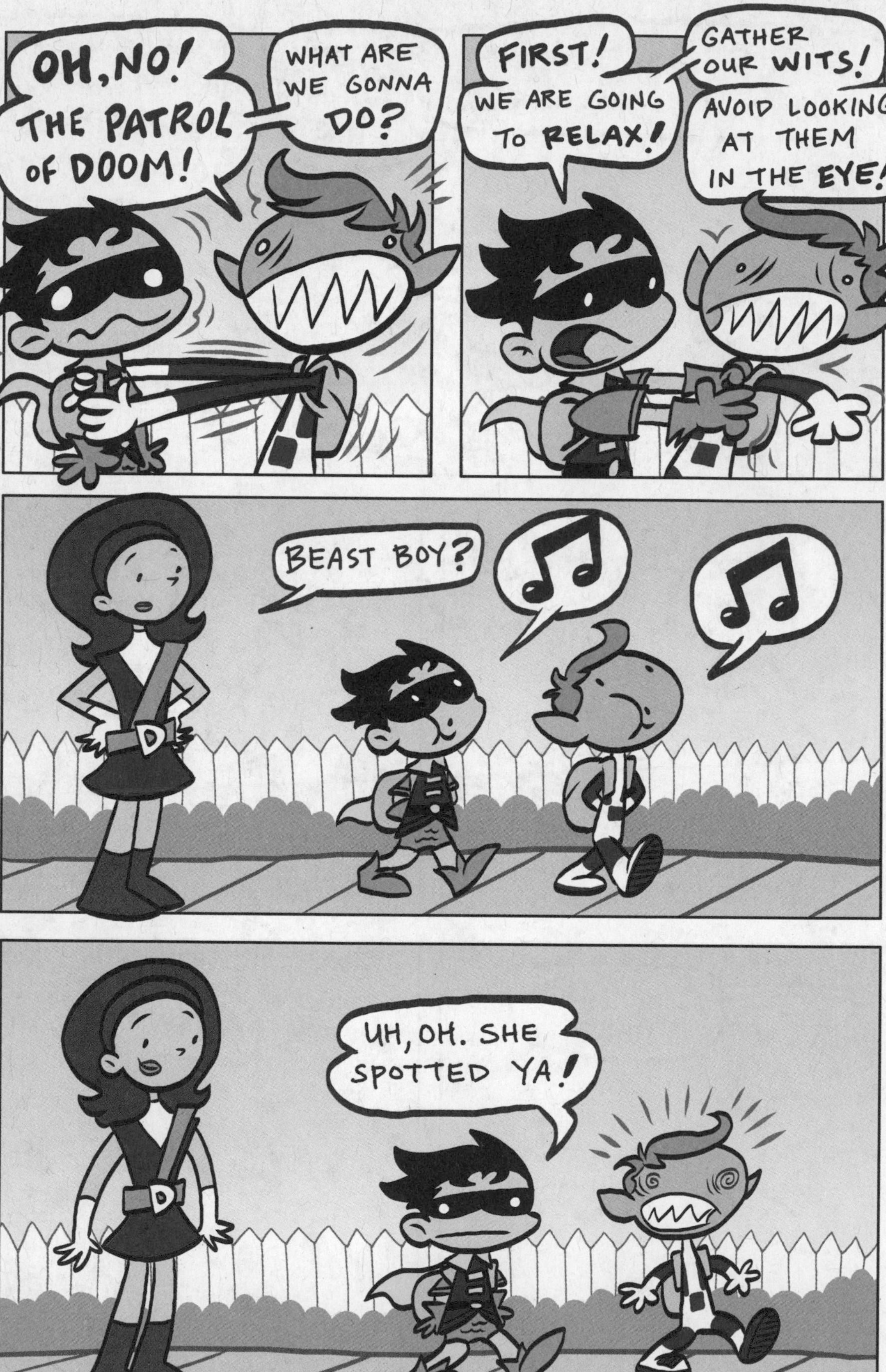
OH, NO! THE PATROL OF DOOM!
WHAT ARE WE GONNA DO?
FIRST!
WE ARE GOING TO RELAX!
GATHER OUR WITS!
AVOID LOOKING AT THEM IN THE EYE!
BEAST BOY?
UH, OH. SHE SPOTTED YA!

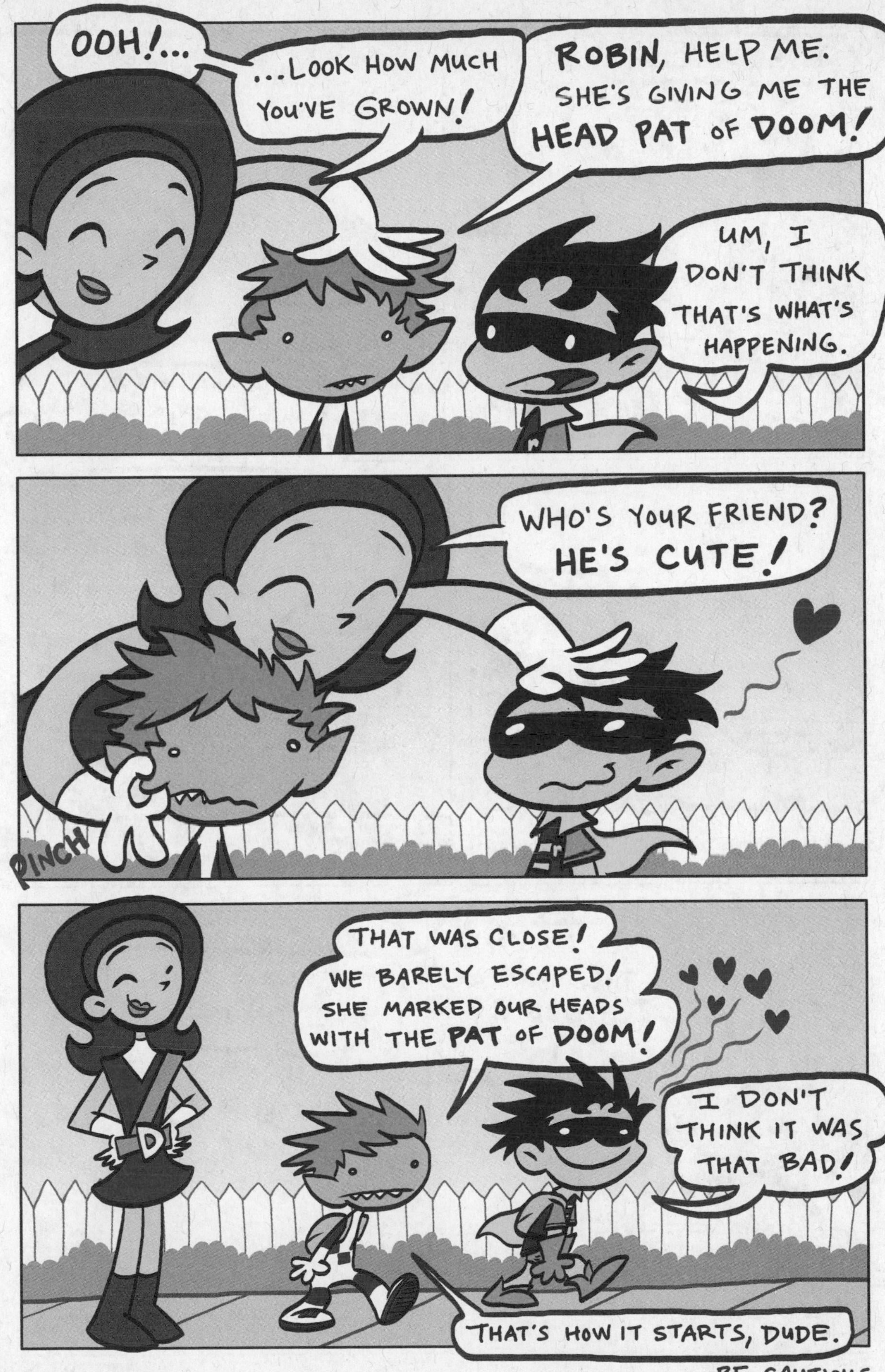
OOH!...
...LOOK HOW MUCH YOU'VE GROWN!
ROBIN, HELP ME. SHE'S GIVING ME THE HEAD PAT OF DOOM!
UM, I DON'T THINK THAT'S WHAT'S HAPPENING.
WHO'S YOUR FRIEND? HE'S CUTE!
PINCH
THAT WAS CLOSE! WE BARELY ESCAPED! SHE MARKED OUR HEADS WITH THE PAT OF DOOM!
I DON'T THINK IT WAS THAT BAD!
THAT'S HOW IT STARTS, DUDE.
-BE CAUTIOUS.

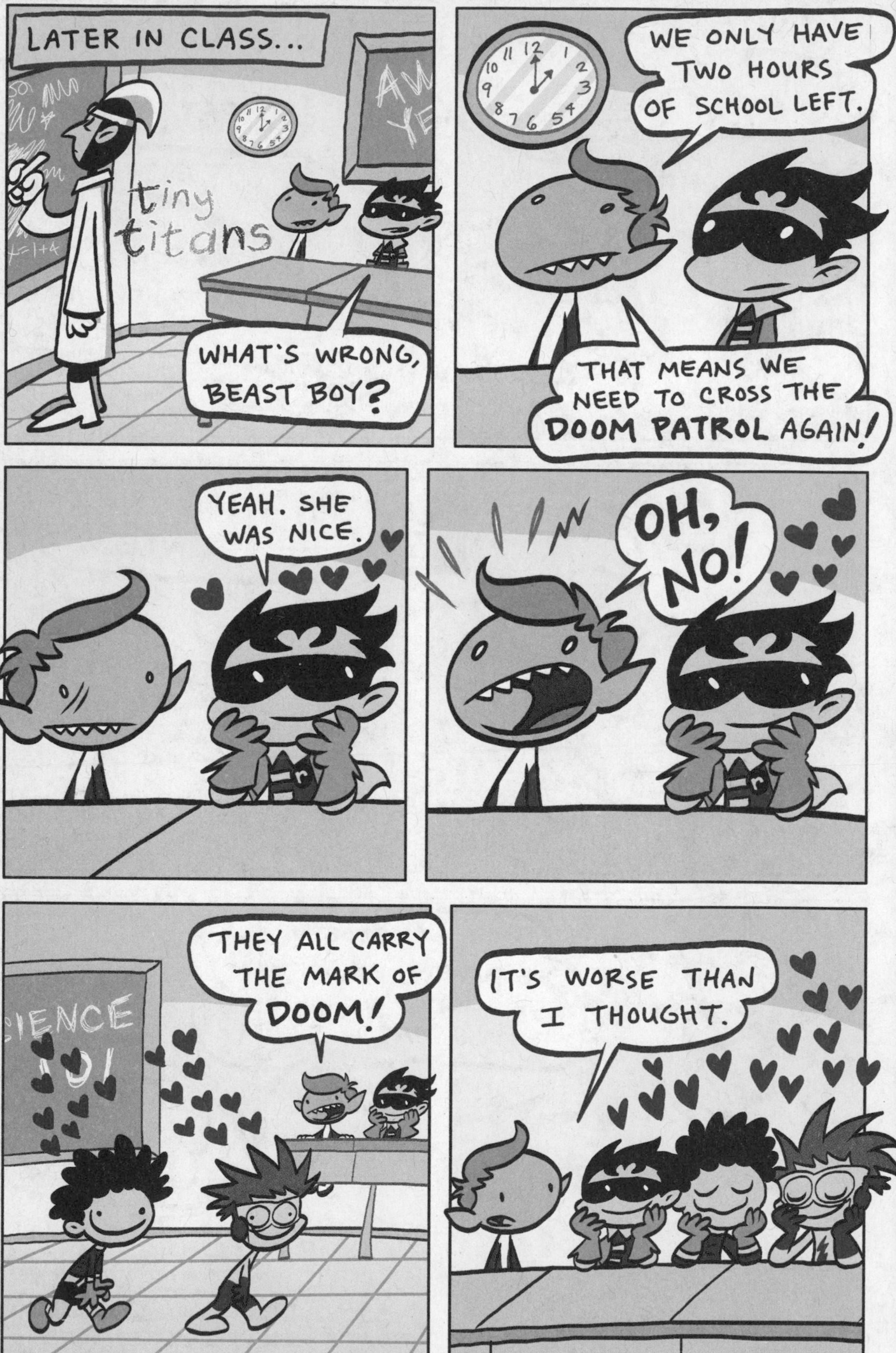
LATER IN CLASS...
tiny titans
WHAT'S WRONG, BEAST BOY?
WE ONLY HAVE TWO HOURS OF SCHOOL LEFT.
THAT MEANS WE NEED TO CROSS THE DOOM PATROL AGAIN!
YEAH. SHE WAS NICE.
OH, NO!
SCIENCE 101
THEY ALL CARRY THE MARK OF DOOM!
IT'S WORSE THAN I THOUGHT.
-HAIR RAISING.

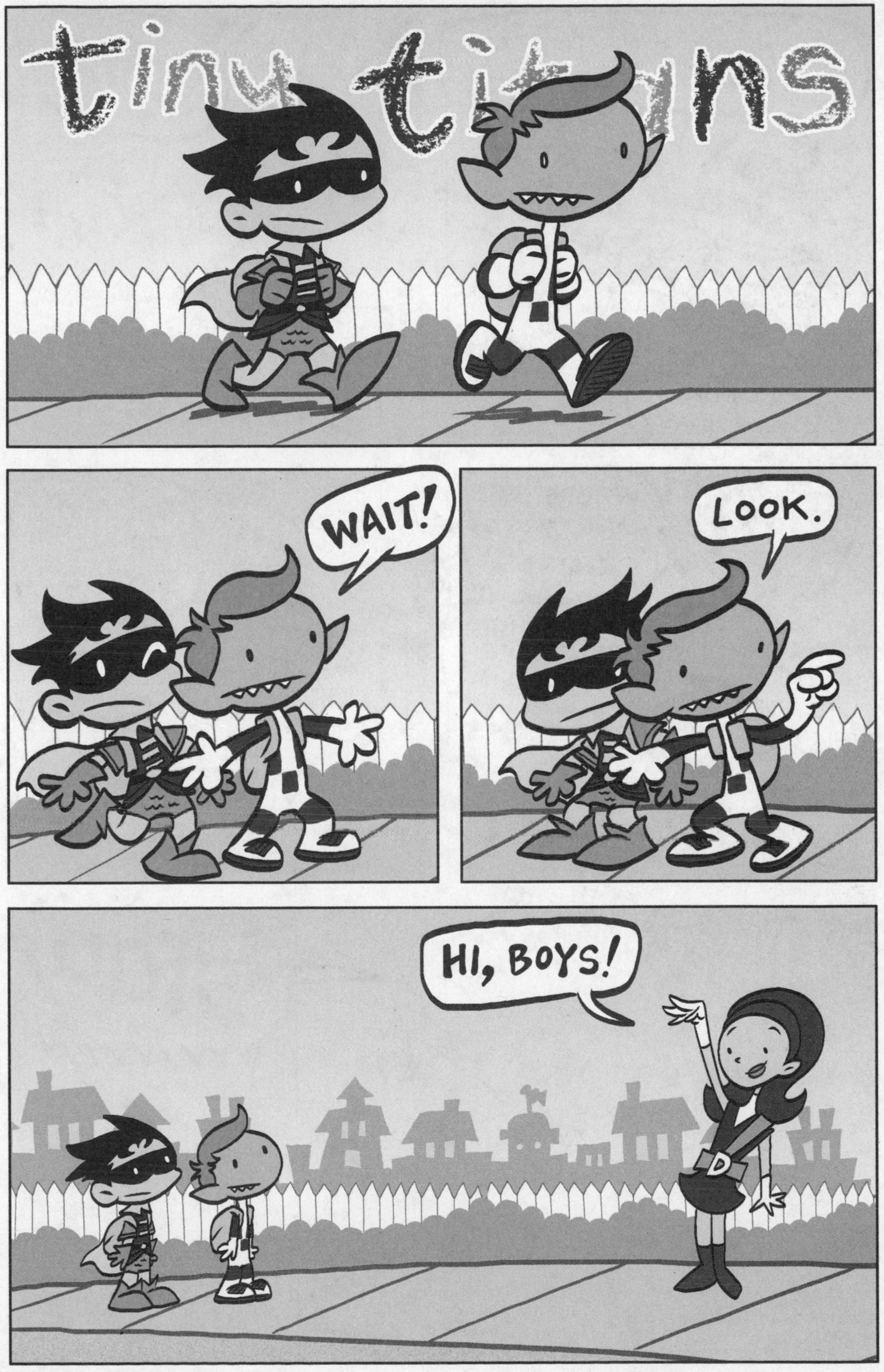
tiny titans
WAIT!
LOOK.
HI, BOYS!

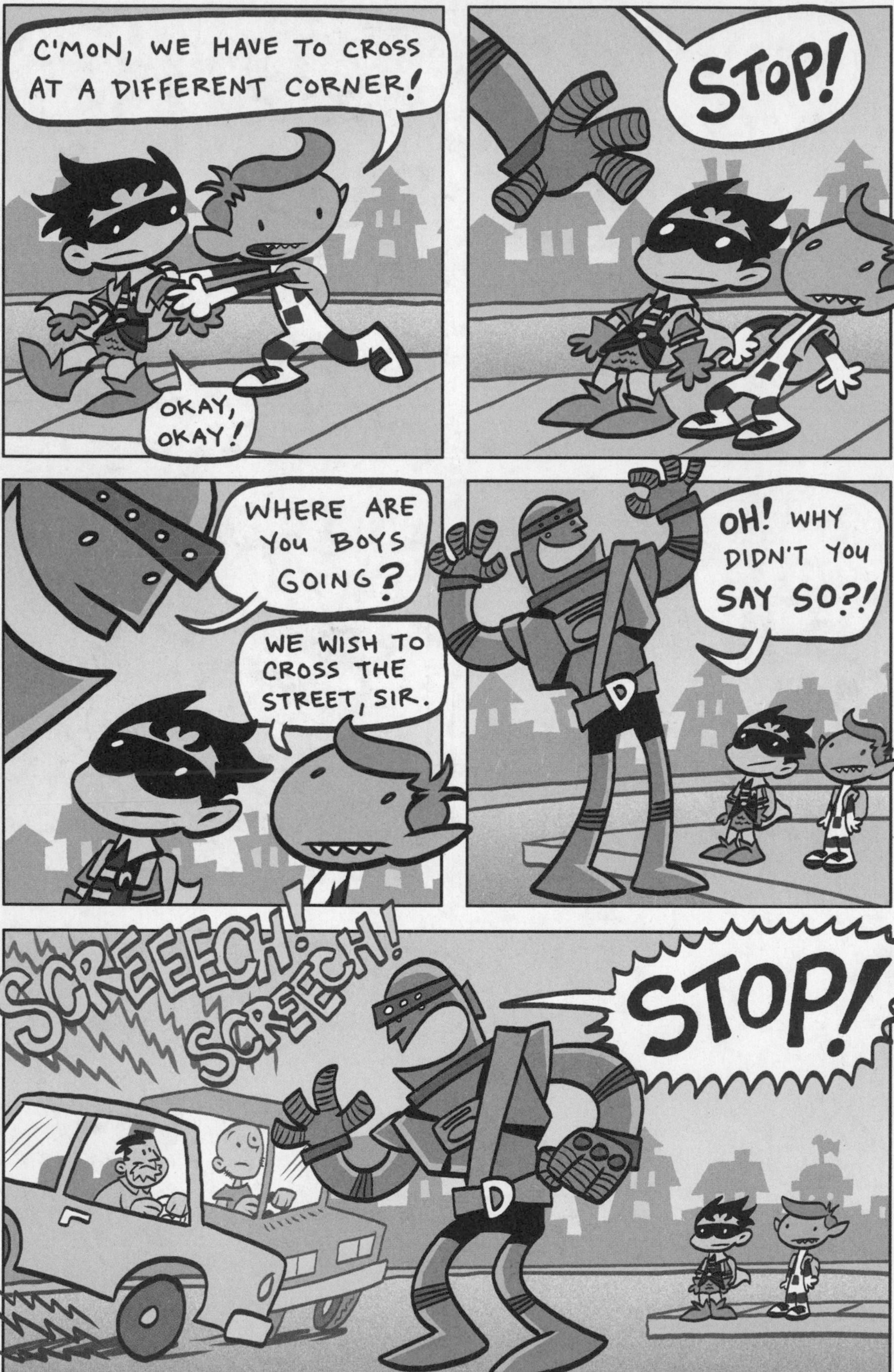
C'MON, WE HAVE TO CROSS AT A DIFFERENT CORNER!
OKAY, OKAY!
STOP!
WHERE ARE YOU BOYS GOING?
WE WISH TO CROSS THE STREET, SIR.
OH! WHY DIDN'T YOU SAY SO?!
SCREEECH! SCREEECH!
STOP!

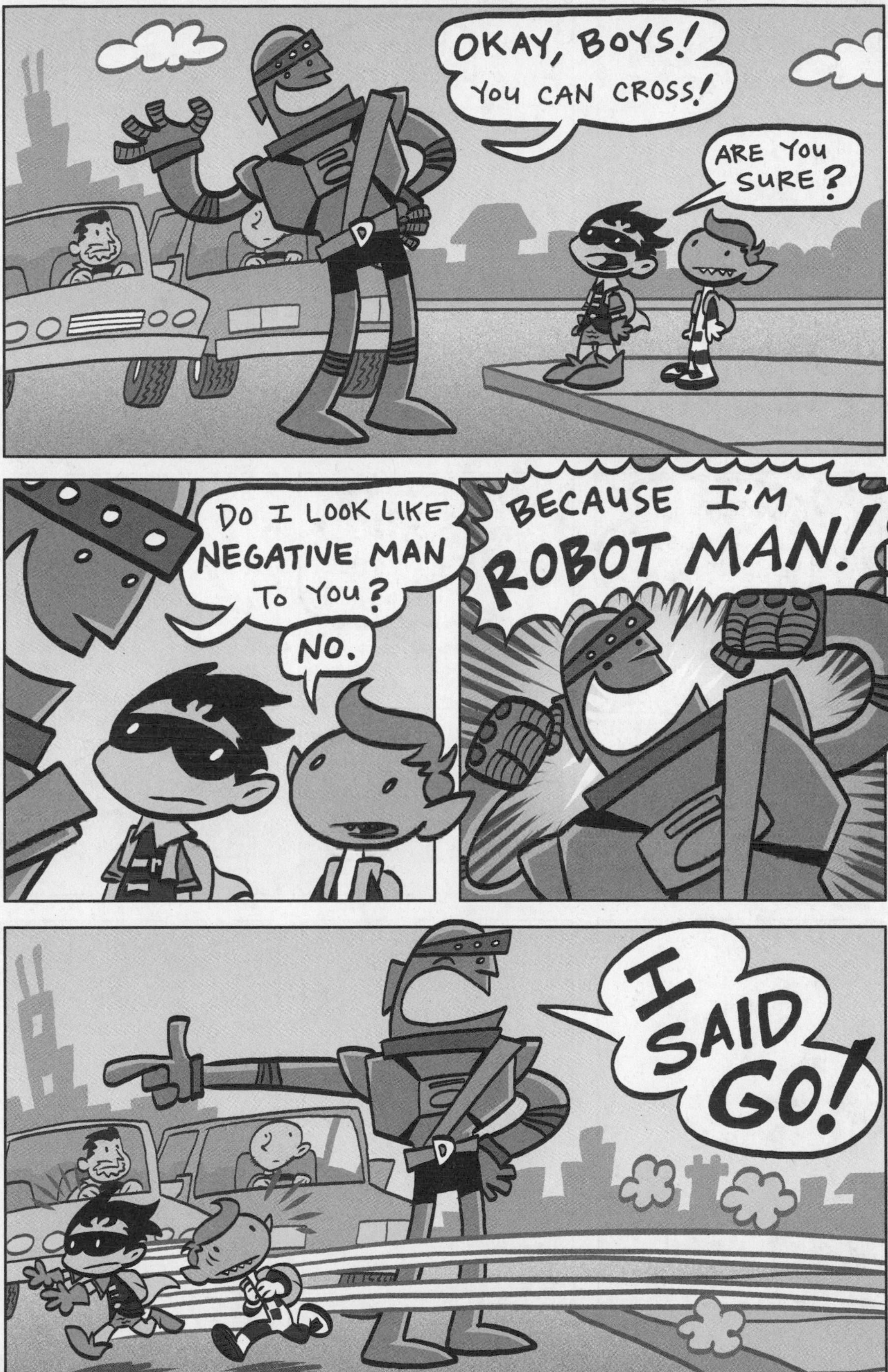
OKAY, BOYS! YOU CAN CROSS!
ARE YOU SURE?
DO I LOOK LIKE NEGATIVE MAN TO YOU?
NO.
BECAUSE I'M ROBOT MAN!
I SAID GO!

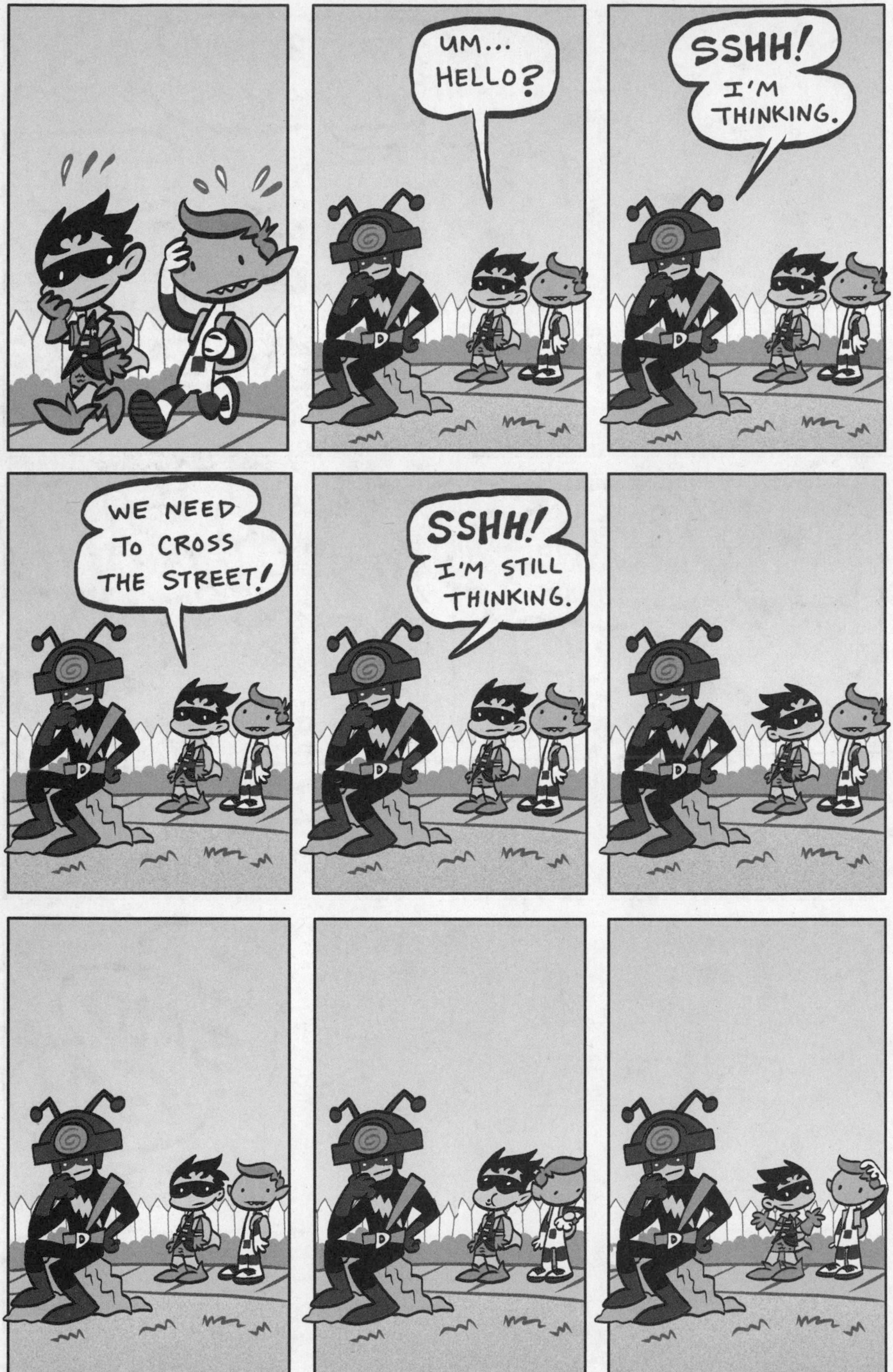
UM... HELLO?
SSHH! I'M THINKING.
WE NEED TO CROSS THE STREET!
SSHH! I'M STILL THINKING.

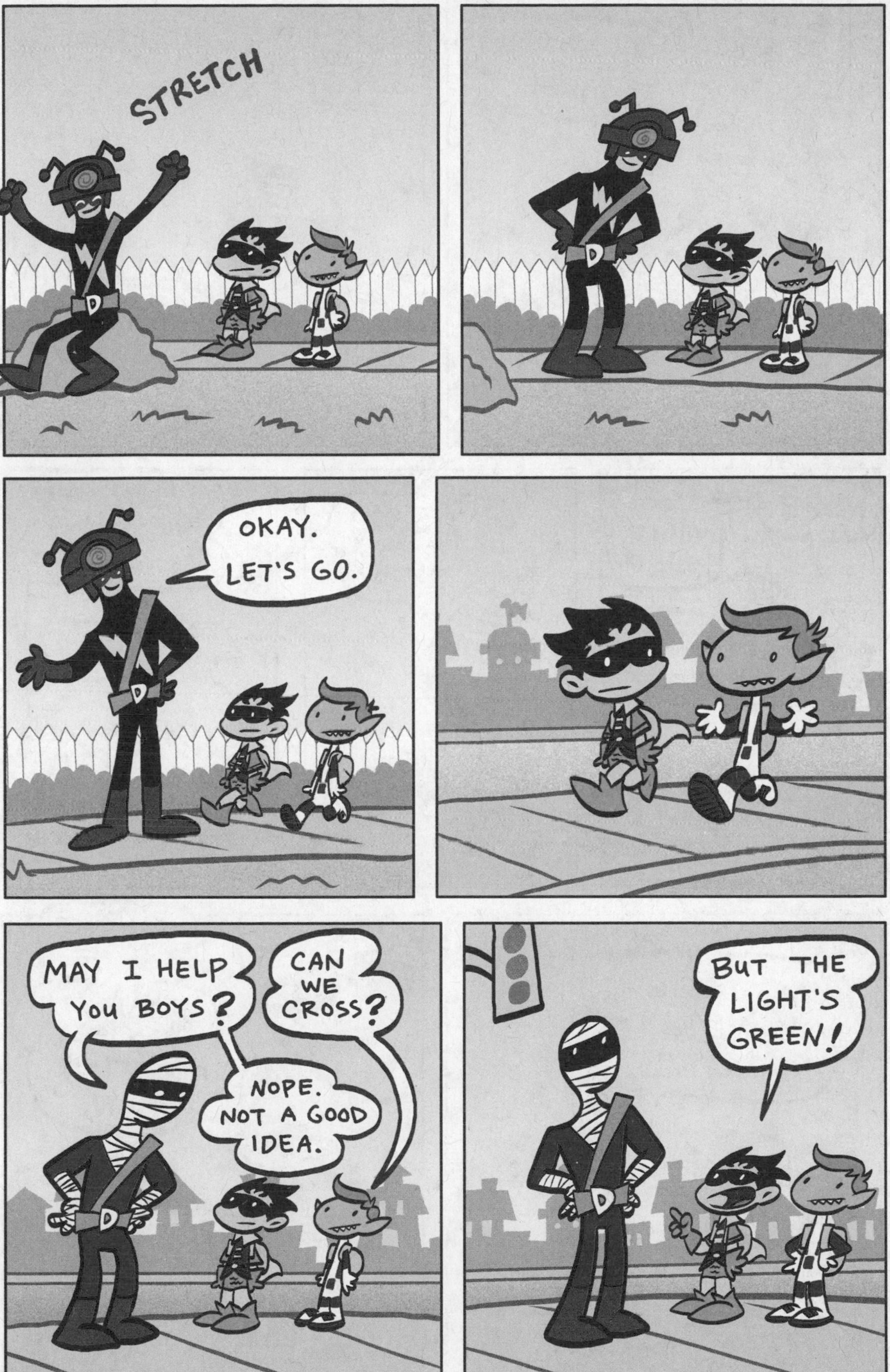
STRETCH
OKAY. LET'S GO.
MAY I HELP YOU BOYS?
CAN WE CROSS?
NOPE. NOT A GOOD IDEA.
BUT THE LIGHT'S GREEN!

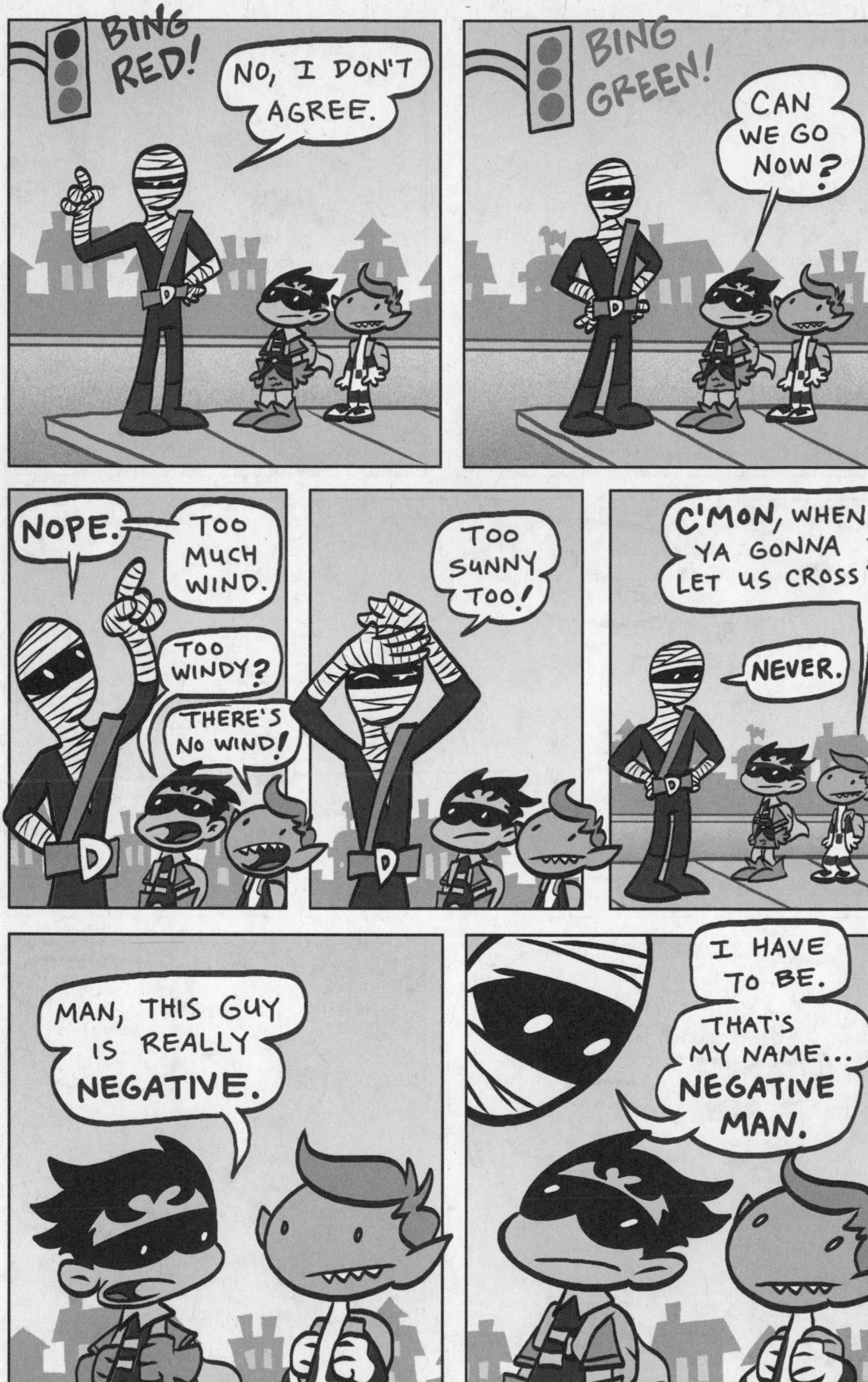
BING RED!
NO, I DON'T AGREE.
BING GREEN!
CAN WE GO NOW?
NOPE.
TOO MUCH WIND.
TOO WINDY?
THERE'S NO WIND!
TOO SUNNY TOO!
C'MON, WHEN YA GONNA LET US CROSS?
NEVER.
MAN, THIS GUY IS REALLY NEGATIVE.
I HAVE TO BE.
THAT'S MY NAME... NEGATIVE MAN.

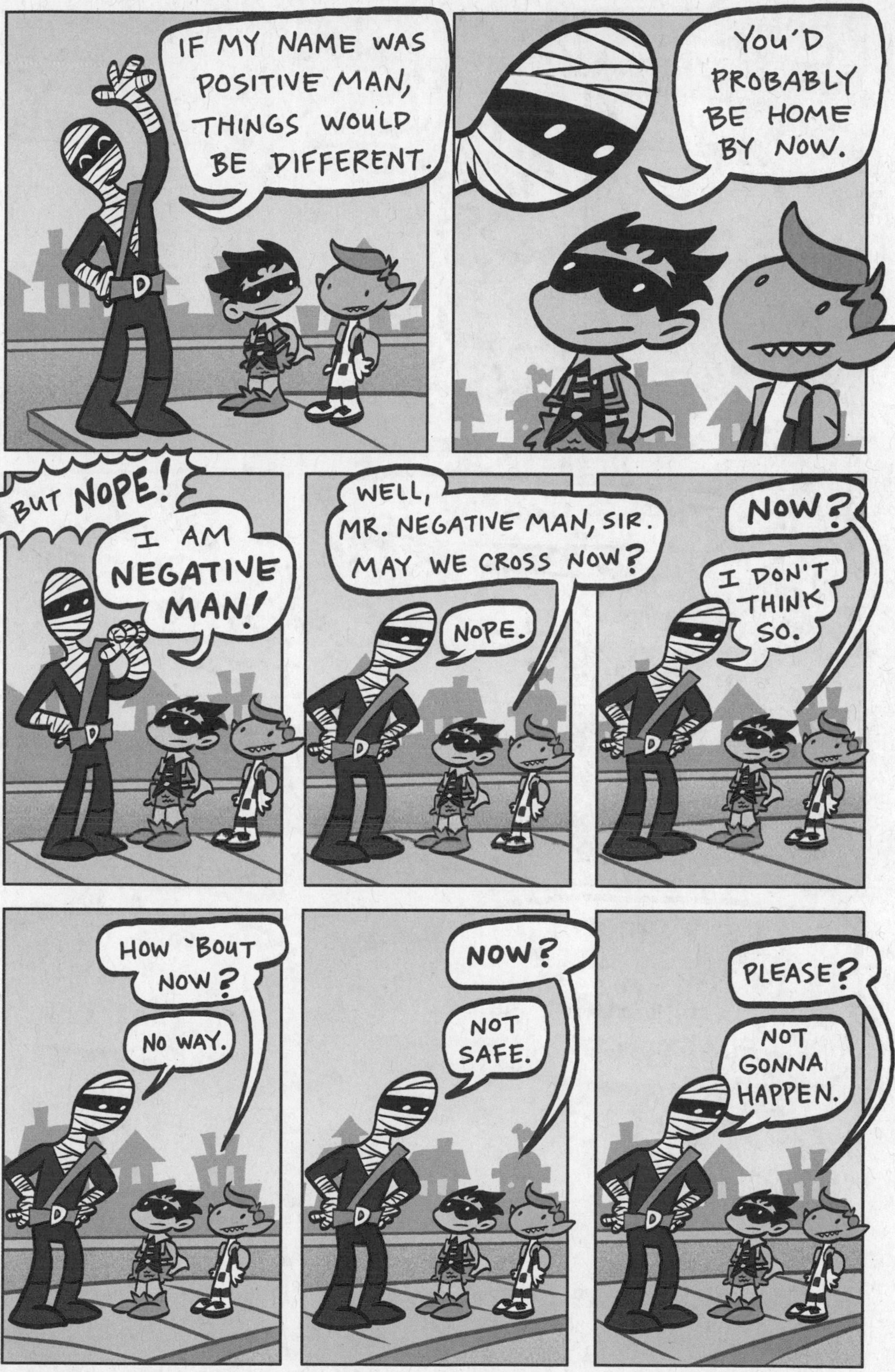
IF MY NAME WAS POSITIVE MAN, THINGS WOULD BE DIFFERENT.
YOU'D PROBABLY BE HOME BY NOW.
BUT NOPE!
I AM NEGATIVE MAN!
WELL, MR. NEGATIVE MAN, SIR. MAY WE CROSS NOW?
NOPE.
NOW?
I DON'T THINK SO.
HOW 'BOUT NOW?
NO WAY.
NOW?
NOT SAFE.
PLEASE?
NOT GONNA HAPPEN.

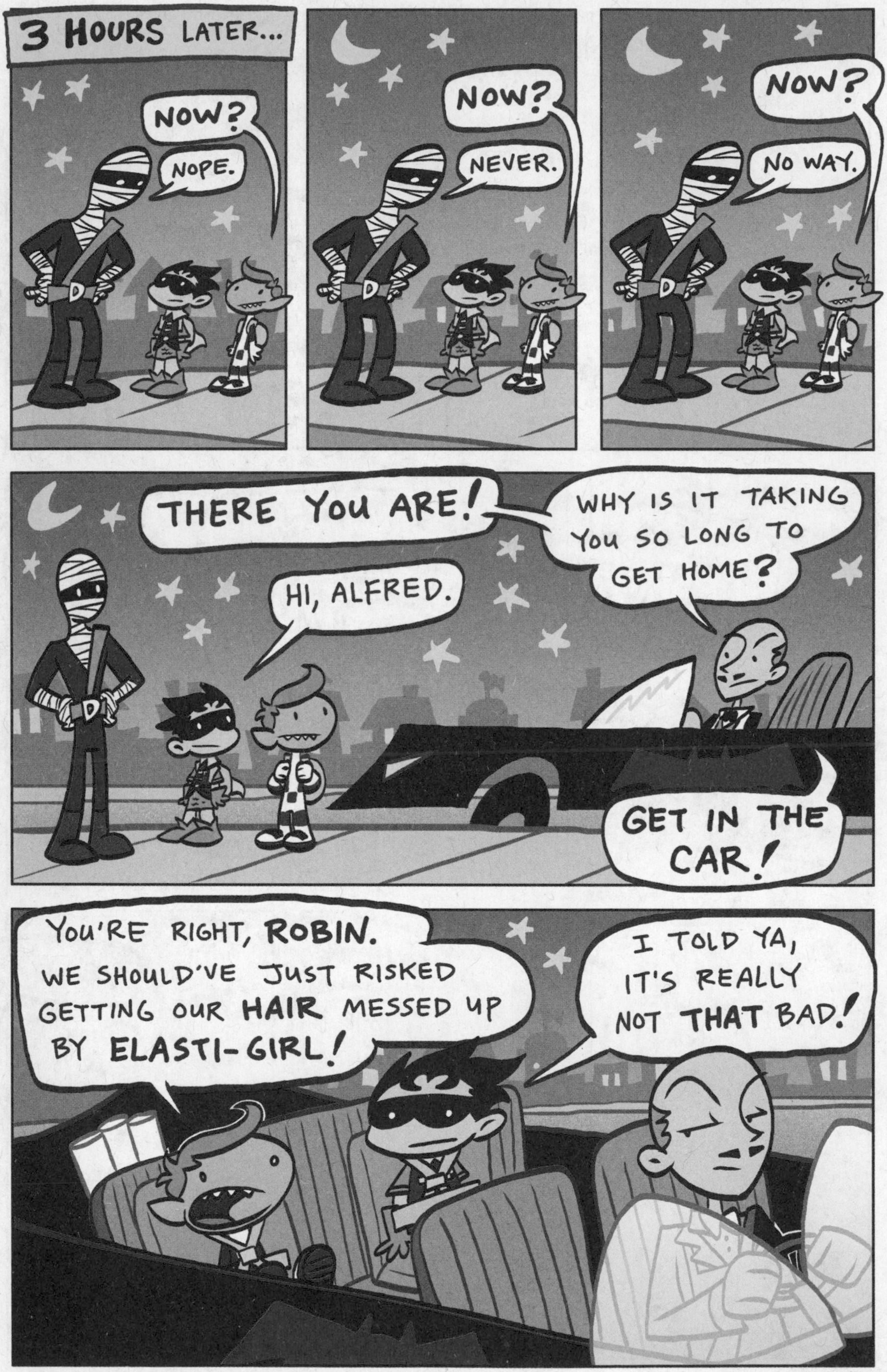
3 HOURS LATER...
NOW?
NOPE.
NOW?
NEVER.
NOW?
NO WAY.
THERE YOU ARE!
WHY IS IT TAKING YOU SO LONG TO GET HOME?
HI, ALFRED.
GET IN THE CAR!
YOU'RE RIGHT, ROBIN. WE SHOULD'VE JUST RISKED GETTING OUR HAIR MESSED UP BY ELASTI-GIRL!
I TOLD YA, IT'S REALLY NOT THAT BAD!

-NOPE.

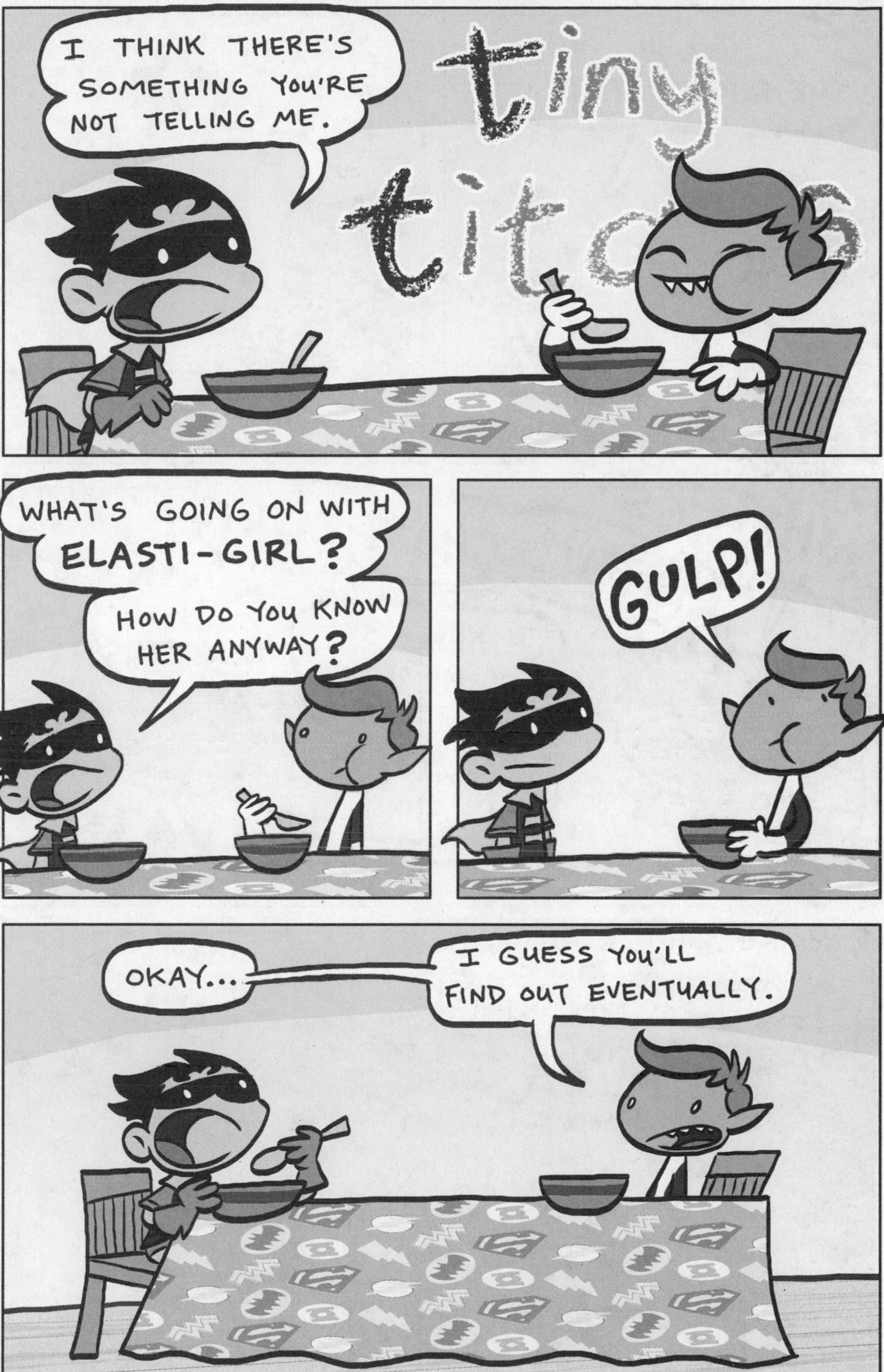
tiny titans
I THINK THERE'S SOMETHING YOU'RE NOT TELLING ME.
WHAT'S GOING ON WITH ELASTI-GIRL?
HOW DO YOU KNOW HER ANYWAY?
GULP!
OKAY...
I GUESS YOU'LL FIND OUT EVENTUALLY.

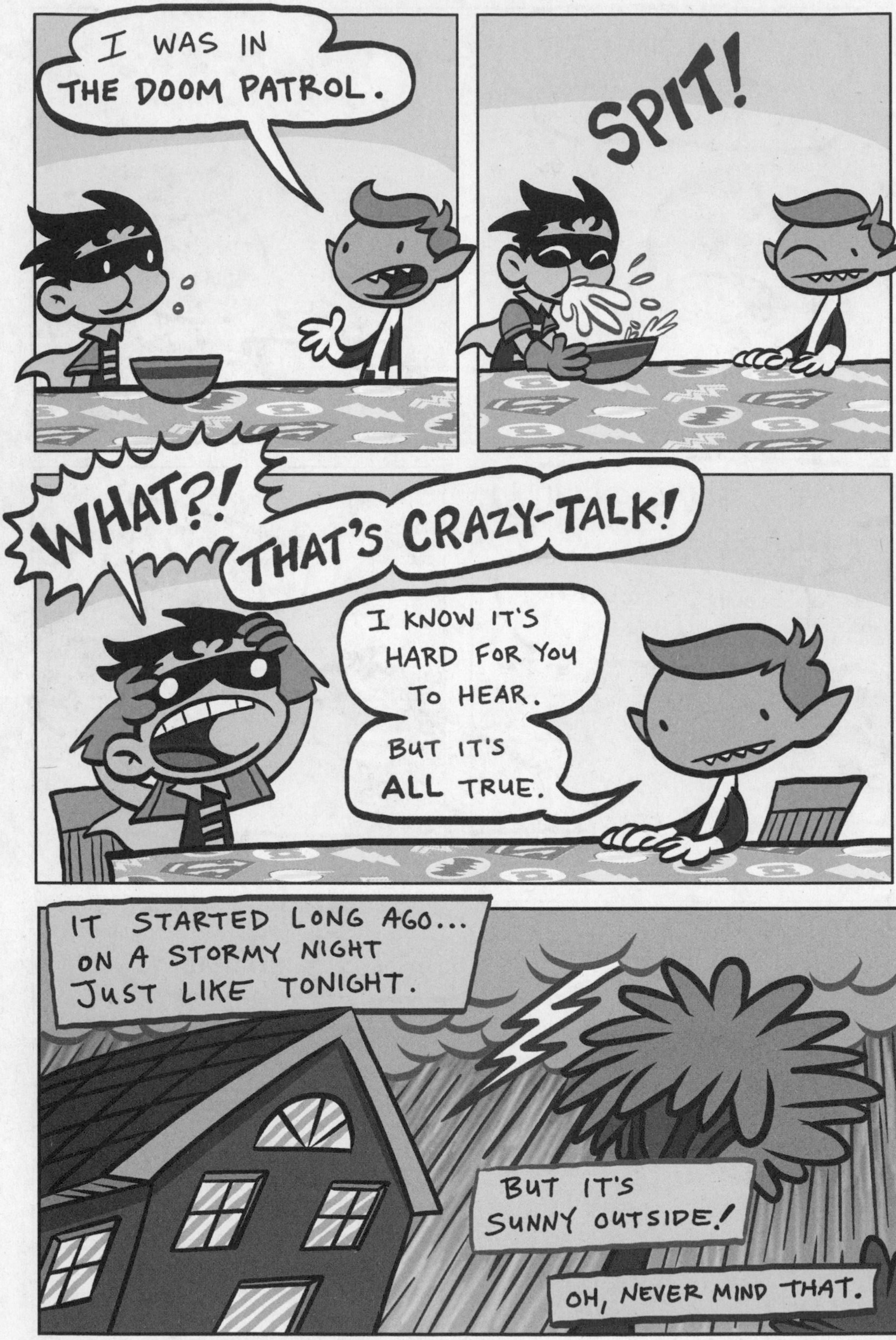
I WAS IN THE DOOM PATROL.
SPIT!
WHAT?!
THAT'S CRAZY-TALK!
I KNOW IT'S HARD FOR YOU TO HEAR.
BUT IT'S ALL TRUE.
IT STARTED LONG AGO... ON A STORMY NIGHT JUST LIKE TONIGHT.
BUT IT'S SUNNY OUTSIDE!
OH, NEVER MIND THAT.

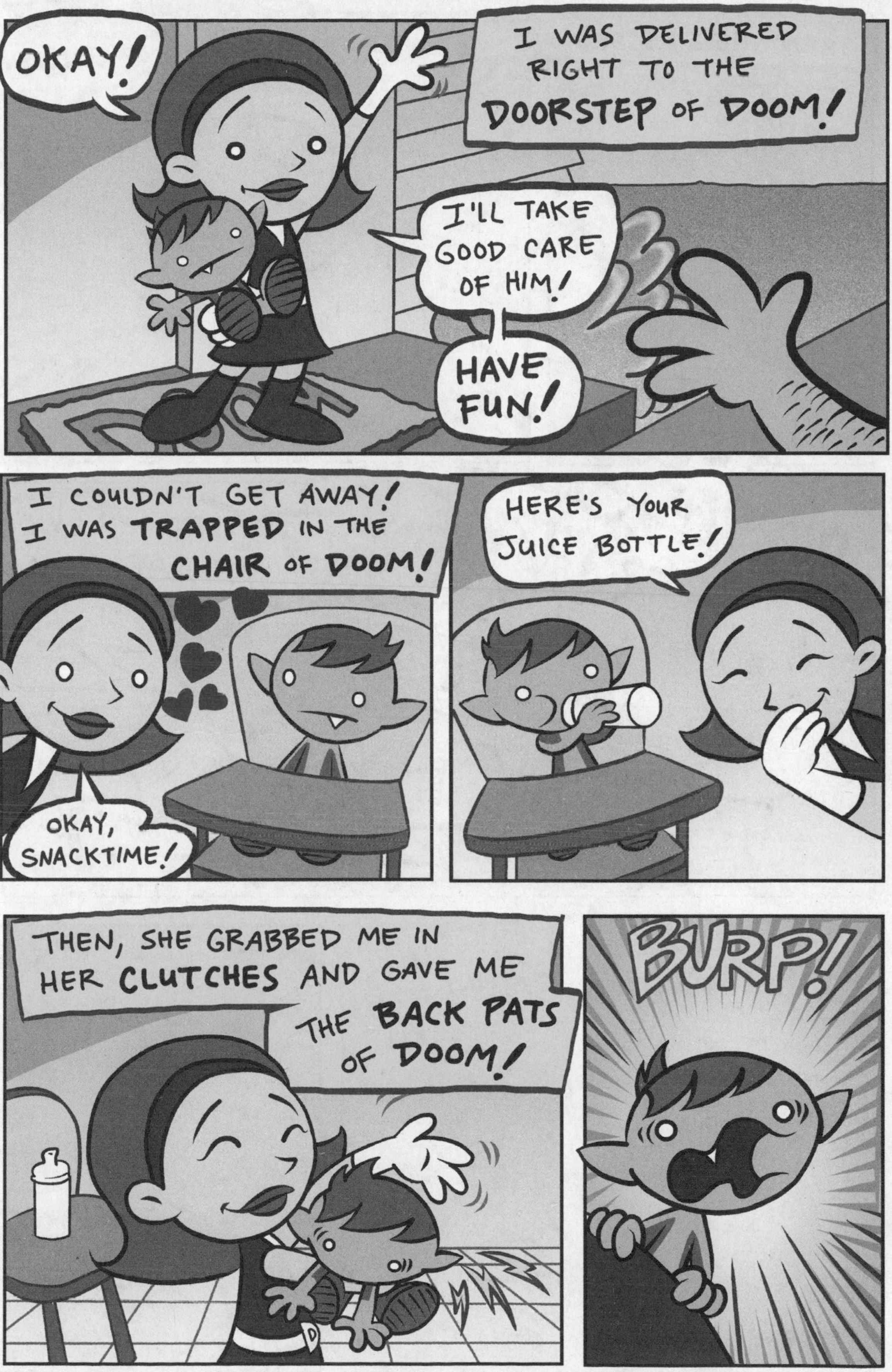
OKAY!
I WAS DELIVERED RIGHT TO THE DOORSTEP OF DOOM!
I'LL TAKE GOOD CARE OF HIM!
HAVE FUN!
I COULDN'T GET AWAY! I WAS TRAPPED IN THE CHAIR OF DOOM!
OKAY, SNACKTIME!
HERE'S YOUR JUICE BOTTLE!
THEN, SHE GRABBED ME IN HER CLUTCHES AND GAVE ME THE BACK PATS OF DOOM!
D
BURP!

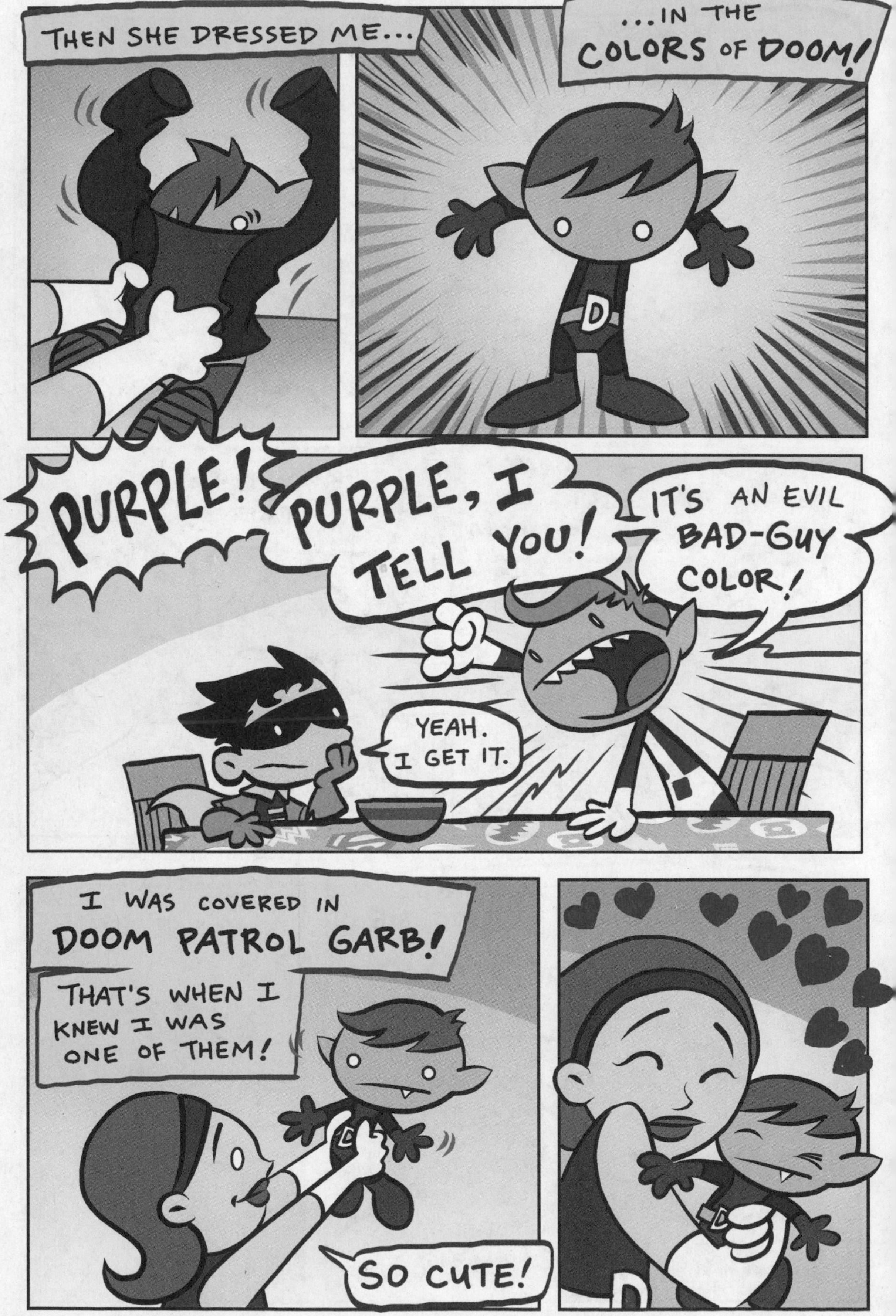
THEN SHE DRESSED ME...
...IN THE COLORS OF DOOM!
PURPLE!
PURPLE, I TELL YOU!
IT'S AN EVIL BAD-GUY COLOR!
YEAH. I GET IT.
I WAS COVERED IN DOOM PATROL GARB!
THAT'S WHEN I KNEW I WAS ONE OF THEM!
SO CUTE!

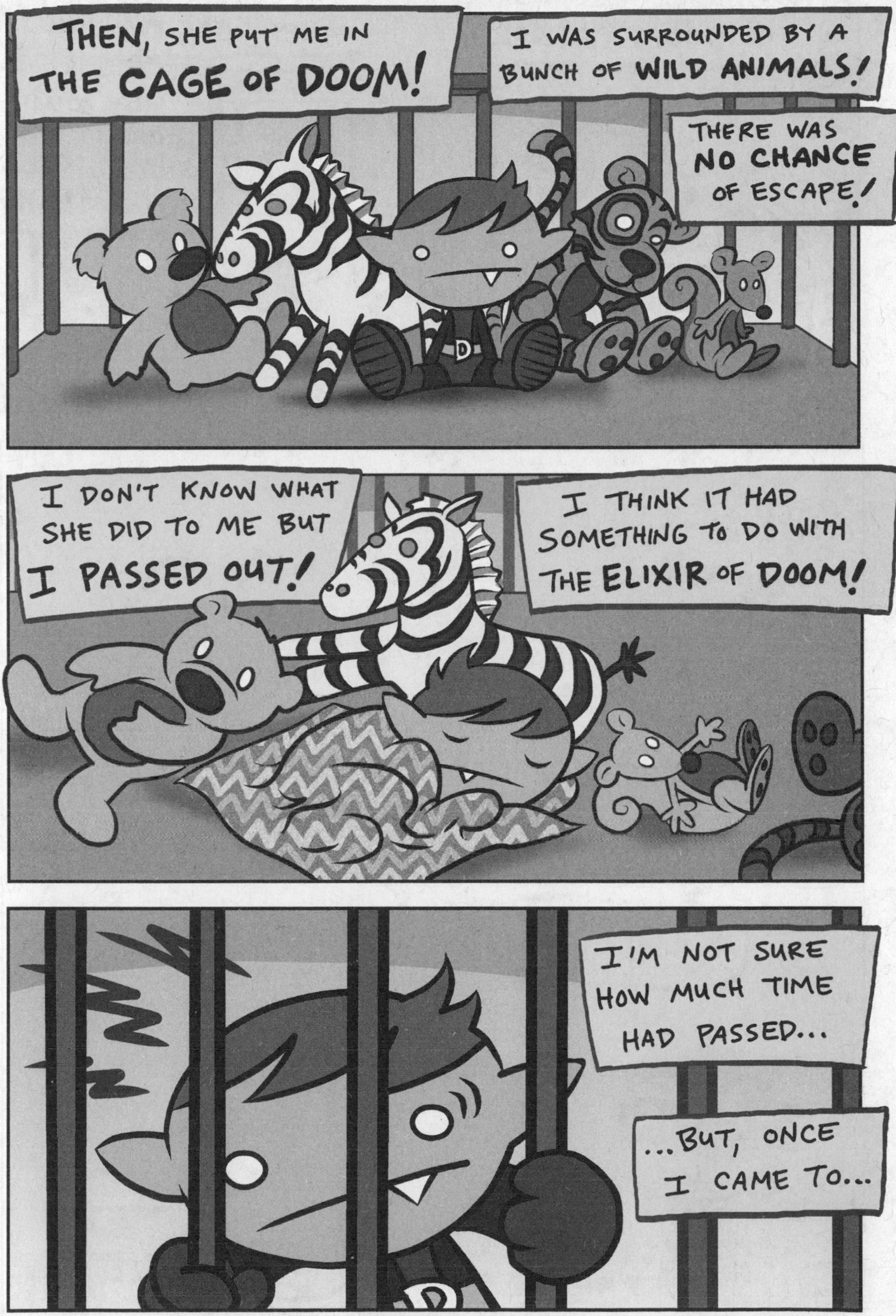
THEN, SHE PUT ME IN THE CAGE OF DOOM!
I WAS SURROUNDED BY A BUNCH OF WILD ANIMALS!
THERE WAS NO CHANCE OF ESCAPE!
I DON'T KNOW WHAT SHE DID TO ME BUT I PASSED OUT!
I THINK IT HAD SOMETHING TO DO WITH THE ELIXIR OF DOOM!
I'M NOT SURE HOW MUCH TIME HAD PASSED...
...BUT, ONCE I CAME TO...

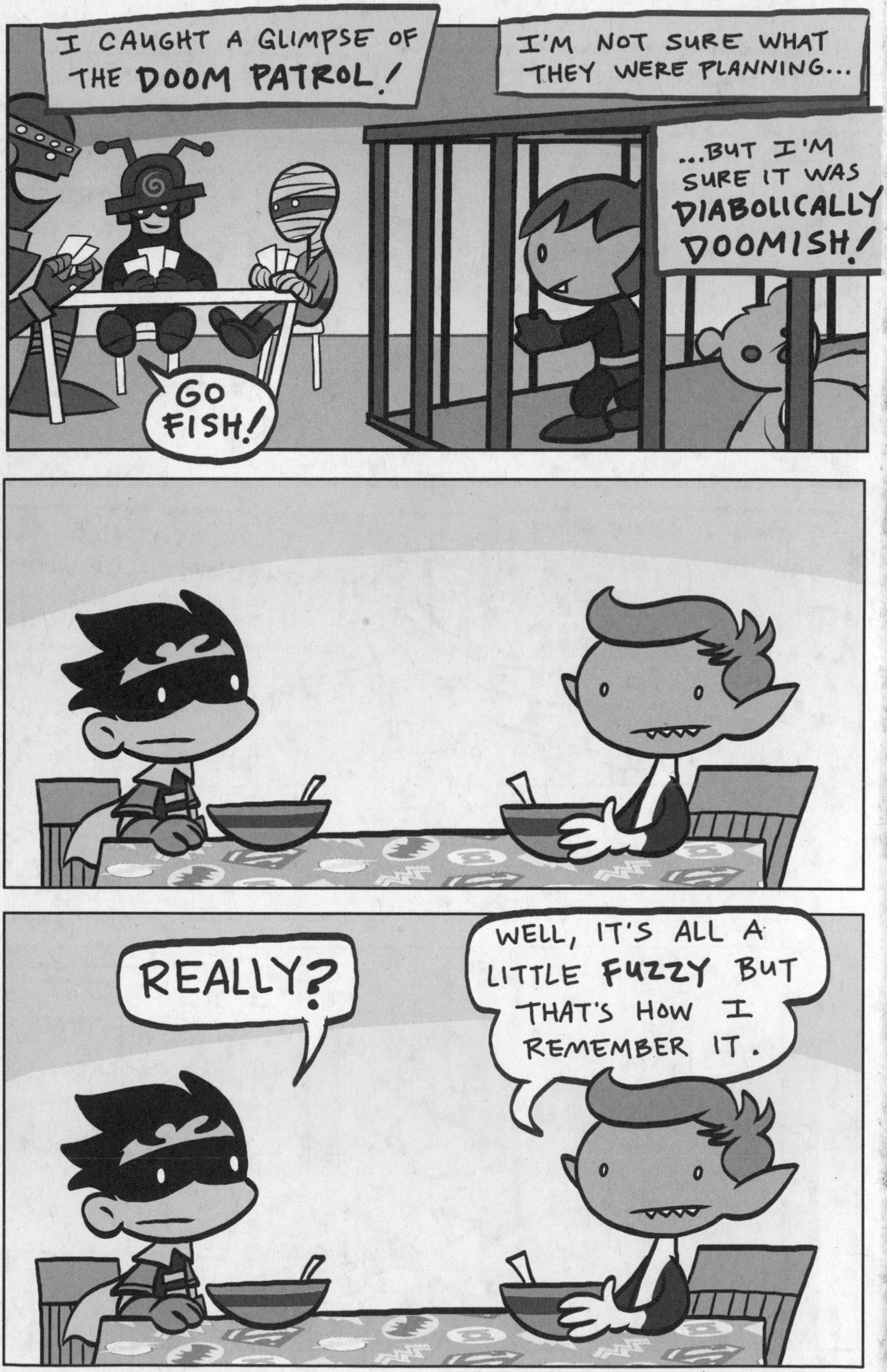
I CAUGHT A GLIMPSE OF THE DOOM PATROL!
I'M NOT SURE WHAT THEY WERE PLANNING...
...BUT I'M SURE IT WAS DIABOLICALLY DOOMISH!
GO FISH!
REALLY?
WELL, IT'S ALL A LITTLE FUZZY BUT THAT'S HOW I REMEMBER IT.

–JUST DOOM IT!